# A RESPECTABLE WOMAN

# A RESPECTABLE WOMAN

*by*

Susanna Bavin

**Magna Large Print Books**
Long Preston, North Yorkshire,
BD23 4ND, England.

British Library Cataloguing in Publication Data.

A catalogue record of this book is
available from the British Library

ISBN   978-0-7505-4580-8

First published in Great Britain by Allison & Busby in 2018

Published in Large Print 2019 by arrangement with
Allison & Busby Ltd.

Magna Large Print is an imprint of Library Magna Books Ltd.

Printed and bound in Great Britain by
T.J. (International) Ltd., Cornwall, PL28 8RW

*To the memory of Barbara Bourke (neé Gourgian, 1922–2017), who was immensely proud that* The Deserter's Daughter *was going to be published. Every time I saw her, she told me how she was going to go to the bookshop on publication day to buy the first copy; then after she had read it, she would write to the papers about it – her equivalent of posting an Amazon review. Unfortunately, Auntie Barbara died a few weeks before* The Deserter's Daughter *was released, and this book is dedicated, with affection and sorrow, to her memory.*

*And to Kevin, my tech elf, who in the six months it took to write* A Respectable Woman, *took over all matters domestic and acted as cat-servant-in-chief.*

# Chapter One

## Annerby, Lancashire, February 1922

'Bye-bye, chick. Be a good boy for Nanny.' Nell dropped on one knee in her mother-in-law's gloomy hallway and Alf's arms snaked round her neck as he put his heart and soul into hugging her. He was a loving child, just like her mock-wrestling, back-slapping brothers had been.

'You'll mek a mother's boy out of that one, if you don't watch out.'

Nell looked over the top of Alf's sandy head at Mrs Hibbert's raised eyebrows and downturned mouth. She didn't want to turn her son into a milksop, but how could she resist wallowing in his boundless affection? Was she foolish to want to ward off the time, perhaps when he started school, when her snuggly embraces might no longer be welcome? If only he had his four strapping uncles to drop comradely hands on his shoulder, to tousle his hair, and teach him by example that physical contact wasn't sissy.

'Don't say you haven't been warned,' said Mrs Hibbert.

No, indeed, that was something Nell could never say. Not about cuddling Alf, or about teaching him his ABC too young, or reading him a bedtime story instead of sending him straight to sleep. Or about wasting her time sticking her nose in a

11

library book or wasting her money taking her knives to the knife-grinder just because he was an old soldier, instead of investing in her own knife-sharpener.

At what point had they gone from, 'Can I give you a spot of advice, love?' to 'Don't say you haven't been warned'?

She was flaming sick of being warned.

She disentangled herself from Alf, catching his hands and pretending to gobble them up before rising to her feet. Her heart turned over as she looked at him. In his knitted pullover and grey shorts and socks, he was so appealing she could have gobbled him up for real.

Mrs Hibbert already had the front door open. 'You're letting the warm out, Nell.'

She gritted her teeth. 'Shut the door, then. I needn't go yet.'

'You don't want to be late.'

'You say that every morning and I never am.'

'Exactly.'

Nell gave up. With a last smile for Alf, she went to the door, with him pattering beside her to wave from the step. She walked a few paces, then turned to wave. She would have preferred to wave from the corner, but she had to get her wave in quickly before Mrs Hibbert could shut the door.

How had she ever imagined this old bag might take Mum's place? Old sorrow washed through her, piercing her with sudden freshness. How could it still do that after six years? Six years, for pity's sake. 1916 – the year her world ended. Dad was already dead; he died in the autumn of '14, believing it would all be over in weeks and the

12

boys would be home for Christmas. But they never came home. Nell liked to think they had all died together, the four of them, Doug, Tom, Eric and Harold, but there was no knowing, and it was probably just her being stupid.

Then Vi died. Nell had never shaken off the astonishment of Vi's death. She was an ambulance-driver. An ambulance-driver! Stretcher-bearers and ambulance-drivers weren't supposed to die. All Vi had wanted was to go on the stage and dance in the chorus at the music hall.

That was the end for Mum. Nell hadn't seen it at the time, but now she knew Mum had died inside. She died for real three months later; of a broken heart, everyone said. She died even though Nell had barely left her side, even though Nell loved her and needed her and always would, even though Nell was only sixteen and not old enough to live on her own. It was hard knowing you weren't reason enough for your mum to stay alive.

Kind neighbours took her in and she handed over her meagre wages for her board. It had been a strange existence, her whole family wiped out and her dumped in this new life that didn't feel like anything to do with her. A new family moved into the Pringles' house and that was hard to watch.

Then along came Stan, a good-looking soldier with his arm in a sling, who liked the look of her and persevered. Gradually, she turned to him. The neighbours encouraged it. Not that they wanted to get rid of her, but they encouraged it.

The thing about good-looking soldiers with

their arms in slings was that their injuries healed and the slings came off and it was only a matter of time before they went back to France. It added a feeling of urgency.

'Don't let him slip through your fingers,' warned the neighbours.

Stan was keen. Would she write? Would she be his girl? Would she meet his mother?

The morning was overcast and spitefully cold. Other folk might hunch inside their coats, with their hats pulled low over their ears, but not Nell. Wrapped inside Mum's faithful cavalry-tweed overcoat, which she had let down as much as she could but still wasn't long enough, she held herself tall and proud as she walked through the cobbled streets. She would pull her teeth out with the pliers sooner than let anyone see how shrivelled-up her job made her feel. Turning the corner, she walked towards the Royal Oak. It sounded grand, but it was just a backstreet pub on the corner of Starling Street and Hawk Street. The front door was on Starling Street, giving it a Starling Street address. Hawk Street would have been better, as in Hawking and Spitting Street.

She pushed open the door, bracing herself for the men's lavs. Some blokes had revolting habits. It didn't matter how coarse you were, everyone knew better than to pee on the floor. And it wasn't just pee either. Her stomach curled up just thinking of it.

'Morning, Mr Page.'

He grunted a reply. She turned to shut the door, snatching a final breath of air before she had to inhale the stench of stale beer and tobacco. It wasn't just the smell. It was the feeling that it was creeping under her skin, into her hair, soiling her clothes.

Lifting the bar-flap, she walked through into the Pages' living quarters to hang her coat and hat on the peg inside the broom cupboard. She rolled up her sleeves, put on her wraparound pinny and tied a scarf round her hair. She called herself a cleaner, but she looked like a charwoman, and maybe she was one. How many cleaners had to scrub stinking urinals?

She returned to the bar. Tables first. The Pages didn't even clear away the glasses before shutting up for the night. Honestly, there were times when she felt like chucking the dirty glasses at Mr Page's head. Mrs Page was seldom in evidence at this time of the morning, or indeed at any time of the morning. Landladies didn't soil their hands with cleaning, so she said. Lazy cat.

Onto the bar went handfuls of glasses. Washing them was Mr Page's job, but he never did it until Nell put them on the bar. She emptied the ash-trays, swept the floor and gave the tables a wipe to get rid of the rings, then set about polishing them. When she went through to the back for her mop and bucket, she took a moment to apply hand cream.

'Always look after your hands, our Nell,' said Vi's voice in her head. 'And don't forget to cream your elbows. To go on the stage, you need nice arms as well as smooth hands.'

Nell smiled. Recalling things the others used to say kept them alive in her heart. She must have been eight when Vi dispensed this advice and, as

15

she wasn't stage-struck like their Vi, it hadn't mattered; but it mattered now. Not her elbows, but her hands and face, especially her face. She had good skin and intended to keep it that way. She made her own lotion from quince blossom and cucumber. She dreaded being old before her time, the curse of the backstreet housewife.

Not that she minded working. She came from a long line of grafters and would cheerfully have scrubbed out urinals – well, not cheerfully, but she would have done it, if it had made a difference. A proper, worthwhile difference; a new shoes and best end of meat difference; a day trip to More-cambe difference; but all her cleaning achieved was to keep their heads above water.

That was why she had her rainy-day fund. Mostly it was money from her knitting. Mrs Dillon in Pigeon Street had a front-room shop and sold Nell's garments for tuppence in the shilling commission. Nell put some of the money into the household coffers so Stan wouldn't suspect, but the rest she stashed in an old tea caddy at the back of the pantry. Quite why she hid it she wasn't sure. It wasn't as though Stan raided the housekeeping jar. No, he just didn't hand it over in the first place. He gave her enough to get by on if she was careful – and the rest he drank. He ought to be a right fat-gut, but he wasn't. Not that that was any consolation to Nell when she was robbing Peter to pay Paul and performing miracles with scrag-end.

'Obviously you can't be trusted with money,' was Mrs Hibbert's opinion. 'Some women are feckless.'

'I'm not,' Nell retorted. Mum had never had so

16

much as a farthing's worth of tick at the corner shop and neither had she.

'Then why won't my Stan trust you with money? It's normal for a man to drink. Nowt wrong with that.'

'But all the money he gets through–'

'If you made his home a happier place, he wouldn't need to go out, would he?'

Nell lugged her bucket into the bar. Mopping the floor was the finishing touch. If this was all she had to do each morning, she would be happy to come to work. She might even be proud of it.

She could already taste the bitter tang in her throat.

Mrs Stanley Hibbert, urinal scrubber.

Who was that knocking at dinner time? If it was one of those door-to-door salesmen, she would give him a piece of her mind. Nell removed the pan from the heat and took Alf to the door. The chilly morning had turned to sleet. One of the district nurses stood outside. She wore a dark-grey cloak over a grey dress with white collar and cuffs and she carried a large satchel. Her bicycle was propped up against the lamp post.

'Mrs Hibbert?' She smiled. She had a round face that was built to look cheerful. 'I've come to see the baby.'

'You what?'

'The baby. I'm Nurse Beddow from the district.'

It wasn't sleet in the air. It was little darts of surprise. 'You're six months early.'

Nurse Beddow looked at her blankly. 'You're Mrs Hibbert, aren't you? Mrs Stanley Hibbert

17

of...' She pulled a sheet out of her satchel. '...of ... oh, lummee.'

'5 Lark Street. What's the matter?'

The nurse laughed, an awkward sound. 'Nothing. Um – nothing. Sorry, love, my mistake.'

'Why am I on your list if–?'

She was talking to thin air. With a flash of leg and sturdy garter, the nurse flung herself onto her old boneshaker and pedalled furiously down the road, the bicycle bouncing on the cobbles.

'Who was that, Mummy?'

'That lady was a nurse.'

'Am I poorly?'

'Well, I don't know, but poorly boys can't manage toad-in-the-hole.'

'I can eat toad-in-the-hole,' cried Alf, darting down the hall to the kitchen.

Nell followed, smiling at his eagerness. Her Alf would walk on hot coals for a sausage. As he washed his hands in the scullery, she looked out of the window. The cat was there again. It was getting bolder. No, that wasn't the right word. Hopeful – it was getting more hopeful. Poor cat. It would be pretty if it weren't so scrawny. It was black, with eyes like gooseberries, and its coat was fuzzy, as if it had fluffed it up to keep warm. It gazed at her from the top of the coal bunker. She should never have started feeding it; but how could she have ignored it?

Soon Alf was at the table, face screwed up in concentration as he manipulated the child-sized knife and fork she insisted he hold correctly, even though Stan said it didn't matter. She ate her bread and dripping slowly to fool her stomach into thinking it was more than it was. She would have her own toad-in-the-hole this evening with Stan, though her portion wouldn't be much bigger than Alf's.

'What do mermaids eat, Mummy?'

While part of her brain wrestled with Alf's question, another part dwelt on Nurse Beddow's mistake. For someone at the district nurses' station to draw up a journey list including a check on a baby that hadn't been born yet was inept, to say the least; but in this case, it wasn't inept so much as clairvoyant, because, after what happened last time, she hadn't as yet told a living soul she was pregnant.

Nell wrapped her arms round her body, hugging herself in delight. It was time to tell Stan he was going to be a father again and she knew just how to do it. First she would puzzle him with the tale of Nurse Beddow, then say, 'But someone down at that nurses' place must have a crystal ball, because Nurse Beddow was right. It was just the date she got wrong.'

Her arms tightened: soon it would be Stan's arms round her.

Thank you, Nurse Beddow.

There was no time to tell Stan when he came in from work. He chomped his way through his toad-in-the-hole and winter greens, practically inhaled the spotted dick and custard, downed a mug of sweet tea and headed out again.

'It's not opening time yet,' she protested.

'It will be by the time I get there.'

No, it wouldn't. Was she now to have the shame

of a husband who queued up outside the pub, champing at the bit for the doors to be unbolted? The front door slammed and he was gone. Nell sewed tassels onto a scarf she had knitted for Alf, then picked up her library book, but she couldn't concentrate. A moth blundered around the lamp – the same as her thoughts, fixed on one important thing, unable to settle elsewhere.

Her excitement at telling Stan had evaporated. Would it return when he came home? It was gone eleven when the front door opened. She snatched up some stray wool and started winding.

'Who did you drink with?'

'The usual fellows. Bed?'

At the foot of the stairs, he unlaced his ankle boots, placing them on the corner of the third stair up. Pairs on the stairs, a Pringle tradition. With eight people crammed into their house, every bit of space had to made use of, and shoes were either on your feet or on the stairs. Nell, as youngest, had had the bottom stair, the position currently occupied by Alf in the Hibbert household; but soon he would move up one, as he should have done a couple of years ago, only Nell had suffered a miscarriage.

That was why it had felt important to keep this new pregnancy to herself. Last time, she had told Stan and Mrs Hibbert early on and had lost the baby a fortnight later, by which time Mrs Hibbert had already informed the world and his wife, and for weeks afterwards all kinds of women were stopping Nell in the street to ask how she was and when her happy event was expected. Even now the memory of stammering to women she knew only by sight, 'Oh ... I...' set her heart pumping and sliding.

This time she had vowed to keep quiet until the third month was behind her. The three months weren't up yet, but today provided the perfect opportunity to deliver her news. Was she taking a chance by telling Stan sooner than she had intended? She hoped not. He had been so upset by the miscarriage that she had felt impelled to put on a good show and had crawled out of bed and donkey-stoned her front step.

'Poor Stan has took it bad,' said Mrs Hibbert.

'So have I,' cried Nell.

'Oh, you. Nowt much wrong with you. You was doing your step the next day.'

She would have to warn Stan not to tell his mother.

She popped her shoes onto the second step, with a telltale crackle of the newspaper that lined them. Stan's boots were silent. The man of the house, the breadwinner, must be properly shod; and so must Alf. Plenty of kids went barefoot or shared shoes, but not her son, not while there was breath in her body, a stash of coins in the old tea caddy and Cherry Blossom in the boot-box.

She changed into her nightie, turned down the bed and picked up her hairbrush. Her hair was the colour of a moth's wings: so Stan had said when she first knew him and she had felt startled to hear something about herself that was nothing to do with loss and bereavement, something that meant life was still there, waiting for her.

She hung up Stan's shirt and slid beneath the bedclothes. The mattress dipped as Stan plonked

21

down on the edge to peel off his socks and pull his pyjama jacket over his vest, his shoulder muscles rippling before disappearing beneath the blue-and-white stripes. He had been thin when they met. Strong, though, in a wiry way. He had filled out since.

'Alf been good?' His back was to her as he did up his buttons.

'He helped me clean out the ash pan. He looked like a chimney sweep when he'd finished.' She smiled: it was time. 'Something funny happened.'

'Oh aye?'

'The district nurse turned up, asking to see the baby, and she had my name.'

Stan looked down, checking his buttons. She waited for his reaction.

'Just a mistake, love. A daft mistake. You'd expect better of them nurses.'

Only he didn't look round as he said it. Nell's skin tingled. To look round, to frown, to laugh – that would have been natural. He hadn't even answered immediately, which you would expect him to do if he was surprised.

She stared at his blue-and-white-clad back.

Stan knew. Something was going on and Stan *knew*.

Nell dropped Alf off with Mrs Hibbert, then went to the Royal Oak, where she made her excuses: she needed to see the doctor. Mr Page wasn't pleased, but she was adamant. She set off at a brisk pace. What was she was doing? She didn't know. And why was she doing it? Same answer. Don't know and don't know. All she knew for certain was that she was boiling with determination as she marched across town to the district nurses' building, known for some reason as their station, which made them sound like railway porters. When she got there, she would … well, she would see about that when the time came.

The nurses' station didn't look all that big from the front, but it must stretch out at the back, because the nurses lived there as well. Poor creatures. Not much chance of meeting a fellow and settling down if you had to shin down a drainpipe to do your courting. Mind you, there was a shortage of men since the war, so maybe these lasses had done well for themselves, having bed and board provided. And no husband meant no one to drink the wages.

As she went in, the smell of disinfectant swarmed up her nose. There was a long corridor, its doors closed, except for one. Nell glanced in: an office, with a woman standing behind a desk, shuffling through a stack of papers. She wore a brown costume that was lifted out of the ordinary by gold buttons and braid, and shiny brown beads, a long set that almost reached her waist. Fancy wearing beads to work!

The woman looked at her in an equally assessing way but without the admiration. 'Can I help you?'

Nell lifted her chin. She wouldn't get a second chance at this. 'One of the nurses came out to me yesterday, but there was a mix-up over the address. Please could you–'

'Your name?'

'Hibbert, Mrs Stanley.'

'One moment.' The woman flicked through the pages in a large notebook. 'Hibbert ... Hibbert. Nurse Beddow was down to see a Mrs Hibbert of 14 Vicarage Lane.'

Nell's innards froze. 'Mrs Stanley Hibbert?'

'Mrs Stanley Hibbert of 14 Vicarage Lane. Is that incorrect?'

She cast an impatient glance at Nell. It pierced Nell's natural respect for authority and made her feel impatient too.

'I'll let you know.'

A big bass drum boomed inside her chest.

14 Vicarage Lane.

Her feet took her through the market square and over the bridge. Courtesy of the dye-works, the river was running blue today, not a natural water-blue, but the colour of peacock feathers. Right colour, wrong shade. Like yesterday with Nurse Beddow. Right name, wrong address.

14 Vicarage Lane.

'Oh, lummee,' said Nurse Beddow's voice in her head.

Vicarage Lane. It conjured up a picture of a winding path and butterflies dancing among the cow parsley, windows thrown open to the sunshine beneath a row of thatched roofs. Mind you, anyone might think the same of Lark Street. Vicarage Lane was pretty much like Lark Street, two long rows of old terraces, though the Vicarage Lane dwellings, being nearer the bottom of the hill, were older and smaller. Lower ceilings.

She ground to a halt at the corner. She wanted to dash home and hide. She wanted to march up

24

Vicarage Lane and demand to know what the ruddy hallelujah was going on. She wanted to pretend Nurse Beddow had never come round, her and her 'Oh, lummee'. She wanted to confront Stan, because he knew. Whatever it was, he *knew*. She wanted it to go away. She wanted it never to have happened.

Anything she wanted had flown out the window when Stan didn't turn and look at her last night.

She forced her feet to take her to number 14.

Except for the number, it might have been her own front door. The same dark green. Someone walked over her grave. Even now it wasn't too late to run away. Yes, it was. The moment Stan didn't turn and look her in the eye last night, it was too late. She rapped hard on the door. A sound on the other side sent a sheen of fear blooming across her skin. The door swished open and there was an answering swish in her stomach.

She looked down at a fair-haired young woman. That was nothing new: she had been looking down at the other girls all her life. This stranger had the soft-edged plumpness that said a baby had recently been born. The tiredness in the face said the same thing, a blissful tiredness that hadn't yet reached the exhausted stage.

Nell peeled her tongue off the roof of her mouth. 'Mrs Hibbert?'

'Who wants to know?'

'Are you married to...?' Her voice failed her. 'To Stan.'

Stan. Nell went trembly all over, as if she was about to crumple on the step.

The other Mrs Hibbert's eyes widened. 'There's

never been an accident at the works, has there?'

'No, no.' Was she actually reassuring this woman? 'Does he work at the furniture factory?'

'Aye, he's an upholsterer.'

'Do you work there too?'

'Nay, I've not worked since we moved in here.' She laughed. 'Well, I say I haven't, but running round after a two-year-old is harder than working on the factory line any day.'

A two-year-old? A two-year-old!

'Who are you?' asked Stan's other wife. 'Why are you asking after my husband?'

*He's not your husband. He's my husband. Go on, say it.* But she couldn't. Didn't want it said out loud, because that would make this situation real. And then it became more real than she could ever have imagined. A small child trotted down the hall to cling to his mummy's skirt, thumb plugged into his mouth. A two-year-old with sandy hair and blue eyes like Stan.

Sandy hair and blue eyes like Alf.

## Chapter Two

By the time Nell had walked up the hill, her marriage was over. No confrontation was needed, not with Stan's fancy piece and not with Stan. There was nowt to say. Well, there was plenty to say, obviously, preferably while chucking the fire irons at Stan's treacherous head, but what was the point? The marriage was over. She

26

had to make plans.

She didn't go into the house the front way, not wanting to be spotted by neighbours who would wonder what she was doing home at this time. Instead she sneaked up the back entry, lifting the latch on the wooden gate. The brown paint was peeling and now she knew why. The stray cat appeared from nowhere and tried to wind itself round her ankles, but she stepped away. A hopeful cat was the last thing she needed.

What she needed was a foolproof plan. What she needed was money. What she *needed* was a trustworthy husband, who could keep the family jewels inside his trousers.

She stopped dead, right there between the privy and the coal bunker. The world tilted up and down, side to side, forwards and backwards, all at the same time. Forget morning sickness. This was full-blown seasickness. Stan wasn't having a fling. This was a long-standing relationship. With a house. And children. Children – plural. Another marriage. Another Mrs Hibbert, who was a housewife, if you please, while the real Mrs Stanley Hibbert waded through phlegm and vomit and excrement and scrubbed out stinking urinals in a backstreet piss-house, and that was bad language, and that was wrong even if it wasn't out loud. Sorry, Mum.

She lurched to the back door, her knees as feeble as underdone rice pudding. She bent to retrieve the spare key from under the flowerpot. The cat appeared and she swatted it away, though not hard. She couldn't abide cruelty or bullying. Thank goodness she had her gloves on. Bare fingers might have felt how cold the cat was. She couldn't be responsible for it.

She let herself into the scullery and leant against the sink. Through the window she saw the back gate, brown and peeling. Her heart froze.

'That back gate could do with a lick of paint,' she had suggested shortly after Stan had painted the front door. 'There'll be enough left over from the front.'

'Nice idea, love, but there isn't enough paint.'

'Is that you trying to get out of doing a job, Stan Hibbert? She slid her arms round his waist and snuggled close. Sometimes Stan took a bit of persuading.

'Nay, love, there isn't enough.'

And there wasn't, either. Later, she found the tin on a shelf in the cellar and prised the lid off with a screwdriver, and Stan was right. The tin was almost empty. She must have been mistaken. It was the only explanation.

No, it wasn't. It was merely the obvious explanation. More obvious than Stan buggering off down the hill to tart up his other front door.

Bastard.

'Bastard,' she whispered.

Terrible word. Their Doug had said it once and Mum had washed his mouth out with soap. There was no stopping Mum when she was riled and never mind that Doug was a strapping fifteen-year-old bringing in a wage.

Talking of wages, Stan's clearly hadn't all gone across the bar at the Royal Oak. All this time, she had marvelled that the man who could drink the brewery dry didn't have a vast beer gut. Now it

28

turned out that he was just a common or garden cheating husband.

Well, no, not a common or garden cheat. A full-blown bigamous cheat with another wife and family and a second rent book. That was where the money had gone. That was why she had had to go out to work, to scrape by in Lark Street while Stan supported Vicarage Lane. The other Mrs Hibbert didn't go out to work. Talk about adding insult to injury.

The other Mrs Hibbert stopped at home with her children.

She barged through the kitchen into the parlour, throwing her coat over the back of the armchair. First things first. She couldn't do anything without money – *no*. That wasn't first. She pounded upstairs into their bedroom. Her ears were crammed with the banging of her heart, but when she stood in front of the chest of drawers, the world fell silent, as though she had fallen into a snowdrift. She took out her little wooden box with the carved top. Grandpa had made it for Nan when they were fourteen. Inside lay Mum's wedding ring. Nell twisted her own ring. She meant to remove it slowly, deliberately, in a moment of deep significance, but it stuck. Fury gripped her and she wrenched it off, almost taking the skin off her knuckle with it. It had meant the world to her, but Stan had rendered it worthless. But she still had a ring that meant the world. Her heart folded in half as she slipped on Mum's ring. This was her wedding ring now – no, her respectability ring. Proof of widowhood.

She looked at her old ring. She felt like chucking

it down the privy, but she wrapped it in a handkerchief and took it downstairs. Now for the money. She opened the sideboard drawer and slid her hand under the linen, feeling for the old frayed envelope containing a week's spare rent, just in case. Stan didn't know about it or about the Mazawattee tea tin at the back of the pantry, where she kept the odd coppers she saved. When your husband didn't hand over his full pay packet, you learnt to hoard, sixpence here, tuppence there. Even a farthing made a difference. Occasionally, she emptied the tin and stashed the money in her post office savings account.

Then she opened the cupboard under the stairs, ducking her head so as not to crack it on the underbelly of the staircase as she reached for the old carpet bag. She took it into the parlour and dumped it on the table. The candlesticks, the clock: they must be worth summat. She stood them beside the bag. Her blue-and-white vase. Her heart gave a sharp creak inside her chest. The vase used to be Mum's, and before that Nan's. When Nell was a lass, Nan had kept it on a high-up shelf and Nell had gazed up at it, loving it even then. Her heart said not to part with it, but what did her heart know? Her heart had said to marry Stan.

What else? A couple of brass ornaments; a stack of sheet music from inside the piano stool. The framed studio portrait of her and Stan on their wedding day, herself skinny with grief but with hope shining in her eyes, Stan handsome in his uniform, and his mother on his other side. Honestly, who had their mother-in-law in their wedding photograph? But she had loved Olive Hibbert every bit as much as she had loved Stan back then.

'Olive Hibbert, widow', was how Mrs Hibbert had introduced herself when Stan had presented Nell to her.

Was she meant to say, 'Nell Pringle, orphan'? That was what she was. Orphaned, everyone dead, her world blown apart. The bleakness had overwhelmed her and she dissolved into tears. Olive Hibbert took her into her arms. Stan put one arm round her, the other round his mother; and Nell had felt safe and loved and wanted in a way she had thought was lost to her for ever. Something stirred inside her broken Pringle heart and she knew she was going to be a Hibbert.

She turned the frame over to unclip the back and flipped the photograph out, depositing it – face up, face down, she didn't look – on the mantelpiece before she reassembled the frame and popped it on the table. From the sideboard drawers she took the boxed set of fish knives, her table linen and spare antimacassars; from the cupboard underneath came the glass bowl she used for her Christmas trifle. How proud she had been to place a trifle on the table for the first time. How married she had felt.

Had Stan dreaded her trifle, her Christmas pudding, her tin of mince pies, knowing he would have to force down the same things all over again in his other house? How long had his so-called wife been in residence in Vicarage Lane? That little boy was two, so say Stan had met her a year before – that would have been almost as soon as he came home for good in 1919. That couldn't be right. She must be mistaken.

But the child's age proved it.

Nell dropped onto the wooden chair next to the sideboard. Two years ago, she had suffered her miscarriage. Stan had been expecting two children at the same time and she had lost hers. No wonder he had been stunned. Was it guilt that had floored him? Now he had done the double again, only this time he didn't know about her baby. And never would. She would put his name on the birth certificate because she and the baby were entitled to that, but that would be the beginning and end of Stan's involvement in this child's life.

When she was gone, he and Mrs Vicarage Lane could have a dozen sandy-haired miniature Stanleys for all she cared, but her Alf would never know.

Dumping the carpet bag behind a crate in the yard round the back of the Royal Oak, Nell went round the front and let herself in. The tables wanted polishing, the floor hadn't been swept, the ashtrays overflowed.

Mr Page was behind the bar. 'There you are at last. Take your coat off and get fettling.'

'I can't. I've took bad ways.'

'You look all right to me.'

'I need medicine. Otherwise you won't see me for a week, like as not.'

'A week? You can't be sick that long. Who'll do the cleaning?'

'If I get medicine, I'll soon be back, but I can't

get it without my wages.'

'I s'pose I've got no choice. You'll not get nowt for today, mind.'

'I wouldn't expect it.' Not from him, the old skinflint. Do someone a good turn? Henry Page? You must be joking.

The drawer of the cash register flew open and he pawed through the little boxes. 'There y'are.' He clattered a handful of change on the counter.

'It's a bob short.'

'I'll add it to your next pay.'

'I'll have it now, if it's all the same to you.'

He slapped a shilling on the counter. 'And who's going to do the cleaning while you've took to your sickbed?'

'Ask Mrs Page.'

Mr Page's mouth dropped open. Mrs Page, with her swaying hips and powdered face, wouldn't recognise a mop if one got up and bit her on the bum.

Nell left, letting the door swing shut behind her. She collected the carpet bag and headed down the hill, using the back alleys, praying no one she knew would see her skulking down to town. The backs of her eyes stung. Oh, the shame. She had never in her life set foot inside the pawnbroker's. Mum must be turning in her grave.

Emerging into the market square, she held her head high, as if carrying a carpet bag was a per-fectly natural thing to do, then dived into the side street where the three balls hung over a door. With a final glance round to ensure she wasn't being watched, she went in.

The dark-suited pawnbroker stood behind a

glass-topped counter, beneath which lay trays of medals, jewellery, cutlery, trinket boxes, christening spoons, you name it. Behind the counter were racks of clothes as well as shelves housing a mishmash of larger items, stuffed animals, wax fruit, boots, hat boxes, vases, kettles – kettles? How could anyone pawn their kettle? She couldn't manage without hers.

'I've a few things I'd like to ... hand in.'

She emptied the carpet bag, putting her items on the counter, where the pawnbroker spread them out. She must look like a travelling pedlar.

'Your husband's suit. I normally take those in on Mondays, not Fridays.' Did he think her another scrimping housewife, pawning the old man's suit till Saturday afternoon, ready for church on Sunday? '...Fish knives, ivory-handled, velvet-lined case ... carriage clock, eight-day movement ... sheets, pillowcases ... more of the same...'

'Some of the sheets have been turned sides to middle, but there's plenty of wear in them.'

'The shroud-maker is always interested in decent sheets ... assuming you don't redeem them.'

How did he know? 'How much will you give me?'

'For the clock, twelve shillings; the candlesticks, ten shillings for the pair; the photograph frame, half a crown; with a redemption date of three months. I'll write slips for these items while you unfold your sheets. I need to see their condition.'

'I told you: sides to middle.'

'I wish to see they're unstained and free of holes. Don't take offence, Mrs...?' He must have caught

34

her hesitation. 'It's seldom advisable to give the wrong name and address to the pawnbroker.'

'Hibbert,' she whispered. 'Mrs Hibbert. 5 Lark Street.'

'Now if you don't mind...'

Unfolding her sheets when anyone might peer through the window made sobs rise in her throat, but she held them clenched there, determined not to give in.

The horrid business dragged on, her skin prickling as the slips mounted up.

'And finally.' He reached for the blue-and-white vase.

'No!'

Her hand snaked along the counter to snatch it back. Pure instinct. Pure stupidity, more like. She needed the money. She needed every penny – every farthing. But she couldn't part with Nan's vase.

'I've changed my mind.' She stowed it inside the bag. 'But there is one more thing.'

She gave him the handkerchief, watching as he unwrapped the gold ring. He glanced at her and she wanted to rip off her glove and cry, 'That's not my ring – *this* is my ring,' just so he would know she was decent and respectable and not in need of pity.

Anger swelled inside her. Damn Stan. She had known he wasn't the best husband in the world; his so-called drinking had brought her down to earth long since; but she had never deserved to be dragged down like this. The anger evaporated, leaving her cold and small. She felt no satisfaction as the pawnbroker counted out the money into her hand. She wanted to run and hide and wake up when everything had returned to normal.

'Mrs Hibbert,' he said as she turned to leave. 'You've forgotten your slips. A word to the wise,' he added when she made no move to take them. 'If you're doing what I think you're doing, you should leave them in a prominent place in 5 Lark Street, as proof you haven't stolen these articles.'

Stolen? *Stolen?* If Stan should dare lay any blame on her, after what he had done–

She stuffed the slips in her pocket and marched out.

'You're late. Where the heck have you been?'

Charming. Nell walked into her mother-in-law's hallway, outwardly composed, inwardly – well, never mind. She was ignoring the inward things now. It was the only way to cope. She threw her arms wide as Alf ran to greet her, hugging him tighter than she had ever held him before. From now on, he had only one parent. She was filled with an acute sense of resolve. She would never let him down.

'Nanny says you're late.'

'Just a bit.'

'Nanny says it's rude to be late.'

'Does she?' She looked at Mrs Hibbert. How many times had this battleaxe put her in her place?

Mrs Hibbert bridled. 'Well, it is.'

'Almost as rude,' Nell said quietly, 'as telling a little lad his mummy is in the wrong.' Turning away from the gawp of astonishment, she released Alf. 'Fetch your things, pie-can.'

Soon they were on the pavement. Mrs Hibbert stood on her step.

'Thank you for looking after him,' Nell said for the final time.

Mum would have said, 'No thanks needed. He's a little love.'

Mrs Hibbert said, 'Aye, well.' Nell had never worked out what that meant, only that it made her feel beholden.

'Give Nanny a big hug.'

*Hug him, hug him, you stupid woman. This is goodbye. You'll be sorry in days to come that all you did was pat his head.*

Or maybe not. She would be too busy blaming Nell.

Nell and Alf walked home, hand in hand, and went in. Would he notice the missing things? No, but he did notice the carpet bag.

'What's this for, Mummy?'

'It's a secret for now.'

'Can I have three guesses?'

His excitement sent a wave of guilt washing over her. How could she take him away? He worshipped Stan.

She prepared dinner. It was meant to be mince and vegetables for Alf, and the same in a pie this evening for herself and Stan. Instead she made a pie for herself and Alf, and pasties for the journey. There was still mince left. Leave it for Stan? Not while there was a more deserving cause. She opened the door. The stray appeared, prancing on tiptoe. She put the plate down.

'Make the most of it, cat. Muggins won't be here to feed you tomorrow.'

It was time to get ready. Her heart turned over.
'We're going on an adventure,' she told Alf.
'Is Daddy coming?'
'No, just you and me. Do you think you could wear your other jumper on top of this one? It's a special way of packing, so you take as much as you can. And we'll each have a blanket round our shoulders over our coats.'
'Like cloaks. Can I bring the sword Daddy made me?'
It was extraordinary how you could tuck your life inside a carpet bag. Extraordinary and pitiful and scary. Stan deserved to rot in hell. Clothes. Knife, fork and spoon each; plates. A towel. The sheet from Alf's bed – and he could carry his pillowcase with some things inside. Knitting needles, some things from her sewing box. As much food as she could cram into her shopping bag. Tins of sardines and peaches. Marmite. Evaporated milk. Bread and cheese wrapped in a tea towel. The tea caddy.
And the important things: Nan's blue-and-white vase, Mum's pitifully small collection of letters from the boys – dear heaven, what was she doing? She couldn't leave. How would the boys find her if they came home? She had to be here.
But they would never come home. Neither would Vi. She knew it in her head. She wasn't stupid. But her heart was stupid. Oh, her heart was stupid.
'Mummy, the rag-and-bone man's here. Is this it, Mummy? Is this our adventure?'
'Yes, pie-can. Go and have a wee, please.'
She bustled him to the back door. Her heart

38

was building up to exploding. She must be mad. Pulling on her coat, she drew the pawnbroker's slips from the pocket and placed them on the mantelpiece, where the clock used to be.

'Mummy, there's a cat asleep on the coal bunker.'

'It's got a full tummy, that's why it's asleep. Coat, scarf, gloves, please.'

'And my sword.'

'And your sword.'

'How do you know the cat has a full tummy?'

'Now, please, Alf.'

She didn't want to leave a note, but the slips weren't enough. She wanted Stan to *know*. On the back of a slip, she wrote *14 Vicarage Lane* and left it on the top of the pile.

'Oh, lummee,' said that damn nurse's voice in her head.

'Who does it belong to?'

'What?'

'The cat.'

'Nobody.'

'Then who fed it?'

'I did.'

'Will Daddy feed it while we're having our adventure?'

'Time to go. Mr Fry is taking us to the station.'

'We're going on a *train?*'

Charlie Fry took their meagre luggage, then lifted Alf onto the seat. Nell climbed up beside him.

'Ready, missus?'

'Yes – wait!'

She jumped down. It was a stupid idea. She had

far too much else to worry about. She fetched her wicker basket, opened one side of its lid and lined the inside with a hand towel. Damn cat. She should never have fed it. She opened the back door.

'Hey, cat.' She stroked it gently. She hadn't touched it before, not on purpose. 'Do you want to go on an adventure?'

## Chapter Three

### Manchester, March, 1924

Posy dreaded Saturdays. You were meant to love them, to spend all week at school looking forward to them. And today was sunny and fine, which should make it better, but didn't.

She spent the morning playing out. 'Don't come back till dinner,' Ma had instructed, same as every other mum in their road, in the whole country, probably. Mums were always sending you out to play – well, except for Mrs Hibbert. She was different. She spent loads of time indoors playing with her Alf and Cassie, even though Gran said she worked all the hours God sent. Sometimes Gran called Alf and Cassie 'them poor little mites', because their mum had to go out to work, her being a widow. Being widowed young was reet buggeration, as Posy was well aware, having heard Mrs Watson next door to Gran say so.

Eh, she did like Mrs Hibbert. Fancy a mum

playing with her nippers. She was careful not to say so at home, though.

'Spoilt brats,' was Dad's opinion of the Hibbert children. 'A nancy boy and a little madam in the making.'

Dad didn't like Mrs Hibbert. He grumbled about her having her feet under Gran's table, though at other times he would tell Ma, 'That Hibbert female is lucky to have a roof over her head, Hilda. The least she can do is fettle for your parents and save you traipsing over there all the time. Your place is here, looking after your husband and home.'

And daughter. Posy had waited for him to say 'and daughter', but he didn't. Maybe that was what grown-ups meant when they said eavesdroppers never heard good of themselves. Not that she was an eavesdropper, as such. Eavesdroppers listened on purpose, but she couldn't help it. With Dad and Ma sitting in the armchairs by the kitchen range, and her sleeping in the scullery, she couldn't help overhearing. It wasn't her fault if they assumed she fell asleep the instant she put her head down. Frankly, she wished she could. It wasn't any great pleasure lying on the board Dad had made to go over the sink, with her legs on the wooden draining board, even though she had a cushion to go under her head and a blanket to wrap herself in.

Whatever Dad thought of Mrs Hibbert, Posy thought she was wonderful. Imagine it – a mum who had been known to play out with the children. She would never have believed it if she hadn't seen it with her own eyes one Saturday when she was at Gran and Gramps's. All the kids in Finney Lane were playing out as usual and Mrs Hibbert had played cricket with them; and by crikey, could she bowl. Afterwards, at the tea table, she had said summat about growing up with older brothers.

Mrs Hibbert was the biggest kid of the lot, according to Gran, though she never said so in front of Dad; but Gran knew she could say it to Posy. She and Gran understood one another. She wished she lived closer to Gran and Gramps instead of a bus ride away, especially now Gramps was poorly.

If only they had enough room to bring Gran and Gramps to live with them, but they had only the downstairs – the front room, which was Dad and Ma's bedroom, the kitchen and the scullery. The house belonged to Mr Warren, who lived upstairs – well, it didn't belong to him, as in owning-belonging. He rented it and he did something called subletting the downstairs to Dad.

Dad didn't like living under another man's roof, but he liked it that Mr Warren had put a runner down the hall and up the stairs.

'It shows the neighbours we're better than they are,' he said, as though the strip of carpet was his personal property.

He liked to go for a walk on a Saturday morning too, just in case anyone forgot that he finished work on a Friday, unlike Mr Unwin and Mr Rutledge who worked in shops, and Mr Greaves and his son who were road menders, and Mr Grey who worked in the sorting office. He never actually said that was the reason for his weekly walk, but from the way he puffed out his chest,

Posy knew.

That was where Dad was now, having his Saturday morning strut.

Saturday.

Posy dreaded Saturdays.

Posy's throat hurt, as if the tough bristles on the clothes brush were lodged in her gullet, making it difficult to eat, even though it was potato rissoles, which was one of her favourites, especially the way Ma made them, with the green bits off the spring onions, the way Gran had taught her. Gran was the best cook in Lancashire, according to Gramps.

She forced in another forkful and tried to chew, but it felt rubbery in her mouth. She ended up chewing too much and it went mushy and tasteless and she didn't want to swallow it. She dipped her head down so Ma and Dad wouldn't see her pulling faces.

'Eat up, Posy.' Ma sounded more fretful than encouraging. 'Dad wants his pudding.'

Posy struggled on. Afterwards there was treacle pudding to plough through. Any other day, she would have emptied her bowl, but not today. After dinner, she sat at the table while Dad and Ma had a cup of tea. At last Ma removed the cups and Dad held out a ha'penny on the palm of his hand. Posy always felt as though her hand would vanish inside Dad's, because his were big and square. He was a big man, was Dad, which was odd when you thought about it, because other dads were taller.

Off she went. Other kids were emerging from

their houses; so were those who wouldn't have had a meal because there wasn't the money, but they went indoors anyroad for the sake of appearances. Games of marbles and hopscotch started up. A couple of lads walked up and down, arms slung round each other's shoulders, singing, 'Hands in the band for staggy ... hands in the band for staggy...' It wouldn't take long for others to join in. Posy was good at staggy, darting about, keeping out of the way of getting caught; and when she was caught, she was good at running with her partner to catch others. Fleet of foot, Gran called her, which made it sound like her feet were in the navy, but Posy knew what Gran meant.

She had to pass three corner shops before she arrived at the sweet shop. Inside, it smelt of wooden floorboards and sweetness, sugary, fruity, sharp. You wouldn't think there could be so many kinds of sweetness, but there were. The smell of the sweet shop used to make her mouth go moist with anticipation. Now it made it go dry.

Two youngsters were oohing over the penny tray with its array of sugar mice, bootlaces, shrimps, blackjacks and fruit salads. Lucky beggars. The glass jars of sweets were all very well, but everyone knew the penny tray was the best thing in the shop.

All too soon it was her turn.

'What would you like?' asked Mr Bennett. 'As if I need ask,' he added in a jokey voice.

'A quarter of caramels, please.'

He took the jar from the shelf. Positioning himself behind the scales, he put the weight on one side and tipped the jar over the dish until the two sides were level.

How many? Please, please.

He returned the jar to its place between the rhubarb and custards and the lemon drops before flicking open a little cone-shaped white paper bag and holding it against the pointy end of the weighing dish. Posy raised herself on her toes, trying to count as the sweets tumbled into the bag. She tried every week, but she never managed.

Mr Bennett folded the top of the bag. 'A ha'penny, please.'

Posy handed him the coin and then took the bag. It was crisp in her fingers. She said thank you and left the shop.

She carried the bag with care, not so loosely that she was in danger of dropping it, but not tightly for fear of crumpling it. She suffered the weekly temptation of opening it, but if she did, the folded-over top would lose its sharp edge. Her fingers twitched, wanting to feel the caramels through the paper, but the bag must get home in pristine condition to show she hadn't tampered with it.

When she arrived, Dad was reading the paper and she had to wait. Her legs felt hollow and her brain buzzed. At last Dad stood up. He held out his hand, as big as a spade. Goosebumps chilled Posy's arm as she gave him the bag. The look he gave her nailed her to the floor. He went to the table. A dark green oil cloth covered the table between meals. A glass vase with silly little pretend-handles that you would be lucky to get a finger through stood in the middle, filled with daffodils.

45

The paper cone rustled as Dad emptied it, letting the caramels in their see-through wrappers slide out, each one landing with a tiny tapping sound.

Here they come, one two three, please please, four five, please please...

Buggeration.

Not six, not six. Not not not six six six.

Dad looked at her and she knew how it felt to be a caramel, because when you popped one in your mouth, it went all soft and melty and you could use your tongue to stretch it. That was how the bones in her arms and legs felt now, soft and waxy and incapable. She would never be able to move again in her whole life.

'Five caramels. When will you learn? Rupert should know what you've done. Go and fetch him.'

And even though her legs were soft and melty, even though she couldn't move, Posy went.

## Chapter Four

'Nell Hibbert! Why do you do that? You want your bumps feeling.'

With a glance after Mr Flynn's stooped figure as he loped away, and another to ensure Miss Lockwood had her back to them as she scrutinised Mildred Shaw's seams, Nell looked across the aisle to where Elsie Jones sat behind the next sewing machine.

'Keep your voice down.' Her fingers hovered

over the polka-dotted navy cotton, ready to feed it through the machine the instant they finished their illicit chat.

'You carry that bloke, you know you do. You know it, he knows it, we all flaming know it. Without you handing him the work rosters on a plate, he'd end up getting the sack.'

'And then I could step into his job, I suppose.'

'You'd be a darned sight better at it than he is.'

'Except I wouldn't get it, would I? It'd go to another man.'

Why did the world assume it was just men who needed good jobs? Yes, Mr Flynn had a wife and family to support, and yes, he had left his nerves behind in Flanders, but she had responsibilities too. A young widow with children needed a decent income every bit as much as a family man did.

A young widow. She almost believed it herself. Mrs Stanley Hibbert, runaway wife of that bigamous cheat, was another person. She was Mrs Nell Hibbert now, hard-working widow, and Respectable was her middle name.

She turned back to her machine. Let alone she couldn't afford the fine should she be caught nattering, she was on piecework. As she fed the bodice pieces through, the polka dots blurred into pinstripes. She was a skilled machinist, having taken to machine-sewing as if she had been born to it. She loved the fabrics, the serviceable flannel and supple wools, silky rayon and light-as-air Crêpe de Chine. She was even trusted with velvet and the best satin.

Miss Lockwood, who had been the overseer in this workshop since dinosaurs roamed the earth, thought highly of her.

'You're one of the best girls I've ever had,' she had said: you could be sixty and you'd still be a girl if you worked a machine.

It was high praise, but you were only as good as your last garment and Nell put all her concentration into every one of hers. She was a Pringle and the Pringles were grafters.

Sometimes she wished she had changed her name back to Pringle when she arrived in Manchester. If Alf had been younger, she might have; but he had known he was a Hibbert. As loving and amenable as ever, he didn't seem to have suffered through not having a father, for which Nell was grateful every time – God forgive her – Alf told someone his daddy was dead.

It had been the only way. How else was she to explain Stan's absence? To start with, Alf had accepted that the adventure was just for the two of them – plus the cat.

Two years ago, she had bumped along to the station on Charlie Fry's cart, boggling at the spur-of-the-moment idiocy that had made her adopt the stray and wishing it would scrabble from underneath the basket lid and leap away into the early twilight; but the cat, its belly full of Stan's mince, and probably as close to warm as it had been since the previous summer, had stayed put.

Her spur-of-the-moment idiocy had turned out to be a master stroke. Alf was enchanted.

'What's his name?'

'Her name. She hasn't got one.'

'Violet,' said Alf.

'What?'

'She's called Violet. She told me. Like Auntie Vi. We've got a cat called Violet Pringle.'

If nowt else, it showed that telling him about his uncles and auntie had sunk in. But Vi would be turning in her grave, wherever it was.

A few weeks later, snuggling down in the bed in which she would later join him, Alf whispered, 'Can Violet stop being Violet Pringle and be Violet Hibbert, so she knows she's ours?'

'I think she knows that already.' The cat knew when she was well off. She had slept almost non-stop for a week beside Mrs Brent's kitchen range when they moved in.

'Good,' said Alf.

And, simple as that, he had gone to sleep. Had he been worrying about the blessed cat's place in the household? Better that than worrying about Stan's being dead or the long hours she had to spend at work.

Forty-eight hours a week. Forty-flaming-eight. Eight till twelve and one till half-six, and seven o'clock on Fridays. Fridays were the worst, because you worked later, then had to queue up in your own time to collect your wages. Her heart broke in frustration and longing every Friday evening. On Friday evenings, she hated Stan for condemning her to life as a working mother.

She didn't hate him the rest of the time. To hate someone, you had to think about them and she didn't waste her time. Life was hard but it was good. She was proud of her work. How had she ever tolerated the Royal Oak?

The hooter sounded for dinner. Nell felt a thrumming vibration in her bones as the whirring

49

sound around her intensified as the women finished their seams. Then chatter filled the room as they pulled out their pink tickets. You bought your tickets on Monday, tuppence each, to exchange during the week for mugs of tea. This was Nell's last week of having tea until the autumn. Starting next week, she would bring a bottle of cold tea or lemonade. Any saving helped when you had to make every penny do the work of thruppence.

'How are your lads getting on at work?' she asked Elsie, putting down her barm cake between bites to make it last. Wish sandwich, Dad had called it, spread with jam or Marmite that you wished was chicken or ham.

Elsie munched a mouthful of pasty. 'They'll each get another sixpence a week when they turn fifteen.'

'Riches! What will they do with it?'

'Give it to me. It's about time they paid their way. And two weeks after the boys turn fifteen, the girls are fourteen.'

'They're all July birthdays, aren't they? My Alf will be six in July.'

'Six? And the little 'un not much more than a baby. You've years to go yet.'

'It can't last long enough for me,' said Nell.

'I couldn't wait for mine to grow up.'

'Well, twins twice, a year apart...'

'The ruddy powers that be didn't help. Putting the school leaving age up to fourteen: what was the point of that? And then stopping twelve-year-olds working half-time – I ask you. How are families supposed to manage?'

'You'll soon have all four of them working. You

won't know yourself.'

'I know this much. My lasses start work the day after school finishes; and the day after that, I'm cutting my hours here.'

'I wish I could cut mine. I'd love to spend more time with the kids.'

'I thought you was happy leaving your nippers with your landlady.'

'Don't get me wrong. The Brents are kindness itself, but it isn't easy knowing that another woman gets to spend all day with my children.'

'You know what you need,' said Elsie. 'Another husband.'

People said that to widows. She had had to get used to it. She never responded.

She finished her barm cake and licked her fingers. She couldn't afford to waste even a smear of food. Providing for the children included going without herself. It was summat mothers got used to.

'Actually,' said Elsie, 'what you look like you need is a good night's sleep. Your Cassie keeping you up, is she?'

'Mr Brent's poorly. I've been staying up nights so Mrs Brent can sleep.'

'What's wrong with him?'

A hot fist tightened in Nell's belly. 'It started as pleurisy, then turned to pneumonia.'

'Poor old boy. Is he getting over it?'

'The doctor told Mrs Brent...' A lump filled her throat.

'Eh, chuck, what is it?'

'The doctor says...' She had to swallow. '...heart failure. He already had it, apparently, and without

51

the pleurisy, he might have lasted who knows how long.'

'But the pleurisy and pneumonia have buggered him up good and proper.'

'Looks like it,' said Nell.

'Any children?'

'A daughter.' And a right waste of space she was an' all.

'So, she'll take her mam in afterwards and that'll leave you right up a gum tree. I'll keep an eye out for cheap lodgings, but you won't have much choice. You did well for yourself when you got took in by them two. Luck like that doesn't come along twice.'

Nell had no intention of waiting for luck to come her way. She had taken charge when she left Stan and now she had to take charge again. It all came down to money. Her piecework earned her two pound ten a week, give or take. Over time, as the trust and affection between herself and the Brents had grown, she and Mrs Brent had reached an understanding whereby she handed over two quid a week, all-in – for the room, contributions to the food, coal and gaslight, and the child-minding Mrs Brent did. With the ten-ish bob she had left, she paid a shilling each into the boot club, burial insurance and the Hospital Saturday Fund; and she always saved summat, even in the leanest week when all she could put by was a few farthings. When she left Stan, she had felt rich with all that money in her pocket – rich and scared, because she had to get fixed up before the money ran out. She still had two guineas of that money tucked away against dire emergency, along with what she had saved since.

Dear heaven, please guard her against dire emergency.

Forget dear heaven. It was her job to guard against dire emergency.

And she knew how she was going to do it.

The first thing Nell saw as she turned the corner into Finney Lane was the depressingly familiar sight of cats outside their house, two black-and-whites lounging in the road, a ginger practically on the doorstep. Violet in season was the last thing they needed. Would Mrs Brent have been too preoccupied to notice the tomcats lurking outside?

She let herself in, experiencing the usual lurch of disappointment. She wanted her children to come running to meet her, but they were tucked up in bed. If only she didn't have to work such long hours. She ran upstairs to the back room, where the children were slumbering: Alf was in bed, Cassie in her drawer on the floor. She had started life sleeping in a drawer from Nell's chest of drawers, then the Brents had lent a larger drawer; but Cassie couldn't stay in it much longer, not without stunting her growth.

Violet, curled up at the foot of the bed, got up and stretched, no doubt flinging come-hither fumes in all directions. Not a care in the world. In danger of landing them with half a dozen kittens, but not a care in the world.

Nell crammed her hat and coat onto the crowded pegs on the back of the door and slid out onto the landing before Violet could get any ideas. The door to the front bedroom stood open. She peeped in. Mr Brent was sleeping, Mrs Brent at his bedside, her spine a curve of desolation.

Nell said cheerfully, 'I'm home. How is he?'

Mrs Brent's spine sprang to attention. 'Oh, there you are, love. He had a bad coughing fit earlier, which wore him out, but he's sleeping now.'

'I'll make tea and bring it up.'

'Aye, love, you do that.'

That in itself spoke volumes. When it was pleurisy, even when it was pneumonia, Mrs Brent would have said, 'Nay, you've been at work all day. You stop with him and I'll pop down.'

Nell brought the tea, skirting round the bed into the strip where they had pulled it away from the wall. It made everything easier, that gap did – moving and washing Mr Brent, adjusting the bedding and sitting either side of him.

'Has he been awake much?'

'He was earlier. We had a good old chat. He can always make me laugh, can my Hedley.' Tears welled in Mrs Brent's eyes, blue blurring to grey.

'He doesn't sound as wheezy.'

'His lungs have mostly cleared up.' There was a rattle of china as Mrs Brent put down her cup and saucer. She rubbed her hands up and down her arms. 'Ten days since, I thought pneumonia were the worst that could happen, but now...'

'You're caring for him beautifully. No one could do more.' And talking of not doing more: 'Did your Hilda come today?'

'For a while. She left to get Edmund's tea.'

'Posy's old enough to do that.'

54

'Edmund likes her to be there to put his meal on't table. You know how men are.'

Stuff that. If she had still been wed to Stan, and her dad had been on his deathbed, she would have told Stan to get his meals off his mother while she took their Alf and went home. But if Mum and Dad had still been alive, would she have married Stan? It was the anguish of multiple bereavements and the huge swell of loneliness that had grown inside her like a new organ that had propelled her into Stan's arms.

'Did Mrs Watson have the children again?' she asked. That was another worry. Mrs Watson next door had a heart of gold, but she also had a colourful turn of phrase and Nell didn't want the children picking up any fruity expressions. Besides, she ought to offer Mrs Watson something for her trouble, but money for child-minding was wrapped up in what she gave Mrs Brent every week. She couldn't ask for some of it back, not with Mrs Brent heartbroken over her failing husband.

'Is that our lovely lodger?' Mr Brent's voice was frail. The face he turned towards her was thin and grey, the skin sunken into the crevices of his skull.

'I see you've not forgotten how to flirt,' Nell managed, though cords of anguish tightened in her throat.

'I've only ever flirted wi' one lass.' He looked at his wife, lifting a shaking hand from the bed for her to clasp. 'The most beautiful girl in the world.'

'Get on with you,' said Mrs Brent.

'You'll always be my pretty, dark-haired lass.'

'Look at me now, grey as can be.'

'Salt-and-pepper,' said Nell.

'Same blue eyes an' all.' Mr Brent turned to Nell. 'I'm sorry you lost your husband, lass. There's nowt better than a long marriage and you're young to go through life with that regret.'

'Don't fret about me.' She felt a complete heel. She wasn't just a lodger to this darling couple. They had drawn her into their hearts and she knew how valued and trusted she was. Trusted. And they believed her to be a widow.

Everyone believed she was a widow – including her own children.

'Do you have any regrets, love?' Mr Brent asked his wife.

'Well, I'd have liked more children.'

'I know, but having just our Hilda made the money stretch further. A man wants to do the best he can for his family.'

'What about you, Mr Brent?' Nell asked. 'Any regrets?' She immediately knew she had said the wrong thing. A sort of flutter passed between the couple. 'I shouldn't have asked.'

'It's all right, lass. It's no secret. My Leonie has always known.'

'Me and Hedley had to get wed because our Hilda was on the way. We'd have got married any-road, of course, but we needed to do it quicker, only my sister–'

'Who were a reet spiteful so-and-so,' put in Mr Brent.

'Our vicar was a strict sort and my sister took it on herself to tell him I were in the family way, so he refused to marry us. He said he didn't marry sinners. I knew my sister was waiting for us to go traipsing round all the churches, begging to get wed, but I wouldn't give her the satisfaction. We went down the registry office and got wed there.' There was a glint in Mrs Brent's eyes and a certain tilt to her chin. A glimpse of the spirited girl from years ago? 'And that were good enough for me, but I've always known my Hedley wished for a church do. I'm sorry, love. I put my fight with my sister in front of what you wanted. If I could take it back, I would.'

And Nell knew exactly what she had to do.

'You did what?' Mrs Brent jostled the milk pan as she turned in surprise. She steadied it over the heat before confronting Nell, eyes snapping. 'You've arranged for us to get married? I'll have you know me and Hedley have been legally wed forty years come August and our Hilda turns forty in November. Or are you one of them as doesn't believe in registry office marriages? Have you got the brass neck to stand in my kitchen, telling me I'm not a respectable married woman?'

'Of course you're married. I didn't make myself clear. It's not a wedding, it's...' There didn't seem to be a word for it. Certainly Mr Stidson hadn't known one. 'The minister said he would do a ceremony for you.'

Mrs Brent's eyes narrowed. 'The minister?'

'Mr Stidson from the chapel.'

'We're not chapel-goers.'

'I know, but the vicar said no.' Actually, he had said she was barking mad, but never mind that now.

'Anyroad, Hedley can't go anywhere, not in his

state. I don't know what you was thinking.'

'Mr Stidson says he'll come here.'

'Then it won't be a wedding, will it? Even I know that, heathen that I am with my registry office marriage.' She tossed her head, her words loaded with scorn.

'Mrs Brent, hear me out – please. I know I took a liberty, but it was done in good heart. There's no question that you're married, but when Mr Brent said about his one regret–'

'And you've took it on yourself to set right what I did wrong nigh-on forty year ago.'

'You didn't do owt wrong–'

'Oh, but I did.' Mrs Brent splayed her fingers over her stomach as if warding off sickness; her wedding band glinted under the gas lamp hanging from the ceiling. 'When our vicar turned us down, I were that riled with our Martha I went straight up the registry. I wouldn't even wait for the banns: I had a special licence. Ha! That were one in the eye for Martha.'

The fight drained out of her and she deflated. Her face sagged and her shoulders rounded. Nell tried to hug her, but with sudden spirit she danced away.

'Nay, don't mind me.' She plonked herself in front of the range, seizing the wooden spoon to stir the milk. 'I'm just the daft old bat who got wed up the registry to spite her sister.' She stirred the milk so vigorously it threatened to stream over the sides.

Nell was struggling to keep up. 'But I thought it was what you wanted.'

'Oh aye?' Mrs Brent picked up the milk pan and

crashed it down on another part of the range. She faced Nell. 'You think I wanted to get married up the registry? You think it were my girlhood dream? Well, it wasn't. I wanted a proper dress and my mother's veil and a lend of my cousin Molly's cream-coloured shoes what she had dyed for her own wedding. But I forgot all that, because I were too busy spitting feathers.' She stopped. Her chin dropped onto her chest. When she raised it, her eyes were sombre. 'You don't make vows in a registry office: did you know that? I didn't. You say summat and you sign summat and that's it. The registrar said, "You may kiss the bride," and I wanted to say, "What about us vows?" but I couldn't, could I, not with me being the one what had insisted. So I put on a brave face and told our Martha to put that in her pipe and smoke it. But I've always been sorry we never made vows. I wouldn't have minded the registry if they'd had vows.' She wet her lips. 'I've never told anyone else and you're not to say a word.'

'I wouldn't dream of it.'

'Especially not to my Hedley. He's always ac-cepted the registry office because it was what I wanted. He'd be upset summat dreadful if he knew I had...'

'Regrets?'

'Reservations.'

'So what should I do about Mr Stidson?'

'What's he going to do?' Mrs Brent gave a sheep-ish half-smile. 'I were too het up to listen properly.'

'He'll say a few words about long marriages, then he'll bless yours. Do you think that might make up a little for not getting wed in church?'

Mrs Brent deflated again. This time Nell held her as she wept.

'Your parents are *what?*'

Wrapped in her blanket in the scullery, Posy sat up, the better to earwig. Something was going on. Ma had been to see Gran and Gramps today and Posy had arrived home from school to find her looking frowny and nervous.

'They're going to have their marriage blessed,' said Ma.

'They're what? Why?'

A tiny silence: Posy imagined Ma pressing her lips together. 'Well, they never had a church wedding, so...'

'Codswallop! A blessing, my foot. About forty years too late, wouldn't you say? What made them think of that?'

'It was Mrs Hibbert's idea.'

'That woman! She should keep her nose out.'

Posy squirmed on Ma's behalf. Even when something wasn't your fault, Dad could make you feel like it was.

'It's this Saturday. Mother would like us there so it's a proper family occasion.'

'And will that lodger be present?'

A pause. 'I think so.' Which meant yes.

'Then it won't be a family occasion, so there's no need for us to put ourselves out.'

'Edmund, please. It means a lot to them.'

'We'll have to see.'

Which meant he wouldn't decide until the last minute. Or rather, he might have made his mind up already, but he wouldn't say owt. He would keep them dangling. Keeping them on their toes, he called it.

Posy lay down, wriggling to get as close to comfortable as she could. The evening gloom was deepening. Behind her head, the curtain shifted in the draught from the tiny hole in the window. Propping herself on one elbow, she pushed a fingertip of curtain into the hole, then settled down again. The copper across from her was a deeper shape of darkness. The scullery had the sharp tang of soda crystals but sometimes, like today when Ma had washed the front room curtains as part of her spring-cleaning, it smelt of soapsuds, which was a much nicer smell. Clean but kind.

What was this blessing Gran and Gramps wanted? That was the trouble with listening in. You couldn't ask questions afterwards. Perhaps Ma would tell her in the morning.

But Ma said nowt on the subject, not the next morning after Dad had left, nor when Posy came home from school that afternoon. Perhaps some encouragement wouldn't go amiss.

'Please may I go round to Gran and Gramps's this weekend?' Posy asked, then fastened her mouth tight shut. Don't say more. Don't say too much.

'I don't know,' said Ma. 'Ask nearer the time.'

Why couldn't she say, 'They're doing summat special on Saturday and they want us there, but it's up to your father'? Posy wasn't stupid. She knew not to say owt to Dad.

Unfortunately, the same couldn't be said for Ma.

Dad arrived home and Ma hurried to put tea on the table. Tripe and onions tonight: was she trying to butter him up?

'Our Posy was asking about going to see Gran and Gramps on Saturday,' said Ma.

Not on Saturday. She deliberately hadn't said Saturday. Posy's throat closed, trapping food in her mouth. Eyes down, she continued chewing, willing herself to swallow, willing Ma to correct the mistake.

'Really?' said Dad and Posy felt his gaze on her. 'And how does she know about Saturday? Did you tell her?'

'No,' said Ma. 'She wants to see them, that's all.'

'And she happens to want to go on Saturday.'

The food in Posy's mouth was a tasteless wodge. Her throat relaxed and she made herself swallow. Her stomach twitched a protest that brought tears to her eyes, but the food settled.

Dad didn't say anything else. Was she safe? You never knew.

Ma took the plates to the scullery and fetched the lemon pudding, its sharp-sweet aroma wafting across the table.

'It'll only take a minute to do the custard,' she said.

'I wonder if Posy deserves pudding,' said Dad.

The kitchen went quiet. Ma didn't move. Then she opened the cupboard and took out the box of Bird's Custard Powder.

'Look at me, Posy.'

The custard powder was in between the Green's Blancmange Powder and Chivers Jelly Crystals. Next to the jelly was a gap where the Criddle's

62

Black Treacle was meant to be. Ma had better get that replaced quick smart and hope Dad didn't fancy any gingerbread in the meantime.

Dad's fist crashed onto the table. Posy jumped. So did the table.

'Look at me when I tell you.'

The air tightened around her.

'You listened in. You had your ear pressed to that door. Well – didn't you?'

'No.'

'Fetch the candle.'

She got up. Her legs wobbled and she almost had to sit down again, but you didn't disobey Dad. Even useless legs didn't disobey Dad.

The candle was on the shelf next to the range. Without looking, Ma pushed it nearer and Posy picked it up. It wasn't much more than a stub, glued to its saucer by wax. Dad took a box of Swan Vestas from his pocket. He slid it open and removed a match, holding it ready to strike. Ma stirred the custard. She kept her back to them. Dad struck the match. There was a brisk *fizz* and the sharp smell as the flame flared and settled.

'You listened at the door, didn't you?'

She was for it, whatever she said. *No* got the candle. *Yes* admitted to lying. Which was worse? She gazed at the flame and her courage failed.

'Yes,' she breathed.

'Speak up. I can't hear you.'

'Yes.'

Ma stirred, her back to them. Nowt to do with me, said her back. Nothing's happening, said her back.

Dad's eyes gleamed. 'First she says no, now she

says yes.' He sucked in a breath through his teeth. 'Which is it? Yes, you did or no, you didn't?'

She couldn't go back to no. 'Yes.'

'And how am I to tell when you change your answer?' He indicated the candle with a jerk of his big square jaw. 'You're saying yes? Hold your hand over the flame. If you're telling the truth, you won't get burnt.'

Ma stirred the custard.

## Chapter Five

Would Hilda show her face? When Nell asked, Mrs Brent said, 'Oh, yes, love. Of course she'll come, if she can,' and Nell had wanted to send her arm snaking all the way to Heathside Lane in Withington to give Hilda a good slap. If she could, indeed! Didn't she understand how much this mattered? But that was Hilda Tanner all over, as much use as the skin off last week's custard.

Mr Stidson was due at three. Nell took Cassie next door to Mrs Watson at half-two. At that age, Alf would have watched with big round eyes, happy to be quiet as long as he could sit cuddled on his mummy's knee, but Cassie was independent, determined, a wriggler. Nell still boggled at how different her children were. She and Alf had always been so natural together that he felt like an extension of herself, but Cassie seemed to think that a name like Cassandra gave her a lot to live up to and there was no harm in starting now.

'Eh, give her to me, the little lamb,' said Mrs Watson.

The little lamb toddled purposefully over the threshold and bolted down the hallway, leaving Nell to hand over a bag of building blocks that Alf used to use for building but which his sister used for banging, throwing, kicking, anything you could think of other than building. With luck, Cassie would make too much racket to notice any undesirable vocabulary Mrs Watson let slip.

Nell went home. Mrs Brent was at Mr Brent's bedside, and Alf was with them. Should she take more chairs up in case Hilda's family came? They were cutting it fine if they were coming. But if she provided chairs and they didn't come, it would look bad.

She had just sat down on the chair between the bed and the wall, and was lifting Alf onto her lap, when the front door opened. Mrs Brent perked up.

'That's Hilda. Hedley, our Hilda's come. I knew she would.'

Footsteps on the stairs, lots of them, then the bedroom door opened and Hilda's family entered. Nell came to her feet. She was pleased to see Hilda – not Hilda personally, but she was glad for the Brents' sake. Edmund Tanner stood in the doorway, filling it. Not that he was tall, but he filled the space, filled the room. 'Brick shithouse,' Doug said in Nell's head. Built like a brick shithouse. Wide shoulders, big chest. Big, square jaw.

'You sit here,' Nell offered Hilda. Holding Alf's hand almost over his head, she shuffled behind him, squeezing along the gap, anxious not to bump the bed.

'Yes, Hilda,' said Edmund Tanner. 'You sit beside your father.'

He looked at Nell. She glanced away quickly enough – she hoped – that it didn't look like she was dodging a staring contest.

'I'll fetch more chairs,' she said. Alf clung to her hand, moulding himself to her leg. 'Stop here with Mrs Brent,' she whispered. Alf was scared of Edmund Tanner. The man had never done anything to him, but he was still scared. Mind you, there was summat about Edmund Tanner. Broad and handsome he might be, with his dark eyes and his black hair, but there was nowt to warm to.

'I'll do it.' With a glance at Alf that bordered on a sneer, Edmund Tanner left the room.

He returned with a single chair. He put it at the foot of the bed and sat down. Nell smiled, pretending it didn't matter.

'What about a seat for Mrs Hibbert?' asked Mrs Brent.

'Oh, is she stopping? I thought this was a family matter.'

Mr Brent stirred. 'We want her here.'

'It were her idea,' added Mrs Brent. 'She should be here.'

'Very well.' But he didn't get up immediately.

'No need,' said Nell. 'I'll fetch my own chair.'

She stepped forward, or tried to. With Alf clinging, it was like having a wooden leg. She had to unpeel him. Behind her was the dressing table. Her chest tightened at the sight of Alf's pleading eyes, but she placed him by the dressing table, catching the hands that scrabbled to keep hold of

66

hers and attaching them to the smooth curve of one of the legs. She turned to leave the room. Edmund Tanner's broad back overlapped the spindled back of his chair. Didn't he realise she needed him to move? Well, she wasn't going to squeeze past.

'Excuse me, please.' She kept her voice cool and polite. 'Shift your ruddy arse,' said Tom in her head.

As she ran downstairs, a rat-tat took her straight to the door to admit Mr Stidson.

'Thank you for coming. It's upstairs, the front room.'

Posy appeared on the stairs. 'I've come for the footstool.'

The bedroom was going to look like a rag-and-bone yard at this rate. 'Shall I bring you a chair, Mr Stidson?' Nell offered.

'I'll carry one up for myself.'

'It's no trouble, honestly.' She couldn't have the minister fetching and carrying. It wasn't respectful.

'I insist.'

So she led the way up, followed by Mr Stidson with a chair and Posy with the footstool from the parlour. Edmund Tanner was obliged to shift his arse once more and, in the bustle of introductions and arranging the furniture, Nell stood in front of the dressing table, at the rear of the proceedings, holding Alf's hand.

She waited for Hilda to call Posy into the gap by the wall, but Hilda said nothing, so Nell said quietly, 'Here, Posy, pop the footstool next to me.'

Posy gave her a beaming smile. 'Would you like

to sit on it, Mrs Hibbert?'

'It's a bit low for me, but thank you for asking. Mr Stidson, would you like me to take your hat?' She put it on the dressing table.

The minister sat down. He had placed his chair at the foot of the bed at an angle so that he could easily look round and include those at the window end of the room.

'Shall we begin? This is a special occasion, not just for this family but also for me. I've never been asked to do this before and I've been reflecting on what an honour it is. I have married many young couples in my time. They come to me, full of love and hope, and I join them in wedlock; but today I have the pleasure of meeting Mr and Mrs Brent, who are not at the beginning of life's journey together, but who have been married for ... how long?'

'Forty years come August,' said Mrs Brent, 'and we was childhood sweethearts before that.'

'A lifelong love,' said Mr Stidson. 'Usually I officiate at marriages by talking about what lies ahead, but today we celebrate this marriage by looking back. Mr Brent, do you feel strong enough to say a few words about your childhood sweetheart?'

Mr Brent's worn face softened and his hand wriggled across the eiderdown to wrap itself round his wife's. 'Eh, she were the bonniest lass in our street. Blue eyes and long dark hair and the tiniest waist you ever saw.'

'Not like that now,' said Mrs Brent.

Nell smiled. She might have laughed but felt constrained from doing so. Edmund Tanner remained impassive and Hilda sat quietly, eyes downcast. She should be looking at her parents.

'You've always been a beauty in my eyes,' said Mr Brent. 'I can see thee now, running down our street with a hoop and stick, your hair flying behind you. You could keep that hoop going all the way to the gasworks and back. I knew then you were the lass for me.'

'You fell in love with Gran because she were good with a hoop?' said Posy.

'Seen and not heard, Posy,' said Edmund Tanner without looking round.

'It's as good a reason as any.' Mr Brent chuckled. It turned into a cough that crackled in his throat. He regained control, eyes watering, his thin chest heaving.

'Have some water.' But Mrs Brent's hand was too trembly to hold the glass to his lips.

For heaven's sake, why didn't Hilda–?

'Shape yourself, Hilda,' ordered Edmund Tanner and Hilda fluttered to life, leaning forward to assist. Nell wiped her face clean of expression. She were nowt a pound, that Hilda.

'Should we stop for a few minutes?' asked Mr Stidson.

Mr Brent waved a feeble hand. 'Nay.' He made circles with his hand. 'Keep going.'

'Very well.'

The minister talked smoothly about long marriages and Nell blessed him for giving the Brents time to recover. Then he looked at Mrs Brent.

'Would you care to tell us how you knew this was the boy for you?'

'That's easy, that is. He started out in the cats'

69

meat shop, this one did. Left school at twelve and became the cats' meat lad. My mother weren't best pleased that I had my eye on him, but he promised me he'd make summat of himself, and he did. When he were fourteen, he got took on as an apprentice by the Corporation and I knew we'd be set for life.'

'It's important for a man to provide for his family,' said Mr Stidson.

'He's been a good provider, has Hedley.' Mrs Brent's voice rang with pride. 'I've never had a moment's worry on that score.'

'Would you like to say something about your parents, Mrs Tanner?' asked Mr Stidson.

Hilda looked flummoxed. 'Well ... they've been a good mum and dad to me...'

Beside Nell, Posy sat forward. Hilda clearly couldn't think what to say. Well, what a surprise.

'May I say something?' Nell volunteered.

'Family first,' said Edmund Tanner. 'Go on, Hilda. What have you got to say?'

'Um ... I've finished.'

'And very nice it was, love,' said Mr Brent. 'No parents could ask for more than to be thought well of by their family.'

Would that inspire Hilda to flights of deathless prose? Apparently not, but Nell smiled at Posy as if her mother had delivered a wonderful speech.

'Can I say something about Gran and Gramps?' asked Posy.

'*May I,* not *Can I,*' said her father. 'And no, you may not. Children should be seen and not heard.'

The moment wobbled on the brink of being spoilt.

'Then...' Mrs Brent looked expectantly at Nell and Mr Stidson turned round with an encouraging glance. Even Edmund Tanner felt obliged to look over his shoulder.

'I'd like to thank Mr and Mrs Brent for taking in me and my Alf when we was in need,' Nell began.

'And Violet,' Alf piped up.

'I thought the baby's name was ... Caroline ... Catherine...?' said Edmund Tanner. Was he interrupting on purpose?

'Cassie,' said Nell.

'Violet's the cat,' said Mrs Brent.

'The cat? I thought that animal was yours.'

'Nay. She came here with Mrs Hibbert.'

'She's an all-of-us's cat,' said Alf.

'Never forget, Posy,' said Edmund Tanner, 'that children should be seen and not heard.'

Nell felt her cheeks darken. 'Anyroad, we couldn't have found a kinder or better landlord and landlady. It takes a special kind of person to accept a widow and a child. The Brents wanted a male lodger, so that tells you how good they were to take us.'

Mrs Brent gazed at her, her eyes shining. She had such kind eyes. You could tell a lot about a person from their eyes, so Mum used to say. You could see the fun in Eric's, the serious thoughts in Harold's, the wry humour in their Vi's.

The emptiness in Mum's after they all quit this world.

'Would anyone like to say more?' asked Mr Stidson.

No one answered, then Mrs Brent sat up

71

straighter. 'Yes, sir. I've got summat to say, sum-mat I've only realised these past few days.' Turning to her husband, she reached for his hands and gazed at him as if he were the only other person in the room. 'You and me didn't make vows, love, because of not marrying in church, but this I do know: the way we've treated one another and looked after each other and done us best for each other – we might not have said vows under God's roof, but we've lived us lives as if we had.'

'Oh, petal,' murmured Mr Brent. 'You're my best girl.'

The loving looks they exchanged made Nell's throat ache. She wanted the moment to last for ever, for their sakes.

'Shall we bow our heads in prayer?' said Mr Stidson.

A few more minutes and it was over. Thanks and goodbyes were exchanged. The minister pressed the Brents' hands warmly, then Nell handed him his hat and Edmund Tanner showed him out, re-turning a minute later to stand in the doorway, not speaking, but by not crossing the threshold sug-gesting it was time for his family to leave. Nell could have crowned him.

'Come and sit down again, Edmund,' said Mrs Brent.

He sat down.

'Mrs Brent looks weepy,' whispered Alf.

Nell kept her voice low, aware that the others could hear every word. 'Today is a funny day, happy and sad at the same time. We're happy because dear Mr and Mrs Brent have had such a long life together, but we're sad too because Mr

Brent is poorly.'

Please don't ask if he's going to die.

Alf looked at her in concern. 'Is it reet bug-geration, Mummy?'

## Chapter Six

Was that...? It couldn't be. But it was – the slender figure, that confident, chin-up walk, the elegant rig-out. *Roberta.*

Jim leant into the top of the ladder, pulling his cap down over his forehead and turning his face away from the women on the crazy-paving path below. Women: that was the wrong word. Ladies, with their tippy-tappy shoes and educated voices. He knew that voice – Roberta's mother. He leant further towards the window pane. He must look like he was getting an eyeful of the Randalls' front bedroom, but he wasn't. He was accustomed to looking at the window, not through it.

Hearing the front door shut, he glanced down. Roberta and Mrs Fairbrother had disappeared indoors. He huffed out a breath and applied his energy to buffing up the window with his chamois. Good job this was the final window. He could be gone in a few minutes.

He descended the ladder, standing at its foot to draw it into an upright position before carrying it down the path and through the gate. His barrow was parked against the kerb. Behind it stood a motor he knew, Angus Fairbrother's beloved old

Austin. He smiled: he would bet any money Roberta had been on at her father to buy something new.

The uniformed chauffeur, leaning against the side of the vehicle, ankles crossed, smoking a cigarette, was unknown to him.

He lowered the ladder onto his barrow. 'Smart motor.'

The chauffeur uncrossed his ankles, turning to pat paintwork the colour of port wine. 'She's not bad for her age.'

'You keep her looking smart.'

'It's worth the effort. Cigarette?' He pulled out a packet of Player's Drumhead.

Ordinarily, Jim would have accepted and passed the time of day, but not this morning, not with Roberta and her mother in the handsome house behind him.

'Thanks, but no. Mustn't keep the customers waiting.'

He returned for his bucket, tipping the water down the drain. The windows looked good in the spring sunshine. No smears, no grubby corners. He was a good window cleaner. Conscientious. Reliable. He had built up a decent reputation. His customers would be amazed if they knew what he used to do for a living.

He skirted the side of the house to the kitchen door, which Mrs Randall's daily had left open on this fine morning. She appeared, wiping her hands on her apron.

'She's give me the money for you. There y'are – a bob.'

'Thanks.' He pocketed two tanners. 'See you

next month.'

He came round the corner of the house – and there was Roberta. Too late to duck out of sight: they were face-to-face. A small parcel dangled by its string from her fingers; she must have fetched it from the motor. Her free hand flew to her chest, her leather-gloved fingers spreading out in a fan, lips parting on a gasp as her eyes widened.

He touched his cap. 'Roberta. I'd hoped to leave without being seen.'

She recovered quickly. Her hand dropped to her side. There was a flush of colour high on her cheekbones. 'You've no business using my first name.'

'I stand corrected, Miss Fairbrother, or is it Mrs?'

The flush on her cheekbones flared a fiery red. 'It's Miss Fairbrother.'

Still.

Oh, Roberta. She had expected the war to send back to her the same man it had taken from her in 1914 and it had hurt her terribly when she realised how he had altered ... and how her future had altered as a result.

'You're still cleaning windows, I see.' Her voice was brittle.

He smiled. 'As you see.' He spread his arms, inviting her to look at him in his shirtsleeves. 'You're looking well, Miss Fairbrother, if I may say so.'

'Don't make fun of me.'

'It was intended as a compliment. I apologise if I spoke out of turn.'

It wasn't what he had wanted to say, anyway. He wanted to tell her how swish she looked, all decked out in a peachy-pinky colour that you would have to be female to know the name of. Jacket, dress, hat, even the tongues of her shoes were the same hue. The jacket was almost long enough to be a coat and had heaven alone knew how many minuscule buttons down the front: it must take five minutes to fasten all that lot. He could imagine her standing there while her maid did the necessary. She would consider it time well spent.

Her hat was one of those cloche things that looked like an upside-down flowerpot and it sported a colossal felt flower on the side. Only the tiniest bit of her hair showed, so she must be wearing it pretty short these days. Pity.

Her eyes narrowed. 'I don't look for compliments from window cleaners.'

She marched indoors. Would she tell her mother about the encounter? Tell her friends? Would she laugh and say, 'I had such a lucky escape,' and shake her head in relief?

Or would she keep silent about it, as if it had never happened?

Jim's next calls were some corner shops in the backstreets. He liked doing them, liked to feel a shining window would tempt customers inside. Before the war, he had never set foot inside places like these, but now he had nothing but admiration and sympathy for the shop owners. A twelve-hour day was nothing. Sixteen hours was normal to many of them.

He did the tobacconist's, then moved along to Bradshaw's, the butcher's on the next corner. As well as chops, sausages and joints, they did tasty pies here. Betty Bradshaw was a dab hand with pastry.

The shop door stood open. He stuck his head inside.

'Save me a meat and tater pie, will you? I'll collect it when I finish my morning round.'

'Will do, Jim. Now shove out o't road and make room for a real customer. Morning, Mrs Watson.'

'Sorry.' Jim stepped aside to let a woman in. She had two young children with her, her grandchildren, probably.

'Ta, love. You got the Brent ham, Arnold?'

'Coming right up.'

'Here's your water.' Betty came round the counter, hefting his bucket.

He took it from her and went outside. The ladder was already in position, but he was going to start at the bottom and work up. With his drying-leather tucked in his belt, he dunked a cloth and set to work.

'Are you a window cleaner?' piped up a voice beside him.

He looked down at the little lad. 'My secret is out. What gave me away?'

'We've come for the ham.'

'So I gather.'

'It's special ham called buried-with-ham. You have it at funerals. But,' he confided, 'it doesn't mean you put ham in the coffin.'

'No, that would be an odd thing to do.'

'My daddy was buried with ham, but I'm not old enough to remember.'

'People set store by being buried with ham.'

'What does *set store* mean?

'What do you think it means?'

The boy tilted his head to one side. 'Does it mean people think it matters?'

'You're a clever lad. What's your name?'

'Alf, and my little sister is Cassie.'

'That's a fancy name.'

'It's short for Cassandra.'

'That's even fancier. You don't get many Cassandras to the pound.'

The boy frowned, unsure, then carried on. 'Mummy wanted Violet, but she couldn't have it because the cat got it first.'

'Is that so?'

'Buggeration!' It was the woman who had brought the children for the ham. 'What's that child doing now?'

Jim turned round, thinking Alf was about to get it in the neck for interrupting him, but instead found the little girl was partway up his ladder. Dropping his cloth, he covered the distance in a single stride. She was at chest-height, a little dot of a thing. He couldn't help admiring her spirit. He plucked her from the rungs and swung her high in the air. Her chubby face was filled with glee and he grinned back. She might be more adventurous than was good for her, but she was a sweetheart.

'What are you doing with my daughter? Put her down this instant!'

A young woman hurried across the street with the light of battle in her eyes. She was tall and had a natural grace that was unimpeded by the cobbles, a full shopping bag and her haste. She wore a cavalry-twill coat that had seen better days and a simple, small-brimmed burgundy hat that revealed frank features and clear skin. Her hair, fringed and bobbed, swinging at a length between chin and shoulder, was the same colour as the crackly brown of autumn leaves.

'Put her down!'

Jim set Cassie on her feet. She immediately set off in the direction of the ladder. He caught hold of her by the woolly bobble on top of her bonnet. She stopped, looking up and turning in a circle, trying to see what was impeding her progress.

'She were halfway up yon ladder,' said the older woman. 'You can't take your eyes off her for one minute without her climbing aboard the tram to Blackpool. She's a little terror, is our Cassie.' She beamed down at the tiny girl, wagging a finger that gave no indication of annoyance.

'This man rescued her.' Alf ran to his mum. 'He's a hero.'

The young woman's gaze flicked in his direction. There was a trace of awkwardness in the glance, but she raised her chin at the same time. 'Maybe I were a tad hasty, but any mother would have re-acted the same.'

'I don't doubt it.'

'Ooh, don't he talk fancy for a window cleaner,' cried the older woman.

Catching hold of Cassie's hand, the young mother gave Jim a brief half-smile that combined thanks with dismissal. He nodded, stepping back to the window, but he was reluctant to let the moment go. That young woman had something about her. Having seen Roberta less than an hour ago, it was impossible not to compare the two, and Roberta won on every count: beauty, clothes, poise and that certain something that came from a life of ease and privilege. But even so, this young woman had something about her.

He dipped his cloth in the water and continued with his work.

'I've got the loaves and butter – and tomatoes – and tea – and more sugar, just in case – oh, and a jar of that extra-strong piccalilli that were Mr Brent's favourite, though whether anyone will fancy it is another matter, but Mrs Brent insisted.'

'Eh, love, you've done all that and all I've done is fetch the ham and lose your Cassie up a ladder. Let's get on home and get these butties made. Mustn't be late for't funeral.'

Jim turned round. 'I hope it goes well – as well as these things can.'

She looked at him, right at him, as if those other glances hadn't really seen him. Her eyes were hazel, a light amber colour. He saw cleverness in them. Not shrewdness, not calculation, but honest-to-goodness intelligence and good humour. His heart bumped.

He didn't want her to go.

Was she still Mrs Hedley Brent? Or did his death make her Mrs Leonie Brent? What it made her was a smaller person, a lesser creature, that was for certain. Her and Hedley, they had been inseparable. Childhood sweethearts, they had spent their entire lives together. Without him, she was less than she was meant to be. Diminished. It felt like she was fading away.

Eh, but she had given him a good send-off and that was summat to be proud of. A fancy hearse with glass sides, pulled by black horses with black plumes, the undertaker walking in front with his top hat and his cane: you didn't get more special than that.

'You've done him proud,' the neighbours said, igniting a fierce glow of satisfaction inside her.

She caught a few murmurs about how much extra the Brents must have stumped up for their burial insurance. She had been allowed to cash in part of her own policy to contribute to Hedley's funeral, but this was a secret. Should she have told Hilda? But Hilda would have told Edmund and he might not approve and she really couldn't be doing with him laying down the law, not just now, not in connection with Hedley's funeral. Hedley's funeral had to be perfect.

And it had been.

What was she meant to do now? Her parlour was full of neighbours and she was sitting in the middle, feeling excluded, separate ... alone. Organising the funeral had kept her going, given her something to focus on, one last thing to do for Hedley; but now it was over and she couldn't think what she was meant to do next.

Mrs Watson leant towards her, her face creased into compassionate lines. Her voice sounded kind, but it was difficult to concentrate on the words. Leonie returned her neighbour's smile with a little grimace, then pretended to let someone else catch her attention. The brass candlesticks on the mantelpiece had a good gleam on them. She had never been scared to use a bit of elbow grease. Hedley liked things to look their best and she had been proud to keep their home sparkling. Someone pressed a cup and saucer into her hand. She put it on the table beside her. It wasn't her cup and saucer. Hers had harebells round the rim, but everyone had mucked in with a lend of their crockery, and this cup and saucer, with its red and gold pattern, belonged to Mrs Foskett.

That green glass vase in the corner – she could get rid of it now, if she wanted. Years ago, Hedley's mother had taken it off the top of her own cupboard and handed it to her. 'For your new home, chuck,' she had said, which sounded like a generous gesture, but Leonie had sensed that Hedley's mother was passing it on just to get rid, because she hated it.

Leonie hated it an' all. It was plug-ugly. The glass was knobbly and the sides were straight. Vases shouldn't be straight. They should be curved and elegant. But she had never been able to say owt, because of it coming from Hedley's mother. She could get rid of it now, though, if she felt like it; only she didn't feel like it. Her limbs felt like dead weights. Her heartbeats were heavy and slow, but at the same time there was something inside her that was pitter-pattering in panic.

Folk were getting up to say goodbye. They pressed her hand and said kind words. She tried to hold onto their fingers, but the hands slipped away. She wanted them to stay and talk about Hedley, to give her a few more minutes with her darling chap, that sweet boy she had fallen in love with all those years ago. Why hadn't she made more effort, paid attention, listened, talked, instead of feeling lost and alone? A fist squeezed inside her chest and her breathing stopped. Raw fear streamed through her.

She wasn't alone. Don't be stupid. She had Hilda and their Posy. Oh yes, and Edmund. And the Hibberts. She wasn't alone.

Yes, she was. Always and for ever.

'Well, that's over.'

Edmund's voice was full-throated and he made the most of it, as if he expected everyone to pay attention because he was worth listening to. He stood in the middle of the room, the better to have all eyes on him. Hilda sank into the armchair. It had been pushed out of the way to make space, so Hilda seemed tucked out of the way too. Posy, dear little Posy, looking pale and washed out in black, sat quiet as a mouse in the corner.

'It went well,' said Edmund.

'Aye,' Leonie began, glad to talk about it and keep it happening, to keep that precious link with Hedley.

'Now we need to decide what's best for you, Mother-in-law.'

Her mind went blank. She had thought they were going to relive the funeral, wringing every last detail out of it, every possible crumb of solace, but instead Edmund – what did he mean, what was best for her?

'This is a big house for you on your own.' He made it sound like she lived in Longford Hall.

'I'm not on my own. There's–'

'Yes, yes, the lodger and her offspring. You can't rely on her. She didn't even stay for the wake.'

'She had to get back to work. She took the morning off to do the shopping and get the food ready and attend the service. She can't take the afternoon off an' all.'

'I noticed she left her children behind for someone else to look after.'

'Well, she can't take them to the factory, can she? Mrs Watson's Annie came round special to sit with 'em next door, and I bet they've been as good as gold.'

'The point is, Mother-in-law, how are you going to manage without Father-in-law's work pension from the Corporation?'

A chill uncurled in her belly. 'There'll be a small widow's pension from't Corporation. I've got to apply.'

'I'll do that. That's my job now, to take the worry off your shoulders. You're lucky the Corporation hands out pensions to its widows – isn't she, Hilda?'

Hilda looked up. 'Yes.'

'I don't know anyone else who gets a widow's pension from their husband's work. Of course, it won't be anything like as much as Father-in-law's pension was. You'll find it hard to manage.'

'There's the rent from Mrs Hibbert,' said Leonie.

Edmund laughed. Hedley not cold in his grave, and Edmund stood there and laughed. It wasn't decent. 'That won't go far,' he said.

'She says if she works extra hard, she can maybe earn as much as three pounds a week.'

'Nonsense. That's a man's wage.'

'It's piecework. She'll fettle faster.'

84

'And produce shoddy work and earn less, not more.'

Didn't he want her to have enough to live on in this beloved house she had moved into as a bride? 'She has to take care not to let her standards slip, she knows that.'

'Even if she does rake in these riches – which I don't expect for one moment – she's young. She'll marry again and then where will you be?'

Leonie pressed her lips together. She and Hedley had never thought of Nell's getting married again. She was busy with her job and her children and that seemed to be her whole life. But she was young and attractive. Who could say?

'Even if she doesn't remarry,' Edmund went on, 'there's this new widow's pension starting next year. Ten bob a week, plus extra for children, so she won't need you. It's time to put yourself first. Let us put you first. It's better to rely on family.'

There was a rich note in his voice and Leonie almost crumpled under the kindness.

'That's what you should remember, Mother-in-law. Hilda and I are the ones you can trust. We'll always be here – won't we, Hilda?'

'Yes,' said Hilda.

It felt like the moment for Hilda to come to her, put her arms round her and make loving promises, but Hilda stayed put. A pair of thin arms slid round Leonie's neck and Posy snuggled her cheek against hers. Leonie breathed her in: Pears soap and cotton.

'I love you, Gran.'

'Oh, chick, I love you too.'

'Seen and not heard, Posy,' said Edmund.

Posy might have melted away, but Leonie pulled her down beside her on the sofa. Posy sat so close their bodies warmed one another. Would Edmund send Posy back to her seat in the corner?

'Posy has the right idea.' He sounded approving. 'You need your family, Mother-in-law.'

'Well...' Yes, she would say it. It had caused her and Hedley heartache over the years, though they had never uttered a word of reproach. 'We've never seen as much of one another as I'd have liked.'

'Now is the time to remedy that, Mother-in-law. We could give up our flat and move in here with you, then you'd never be on your own again. What do you say?'

## Chapter Seven

Saturday. The day she dreaded. Posy spent the morning being optimistic. That was her new word. She had learnt it from Miss Claybourne and now she wanted to use it as much as she could, but it was proving tricky. Not like last week's new words: *with gusto.* Miss Claybourne had set the class a composition about a visit to the zoo and Posy had produced a thrilling tale of lions roaring with gusto and elephants trumpeting with gusto, and a burglar came to steal the head zookeeper's watch and chain, so a quick-thinking girl unlocked the lions' cage and a lion pounced on the burglar and ate him with gusto and the King awarded the lion a medal. It was a ripping story and Miss Claybourne had read it out to the class.

The expression hadn't gone down so well at home. When Ma put a plate of bubble-and-squeak in front of her and she said, 'Thank you, Ma. I'll eat it with gusto,' Dad had made her stand in the corner for being cheeky. That was the trouble with new words. You needed to use them as much as you could because they improved your brain and made the world a better place, but other people didn't always appreciate them.

She had managed to work *optimistic* into a conversation – in Dad's absence, just in case.

'Are you optimistic that we'll go and live with Gran?' she asked Ma.

'Am I what?'

'Optimistic.'

'Lord, Posy, was there ever a child like you? How do you know about that, anyroad?'

'Dad said it after Gramps's funeral. So are you? Optimistic?'

'I don't know, love. We'll see.'

Ma never knew. Dad did all the knowing, all the thinking and deciding. Posy wasn't going to get married. She was going to do her own thinking and deciding.

She had vowed today to be optimistic. It was selfish to dwell on her own fears when Gran was sad because Gramps had died and gone to heaven. Besides, with her and Ma going to see Gran this afternoon, maybe Dad wouldn't send her to get his caramels.

But he did.

Oh, buggeration, he did.

It was the usual palaver, with Mr Bennett asking her what she wanted even though he knew perfectly well, then saying, 'As if I didn't know,' with a ho-ho sound in his voice.

She carried the bag home. Perhaps there would be six today. Don't ever let it be said that Posy Tanner didn't make full use of her optimism. Six caramels. Please let there be six.

Out they tumbled onto the green oilcloth. Six, please, six. One, two, three ... six, please, six ... four, five–

Dad gave the bag a shake, as if trying to dislodge a sixth caramel. Nothing fell out. Of course not. He was only doing it for show.

'How many are there, Posy?'

Five. Her throat closed. The word got stuck.

'I said, how many?'

'Five.' A tiny croak.

'I didn't hear that.'

'Five.'

'Are you certain? Count them. Let me hear you count them.'

'One, two, three, four ... five.'

'And how many should there be?'

'Five! There should flaming well be five, because that was what Mr Bennett had measured out.

'Six,' she whispered, hating herself, hating him, hating Rupert.

'You never learn, do you? Every week, you think you'll get away with it.' He breathed in through his nose. His nostrils flared and his chest expanded. 'Fetch Rupert.'

Posy's knees turned to blancmange, but somehow she walked across the room. She looked at

Ma, but Ma was bent almost double over her darning. She willed Ma to look. Even a sympathetic glance would help, but Ma kept her head down. Posy opened the door and stepped across to the side of the staircase, reaching between the balusters. With clammy fingers, she prised the stair rod free and carried it to Dad. He stood there, big and relaxed, letting her offer it until it suited him to take it.

'Turn round.'

She obeyed, locking her knees so they couldn't buckle. Then it came. A sharp swish cut the air and a hefty clout slammed into the backs of her legs, nearly knocking her off her feet. She staggered forwards, but righted herself at once. The pain plunged deep, a hard, full, rounded pain with a cruel, biting edge to it, as he administered six of the best, pain that would linger for hours in the depths of her muscles and bones.

He held out the stair rod. 'Say thank you to Rupert.'

'Thank you, Rupert.' She dropped a trembly kiss on the stair rod. She had once tried to kiss the air above it instead, but Dad had punished her again. Now she kissed Rupert even though it made bile rise in her throat to do so.

'You may put Rupert away.'

She was weak all over, but she knew better than to let Rupert slip through her fingers. She was dislocated from the world around her, but it was important to walk steadily so as not to be accused of being dramatic. She headed for the door.

Look at me, Ma. Look at me.

But Ma was engrossed in her darning.

'There's no need for you to leave just because Hilda's come,' Gran assured Mrs Hibbert, but Mrs Hibbert was already leaving the kitchen table.

'I'm sure you've got family things to talk about,' she said. 'We'll go upstairs and Cassie can have a nap while Alf and I play happy families. Would you like that, Alf?'

Posy was impressed. No one ever asked her what she wanted. Dad said Mrs Hibbert was an idiot who spoilt her children, but Alf and Cassie weren't spoilt.

'Does Posy enjoy playing cards?' Mrs Hibbert looked at Ma. 'Would she like to join us?'

'She'll be fine down here, thank you,' said Ma. 'She ought to be with her gran.'

'Of course.' Mrs Hibbert gathered up her children and disappeared.

'Don't you want to sit down, Posy?' asked Gran.

'I like standing.' The backs of her thighs were giving her gyp. 'Where's Violet?'

'Upstairs,' said Gran.

'Is she still on heat?'

'Posy!' Ma exclaimed. 'That's not polite conversation.'

Gran did funny things with her mouth, like she was stopping a smile breaking out. 'We don't think so, but we're giving it another couple of days to make sure.'

'Honestly, Mother, you encourage her.'

Gran squeezed Posy's hand. Posy slipped her arm round Gran's neck, her heart overflowing. Gran was special. She and Posy were linked together in a way that didn't need words.

'If we moved in with Gran, you could see Violet every day, Posy,' said Ma. 'You'd like that, wouldn't you? Have you given it any more thought, Mother?'

'There's a lot to think on.'

'You could keep your little pension. Edmund would be the man of the house; he'd pay the rent and the bills. Just imagine saving your pension.'

Gran put her cup to her lips, but that was for show. Her eyes were thoughtful. Wouldn't it be wonderful to live with her now she was all alone without Gramps? But underneath Posy's pleasure was a niggle she couldn't ignore. It sounded perfect: live with Gran and have all the family together.

Perfect.

No, it wasn't.


'Miss Lockwood, might I have a word? It's these skirt lengths. They seem a bit on the short side.'

Miss Lockwood stopped beside Nell's machine. 'I might have known you'd notice, Mrs Hibbert. It's next season's fashion, and that won't be the end of it. I was informed by one of the buyers that skirt lengths will get shorter still. Most unseemly, if you ask me.'

Was that a shudder of disapproval? As an overseer, Miss Lockwood wore a plain black dress, with fresh white collar and cuffs every day. Her skirt length was still pre-war. She was that kind of age. Older ladies still favoured ankle-length or even floor-length skirts and probably would until their dying days.

Nell was doing her best to work more speedily

91

so as to increase her wages, but it wasn't always possible. Hurrying could be disastrous if you were doing fur trimming or putting the tiniest of pleats into silk. Skilled work earned a higher rate but also took longer.

As well as working faster wherever feasible, she tried to work extra in other ways. When the hooter sounded for breaks, you had to finish the seam or detail you were in the middle of. While others around her stood up and started chatting, Nell kept going a bit longer, finishing what she was on and then starting the next bit, which meant finishing it too.

Dinner hours were purgatory. She didn't need an hour. She didn't even need half an hour. While everyone else gossiped over their barm cakes, she had to sit with her back to the clock or else she couldn't wrench her gaze away from it.

Miss Lockwood didn't stop for dinner until she had finished checking the morning's output. Nell excused herself to the other women and returned to the workroom.

'I'm sorry to disturb you, Miss Lockwood, but I've a favour to ask.'

'I hope it's not more time off.' She made it sound like Nell had gone to Rhyl for a fortnight, not taken half a day for a funeral.

'I was hoping you'd let me work longer.'

'You're already full-time.'

'Could I work from half-twelve till one each day? You wouldn't have to supervise me. You know I'd get on with it.'

'No one has asked that before. I'll have to find out.'

A flutter of hope lifted Nell's spirits. It would do wonders for her earnings.

That afternoon, when her colleagues were filing out for their tea break, Nell carried on for an extra few minutes, pushing the additional time as far as she dared.

Miss Lockwood appeared at her side.

'I took your request to the office and it was refused. You're not allowed to work more than forty-eight hours. Don't be too long finishing that sash. Everyone else has gone.'

'Yes, Miss Lockwood.'

Left alone, Nell finished the waterfall effect. She could murder a drink of tea, but these days she was providing her own refreshments. She went to the back of the room to the shelf where they were allowed to put the bottles of cordial or cold tea they brought from home. Hers was the only one left.

'There you are, Mrs Hibbert.'

Mr Flynn appeared. She knew what was coming next.

'Can I help you, Mr Flynn?'

'Well, now you mention it.' He always made it sound like he had never asked before.

She was tired and gasping for a drink, but Mr Flynn had that panicky look in his eyes. Suppose her brothers had survived and one of them had come home unable to cope with even the smallest amount of pressure. It might have happened to Tom; he had always been a bit of a dreamer; or maybe to Harold. He was big and steady and reliable, but you never knew. She would want her afflicted brother to receive kindness and support.

'It's next week's rosters.' Mr Flynn waggled his clipboard. 'I've made a start.'

Made a pig's whisker, more like. Nell looked through the orders. 'This one's substantial.'

'You remember those flower-printed dresses we did in March? It's a similar order, but bigger. We'll be working flat out, only I can't quite...'

'Put that order in this workshop and get next door to do the underwear and the children's coats...'

In two minutes she had sorted out the lot and sent Mr Flynn on his way. The flutter of hope she had experienced earlier returned, this time settling into a glow of inner calm. That big order would be a doddle. Unfitted bodices, low-waisted straight skirts, scooped necklines with casual collars: she could churn them out in her sleep. If she was ever going to make three pounds, next week was the week.

Posy knew what Dad and Ma were up to. No, it was difficult to imagine Ma getting up to anything; she was just following orders.

'Did you say what I told you to say?'

That was the moment when Posy knew. She was lying on her board over the sink, rolled up inside her blanket, and Dad's question floated through the closed door.

'Did you say what I told you to say?'

And Posy knew. All those considerate things Ma had said to Gran since Gramps died hadn't been said out of the kindness of her heart. She had said them because Dad told her to. He had thought them up and she had done as she was told. All that about Dad supporting them and Gran saving her pension ... having company all day because Ma didn't go out to work ... watching Posy grow up...

Posy knew what had been said, because school had broken up for Easter on Wednesday instead of Friday because of burst pipes; and she had gone with Ma to visit Gran each day. How proud she had felt of Ma for paying Gran so much attention, for being worried about her now she was on her own without Gramps. Posy had thought it was all real, everything Ma said. Did Gran think it was real too?

If she let them move in, she would live to regret it.

Everyone lived to regret it where Dad was concerned.


## Chapter Eight

Nell blessed Mr Flynn's fractured nerves as she worked through the order of day dresses. They were a pleasure to make. Not long ago, the machinists used to groan at being told to make up an order in rayon, but already it was being made to a higher standard.

'Art silk, they're calling it now,' said Mildred Shaw with the air of one in the know.

'Aye, them with nowt between their ears,' scoffed Elsie. 'Art silk only means artificial, you daft ha'porth.'

'I know that,' sniffed Mildred.

'Eh, you two,' chimed in another voice. 'Stop your bickering and eat your butties.'

Nell joined in the laughter. She felt light-hearted and fired up in a way she never had before. Ambition: that was what it was. She had never had an ambition before. Well, she had in a general way – do her best for the children, that kind of thing – but this time she had a specific aim to earn three whole pounds in one week. Today was Wednesday: she knew she could do it.

'Aye-aye,' said Elsie. 'Here comes her ladyship. Who's for it this time?'

Nell was as surprised as anyone when Miss Lockwood stopped at her side. She hadn't fudged any of her garments. She knew she hadn't – had she? Her cheeks tingled as she followed the over-seer. Miss Lockwood stopped in the corridor.

'You've done nothing wrong. You're one of the best girls I've ever had, and certainly the quickest.'

Relief brought words flooding out. 'I need to earn three pounds a week. I managed two pounds sixteen and eight last week.'

'I'm aware of what you earned last week and so is Mr Cooper. He'd like a word, but don't worry. I'll be with you.'

Worry? Why would she worry at being congratulated by the boss? She trotted up the stairs behind Miss Lockwood, who knocked on the office door and led her inside. Mr Cooper, a paunchy man with a serious air, sat behind the desk, Mr Flynn standing by his side.

'This is Mrs Hibbert, Mr Cooper,' said Miss Lockwood.

'Ah – yes. You earned a substantial sum last week.' He held up his hand and waggled his fingers.

'Two pounds sixteen and eight,' said Mr Flynn.

Nell beamed. 'I'm determined to make three pounds this week, sir.'

'Ah – yes. The thing is, it won't do, Mrs Hibbs, d'you see?'

Mr Flynn cleared his throat. 'Mrs Hibbert, sir.'

'What? Yes, yes. We can't have you earning that much.'

'Why not, if I produce the work? I don't skimp, sir. Miss Lockwood will tell you my garments are of the highest standard.'

'My good woman, you're missing the point. I can't pay a female worker that much. That's what a breadwinner earns.'

'I'm a breadwinner. I'm a widow with young children.' She darted a look at Mr Flynn. How many times had she helped him out? But he wouldn't meet her gaze.

'You can't earn three pounds and that's all there is to it.'

'But if I do the work–'

'If you do three pounds' worth of work, I'll have to cut the piecework rates so you earn less; and I can't cut your rates without cutting everyone else's. So, what's it to be, Mrs Hibbs? Do I cut everybody's rates or will you restrict your earning?'

'It's a good job our Posy's not a jealous child.'

Those were the words that tipped the balance. Leonie had struggled – oh, how she had struggled with the problem. She loved Nell and the children, but she had her own family to think of. And herself.

'You have to think of yourself, Mother,' Hilda had urged. 'It's what Dad would have wanted: all of us to be together.'

Was it? It would feel good to do what Hedley wanted. She missed him with a wild ache of fear and pain, prowling the house in the dark, unable to settle, feeling herself going slowly mad. Would things be easier if the Tanners moved in? It was hard looking after Alf and Cassie. She felt so worn down.

'You have to think of yourself, Mother,' said Hilda, 'especially at your age.'

'I might never see sixty again, but I'm not in my dotage yet.'

'You know what I mean,' Hilda muttered.

Leonie felt a pang of disappointment. Times were when the two of them would have roared with laughter at Hilda's tactless remark, but not now. Hilda had been a sunny child, but in adulthood she had gone wishy-washy. Was it because of those ten childless years before Posy came along? Sometimes Leonie felt an obscure need to apologise to Edmund for being saddled with a wife who had turned out to be such a wet lettuce. Eh, he must be disappointed.

And that was another problem. Leonie couldn't keep her mind fixed on anything these days. She had an important decision to make, but she couldn't get her thoughts together without Hedley to support her. Not that she had been one of those wives who let the husband do all the thinking, but they had been best friends, discussing everything.

While she floundered, failing to make decisions, Hilda uttered the crucial words.

'It's a good job Posy isn't a jealous child.'

Coldness spread through Leonie's chest. 'What makes you say that?'

'All the attention you give those children.'

'I look after them. Of course I give them attention.'

'And the amount you talk about them.'

Did she talk about them more than she did about Posy, her own granddaughter? She looked away from Hilda, the coldness in her chest turning to a hollow feeling. Her own granddaughter. It wasn't her fault the Tanners lived a tram ride away instead of round the corner. But that wasn't the point. Her own granddaughter.

Later, before Hilda and Posy set off for home, Posy hugged her.

'To keep you going until next time, Gran.'

Leonie caught Posy's face between her hands. There wasn't much of Posy on the outside. She was skinny with a pinched little face but, by heck, there was loads of her on the inside. Imagination and courage and, most of all, heart.

And just like that, as if she had rolled up her sleeves, the choice was made. She loved Nell and the children, but she loved Posy more.

Nell trudged home. Well, no − that would have meant walking slowly, and she didn't have time for that. She had left Stan at a brisk pace and that pace had never let up. If anything, it had increased. But in her heart, she was trudging. They weren't going to let her earn three pounds a week.

They knew she could do it and they wouldn't allow it.

She rounded the corner into Finney Lane. Would Alf still be awake? Would she have the chance of a cuddle or even a story before he snuggled down? Violet scampered beside her, darting inside as she opened the door. The pungent aroma of fried onions brought her stomach wide awake and clamouring. The kitchen door was open and Mrs Brent stood at the range, steam rising from a couple of saucepans.

'I'll be down in a minute,' called Nell.

She ran upstairs, shrugging off her coat. Cassie was tucked up in her drawer. Nell's heart melted. Cassie was a little monkey when she was awake, but slumber turned her into an angel.

Alf stirred. 'Mummy?'

She felt as if she had earned a victory lap around the playing field. 'I'm here, chick.'

'Good.' He turned over and went back to sleep.

She laughed. She made herself laugh. So much for the cuddle and the story.

She hung up her things on the back of the door, tidied her hair in the speckled mirror propped up on the chest of drawers, and headed downstairs.

'Smells good.'

'Onion gravy. I made rissoles with the leftover cottage pie.'

Nell's mouth watered so much she was scared of dribbling. Could she afford something more sustaining than jam in her midday barm cake? Cheese would be more filling. But she kept her own food to a minimum for a reason, and that reason was even more pressing now.

She helped dish up, then ate her meal as daintily as any fine lady enjoying afternoon tea at the Midland Hotel, but it was an effort. Every evening she wanted to fall on the food and shovel it down. Anyroad, it was better to eat slowly. It made you feel fuller longer. So she told herself.

Mrs Brent cleared away the plates and, protecting her hands with a cloth, removed a bowl from the oven.

'Roly-poly pudding.'

'Before you put custard on, may I cut my helping in two and save half to take to work?'

'I'm always telling you you need more inside you at midday.'

'What would I do without you to keep an eye on me?'

'Get away with you,' Mrs Brent said gruffly.

'Did your Hilda come today?'

'Aye, she did.'

Good. Hilda might be a drip, who hadn't paid her parents anything like the attention they deserved during her father's lifetime, but she had come good since his death.

'And Posy?'

'She took your two outside to play in the street with the other children.'

'That was sweet of her.'

'She's a sweet child.' Mrs Brent threw down her spoon. It clattered against the rim of her dish and sank into the custard. 'It's no use. I can't pretend everything's the same.'

Nell's heartbeat picked up speed. 'What's happened?'

'Eh, lovey, I'm that sorry. I know me and

Hedley told you to look on this as your home, but ... our Hilda's moving in with her family and so...'

*You want me to move out.* Nell couldn't say the words any more than poor Mrs Brent could. She dropped her hands into her lap, clasping them together beneath the shelter of the table. She forced herself to say the right thing. She owed this dear lady so much.

'I understand.' A crackle invaded her throat. 'When...?'

Mrs Brent's eyes were swimming. She sniffed, her hands fluttering in search of a hanky. 'There's no hurry. I'll tell Hilda they can't come until you're sorted. And I'll still do your child-minding for you. I wouldn't give that up for anything.'

Nell nodded. Her heart was going to explode with panic.

'I wouldn't do this if I wasn't certain you'll be all right.' Mrs Brent's voice wobbled. 'But with you all set to earn three quid a week ... and there's this widow's pension starting next year...'

Another nod. The rest of her was frozen to the spot, but her stupid head nodded as if everything was fine.

What was she going to do now?

Nell spent Thursday and Friday in a haze of panic, relying on her experienced fingers to make the rayon day dresses. She spent both evenings racing round like a mad thing, trying to find somewhere to live, not even stopping to have her meal first, much to Mrs Brent's distress, but she couldn't have forced anything down anyway.

She gazed into every shop window where customers advertised on postcards, copying the addresses offering rooms. Some folk shut the door on her for daring to knock in the evening. Others didn't want a woman. 'Breadwinners only, love.' Some wouldn't take children. She didn't dare mention Violet.

On Friday night she lay awake, bouncing the curve of her knuckles against her mouth, fear pinning her to the bed.

She spent Saturday morning with the children, anxious to keep things normal for them, but that afternoon she would have to take them for a walk past the stationer's on Beech Road in the hope of seeing some likely for-rent postcards.

As they finished their dinner, the Tanners arrived.

'Hilda has some shopping to do, Mother-in-law,' said Edmund Tanner. 'Would you like to go with her?'

'Yes, go,' said Nell. 'I'll clear away. You'll help, won't you, Alf?'

'So will I,' said Posy.

'Mrs Hibbert can manage,' said her father. 'You may go out to play, Posy. I've brought yesterday's *Evening News* with me. I'll read it in the parlour.'

Everyone dispersed. Nell took her children into the scullery to wash up. When they finished and were putting things away, Edmund Tanner, newspaper under his arm, appeared in the kitchen doorway. 'Built like a brick shithouse,' said Doug's voice in Nell's head. Standing in front of the wall cupboard where the crockery was kept, she made a point of adjusting the small stack of plates, just to show she wasn't fazed.

103

Cassie came toddling through from the scullery, clutching Mrs Brent's saucer.

'Thank you, chick.' Nell took it from her.

'Here's the last one, Mummy.'

Alf appeared, Mrs Brent's harebell teacup half-wrapped in the tea towel. At the sight of Edmund Tanner, he stopped dead. For a breathless moment, the cup got tangled in the tea towel before slipping through and dropping to the tiled floor. A musical *ting* bounced into the air, mixing with the sharp-sweet aroma of the spicy apple pie Mrs Brent had baked that morning.

Nell swooped. Please don't let it be broken. It wasn't. She expelled a huge breath, but her relief was swept aside as the sight of Alf's huge eyes made her heart turn over.

'Don't worry. It isn't broken – look.'

'Let me see.' Edmund Tanner's voice was hard. Disbelieving, accusing.

She stood up straight. 'No need,' she said quietly. 'It's fine – but it's been on the floor, so it needs washing again, doesn't it, Alf? Come and help me.'

'You've no idea how to bring up a boy.' Edmund Tanner's voice was loaded with scorn.

Shepherding her children into the scullery. Nell tried to make light of washing the cup, but Alf had sunk into himself. Cassie didn't care. Nothing bothered her. She watched and listened and took everything in and one day she would kick the Edmund Tanners of this world where it hurt.

Nell washed the cup, but Alf wouldn't dry it or carry it into the kitchen.

'You should make him do as he's told,' Edmund

Tanner remarked as she put the cup away.

'Do you want something?' she asked, her voice carefully controlled.

'You can make me a cup of tea.'

'You what?'

'Milk, two sugars, and make sure it's properly brewed.'

*I'll do no such thing. Bugger off. How dare you scare my son? I'll set my brothers on you.*

But maybe he was entitled to ask since Hilda and Mrs Brent were out.

'Well, put the kettle on,' he said.

Nell balled her hands into fists at her sides, but she had no choice. He was Mrs Brent's son-in-law and he was entitled to be here. She pulled her shoulders back: she was entitled to be here an' all.

For now.

She put the kettle on, smiling at the children, keeping her face averted from Edmund Tanner. She might be obliged to make his dratted tea, but she wouldn't acknowledge him in the process.

'I want you out of this house by midday next Saturday.'

*Whump.* She felt it as a punch in the stomach. 'Mrs Brent said I could take as long as I needed.'

'My mother-in-law has just lost her husband of forty years. You can't expect her to think rationally. If you take your time, who knows how long you might spin it out? My family takes up residence here next Saturday, so I will require you and your brood to be out by midday.'

'But–'

'Don't forget to allow time to give your room a

105

thorough spring-clean.'

'Mr Tanner–'

'You can bring my tea to the parlour. After that I'll take a stroll with Posy to find the nearest sweet shop. Oh, and you can have this.' He threw the newspaper her way. It landed on the floor, its pages fanning out across the tiles. 'Pick it up, boy.'

Alf flattened himself against her legs. Nell picked up the paper and dropped it on the table.

'I've circled some rooms for rent,' said Edmund Tanner. 'Just in case you need helping on your way.'

After she had made this horrible bully his tea, Nell took the *Manchester Evening News* upstairs, cut some pages into strips and set the children making paper chains. Alf was meticulous about it, while Cassie cheerfully slathered herself in flour-and-water paste.

Nell read the small ads, fighting to keep her spirits up as the locations of the rooms for rent sank in. Fallowfield, Levenshulme, Gorton ... Oldham. The thought of moving so far made her want to weep, but it was no use getting upset. She brushed her hand across her eyes and looked again at the paper, but she had lost her place and found herself scanning the jobs. A boxed advert headed INGLEBY'S caught her eye.

She knew Ingleby's – didn't everyone? It was a big shop on Market Street, endlessly fascinating to anyone interested in needlework and dressmaking, with its vast array of fabrics and everything a dressmaker could possibly need, including acces- sories – hats, gloves, brooches – to wear with what you made, though plenty of their customers patronised their famous dressmaking service.

Ingleby's wanted women who could demonstrate how to use a sewing machine. Nell sat up. She could do that standing on her head. Interested parties were invited to present themselves this afternoon at three o'clock.

This afternoon!

Her heart thumped. She should be out looking for a new home, not dashing off in pursuit of a new job. Yet she needed another job too, one with more favourable hours. Finding a new home close by had so far proved impossible, which in turn meant Mrs Brent wouldn't be able to look after the children. The thought of new child-minding arrangements set her instincts ringing alarm bells and demanding she didn't work such punishing hours. It was one thing to entrust the children to Mrs Brent's care for forty-eight factory hours plus travelling there and back. She couldn't countenance leaving them all that time with a new person, no matter how kind or loving.

A job with shop hours would make a significant difference to her circumstances. Did she stand a chance?

# Chapter Nine

Saturday. Best day of the week. Jim felt he was doing something worthwhile, repaying a fraction of the debt he could never pay back. How did you repay the world for your life when unimaginable numbers of men had perished? And for some unfathomable reason, he had survived. It hadn't felt like surviving at first. How could it, when, instead of a soul, he now had a pit of loss and lament? How did you repay all those bereaved families? How did you justify your own existence? That was why he lived this outdoor life. Being outside, working at a job that was all physical, no brainwork required, helped him, though dashed if he could explain how.

All he had known when he returned from the war was that he couldn't step back into his old life. God knows, he had tried. He had returned to the offices of Fairbrother and Pepperdine, in Rosemount Place off Market Street in the middle of town, and stood in his old office doorway, looking into his well-appointed room, with his oak desk with the maroon inlay. It was his ... yet not his.

Mr Fairbrother had slapped him on the shoulder. 'Fairbrother, Pepperdine and Franks: how does that sound, my boy? I'll have the brass plate changed while you're on your honeymoon.'

Roberta had the wedding dress ready – dress,

veil, pearls, going-away costume. A something-borrowed bracelet, a something-blue pair of sapphire earrings. God, the trouble she had gone to. And who could blame her? She had spent years planning this. Her mother had drawn up the seating plan in 1915.

'Of course, there have been some amendments,' said Roberta, oblivious to his silence. 'Uncle Rodney and your parents passed away, and poor Cousin George ... well. You know.'

Well. You know. That was one way of putting it. Perhaps they should have used it on the telegrams. WELL STOP YOU KNOW STOP. Because everyone had known, all the wives and mothers and sweethearts at home, hoping and praying for their boys. They had seen the telegram lad and they had known.

He had tried explaining to Roberta what was inside him, but how could words express deep-rooted loss and lament? She understood ... up to a point; was sympathetic ... up to a point. But she had waited for a long time and she wanted everything she had waited for. The smart wedding, a home of her own, and darling James working alongside Daddy; the life that, as daughter of Angus Fairbrother, she was entitled to.

They had been engaged since early '14. If she had wanted back then to marry him before he went off to war, he would have agreed, but she hadn't wanted it – then. She had wanted the perfect, polished wedding of her dreams, not some rushed affair with a couple of dozen hastily assembled guests.

As the war dragged on, she had changed her

109

tune, angling for a wedding while he was on leave, but now it was he who refused.

'Suppose I don't come back?'

'All the more reason to get married.'

Was it? Many a wartime marriage had been undertaken in that spirit, but to him, it hadn't felt right. Marriage was a celebration of the future and, this time next week, he would be back in a world of death and destruction. He couldn't marry her.

So Roberta had waited ... and waited. They had got engaged on her twentieth birthday and she had turned twenty-six before he came home in the spring of 1920 after volunteering to work as a medical orderly during the influenza epidemic.

'I'm twenty-*six!* You *have* to marry me,' she cried when it sank in that he meant what he said about not going through with it. 'And you have to come back to Fairbrother and Pepperdine's. Mummy and I have been telling people for *years.* What do you think you can do instead, anyway?'

So he had told her.

'You're going to *clean windows,*' she hissed. 'You can't. What will people *say?* I forbid it.'

But cleaning windows had been right for him, giving him fresh air, physical labour, time to think or not think, time to be. There were occasions when his sense of loss and lament was overwhelming, when he thought he would die of it or run mad, but he didn't do either. He just carried on. Loss and lament.

Mondays to Fridays he cleaned middle-class windows and shop windows, and on Saturdays he did windows free of charge for hard-up war widows and the mothers of dead soldiers. Saturdays afforded him some satisfaction, though he wasn't sure he deserved any.

Today he had a plan, though that was rather a grand name for it. Made it sound deliberate. Well, it was deliberate. Fool others if you want, Jim Franks, but don't fool yourself.

It was a mild spring day, perfect for the Easter weekend. He had ventured out early for a tramp across the meadows that ran alongside the Mersey. This was why he had chosen Chorlton for his home. An old, small township that was now a growing suburb, it provided him with ample work, while the meadows gave him the fresh air and sense of space he craved.

After the morning's work, he dropped into Bradshaw's. The plates of sausages, mince and chops were nearly empty and Betty's pies and pasties were gone.

'Hoping for a pie, were you?' she asked.

'You have to be quick off the mark to get one of my Betty's pies,' said Arnold.

'I've still got some sausage rolls,' said Betty. 'Would a couple of them do you?'

'Thanks. How did that funeral go?'

'Funeral?'

'When I last did your windows, there was a woman here collecting the ham. She had a couple of nippers with her that belonged to a young widow.'

'Oh, the Brent funeral. Poor Mr Brent.'

'I didn't get the impression it was Mrs Brent I saw.'

'No, that were Mrs Watson, her neighbour.'

111

'And the children's mother...?'

'Mrs Brent's lodger, Mrs Hibbert. What's this about, Jim? Not like you to gossip.'

'It's not gossip. Mrs O'Connor from Brundretts Lane has gone to live with her eldest, so I've got a slot free.'

'And you're looking for another soul to help. You're a good bloke, Jim. Why don't you try Mrs Watson? She lost her Bill at Wipers.'

'Does she live in one of Mr Dawson's houses?'

She did, which made it easier. Dawson's rent man, Mr Miles, knew him and had provided introductions in the past. He caught Miles as he was about to set out on his Saturday afternoon collection round and Miles took him to Mrs Watson's house in Finney Lane.

Jim hung back discreetly as the rent man explained to Mrs Watson and vouched for him.

'It'd save me a job.' Mrs Watson eyed him and he touched his cap to her. 'I take my life in my hands, sitting on that upstairs window sill to wash my bedroom window. You can start round the back and I'll give you a cup of tea before you do the front.'

'Deal.'

He did the back, then came down his ladder and knocked on the door.

'It's open,' called Mrs Watson.

Removing his cap, he entered the scullery. In the kitchen, Mrs Watson wasn't alone. His heart gave a leap of pleasure – Mrs Hibbert. Such beautiful eyes: the colour of smoky quartz. She wore no hat and coat this time and her hair, the same soft, warm hue as a meadow brown butterfly, was thick and shining. She wore a paper chain round her neck. Her dress flattered her tall, slender figure, though its simplicity didn't do her justice. In a stylish gown, she would be a stunner. What was that new expression that made his young nieces collapse in giggles? The bee's knees.

The women looked round.

'I didn't mean to interrupt,' he said.

'I'm just leaving,' said Mrs Hibbert. 'Pleased to see you again.'

Her fine eyebrows drew together in a frown.

'This is Jim, the window cleaner,' said Mrs Watson.

'Oh yes, from outside the butcher's.' She gave him a nod. Something inside him yearned towards her, but already she was turning to Mrs Watson.

Desperate to grab her attention, he said, 'I like the paper chain.' God, what a stupid thing to say.

She looked bewildered, then glanced down and laughed. 'Are you poking fun at my family heirloom?'

'Make sure you take it off before you go,' teased Mrs Watson.

Mrs Hibbert smiled. 'Thanks for helping out. I always seem to be putting on you.'

'It's what neighbours are for, love.'

She left. Wasn't she aware of him? Evidently not.

'Poor lass,' said Mrs Watson. 'She's having a rough time. She's got to quit her lodgings by this day week, which won't be easy with two little 'uns. She'll be back in a mo to drop them off.'

'So she can look for a new home?'

'A new job– Hush. Here she is.' Mrs Watson put

113

on a jolly voice. 'Where are my two pie-cans?'

'Forget the tea,' said Jim. 'You'll have your hands full.'

He carried his ladder along the back entry and round to Finney Lane where he propped it up before starting on the downstairs window.

'Hello, mister. Is that you again?'

'It was last time I looked.' He smiled at Alf's earnest face.

'Can I help?'

'You can stand at the foot of the ladder and hold it steady when I'm up it. You have to make sure I don't fall off. But most of all, you have to stop your pet monkey climbing up.'

Alf's face screwed up. 'I haven't got a monkey. We've got a cat.'

'You had it with you last time. It climbed up my ladder.'

'That wasn't a *monkey*. That was my *sister*.'

'Sisters can't climb like that. It was a monkey. It was a ladder-monkey.'

'Cassie's a ladder-monkey,' cried the child, his solemn face bright with glee.

Jim had a job not to laugh. It seemed he had won over this little lad, but what were his chances of being noticed by Alf Hibbert's lovely mother?

Nell sucked in a deep breath before walking into Ingleby's. The ground floor sold ready-made garments for the well-to-do middle class: pretty day dresses and smart evening wear, warm coats for motoring and cool linens for sports; the sort of garments Nell made at the factory, fine fabrics and attractive styles that weren't for the likes of

114

her. A notice on the wall informed her that Drapery and Haberdashery were to be found on the first floor. Below it, another notice invited her to visit 'our new Sewing Machine Department'.

Beside a caged lift stood a uniformed lad, but today of all days was a time for sticking with what she knew, so she went up the stairs into an Aladdin's cave of ribbons, braids, beads and buttons. It would be a joy to linger and explore, but she saw a sign for the Sewing Machine Department and wove her way towards it, her heart speeding up.

Several sewing machines sat on their custom-built tables. Along one wall was a line of chairs where two women sat looking stiff and nervous. Two middle-aged women, wearing smart black shop dresses, were on their feet. One had faded red hair and a beaky nose, the other was willowy with an oval face and silvery hair.

'Good afternoon,' said Nell. 'I saw the advertisement. Have I come to the right place?'

'Yes,' said the redhead. 'What's your name and address?'

Nell gave her details and sat down. She and the other women glanced at one another but didn't speak. Another applicant arrived, then another.

'It's three o'clock,' said the silver-haired woman. 'I'm Miss Collier and this is Miss Moore. The advertisement gave no instructions as to where to present yourselves, so how did you come to be here in our department?'

Nell frowned. Was it a trick question?

'It was the obvious place,' said one of the candidates.

'How did you find it?'

'I saw the notice on the ground floor,' said Nell.

'I asked a sales assistant downstairs,' said someone else.

'Good. We're looking for initiative and common sense.'

'Excuse me.' A young woman in a pillar-box-red coat approached. 'Is this the right place for the sewing machine demonstrators?'

'It is,' said Miss Collier. 'Are you an applicant?'

'Yes.' She smiled winningly.

'The advertisement stated three o'clock. Thank you for coming, but I'm afraid you won't be suitable. We require our employees to be punctual and reliable.'

Nell's heart swelled for the young woman, whose face had turned as red as her coat. She left and Nell was aware of the remaining candidates, including herself, sitting up straighter.

'How did you make your way up here?' asked Miss Moore.

'I used the staircase,' said the woman next to Nell.

'So did I,' said Nell.

'I came up in the lift,' said another.

'The lift is for the benefit of our patrons,' said Miss Collier, 'not for our employees or those seeking employment with us. I'm sorry, Miss Peyton, but you are unsuitable. Thank you for attending.'

Miss Peyton slunk away. Nell shifted on her chair. So much for thinking she could do this job standing on her head.

'Please hang your coats over there,' said Miss Moore, 'then sit at the sewing machines and thread them.'

They sewed seams, attached a sleeve, sewed an inset pocket, did gathers and pleats, and attached the fiddliest braid known to man. Working her treadle at a steady pace, Nell refused to be put off when Miss Collier or Miss Moore looked over her shoulder.

When everyone had finished, Miss Moore and Miss Collier had a whispered conversation. Then one of the candidates, a middle-aged woman with roses in her cheeks, was asked to leave, though this was done more kindly than the blunt way in which the others had been rejected.

'Your skills aren't up to our standard, Mrs Kennedy, but should they improve, come back and try again.'

There were three of them left now.

'Unthread your machines, please,' said Miss Collier. 'Miss Ashton will join us. She, Miss Moore and I will play the part of customers learning to use the machines.'

Nell found herself 'teaching' Miss Moore, correcting her deliberate mistakes and fielding a stream of questions, some of which were downright stupid. She remained patient and polite and at the end congratulated Miss Moore on being a good pupil.

Miss Moore and her colleagues disappeared through a door. A few minutes later, Miss Ashton came out, whispering, 'Well done, all of you,' as she left.

Miss Collier appeared. 'I'm pleased to say you've all impressed us. You'll now be interviewed. Mrs Hibbert, would you come first?'

Nell followed her into a small office. Miss Collier squeezed behind the desk beside Miss Moore.

'Have a seat,' said Miss Moore. 'You're obviously an experienced machinist.'

Nell explained about her job. 'So I'm also familiar with using a range of fabrics. Miss Lockwood, my overseer, trusts me with anything tricky.'

'I hope you're not exaggerating, because we'll require a reference from her. Let me tell you about the work we're offering. Our dressmaking service will continue, but we also wish to support the customer who invests in her own sewing machine.'

'I'd like to help your ladies learn to use their sewing machines.'

It was the right thing to say. 'And we believe you'd be good at it. Sometimes we'll require you here in Ingleby's, but mostly you'll be visiting our customers in their homes. Your travelling expenses will be met, naturally.'

Travelling around? She liked the sound of that. Something different.

'Every customer receives six lessons. You'll take with you a variety of threads, ribbons and so on and will receive a small commission on anything you sell, which might be worth an extra two shillings a week.'

'And the hours?'

'If you're required here, you must arrive for an eight-forty-five start. We open our doors at nine and close them at six. The departments have to be tidied before the staff may leave, but tidying may be started before six if there are no customers present; and of course, nowhere should ever be untidy in the first place.'

Getting here by quarter to nine would be dead easy after having to clock in before eight under threat of forfeiting a half-hour's pay if she clocked in even a minute late.

'And if I'm out and about?'

'We wouldn't expect a morning appointment to start before ten and afternoon appointments must finish by five. The lady of the house needs time to prepare for her husband's return.'

'At the moment I work a forty-eight-hour week This sounds less.'

'It is. Our employees work a forty-hour week. In the shop, that means five days, with a dinner hour. You would have to be flexible, spreading your hours over six days if necessary. This post requires someone who will put the customer's convenience first.'

'Is travelling time counted as work?'

'It is.'

'May I ask about the salary?'

'One pound eighteen a week. Being a superior establishment, we pay more than other shops.'

'I earn over two pounds where I am now.'

'You also work eight hours longer. Perhaps you should discuss it with your husband.'

'I'm a widow.'

'Have you any children?'

'I have two young children whose child-minder is also our landlady, so you needn't worry about my being unreliable.' How true would that be this time next week?

'We have two posts,' said Miss Moore, 'one to

119

cover the area to the south of town, one for the north. The other two candidates both live to the north, so we're pleased to offer you the position covering the south, subject to satisfactory references. We'll provide you with a letter to hand to your overseer, and we also require a personal reference. Perhaps your landlord?'

'He passed away recently. I'm sure my landlady would oblige.'

Miss Collier and Miss Moore looked doubtful, as if Mrs Brent's word carried less weight, which made Nell all the more determined to ask her.

'Are you on a week's notice?' Miss Collier asked. 'You could resign on Monday – no: it's a bank holiday. You could give notice on Tuesday. They'd probably let you leave on Friday and start here a week on Monday.'

'Mrs Hibbert hasn't accepted the position yet,' murmured Miss Moore.

They looked at her. Nell performed violent mental calculations. A lower wage ... but with some commission. Fewer hours. More time with the children. Even with less child-minding to pay for, they would be hard up.

But – more time with her children.

Could she afford it?

'Mummy, what did Mr Tanner mean about moving in? Is he coming to live here? In our house?'

A knot tightened in Nell's stomach. Had Alf been fretting all this time? Cassie, after a hectic afternoon running Mrs Watson ragged, had climbed into her drawer, flung her arms round Violet and plunged into sleep with the same

single-minded determination she applied to everything else, but Alf was a worrier underneath. He
sat next to Nell on the bed. She had got him
cuddled up close to share her news and instead he
wanted to know about Edmund flaming Tanner.
The thought of that man coming to live here probably terrified him.

'Oh, chick, have you been worrying about that?'
She hugged him tighter. 'I'm sorry if you've been
upset.'

'Is Mr Tanner coming to live here?' Alf persisted.

'Yes.' Her heart twisted as he flinched. 'But you
mustn't worry, because ... we're going to live
somewhere else.'

'We're *leaving?* But this is our home.'

She was doing this all wrong. 'Since Mr Brent
died, Mrs Brent has felt lonely and unhappy, so
she wants the Tanners to live with her.'

'She's got us.'

'She loves us, but they're her family.'

'I don't want to leave.'

'There isn't room for all of us.'

'But why do we have to go? Why can't they stop
where they are?'

'They want to live with Mrs Brent and look
after her.'

'We can look after her.'

Nell rubbed the back of her neck. Alf was the
most amenable child in the world – but not today,
not over this. She injected a bracing note into her
voice. 'I'd like nothing better than for us to stop
here and take care of Mrs Brent, but the Tanners
are moving in, so we have to leave. Try not to
worry, pie-can. We'll find a comfy new home–'

121

Her arms were suddenly empty as he wrenched himself free. He stood on the rug, facing her, eyes bright with tears.

'I'm not a pie-can and I don't want a new home. I want this one!'

He was out of the room before she could grab him. He clattered downstairs with her flying after him. He hurled himself through the kitchen door, already bawling at a startled Mrs Brent, seated at the table with a cup of tea.

'I don't want to move out and I hate you!'

Nell grasped his shoulder and he flung himself round, burying his face in her skirt and sobbing as though his heart was falling to pieces.

'I'm sorry.' Nell looked at Mrs Brent. 'I've just told him…'

Mrs Brent released a shaky breath. 'Poor little chap. I wish there was a way…'

Nell spoke brightly, fixing Mrs Brent with a meaningful look. 'I think we should be cheerful, don't you?'

Mrs Brent sat up straighter. 'Where's that boy of mine? Alf, you've squashed Mummy half to death, hugging her so hard. I wish I had someone to hug me.'

'I will,' cried Alf, launching himself at her.

Mrs Brent gathered him to her, raining kisses into his neck, making him chuckle in spite of himself. He pretended to try to squirm away, but really he was squirming closer.

'You still love us, don't you?' His voice was muffled against Mrs Brent's shoulder.

She cast an anguished look at Nell. 'Of course I do.'

'But you want us to go.'

'I don't *want* you to, but things change when someone dies and people sometimes have to live somewhere else. Like when your daddy died and you and Mummy came here.'

'And Cassie,' said Alf. 'Do you love Posy more than Cassie and me?'

'I love all three of you, but Posy is special because I'm her gran.'

'I haven't got a gran.'

Olive Hibbert.

Usually, when Alf remarked on not having grandparents, it was Mum and Dad who sprang to mind, but today Olive Hibbert arrived plonk in the middle of Nell's head. Olive Hibbert, crabby mother-in-law and not exactly the most loving grandmother ever to walk the earth. Or was she? Just because she was different to how Mum and Dad would have been didn't mean she wasn't loving in her own way. How had she felt when Alf disappeared? Or had those extra grand-children down the hill made up for the loss?

'Will you be my gran?' Alf whispered. 'Cassie hasn't got one either.'

Nell laid a hand on his shoulder. She couldn't have him putting Mrs Brent on the spot. 'See if Cassie is still asleep.'

He scampered away and she sagged into a chair, feeling as if she'd gone twice through the mangle. 'That was building up all afternoon, I think, ever since...' Yes, she would say it. '...since Mr Tanner said they're moving in next Saturday.'

Mrs Brent looked uncomfortable. 'I know it doesn't give you much time, but Edmund said he'd given you some for rents to follow up and there's Posy's schooling to think of. If they come next weekend, she can start school here on the first day of term.'

Rubbish. Posy was nine years old, not a School Certificate candidate. It didn't matter in the slightest when she changed schools.

'Anyroad, I'm sorry about Alf. I don't know what you must have thought when he came flying in like that.'

'I thought – nay, it doesn't matter.'

Nell's flesh tingled. 'Go on.'

'I wasn't going to say owt, but, well, I thought he were upset about the cup.'

'The cup?'

'My teacup.'

The precious harebell teacup. It sat on the table in front of her. Nell went cold.

'What about it?'

'Oh, it's nothing, really, just the tiniest chip, and it's not on the side I drink from, so it's silly to care...'

Nell picked it up and, yes, a minute chip had been knocked out of the rim. It hadn't happened when Alf dropped it. She knew it hadn't.

'So I thought that's what Alf were in a state about,' said Mrs Brent. 'I thought if he'd helped you wash up, and the cup got dropped...'

Had Edmund Tanner chipped the cup? She would stake her life it hadn't happened when Alf dropped it.

'Did Mr Tanner tell you that?'

Mrs Brent frowned. 'Why would he? I didn't even find the chip until a few minutes ago.'

Oh, that was clever. Mr Brick Shithouse had chipped his mother-in-law's beloved cup, then taken his family home, leaving her to find the damage later.

There was nothing to link Edmund Tanner to it, aside from Nell's suspicion, and what could she hope to achieve by speaking out? Best if she took it on the chin.

'I'm sorry, Mrs Brent. I know how much you love that cup.'

Mrs Brent waved her apology aside, but Nell wasn't fooled. She could see the hurt in Mrs Brent's eyes.

'It's just that my Hedley bought it for me and I've kept it safe all these years. But it's only a cup. It's not as though owt important has happened.'

There was a golden tinge to the late afternoon light that spoke more of June than April, but Jim couldn't spend the evening walking across the meadows, followed by enjoying a pint at the Horse and Jockey. He had a plan. As he pushed his barrow home, some scruffy lads, all holey clothes and scraped knees, were playing football in the road, their ball a bundle of rags. Parking his barrow at the kerb, he plunged into the match, causing hoots of excitement. He darted around, careful how he tackled, aware of his sturdily shod feet in a game where several boys were barefoot.

When he set up a goal for one of the youngest boys to score, he scooped the lad onto his shoulder and jogged around, starting a cry of 'Champion, champion', and the others joined in the chant. When he set down the skinny goalscorer, the boy's face was shining.

Jim gave him a pretend clip round the ear. 'See you next time.'

He went on his way. Oh, the temptation to buy these kids a proper football, but even providing a second-hand one would be inappropriate. He had arrived among these folk as a window cleaner. His educated voice marked him out as different, but his Saturdays spent helping the hard-up widows and mothers of soldiers had given out a general idea of his having had a bad war and his choice of job was accepted. Had he had a bad war? Christ, everyone had. His was no worse than anyone else's and better than most. He hadn't been gassed; he had come home with his limbs intact. That was as much as you could ask.

Halfway along Beech Road, opposite one corner of the hedge surrounding the rec, was Riley's Farm, a small place round the back of which was a row of old cottages. He pushed his barrow along the path past the line of kitchen doors to the far end.

He went in through the back door, stepping across the minute scullery with its slop-stone, into the kitchen, crossing it in zigzag fashion to avoid cracking his head on any of the saucepans hanging from the low beams or getting a faceful of dried herbs. Mrs Jeffrey might not have much space to call her own, but what she did have, she made the most of.

She stood at the range, stirring a pot, the spoon sticking out awkwardly from her arthritic fingers. The mingled aromas of onions and fresh bread made Jim's mouth water.

'Smells good in here, Mrs J. I know what that means. One of your stews, with a crusty loaf to mop it up.'

'It's ready when you are.'

He glanced at the bucket next to the range. 'I'll fetch water while you dish up.'

Collecting the second bucket from the scullery, he went outside to the pump to fill them, then stood one bucket beside the shelf he had rigged up in the scullery, with a bowl on it for washing up. He couldn't have Mrs Jeffrey using the slop-stone on the floor. What he really wanted was for her washing-up bowl to be in the kitchen, but the suggestion had appalled her. Kitchens were for cooking and eating and living in. Dirty dishes and soiled clothes went in the scullery.

'Sit thee down,' said Mrs Jeffrey.

It was all he could do not to hold his breath as her deformed hands transferred the dishes one at a time, each one landing on the table with a clatter but no spillages. He tucked in. Mrs Jeffrey was a good plain cook and kept him well fed. He downed the stew, using hunks of bread to clean his plate, an aspect of lower-class life that, as a hungry working man, he heartily approved of.

'You off out this evening?' asked Mrs Jeffrey.

'Shortly. I'll have a wash first.'

'I'll boil some water for you to tek upstairs.'

Armed with the kettle, he thanked her for the meal and opened the door to the stairs. The day he came here to see the room, he had been startled when his prospective landlady seemed to walk into a cupboard before he realised it was an enclosed staircase, with horribly steep steps that even now

127

put him in mind of broken necks.

The whole of the upstairs was his, such as it was. He used to have one room, but when the other lodger left, he had taken over the front room as well, so now he had a bedroom and a sitting room. Very grand. He smiled wryly. The entire first floor could fit inside Roberta's mother's drawing room with space to spare. Was it hypocritical of him to have two rooms? A real window cleaner would be grateful to have one to himself.

This evening, he was going to step back into his old life, something that was normally reserved for Sundays, when he joined his brother's family after church. Putting down the kettle on the scarred wooden washstand, he peeled off his clothes before pouring hot water into the bowl, topping it up from the china jug. He worked up a good lather on his flannel and gave himself a strip-wash. Before the war, his idea of luxury was the best seats at the Free Trade Hall, listening to the Hallé playing 'Fantasia on Greensleeves', followed by a late supper at the Midland Hotel. These days, luxury meant a double session in the public baths.

Dressed in trousers and vest, he used the last of the hot water to have a shave. Not that he specially needed one – he had never been prone to five o'clock shadow – but it was an automatic part of stepping back into his old life. Look your smartest at all times. He drew on his shirt. In went the gold cufflinks that had once been his father's and he slipped the sleeve-garters up his arms. As he attached his collar and inserted the studs, he felt an unaccustomed squeeze around his neck: he had got used to dressing casually. He slipped into his waistcoat and jacket, then slid his fingers beneath the leather strap attached to the back of his hairbrush and tidied his hair. His only looking-glass was his shaving mirror, but he didn't need a full-length reflection to show him how he looked. He could feel it. He was no longer Jim the window cleaner. He was James Franks, professional gentleman, solicitor. Former solicitor, anyway, though he kept abreast of changes to the law, hoping it would deal more kindly with the working man who had served King and country.

He ran downstairs.

'I'm off, Mrs J.'

She turned, her motherly smile transforming into a distant expression. Nothing quite like appearing in your landlady's kitchen dressed as a toff to throw up the barriers.

He set off. Mr Dawson lived near Longford Park in a handsome three-storey house. Did he own it or did he, the well-heeled landlord who lived off the rents of scores of humble properties, rent his gracious home off an even better-heeled landlord?

He checked the time before ringing the bell. If the Dawsons were going out, or hosting a dinner party, Mr Dawson could fit him in first – or so he hoped.

He was in luck.

'Good of you to see me,' he said as they shook hands. 'A few minutes of your time is all I ask.'

'More than a few, if you want them,' was the genial reply. Dawson was every inch the prosperous gentleman. 'Have a seat.'

Mr Dawson waved him towards a wing-back armchair, one of a pair in front of the splendid fireplace with its three overmantel shelves and attached candelabra. Jim sat down, his hard-worked muscles urging him to sink back into the upholstery and relax with his feet up.

Mr Dawson stood at the sideboard, decanter in hand. 'Scotch?'

'Please.'

'Dare I hope from your get-up that you've returned to a proper way of life?'

'I'm hardly going to present myself here in my window-cleaning gear.'

'To what do I owe the pleasure?'

Jim took a sip, gaining himself a moment. He and Mr Dawson knew one another from way back. Jim had started his career in the offices of Winterton, Sowerby and Jenks, where Mr Dawson was a client. Since Jim had landed up in Chorlton after the war, Dawson had never snubbed him and had benefited from off-the-cuff legal advice as a result. Would he help out now?

'I'm in search of a favour.'

'For yourself?'

'For an acquaintance. Hardly that, really. Someone I know of, who is in a fix. A widow in need of a new home by this time next week.'

'Pretty, is she?'

Heat etched his cheekbones. 'It's nothing like that. I'm not setting up a mistress. She barely knows I exist.'

'One of your war widows, is she?'

'No, just someone who needs a good turn, her and her youngsters. I heard of her plight from a woman who lost her son in the service of his country. Will you help?'

'Have you got a name and address for me? I'll get Miles to look into it.'

'Quickly – if you'd be so kind.'

'I'll see what I can do.'

## Chapter Ten

Posy drew a flower in each corner of the page and coloured them in carefully. Then she reread her letter. She didn't need to read it, because she knew it by heart, but she still wanted to.

*Dear Miss Claybourne,*
*Thank you for being my teacher. I will never forget you and will do everything with gusto and an optimistic heart.*
*Yours sincerely,*
*Posy Tanner (Miss)*

Was there time to deliver it? Did school have a letter box? If she slid it under the front door, would it vanish under the mat, never to be seen again?

'What are you doing, Posy?'

'Nothing, Ma.' She folded the letter. It was private.

'Have you packed your clothes?'

'And my jigsaw and my plasticine.'

*Thwack!* She jumped out of her skin as Dad's

hand slapped down on the table.

'That's no way to speak to an adult. The correct answer is *Yes, Ma,* not *I've done this and that as well.* That's answering back and I won't have it.'

The shaking started as a distant hum that expanded to a deeper vibration that made her innards go higgledy-piggledy. She tried to keep the shaking on the inside, but her body trembled and the table vanished in a blur of tears.

'What do you say to your mother?'

'I'm s-sorry, Ma.'

*'What do you say to your mother?'*

Panic panic panic.

'I'm sorry and I w-won't do it again.'

*'What do you say to your mother?'*

Panic panic panic. How was she supposed to know if he didn't tell her? Panic panic – stillness as she sensed the change. He wasn't looming over her any more. What did that mean? Inside her head was a white swirl of panic panic panic. He heaved out a breath, not a real one, a pretend one, as if it made him sad to punish her, but it didn't. He liked being angry.

'New home, new school ... same stupid Posy. I think Rupert will have something to say about this.'

A flutter across the room made Posy dart a glance that way, but Ma was heading for the door. She was never there when it happened. Even if she was in the room, she wasn't there. Posy's tummy curled up tight, squeezing hard on her breakfast, threatening to send it scudding up her gullet to explode out of her in all directions, from her mouth, down her nose.

'Morning! Removal men are here.'

A knock, a door opening – the front room. Then another knock and the kitchen door opened to reveal a burly fellow with a weather-beaten face.

'Sorry to barge in, but the front door was open.'

'Good morning,' said Dad. 'I propped it open so it won't swing shut while you're at work.'

'I see you're ready to go.'

'Indeed we are. I want to arrive on the dot of twelve, not a moment later. I hope you can oblige.'

How did he do it? She was sick and trembly and probably as pale as someone on their death-bed, yet he could instantly change and be all hail-fellow-well-met, friendly and in charge at the same time. Bonhomie, he called it. Posy wasn't sure what bonhomie was, but that didn't matter. She didn't want to use the word anyhow.

'Can you start in the bedroom?' said Dad. 'I've something to attend to in here.'

Something to attend to. So she wasn't to be reprieved.

'Fetch Rupert.'

She dragged herself into the hall. Her fingers were greasy with fear, but she managed to unclip Rupert and take him – it – to Dad.

Ma delved into a box of crockery. The news-paper wrapped around each piece rustled as her fingers poked about. Posy yearned for Ma to look her way. Even a glance would help, but Ma wouldn't even provide that.

Posy braced herself, fastened her mouth shut, held her breath; but after the first couple of blows, snot spurted from her nostrils and her eyes nearly popped out of her head. Her mouth flew wide open, the breath bursting out of her at the same time as she tried to suck in air to hold her steady. She choked, automatically bending forwards, and received a blow to her back that nearly felled her.

'Stand up straight,' Dad barked.

She lurched upright, staggered, brought herself back into position. You had to stay in position. It was worse if you didn't.

It finished.

Funny how you could feel shrivelled and enormous at the same time. Shrivelled, because you made yourself as small as you could, even if it was only on the inside; but huge as well, because that was what a thrashing did to you. It left you feeling puffy and swollen and bloated to twice your size. It made you feel surprised to look down at yourself and see you were the same size you always were.

'Kiss Rupert and say thank you.'

A trembly kiss. 'Thank you, Rupert.' And may you rot and burn in hell.

'What's this?'

Dad picked up her precious farewell letter to Miss Claybourne. Posy's heartbeat turned to sludge. Would she get into trouble for writing it? But Dad didn't unfold it, didn't read it, just gave it to Ma.

'Something for the dustbin, Hilda.'

The pain from the beating went numb. Miss Claybourne would never know she had wanted to say goodbye, would never know she was going to keep on using her best words.

'Kiss Rupert goodbye, Posy.'

She wanted to mourn Miss Claybourne, but there wasn't time. Kiss Rupert goodbye? Well, that was one good thing, at least. Rupert wasn't moving house with them.

A glimmer of optimism stirred in her heart.

Jim slept with his window open and his bedroom was bright with the fresh green scent of a rain-washed morning. Beneath his dormer window, the soil in his vegetable patch was dark with moisture and the field beyond glistened. A few years ago, someone standing here would have seen more fields beyond, but now, beyond Riley's field, were the backs of a road of red-brick houses.

He bolted down a hasty breakfast and set off, pushing his barrow. He didn't know what time Mrs Hibbert was moving, but he would put money on its being early. The purposeful young widow who had filled two bags of shopping in the time it took Mrs Watson to get the ham wasn't the sort to hang about.

He called at the houses on this morning's round, promising to fit them in another time, then headed for Finney Lane, with a smile that couldn't be contained; he would have to get that under control before he arrived. Would she be pleased to see him? The soppy grin simmered down into a wry expression. Would she recognise him? He had barely warranted a glance on the two previous occasions.

He knocked and she opened the door.

'Yes?' She hooked some hair behind her ear. 'Can I help you?'

'Actually, I'm here to help you.'

'Mummy, it's the window cleaner.' Alf tried to push past her, but she held onto his shoulder. 'Cassie climbed up your ladder.'

'So she did. The ladder's on the barrow, so you'd better keep her away or she'll be using it as a see-saw.'

Alf hooted in delight. His mum cast her gaze up to heaven, but it was only pretend: she was smiling too.

'You think that's a joke,' she said, 'but I wouldn't put it past her.'

Her face softened. She had beautiful skin, smooth and radiant. Her eyes softened too and his heart bumped. She bent to pick up her son; Alf wrapped himself around her, watching Jim with interest.

'Cassie's a bucketful of trouble,' she said. 'This here's my sensible one.' She pressed a kiss onto Alf's forehead. 'He's a bit big to be picked up now, but I'm making the most of it while he still lets me.'

'I don't blame you.'

That earned him a smile. 'Are you touting for work? Mrs Brent already has a window cleaner.'

'I heard you were moving and I'm here with my barrow, if you need it.'

The look on her face suggested refusal, but she hesitated and when she spoke, her voice was friendly. 'Thank you. Mrs Watson has told me you do good turns for folk in need and that's certainly me today.'

He felt ridiculously pleased. 'The kindness of strangers.'

She nodded, accepting this. 'I'm Mrs Nell Hibbert.'

Helen? Helena? She deserved a beautiful name. No chance of shaking hands while she was holding the child. 'How do. Jim Franks.'

'This is Alf.'

'We've met. He's got a pet monkey.'

Alf chortled. 'She's my *sister.*'

Mrs Hibbert – did he dare think of her as Nell? – put Alf down. 'Tell Mrs Brent we've got help.' As he vanished down the hallway, she added, 'I'm sorry if I was abrupt. Things are rather fraught.'

'It's a big undertaking, moving house. I took the liberty of bringing a couple of tea chests and some boxes from the cardboard box factory on Beech Road.'

'You don't do your good deeds by halves, do you?'

'Best way.'

Alf reappeared, dragging an older woman of a similar age to Mrs Watson. Her clothes looked loose, as if she had lost weight recently.

'It's the window cleaner,' cried Alf, 'and he's brought his barrow.' He made it sound like a golden carriage drawn by the finest horses.

'Where are your belongings?' Jim asked.

'Upstairs.'

'I'll take the boxes up. Do you happen to have a strong young chap who can lend a hand?' Alf bobbed up by his side. 'Let's see your muscles.' Jim bent his elbow and clenched a fist. Alf copied and he made a show of testing the tiny muscle and being impressed. 'Can you carry this cardboard box upstairs? Slowly, mind. There's no

137

time for falls and broken bones today.'

He shouldn't have been shocked by how little they had, but he was. Clothing, bedding, some bits and pieces of crockery and cutlery. He tried to keep his expression neutral, but something must have shown.

'We haven't got much – as you can see.' Nell's voice was bright, but there was a steely edge to it, daring him to feel sorry for her. 'We haven't needed our own things, living here. I'll go down the second-hand furniture shop on Beech Road this afternoon and see what I can get.'

'I'll go with you and ferry things back on my barrow.'

'Don't you have to get back to work? Mrs Watson says you spend Saturday helping the poor.'

'I'll do it another time. I've already told my morning calls.'

Her eyes were troubled, filled with second thoughts.

'I know it seems odd,' he said quickly, 'my helping you like this, but since the war...'

'*Oh.*' Her face shone. 'I'm the same. All my brothers – and my sister...' She pressed a hand to her throat. 'Sometimes the only way... I do summat for someone else and it's like doing it for them.'

Her distress, though controlled, was audible. He wanted to take her in his arms, to offer comfort and understanding, one bereaved person to another, to give her someone to lean on. She shook her head and the moment vanished. She was all business.

'Mrs Brent is letting us take this bed. Her daughter's family is moving in and they're bringing their own.'

'I'll take it apart. I've brought tools.'

'I was going to do it myself.'

His face cracked into a grin. 'I can see where your daughter gets it from.'

Before long, the room was empty, apart from the chest of drawers and the hanging cupboard. What was Nell thinking? Feeling? Sadness? Anger at having to make way for others? Impossible to tell.

'I have to give the room a thorough clean before we go,' was all she said. 'There are things in the parlour and food in the kitchen. I went out early to buy it.'

In the parlour was an assortment of items: a bread bin, a small table, an oil lamp, two candlesticks – not a pair – a jug, a chipped platter, some dishes of varying styles, a three-legged stool, faded curtains, a posser, a pair of bellows.

'All given by neighbours,' said Mrs Brent. 'Mrs Watson started it. Everyone tried to give something. I wish I'd thought of it.'

'Cheer up. You'll have your family round you before you know it. That's what this is about, isn't it?'

'Obviously I want them here. It's just that the Hibberts feel like family an' all.' She clapped a hand over her mouth. 'Don't let on to my daughter I said that. She'd be so hurt.'

Jim finished loading his barrow as Nell came downstairs.

'I can't take it all in one go,' he said. 'Let's take this lot, then you and the children can stay in your new place while I come back for more.'

'I haven't finished the room yet. There's the skirting boards to wash, and the picture rail, and the drawers ought to have fresh lining paper.' She blew out a breath. 'And we have to be away by twelve.'

Distress flickered across Mrs Brent's face. 'Me and Mrs Watson will finish the cleaning. Don't argue. You've got enough to do.'

There was a charged moment as the two women gazed at one another, pain and sorrow raw in their faces. Jim hoped Mrs Brent was going to get endless pleasure from living with her family, because she was clearly paying a high price for it.

'I'll check the barrow,' he said. 'The kids can help.'

He took them outside and made sure everything was secure.

'We've got a box of linen here, and that's a box of food. Where's the box with the monkey?'

'I keep telling you,' cried Alf. 'She's not a monkey.'

He scooped Cassie up and popped her into an empty box. 'A special box for monkeys.'

'Can I go in a box?' begged Alf.

'You can sit here.' He lifted the boy onto the barrow, between the handles, so he was sitting with his legs dangling. 'Now we just need your mum and we can go.'

Nell and Mrs Brent came outside, wiping away tears.

'Look at me, Mummy,' Alf called. 'I'm riding on the barrow. It's like when we left our other house and went on the horse and cart.'

She looked startled. 'Do you remember that?'

'If I'm in competition with a horse and cart,' said Jim, 'I'd best turn the barrow round and pull it. I'll be the horse and you, Master Hibbert, are the driver, so I hope you're going to be kind to poor old Neddy. Where to, Mrs Hibbert?'

'Wilton Lane. Wouldn't you rather push than pull?'

'I won't do any pulling until the driver says *Giddy up.*'

'Giddy up, Neddy,' yelled Alf.

As they went, Nell told him about the new house.

'I'm getting it cheap because it has problems. After the last tenants moved out, there was a spell before the new family was meant to move in. Evidently there was a crack in the lead flashing round the chimney stack and water got in and because the house was empty, no one knew, so it got quite bad. When the new people arrived, they found one corner of the front bedroom ceiling had come down, so Mr Miles found them somewhere else.'

'How bad is it?'

'There's the bedroom ceiling, and the wall is saturated, and part of the floor, and it soaked through into the parlour below. That ceiling hasn't come down, but there are huge stains on the ceiling and down the wall. It'll all be made good, but first it has to dry out.' She glanced at him. 'The other bedroom and the kitchen are fine. I wouldn't take my children there if not.' She huffed a sigh. It wasn't a sorrowful sound, more a worried one. 'I feel guilty. I want better for them.'

141

'Give it time. Like you say, it'll be repaired.'

'Aye, and then the rent will go up. I'm sorry; I shouldn't burden you, especially when you're being so kind. Anyroad, if I'm guilty, I'm grateful too. Mr Miles came round himself and offered it. I can't think how he knew. Mrs Watson, I suppose. Here we are.'

It was the same as every other terraced two-up two-down: front door with a step and a sash window beside it, another window above.

'You go in,' said Jim, 'and I'll unload.'

Unloading took no time at all. He tried hard not to find it pathetic. She would be outraged if she thought he felt sorry for her.

There was a musty smell.

'Pooh.' Alf wrinkled his nose.

'That's the damp,' said Nell. 'We'll open the back door and the windows to let in fresh air. You're allowed in the parlour, but you mustn't go in the front bedroom. We'll stand at the door and look at the damage, but you mustn't go in there on your own.'

Jim stowed a few things in the cupboard under the stairs and carried the rest to the kitchen.

'I can't unpack anything until I've cleaned through,' said Nell. 'Even then, I have to wait till I've got furniture. All I can do for now is put the food in the pantry once I've cleaned the shelves.'

'I'll fetch the rest of your things.'

Was there time to run round to the coal merchant? The house needed fires as well as fresh air. Nell wouldn't worry about an unexpected delivery of coal if she thought Mr Miles had organised it because the house needed drying out.

No, there wasn't time now, but Jim wouldn't forget. He would order coal and tell Miles to say it was from the landlord.

Back in Finney Lane, Mrs Watson jollied along a tearful Mrs Brent. Jim loaded the remainder of the Hibberts' belongings, except for the mattress, and returned to Wilton Lane.

Alf greeted him at the door. 'Mummy says you're just in time. She's got the kettle on.'

The man from next door appeared and helped him carry the parts of the bed upstairs.

'The lady next door popped round with a jug of milk,' said Nell. 'Wasn't that kind?'

'That were my wife,' said the helper. 'We're the O'Rourkes.'

'We could all do with a neighbour like Mrs O'Rourke,' said Jim. 'And like you.'

'The kindness of strangers,' said Nell. Her smile turned his heart over. 'Can I offer you a cup of tea, Mr O'Rourke?'

'No, I'll leave you to it. Give me a knock if you need help putting the bed together,' he added to Jim.

'Thanks.' He waited for the front door to close. 'Looks like you've got good neighbours.'

She handed him his tea. He accepted it with exquisite care, determined not to brush her fingers.

'Sorry I can't offer you a seat,' she said, 'unless you fancy that little stool.'

'There's plenty of seats – at least, I think there are. Alf! Count the stairs. Are there enough for all of us?'

Alf flew off to perform the task. 'We can have

more than one each,' he reported.

They sat on the stairs.

'So she can sit still, then.' Jim nodded at Cassie. 'Make the most of it. It doesn't last long.'

'When d'you think you'll finish unpacking? I'll come and take the boxes away.'

'Don't forget we have to keep a box for Violet,' said Alf.

'I won't,' said Nell. 'Violet's the cat. She's staying with Mrs Brent for now, because we'll have to have the windows open to air the house.'

'When Violet comes, she has to stay inside until she learns this is her new house,' said Alf, 'so she has to wait until we can shut the windows.'

'Good luck putting Violet in a box,' said Jim. 'I hope you've got a suit of armour, young Alf.'

'Violet came to Manchester in a basket and she was good as gold,' said Nell, 'though I doubt it'll be so easy this time.'

'Violet came in Mummy's wicker basket,' said Alf, 'and Cassie came in the doctor's black bag.'

A snort of laughter almost made Jim spit out his tea. Oh, that would have looked good, wouldn't it, tea spewing out of his nose.

'Alf, you don't say things like that,' said Nell.

The front door opened. 'Knock-knock,' called a woman's voice and three middle-aged women and a younger one trooped in, carrying an assortment of mops and buckets. Nell sprang up. Jim crushed himself against the balusters to let her past before he came to his feet.

'Elsie!' she cried. 'Mildred! What are you doing here?'

'What does it look like?' demanded their leader

– Elsie? She brandished a mop. 'We wanted to do summat for you in your new house.'

'So that's why you never stopped asking about my move.'

'Aye,' said Elsie. 'I thought you'd never spill the address. We've brought carbolic and rags and soda crystals and when we've given the place a good going-over, we've got lavender polish.'

'I haven't got owt to polish yet,' said Nell. 'I'm getting furniture later.'

'Fetch it now,' ordered Elsie.

'I can't leave you doing the work.'

'Do as you're told. We've come to do a job and we're not leaving till it's done proper.'

'Aye,' said another, 'and we've got husbands at home what are expecting their tea on't table at the usual time, so we can't hang about.'

Nell turned to Jim. 'Would you mind if we went to the furniture shop now?'

'I ought to fetch the mattress first. Time's getting on.'

'Aye-aye, the mattress?' quipped one of the women.

'That's enough of that.' Nell cast a warning glance in Alf's direction. 'This is Mr Franks, the window cleaner. He's kindly helping us move in.'

She looked awkward, and more awkward still when a couple of her friends nudged one another. He couldn't have her feeling uncomfortable. What if she decided he wasn't worth the trouble? He came downstairs and waggled his eyebrows roguishly at the women.

'Ladies, I am a single man.'

They tittered and the moment turned to a joke.

He had established himself as a decent bloke doing his good deed for the day. Nell's shoulders relaxed. Good. And not so good. He wanted to be more than that. Best if he got out of the way and let Elsie and her merry band get on with their task. Once they started on the cleaning, they would be too busy to make teasing remarks ... he hoped.

'C'mon, kids,' he said. 'Let's go and fetch the mattress.'

'I was dreading today,' Nell told her friends. 'Leaving a home where we've been happy and settled...' She shook her head. 'But you've come to lend a hand; and the neighbours have been kind; and as for Mr Franks...' She turned to him. 'What can I say? It's the sort of thing my brothers would have done.'

The words were spoken as if this was the highest compliment she could bestow, and maybe it was. Jim was deeply touched, but at the same time, being compared to her brothers was the last thing he wanted.

'You did say one of the good things about us coming here was that Posy would have a bed.' Hilda sounded peevish. 'You said that, Mother.'

Yes, Leonie remembered saying it, and she had meant it an' all. 'I thought, a little bed in the parlour. We could put it in the back corner, with furniture in front of it in case of visitors. Not that visitors use the parlour. We always sit in the kitchen.'

'That's the point, Mother-in-law.' Where had Edmund sprung from? 'The parlour is kept for best. You can't have a bed in the room that's used for best.'

'Well...' She needed time to think. This had been dropped on her with no notice.

'So Posy will sleep with you. I thought that was what you wanted,' said Edmund. 'Didn't you say you wanted her to sleep in a bed?'

Were they ganging up on her? Of course not. They assumed, with good reason, that Posy's sleeping arrangements had been agreed, and now here she was, rocking the boat. Her gaze fell on Posy. She ought to be bonny and excited at moving house. Instead her eyes were anxious. Leonie bit her lip. Did Posy think she wasn't wanted? Pushing past Edmund, she gathered her beloved granddaughter into her arms.

'Of course you can sleep with me.'

'If you prefer,' said Edmund, 'we could get a single bed for Posy and put it in your room, but it'll be a squeeze.'

That made her feel worse. 'Don't be daft. We'll be snug as two bugs in a rug, won't we, Posy?'

'You're a good sort, Mother-in-law.'

Edmund's voice was rich and kind. It was good to have a man in the house. It made her feel secure.

'Posy, let's put the kettle on. Those men will be gasping when they've brought your mum and dad's bed inside and put it together in their new room.'

'That's another thing,' said Edmund. 'Before they bring it in, don't you think they should move yours?'

'Mine?' What was going on?

147

'I thought it was understood.' He frowned but looked genial at the same time, as if it was amusing that a mistake had been made. 'The married couple should occupy the master bedroom. It makes sense, don't you think, Mother-in-law? Two adults in the bigger bedroom, one in the smaller.'

Well, put like that... 'I suppose so.'

Edmund placed his hands on her shoulders. 'You don't sound sure. You have to be sure.'

How could she? No one had said owt to her about giving up the bedroom she and Hedley had shared. But that was the point, wasn't it? A big room like that was meant to have two people in it. The least she could do was give it to Edmund and Hilda, show them how welcome they were.

'A room that size isn't meant to have just an old biddy rattling around in it.'

Edmund threw back his head and laughed. He had a rich laugh that made you think he must have a wonderful singing voice. 'And we'd better stop talking as if the back room is poky. It's not that much smaller. Goodness, you had a whole family living in it until this morning.'

Leonie went to make tea. What had just happened? She had given up her bedroom and acquired a bedfellow and it was barely half past twelve. And didn't that make her sound like a grumpy old so-and-so? It had grieved her for years that Posy didn't have a bed. She should be grateful to do summat about it. But she felt all prickly and bothered. This morning, she had been mistress of the house. Now Hilda and Edmund were here and she had been relegated to the back bedroom, the granny sharing with the little 'un to save space.

'What's that cat doing here?' Edmund sounded vexed. 'Throw it out.'

Leonie banged the kettle down on the range in her haste to leave the kitchen. Posy darted into the hall. Leonie glimpsed a black blur flying upstairs. Edmund's hand was clamped onto the rounded top of the newel post, his foot on the bottom step.

'That's Violet, the Hibberts' cat,' said Leonie.

'Posy, put it out and shut the door.'

'She won't know where her new house is,' Posy protested, distressed.

'It'll find it soon enough when it's hungry. Do as you're told.'

Leonie stepped forward. 'Violet is stopping here for now, Edmund. The Hibberts' house has problems with damp, so they need to have the windows open as much as they can. They can't have Violet yet, because of her getting out.'

'It's a cat. It's meant to be out.'

'Only when she knows where to go home to. I promised to keep her here. You wouldn't want me to break a promise.'

'Well, keep it out of my way.'

'Violet's a she, Dad, not an it,' said Posy.

'Cats are it. And don't get smart with me.'

'Posy, why don't you bring Violet down to the kitchen?' Leonie struggled to keep her voice normal. Her heart was beating hard. 'There's a good girl.'

Posy scampered upstairs. Leonie returned to the kitchen. She should get on with making the tea, but instead she sank onto a chair. What with one thing and another, her new life hadn't got off to the best start. Losing her bedroom, gaining Posy in her bed – not that that was a bad thing, but it was unexpected and now Edmund not wanting Violet. But things happened in threes, didn't they? And that was three difficult things over and done with in one go.

Everything was going to be fine from now on.

## Chapter Eleven

Nell could barely believe it. Since starting at the factory, she had lurched out of bed every morning at ridiculous o'clock and stumbled back to bed at half-past shattered. In her new job, she had time in the mornings. She could even take Alf to school if she wasn't expected at Ingleby's first thing. She had time of an evening too; time to be with her children, time to play with them, feed them, wash them and put them to bed. It was the best gift anyone could have given her – and it came courtesy of her job. Imagine that.

The cherry on the cake was that she loved the work. She enjoyed the variety of being sometimes in the shop but mostly in ladies' homes and she discovered an aptitude for teaching. She planned a series of six introductory lessons. Ingleby's expected the customers to have one lesson a week, but at the end of Nell's first week, one of her ladies, Mrs Liversedge, asked for two.

She was taken aback. Should she refer the question to Miss Collier? But here she was, in Mrs Liversedge's back room, with its opalescent glass lampshades and wooden Venetian blinds, and Mrs Liversedge was looking at her expectantly.

Well, the customer was always right. 'I'll be glad to come twice a week. I suggest lessons two or three days apart so you have time to practise.' She produced her diary. Already it was the most important tool she possessed. 'I can come next week on Tuesday and either Thursday or Friday.'

'What if I want more lessons after I'd had the six?'

'I'll enquire for you when I go to Ingleby's this afternoon.'

Later she put the question to Miss Collier.

'We're going to start lessons for small groups of ladies in the sewing department,' said Miss Collier. 'How to sew a collar or an inset pocket, that kind of thing. Mrs Liversedge is welcome to put her name down.'

'What about further lessons in her own home?' asked Nell.

'No. We include six lessons in the cost of the machine and that's all.'

How would Mrs Liversedge take the news?

When Nell saw her again the following Tuesday, she was annoyed.

'Really, I expected better of Ingleby's.'

'We don't have the staff to provide unlimited lessons,' Nell said politely. 'You'd be welcome at the group lessons. If you like the way I teach, I'll be taking some of the sessions.' Was that big-headed? If you like the way I teach, indeed.

'What I was hoping for was some long lessons,

151

say three hours each. I want you to guide me while I make my first dress, starting with cutting out the pattern. Do you do private lessons? Please say you do or my lovely material will stay in the cupboard until it rots.'

Private lessons? She was about to say no, but if it didn't impinge on her Ingleby's hours, why not? Providing furniture had eaten into her savings. It would be good to get more money behind her. She flicked through her diary, giving herself time to think. She wasn't working on Saturday. As for the fee, Ingleby's were going to charge five bob for a two-hour lesson. That was half a crown an hour, while she earned less than a shilling an hour. But if the likes of Mrs Liversedge were happy to cough up two and six an hour for lessons in the shop, then...

'I charge one and nine an hour in the week or two shillings an hour on Saturdays. I can come this Saturday at half past one and stay until half past four. Will that be satisfactory?'

'So, I'm teaching a private lesson on Saturday afternoon.' Did she sound conceited? But Mrs Brent looked pleased and impressed and Nell felt a glow of pride.

They were sitting in her kitchen at her new – new to her, but old as the hills – kitchen table. It hadn't been the best in the second-hand shop. It was scuffed and a boy called Tommy had carved his name on it, but her Pringle heart had yearned for its large size, just right for a family crowd.

'I hope you're going to ask me to mind the children,' said Mrs Brent.

152

Should she say it? Could she? The hurt it would cause Mrs Brent made her pause, but her first duty was to her children. Over her dead body would they set foot in the house where Edmund Tanner lived. She couldn't send Alf there, not even for an afternoon.

'This isn't easy to say, so I'll just say it straight out. We love you, the children and me, we all love you; but Alf is frightened of Mr Tanner.'

'What's Edmund ever done to him?'

'Nowt. Alf's scared: that's all there is to it.'

Dipping her chin, Mrs Brent broke free of Nell's gaze. When she looked up again, her eyes were bright. 'Things have changed, haven't they?'

'Yes, but we're still friends. I don't know what I'd have done without you and Mr Brent when me and Alf arrived here. I'll always be grateful.'

She reached across and Mrs Brent's hand grasped hers in a warm squeeze.

'Why don't I come here to look after the children? I'd hate never to be run ragged by Cassie again.'

Nell laughed. 'That'd be perfect. Thank you.' Her shoulders relaxed. 'Things are different, but we still have one another.'

'Aye. It's a credit to you, what you've done with your new home.'

'And I bet you love having the Tanners with you.'

'Of course I do.'

*But.* There it was in Nell's head. But.

'Everything all right?' She pushed the plate of home-made gingerbread closer to her visitor to show it was a casual question.

Mrs Brent's hand hovered as if she were about

153

to take a slice, then dropped away. 'Oh, it's nowt. Just me being an old fusspot.'

'If you can't tell me, who can you tell? You've seen parts of me seen only by the midwife.'

That made Mrs Brent laugh. Good. Would she share what was mithering her?

'It really is nowt. Edmund suggested me and Hilda divide up the jobs, one of us to do the housework and one to do the cooking.'

'What's it got to do with him how you organise yourselves?'

'He wanted to help us.'

Wanted to boss them, more like, but Nell kept her mouth shut.

'Anyroad, he suggested I do the housework and Hilda does the shopping and the cooking, because the shopping is heavy.'

'Oh aye,' said Neil dryly, 'and cleaning isn't heavy at all.'

'I'd far rather do the catering.'

'Did you say so?'

'How could I? It would have looked like I thought our Hilda can't cook.'

'No, it wouldn't. Have a word with her. Share all the jobs. That's fairest.'

Mrs Brent frowned. 'Hilda wouldn't go against Edmund.'

'It isn't going against him. Besides, what does he care? His job is to bring in the money and yours is to run the home – yours and Hilda's.'

'Edmund isn't like my Hedley. Hedley left the domestic side of things to me, but Edmund is ... well, he's more in charge, if you know what I mean.'

Nell was all too afraid she did know, and she didn't like it. She composed her next words with care and spoke them gently. 'It's your house, remember.'

'It's theirs an' all now. They're family and they're entitled to make decisions.'

'I'm sure your Hilda wouldn't want to do that at the expense of your peace of mind.'

'Anyroad, that's enough about me. I want to hear about you. How are the children?'

'Fine. They're playing in the front room. Mr Franks unfolded one of the cardboard boxes for them and Alf pretends it's a raft and sails all over the world on it.'

'He has a way with children, yon window cleaner,' said Mrs Brent.

'He left a couple of boxes too, which they use for boats and caves and goodness knows what.'

'As long as the damp doesn't get onto their chests.'

'The chimney stack was mended as soon as the damage was found, so no rain has got in since then. Besides, Mr Miles sent the coalman round to fill the bunker. He said I had to keep the house warm. I felt rotten bringing the children to a damaged house, but it's far better than I thought.' She gave Mrs Brent a nudge. 'Do you want to hear something exciting? I'm getting a sewing machine.'

'Nay! You'd never afford it, lass.'

'Not to buy; to hire. I'm going to give lessons to backstreet women, then they can pay to use the machine when they need it. What do you think?'

'I don't know.' Mrs Brent sounded huffy. 'All

them women traipsing through the house.'

'They won't be traipsing. You know they won't.'

'Of course I do, love. I'm sorry. I'm a bit out of sorts because of things at home, but I'm glad for you. You deserve to do well. Lord knows, you work hard enough. I wish you well, I really do.'

'Thanks. That means everything to me.'

Excitement bubbled up inside her. She, Nell Hibbert, the girl who got safely married, unlike her sister, who had gone off to drive ambulances; the downtrodden wife who was betrayed in the worst possible way; the sewing-machinist who wasn't allowed to earn the salary she was capable of … she was going to forge her own path. She was going to make something of herself.

How could she have been so mean? Leonie's throat thickened with shame. Women traipsing through the house, indeed. As if Nell would do anything iffy. She was the most respectable person Leonie knew. But oh, the bitterness she had felt in that moment. Jealousy was meant to stab you, but hers had burnt. Her chest had felt hot and raw. Imagine being jealous of a friend, and such a dear friend at that.

And she wasn't jealous, not really. It had been a momentary aber-aber-whatever the word was: she knew what she meant. Nell deserved all the good luck she could get and Leonie was delighted for her, but she couldn't pretend that surge of envy hadn't happened, that knowledge that her old lodger, who had spent the past two years being beholden to her, was on the up, while she … wasn't.

She had accepted the new bedroom arrange-ments with good grace in the interests of getting them off to a good start. But then Edmund had stuck his nose into the running of the household, giving Hilda the best job and reducing her to the rank of cleaner. Not that there was owt wrong with cleaning. She had always kept her house spick and span, but she wanted to do more than clean.

Nell said it wasn't up to Edmund and, sitting in Nell's house, Leonie had thought so too. She vowed to tackle Hilda the moment she got home. They would soon sort it out. Honestly, she was so silly. She had blown the whole thing out of pro-portion when all it needed was a couple of women to put their heads together.

She opened the front door to the aroma of frying onions and boiled bacon, but without the accom-panying scent of herbs, even though Hilda had learnt her cooking from her. It didn't smell like her house any more. She hung up her outdoor things and went into the kitchen, her skirt swishing round her ankles. She had never shortened her skirts. It was all very well for young women to flash their ankles, and more than their ankles these days, but at her age, she had more dignity, not to mention more sense.

Hilda looked up from stirring onion round the frying-pan. 'All well in Wilton Lane?'

'Aye. They've settled in nicely.'

She would have loved to say more; she would have loved to take Hilda with her when she went to Nell's, but Hilda and Nell, though they were civil, had never hit it off, even though Nell had made friendly advances back when she first

157

moved in here. In those days, when Leonie had realised how much she liked her young lodger, she had treasured visions of the three of them clustered round her kitchen table, enjoying a good natter. Wouldn't that have been grand? Almost like having two daughters.

Hilda tipped the onions into a saucepan and sprinkled salt and pepper. Leonie itched to help as Hilda added milk, flour and mashed potato, mixing it all together to make a creamy sauce.

'I'd pop in some sage, if it was me.' She smiled to show she was being helpful, not critical.

'This is how Edmund likes it.'

And that was the end of that suggestion. The man of the house, the breadwinner, got to make all kinds of decisions, including, it seemed, what seasoning was allowed. Hedley had never had opinions like that. His only opinion about her cooking had been how delicious it was. Maybe other husbands weren't so easy.

'Do you like cooking?' Leonie asked.

'You know I do.'

Stupid question. She should have come straight out with it. 'I miss it now we've divided up the housework.'

'Mother, it's only been a few days.'

Right. This time she really would come straight out with it. Nell had said, 'I'll just say it straight out.'

'What would you say to changing jobs?'

'What, you do the cooking and me do the cleaning?'

'No.' Cautious hope made her bite her lip. 'Let's go halves.'

158

Hilda gazed fixedly into the saucepan. 'I don't know. Edmund...'

'What's it to him?' she asked cheerfully.

'Let's leave it as it is, shall we? For now.'

For now? Did she mean that or was she just saying it? And how much did it matter, anyroad? The last thing Leonie wanted was to upset Hilda. She tugged her earlobe, doubt creeping through her.

'Don't say owt to Edmund, will you?' said Hilda.

'Not if you don't want me to.'

'He'd be upset if he thought we didn't like how he organised us.'

He shouldn't care. Hedley had never laid the law down. He had gone out and earned their daily bread and left everything at home to her and that had suited them both. Their Hilda had grown up with that as an example of how to live together as man and wife, but she now accepted a different set of rules. Would Leonie have to accept these rules an' all? It looked like she would, if she intended them all to live in a happy home.

It was difficult not to feel resentful. Leonie forced a smile. No one liked a sour face and it would set a bad example to Posy. Besides, what if anyone realised why she was vexed? Posy would be dreadfully hurt and she couldn't bear the thought of causing that.

But Edmund had specifically said that Posy couldn't have a bed in the parlour because of keeping it for best. Yet here they were, sitting in the parlour in the evening, and it wasn't for the first time either. They had done it on the Tanners' first evening here, because Edmund said it was a special occasion, and then they had carried on doing it and now it was part of the routine. What must the neighbours think? She quaked every time someone walked past the window. She dreaded being saddled with a reputation for getting above herself. Living in the parlour, indeed. Very swanky.

But that wasn't why she felt resentful. No, the reason for the tension in her shoulders and the hot bubbling sensation in her stomach was that if they weren't keeping the parlour for best, then why not put a bed in the corner for Posy? Only she couldn't say so, because poor Posy would feel her gran didn't want to share with her.

So she was lumbered with it.

Edmund took pride of place in the armchair. The front room had just the one armchair. Why splash out on a pair when the room was used only on high days and holidays? That had been Hedley's opinion and she had agreed.

'Far more important to have two cosy chairs by the kitchen fire,' Hedley had said.

So, Edmund sat smoking in the armchair and she and Hilda sat on the settee, while Posy sat on the footstool, her knees bunched up since she wasn't allowed to stretch out her legs.

'Sitting with us before bed is how she'll learn to make conversation,' according to Edmund, but this apparently was to be achieved purely by listening, since the child wasn't allowed to speak unless spoken to. Anyroad, as Leonie had learnt by sharing a room with her, Posy was nothing if not adept at conversation.

Hilda pushed the darning mushroom into the heel of one of Edmund's socks. Leonie had undone one of Hedley's pullovers and was knitting it up into a cardy for Posy. It had hurt to unravel something of Hedley's, but waste not want not, and who better to rework it for than Posy?

'Did you visit Mrs Hibbert today?' asked Edmund.

'Yes. She's well; so are the children.'

'I hope you kept yourself wrapped up warm, Mother-in-law, in that damp environment. We don't want you falling ill.'

'It isn't at all bad. It's only the front two rooms and they're not lived in for now. The upstairs room is worse by far.'

'I'm only concerned for your welfare.'

'Thank you.' She felt a pleasing inner glow. It was nice to be watched over by a man.

'I know Mrs Hibbert had to leave here at short notice,' said Edmund, 'but that's no excuse for taking her children to live in a place like that.'

'She had no choice,' Leonie protested.

'I'm sorry to contradict you, but she had ample choice. I myself provided a list of rooms from the paper. Are you telling me they were all worse than the house in Wilton Lane?'

'She didn't try them, because Mr Miles offered Wilton Lane.'

'Warts and all,' said Edmund. 'She might have done better to visit some of my places. Don't you agree, Hilda?'

Hilda mumbled something. She held the darning close to her face, inspecting it minutely.

'The Wilton Lane house wouldn't do for my

family,' said Edmund. 'It's a question of stand-ards.'

Leonie couldn't let that pass unchallenged. 'Mrs Hibbert has standards.'

'If you say so, Mother-in-law.'

I do say so. But that would sound argumentative and what sort of example was that to set Posy? So she said nothing, but it hurt to hear her friend dismissed. Edmund had a point, though. As a responsible husband and father, naturally he was riled at the thought of someone taking their family into a damaged house. He obviously pictured it as far worse than it was. Perhaps he could be brought round.

'I'm looking after the Hibbert children on Saturday afternoon.'

Edmund looked at her. 'Where? Here?'

'No, round there, to help out while Mrs Hibbert is working.'

A frown clouded Edmund's broad brow. 'It was one thing to mind them when they lived here – and I never approved, as you know – but it's worse if you have to drag yourself round there. She shouldn't ask it of you.'

'She didn't.' Her knitting needles clicked more quickly. 'I offered.'

He blew out a stream of smoke. 'She's taking advantage of your good nature.'

*Click-click* went the needles. Would he try to forbid her to go? *Click-click*. But she mustn't argue in front of Posy. Even if Posy hadn't been there, she wouldn't have argued. They were one family and they must get along. Give and take. Listen to others. Mind your manners.

'Mrs Hibbert is an independent soul,' she said mildly, 'but she needs a hand with the children. I've known young Alf since he were knee-high to a grasshopper and I helped bring Cassie into this world–'

'Did you?' Posy exclaimed, entranced.

Hilda came to life. 'What Gran means is, she opened the door to the doctor when he brought the baby in his black bag.'

'Seen and not heard, Posy,' said Edmund.

'It wouldn't be right to give them up,' said Leonie. 'Alf and Cassie: it wouldn't be right.'

Edmund gazed into the fireplace, as if there were a fire crackling away and he was hypnotised by the flames. Had she won him round? Her row ended. She turned her knitting round, ready to start again. *Click-click.* Not so fast now.

Edmund fetched a deep sigh. His chest expanded and settled. He flicked his cigarette end into the fireplace. She wished he wouldn't do that. Throwing cigarette ends in the fire during the winter was fine, because they got burnt up, but chucking them in the empty summer fireplace was dirty. She was surprised at Hilda for not forbidding it on day one of their married life. She would have to say summat, but now wasn't the time, not in front of Posy, and not when she had hopes of Edmund's feeling more kindly towards Nell.

He looked at her and shook his head. Her heart quickened. *Click-click.*

'I'm sorry to say it, Mother-in-law, but I'm disappointed.'

Disappointed? *Click-click.*

'I suppose it was inevitable that a loving person

such as yourself would become attached to those children when they were under your roof. I warned you against it at the time, because I could see it gave Mrs Hibbert the opportunity to push her luck.' He held up a hand. 'Please allow me to finish. I admired your affection for those poor fatherless children, but I also – yes, I will say it – I also resented it, because it worried me that my daughter would be pushed out.'

Pushed out? *Click … click…*

'Oh, Edmund – Posy…' She looked from one to the other. Her lips moved as she struggled for the right words.

'I thought that when we came here, Posy would get more of a chance. You were generous about letting her sleep with you and that seemed like a good start. But now…' He shook his head again, giving her a half-smile that suggested acceptance of a sad situation. 'I see how much those children mean to you. I just wish you'd pay more heed to your granddaughter now she's under your roof. I thought she'd matter more.'

Her knitting collapsed onto her lap. 'Posy…' She could barely get the name out. There was a gurgle in her throat. Her eyes stung, but she mustn't weep. She must be strong. She was the adult. It was her job to reassure Posy.

The child sat bolt upright, eyes wide, apprehensive. Waiting. They were all waiting. Hilda fiddled with her darning. She didn't look up. If only Hilda's fingers would creep across and squeeze hers. Posy shifted like a puppy that had been trained to sit and stay but was desperate to run to its master.

'I'm sorrier than I can say, Hilda and Edmund, if you believe I've neglected Posy. I promise it won't happen again.'

Edmund nodded. 'I'm pleased to hear you say so – aren't you, Hilda?'

'Yes,' Hilda whispered.

'That's that, then. We'll say no more about it.' Edmund sounded almost jovial. 'I'm glad we've cleared the air. Shall we get off to a good start by saying you'll take Posy to the park on Saturday afternoon, Mother-in-law?'

Her breath caught. Had he forgotten? He must have. Oh, lord, what was she to do?

Posy said, 'Oh, but, Dad–'

'Seen and not heard, Posy.'

Posy gazed at Leonie, her eyes imploring.

'Maybe this once, Edmund?' Leonie asked.

He granted permission with a wave of his hand.

'I always run an errand for you on Saturday afternoons, Dad,' said Posy.

'So you do,' said Edmund. 'It's important to keep to routine. Gran can take you out another time.'

Tears welled behind Leonie's eyes. Posy had pulled her out of a hole. The dear child. After her father had cast doubt on her gran's love for her, she still showed love and protectiveness. Oh, Posy.

'Are you quite well, Mother-in-law? You've stopped knitting.'

*Click-click. Click-click.*

# Chapter Twelve

'How do you like your new home, Posy?' asked Mrs Watson, sounding all proper, as if she had never said *reet buggeration* in the whole of her life.

'I love it, thank you,' said Posy and squeezed Gran's hand. She was a big girl now and didn't need to hold hands, but holding hands with Gran was to do with treasuring one another and feeling warm inside. 'I like sleeping in a real bed, and having a cat, though she's not really ours, just on loan because of the damp, and having Gran there all the time.'

'Having Gran there is good, is it?'

'It's more than good, since you ask,' said Posy. 'It's good with gusto, if there is such a thing.'

'School is good an' all, isn't it, Posy?' prompted Gran.

'Yes.' It was the expected reply. Grown-ups were like that. They picked on something you were doomed to do, then asked whether you liked it. She had made some friends, but Mr Allan wasn't like Miss Claybourne. He was more interested in noses to the grindstone.

'Is Posy helping you with the shopping this morning?' said Mrs Watson.

'No, our Hilda does the shopping,' said Gran. 'We're going to the meadows to find flowers to press. Posy has never pressed flowers before.'

'Fancy that,' said Mrs Watson. 'I won't keep you.'

They set off. The mild day was warming up. As they crossed Chorlton Green, the pungent scent of freshly cut grass filled Posy's heart. That was what optimism smelt like. It was a perfect May morning, except for the fact that Saturday morning was followed by Saturday afternoon. Earlier this week, she had rescued Gran from a tricky situation by reminding Dad of her Saturday errand and she couldn't regret it. If she hadn't saved the day, Gran might have had to give up minding Alf and Cassie this afternoon. Gran loved the Hibbert children, but that was all right because Posy trusted Gran to love her best. Besides, if Gran was safely out of the way, she wouldn't see what happened on Saturday afternoons. She had to be protected from that.

'Are you sure you wouldn't rather have gone to the park and played on the swings?' Gran asked.

'I like the swings and the roundabout when I'm with my friends,' said Posy. 'I'm a bit old to want you to watch me play. Anyroad, if I'm playing, we can't talk and I like talking.'

'So I noticed.'

'Dad doesn't like Violet, does he?'

A pause. Gran might have thought she didn't notice things, but Posy had ears like a hawk, supposing that hawks had ears.

'Some folk aren't fond of pets,' said Gran. Grown-ups found wishy-washy ways of saying things, as if children weren't perfectly well aware of the truth.

'Violet isn't just a pet,' said Posy. 'She's a mouser, so she earns her daily bread ... daily piece of pluck.'

'I know, chick, but Dad isn't keen on her, so we

167

have to keep her out of his way.'

They walked down the wide part of the road, where grand metal gates stood on either side between stone pillars. Both pairs of gates were open, giving access to long driveways, leading to handsome buildings. The local toff family lived in one and the other was a hospital.

'I hope you'll enjoy pressing flowers, chick.'

'I like new things and even if I don't, I'll still like it because I'm doing it with you.'

A few more minutes brought them onto the meadows. Posy's eyes prickled and so did her nose. She sneezed, then her eyes got used to it and her nostrils cleared.

The grass was dotted with yellow.

'Buttercups. Stand still, Gran. Let's see if you like butter.'

Gran lifted her chin and Posy held a flower beneath it. A faint glow appeared on Gran's skin.

'Yes, you do. Do I?'

'You do too,' said Gran. 'That's a relief.'

'There are more flowers here.' Posy stopped to examine a cluster of yellow flowers that drooped instead of standing up straight. 'Are they primroses?'

'Primroses hold their heads up. These are hanging over, so they're cowslips.'

Gran showed her how to remove one of each flower. 'That's all we need. We'll build up a scrapbook and one day you'll show it to your grandchildren and say, "I did this with my gran." I'll be their great-great-grandmother.'

'I won't have grandchildren, because I'm not getting married. I don't want a husband telling me what to do.' She was a primrose, holding up her head. Ma was a droopy cowslip. 'Let's try the hedgerow.'

They found white campion, all starry flowers and soft, fuzzy leaves, and cow parsley, its teeny-tiny flowers massed together into umbrella-shaped flower heads.

'Everything is white or yellow,' said Posy.

Gran gave her a nudge. 'Down there.'

It was the bluest blue she had ever seen.

'Speedwell,' said Gran.

'You're so clever. How do you know all the names?'

'Some I've always known and some Mrs Hibbert told me. She used to live on the moors.'

'Was she a shepherd?'

'Not on the moor, but in a town on the moor.'

'Oh.' That wasn't half so exciting.

'We've got five flowers now. Let's take them home and start pressing them. I don't want to keep Mrs Hibbert waiting and you don't want to be late doing your Dad's errand.'

Posy stopped in the hall on her way back from the outside lav. Gran had gone to Mrs Hibbert's and Ma and Dad were in the parlour. Posy had just had to visit the lav for the second time in fifteen minutes. Saturdays were like that. The parlour door was closed. It was only now that they weren't living in the flat any more that she realised how much listening she used to do. Not that she had crouched at the door with her ear glued to the keyhole, but she had heard an awful lot through the scullery door.

Now she stood in the hall and listened. On purpose.

'Oh, Edmund...' said Ma, sounding like a droopy cowslip.

'It will be better coming from you than from me; easier for her.'

Was she being sent back to sleep in the scullery? Posy's bones ached in protest. Then she thought of Violet, who was also doomed to sleep in the scullery now. They could console one another.

'If you say so,' said Ma.

'I do say so. It will be better for all of us if my name is on the rent book.'

'Yes, Edmund.'

So she wasn't being consigned to the scullery, after all. That was something. Not enough to stop her tummy doing its Saturday somersaults, but something.

She looked at the staircase. She hated him – it – even more than she had hated Rupert. Leaving Rupert had been one of the best bits about moving house. Leaving Rupert had put optimism in her heart that he wouldn't be replaced. Gerald was worse, because she had tasted freedom from Rupert.

On a surge of pure hatred, she spat at Gerald. Then she went to say goodbye to Ma and Dad before going to the sweet shop.

Nell's sewing machine stood towards the back of the parlour, well away from the water damage. Her machine, in her house. She felt like shouting it from the rooftops. Her fingers wandered over its

170

smooth curves before lightly turning the handle, setting the needle whirring with the sound of the garment factory. No, the factory sound had been loud, forty machines in her workshop alone. This machine whispered by comparison. Her machine, her business partner.

Her feet settled on the treadle underneath, finding a comfortable position and taking over from her fingers on the handle. Oh, it was bliss. She slowed and stopped, her gaze roaming over the table with its two sets of drawers, far enough apart to allow ample legroom for working the treadle, and – how clever – the flap that lifted up at the side and fastened underneath to give extra space.

She wasn't alone in worshipping at the shrine. All afternoon, women dropped in, curious to see a real sewing machine. The neighbours came, as did women from streets further away, and after they left, they came back with friends and sisters and daughters-in-law. Mrs O'Rourke brought her teapot round and spent the afternoon brewing tea alternately in Nell's pot and her own. Neighbours lent cups; wooden chairs were ranged around the machine. Mrs Clancy up the road, who had enjoyed a private viewing this morning, looked after Alf and Cassie.

For some, it was a sightseeing trip, coupled with the chance to find out the latest about Minnie Wentworth's twins and that female from't greengrocer's, who was no better than she should be; but plenty wanted lessons and the chance to use the machine to run up a pair of curtains or a new skirt or a First Holy Communion dress out of a tired sheet.

When Nell closed the front door on the last of her visitors, she flopped against it, palms flat on the wood. It was happening. It was really happening. She went into the kitchen. Her wonderful neighbours had washed up and returned the borrowed crockery and chairs. There was nothing for her to do except collect her children.

'How did it go?' asked Mrs Clancy. 'Come in and tell me what I missed.'

The children rushed to meet her and she hugged them before settling Cassie on her hip and following Mrs Clancy into her kitchen to tell her about her successful afternoon.

'Good for you,' said Mrs Clancy. 'There's plenty who'd solve their problems by latching onto the first bloke what came along, but not you. You're standing up for yourself. It's lucky you weren't at work today.'

'I don't work on Wednesday afternoons because of half-day closing, even if I'm not in the shop; and I didn't have any appointments this morning because I'm working a half-day on Saturday. Have the children been good?'

'Eh, she can get about a bit, your Cassie, can't she? Never stops moving.'

'I hope she hasn't been any trouble.'

'Has she heck as like. She's a little angel.'

Nell laughed. 'Maybe when she's asleep. Even ladder-monkeys go to sleep sometimes, don't they, Alf?'

She took the children home and made bubble-and-squeak for tea. Then she placed a bucket of 'hot but not too hot' water, as Alf called it, on the kitchen hearthrug and gave the children an all-over wash before bundling them into their night-clothes.

Cassie was put to bed right away. Nell had bought a cot from the second-hand furniture shop, but it had turned out to be the worst purchase ever, since Cassie hauled herself out of it every time she was lifted in. Even if you waited for her to drop off to sleep before putting her in, she would be out of it before you turned your back. So now there were three of them scrunched into the bed together, children at one end, her at the other, though both children generally switched ends during the night and it was impossible for her not to revel in having their little bodies cuddled up to her.

Alf had a story, then he said his prayers, ending with his nightly plea for the house to dry off so Violet could come home.

Downstairs again, all Nell wanted was to take the weight off her feet, but she needed to run to the corner shop or there would be no sugar in the morning, not to mention the cup of sugar she owed Mrs O'Rourke from this afternoon. She threw on her coat and hat and hurried out. It wouldn't be long before the days grew too warm for her old cavalry-twill. Would she have time to make herself a jacket? Or maybe one of those long, edge-to-edge jackets, like a cross between a coat and a jacket, that she had sometimes made at the factory. No, things like that weren't for the likes of her.

But why weren't they? Why shouldn't working-class women dress with a bit of flair?

'Hello, Mrs Hibbert.'

173

She stopped. 'Posy – and Mrs Brent. This is a nice surprise.'

'Our Hilda is feeling poorly, so we're getting her a bottle of Wincarnis tonic before Posy's bedtime.'

'I'm going to the shop an' all.'

She matched her pace to theirs and they headed for the shop. There was a girl of Posy's age inside, carrying a bag nearly as big as she was. Posy knew her and they were soon engrossed in conversation.

'So what's the matter with your Hilda?' asked Nell.

'She's under the weather. She says she has a lot on her mind and she's tired from the move. A tonic will buck her up.'

Aye, and so would a kick up the backside. Nell hung onto her eyebrows to stop them climbing up her forehead. How two such sensible folk as the Brents had managed to produce a lame duck like Hilda beggared belief.

It was Posy's friend's turn to be served and Posy gravitated towards her gran.

'How's Violet?' Nell asked. 'I'm sure you're taking good care of her.'

Posy's face crinkled into troubled lines. 'Yes, but she doesn't like sleeping in the scullery.'

'In the scullery?'

Mrs Brent looked awkward. 'It's Edmund. He–'

Edmund! It would be. She didn't listen to the rest. 'It's not your fault,' she assured her friend. 'I know we spoilt her. You won't need to keep her for much longer.'

'I know how she feels,' said Posy, 'because I never liked sleeping in the scullery in our old flat, but I sleep in a real bed now with Gran.'

'Do you like that?'

'Oh, yes. I'm like the Princess and the Pea, but with one mattress.'

Her annoyance vanished like morning mist. 'Your mum's lucky to have you. So is your gran.'

'Let's get you home, miss,' said Mrs Brent, 'before your head swells so much you can't get through the door.'

'Can that happen? Would I have to pin my ears back?'

Nell laughed and saw them on their way. Armed with her blue bag of sugar, she walked home, turning the corner into Wilton Lane to see someone at her door – a man taking a step backwards as if realising no one was home. Please don't let his knock have woken the children. He turned from the door: Jim Franks.

'Were you looking for me?' She hurried along the pavement. What did he think he was doing, knocking on a woman's door of an evening? Did he want to get her a bad reputation?

He came to meet her halfway. He looked neater than he did when he was working, in a tweed jacket, with his shirt done up to the collar, round which was a tie. Lord, he hadn't togged himself up for her, had he? Don't be stupid. He was wearing ordinary clothes, the same as every other decent working man at the end of the day.

'I shan't keep you,' he said. 'I've got a friend who lost both legs in the war. He makes wooden toys and they're rather good. In his latest batch is a little monkey figure that flips its way up a ladder and down again when you turn a handle, and I thought–'

'Cassie.' The ladder-monkey. Her heart turned to putty. What a kind man. Then she panicked. 'You haven't bought one, have you? I couldn't–'

'I thought I'd tell you about it and where my friend lives.'

Tension seeped away. He had known the appropriate thing to do. They had gone from the kindness of strangers to the thoughtfulness of a real friend. Warmth filled her. Gratitude. Appreciation. Pleasure at the thought of the children's delight.

And an unaccustomed fluttering inside her chest, such as she hadn't experienced since she was seventeen years old and meeting Stan Hibbert for the first time.

'Are you feeling better, Hilda?' Leonie asked. 'I could do the shopping if you don't feel like it.' Her heart leapt in anticipation. She missed her daily toddle round the shops, passing the time of day with the other housewives.

'There's nowt wrong with me, Mother.'

They were sitting at the kitchen table. Edmund had gone to work, Posy to school. Breakfast had been washed up – and Leonie had popped the kettle back on to top up the pot for another cup. She did this every morning now. Anything to postpone the housework, which was odd because she had never minded housework before; but now that it was all she did, she hated it. She felt bored and taken for granted, which was another odd thing, because Edmund made a point of praising her cleaning. At first she had appreciated his compliments, but the other day, the thought had flashed across her mind: *Who are you to comment on the cleaning I do in my own house?*

'You didn't need to fetch that tonic,' said Hilda.

'You looked peaky.' Trying to sound casual, she added, 'You said you had things on your mind.'

Hilda bit her lip and suddenly she was a little girl again, but in those days the bitten lip would have been followed by an endearing smile and a gurgle of laughter. Now it was followed by downcast eyes and a huff of breath.

Leonie poured the tea. She wouldn't get anywhere if she pushed. Hilda the child had been an open book. Hilda the adult was a stranger. Was it her fault? Had she failed as a mother?

'There's summat I want you to think about,' said Hilda, 'only I don't want you to take it the wrong way.'

Lord, surely not a complaint about her cleaning? And from her own daughter.

The moment stretched.

'What is it, love?' Leonie asked gently.

'You wanted us to move in with you.'

'Yes,' she agreed. Hilda made it sound like she had begged them to, but she let that go. They had all wanted it.

'And for us all to live together.'

'Yes.'

'But it's like we're your lodgers, Mother.'

'Lodgers!' She hadn't expected that. 'What are you talking about?'

'It's your house and–'

'Well, there were no room for me in your flat. I could hardly have slept in the scullery with Posy.'

Hilda flushed. 'It's like we're nothing more than the Hibberts. You've swapped one set of lodgers

177

for another.'

'Oh, Hilda, never. You're family.'

'Aye, but we're living under your roof.'

'That's what you wanted. It's what we all wanted.'

'Your roof, Mother, not ours.'

Her eyebrows squeezed together. 'I don't know what you're on about. All this talk about lodgers and whose house it is.'

'You must know.'

'Well, I don't.'

Hilda got up and started to clear the table even though they hadn't finished.

'Hilda, love, sit down – please. That's better.'

Leonie rested an elbow on the table, leaning forward. They mustn't have words. They had never had words, but they seemed on the brink of it now. She smiled and picked up her tea. Sharing a cup of tea was chummy. It had gone cold, but that didn't matter. Two women having a cosy chat over a cuppa could sort out anything.

'What's this about?' She used a kindly, humorous voice. 'I won't know if you don't tell me.'

Hilda didn't look up. She picked at the oilcloth.

'You and your little lot, you're my family,' said Leonie. 'I'd do owt for you.'

Hilda's fingers stilled. 'Would you?'

'You know I would.'

Hilda looked straight at her. 'Will you put Edmund's name on the rent book?'

The children adored the wooden monkey. Alf never tired of making it clamber up and down the ladder, repeatedly telling Cassie, 'That's you, that is. You're the ladder-monkey,' making her crow with delight. Nell had also bought a wooden spinning top from Mr Franks's talented friend. He had painted it in vivid stripes, which merged into a wonderful rainbow blur when the top whizzed round.

That was how her life felt. She had its separate parts all sorted out, the children, her Ingleby's job, her private work, so it ought to feel straightforward; but actually it felt more of a whirling blur, with everything mixed up together and although she had more time in the mornings and evenings, her days rattled by at top speed.

But that was good. It meant she was busy, making more money and providing a secure home for her children; and best of all, watching them grow up. She didn't want them one day looking back at their childhood and remembering their childminders. She wanted them to remember her and everything they had done together. So she played cat's cradle and snap and hide-and-seek; she sang songs and told stories; took them for walks, let them help in the kitchen and, one surprisingly warm teatime, she set up the tin bathtub in the backyard and filled it with water so they could play at seasides.

If Stan had been a better husband and father, if he had done right by them, she and the children might have had all this and more right from the start. Imagine not needing childminders. Both her kids had been looked after from day one.

It was rare to think of Stan these days. He was dead in every way that mattered. Occasionally she was obliged to talk about him when Alf had

179

questions – the same questions time and again, to which she gave the same answers, rather like telling a favourite bedtime story. Daddy had fought in the war and been a brave soldier; Daddy was clever with his hands and had made furniture. They all used to live together in a valley at the top of the hill on the moors. One of Alf's favourite games was to go onto the meadows that bordered the Mersey and pretend they were on the moors.

As for the inevitable question, 'How did Daddy die?', that was set aside with a quiet, 'I'll tell you when you're old enough,' something that good-natured Alf happily accepted, though Nell suspected she wouldn't get off so lightly when Cassie started asking questions.

Was she thinking of Stan because ... because she had no business thinking of Jim Franks?

She couldn't think about him. She mustn't. Everyone in this new life she had built for herself and her children believed her to be a widow – even the children believed it. But she was a married woman.

She had fought hard to create this new life. It wasn't easy for a woman on her own, especially one with a young family, but she had done it. They had their own roof now; she had more time at home; her private work made the future feel brighter. The last thing she needed was ... complications.

# Chapter Thirteen

Saturday rolled round again. When Mrs Brent had looked after the children last Saturday, they had loved it ... until the time came for her to leave. Then Alf welled up and started to snivel. Nell hadn't minded that: it was easy to jolly him out of it. But the big surprise was stolid little Cassie, who opened her mouth to its fullest extent and howled her head off as if she were being butchered. Still wincing at the memory of her daughter's spectacular performance, Nell made child-minding arrangements with Mrs Watson's Annie for Saturday afternoon when she was due to visit a new customer in Parrs Wood. Annie was the children's regular minder now and if she couldn't manage it, Mrs Clancy stepped in.

Nell packed their usual bag of things to take.

'Can I carry the ladder-monkey?' Alf begged. 'I won't drop him. And Cassie can carry something too,' he added as his sister popped up, fingers at the ready.

'Cassie can carry the spinning top,' said Nell.

She checked she had everything for her new pupil's first lesson, then they set off.

'Well, if it isn't my favourite children ... after Posy, of course.' Mrs Brent crossed the road to greet them, a shopping bag over her arm. 'I'm taking my library books back. Where are you off to?'

'Mrs Watson's Annie's,' said Alf, 'because Mummy's working.'

Nell rolled her eyes. 'I've told you before, Alf. She's Mrs Lipton to you.'

'I know, but Mrs Brent might not know who Mrs Lipton is compared to Mrs Watson's Annie.'

Leonie laughed. 'I know who Mrs Lipton is. What's this you've got?'

Alf displayed it proudly. 'The ladder-monkey.'

'Is it yours?'

'It's both-of-us's.'

Mrs Brent raised her eyebrows at Nell. 'Carrying toys in the street, for all to see? That's a bit–'

A flash of anxiety. 'A bit what?'

'Nay, lass, forget I spoke. It's nowt. I wouldn't dream of criticising.'

Something fluttered inside Nell. Was she being showy? There were plenty of kids hereabouts who would regard the ladder-monkey and the spinning top as riches.

'I'll see the children round to Annie's,' Mrs Brent offered, 'and you can get on your way.'

It would make a difference of all of two minutes, but even that would help. A last-minute wee by Cassie had broken into her timetable and she could barely spare these moments to stand here, talking. But – and it was a big but – she didn't want to be known as one of those working women who fobbed off their children onto someone else every chance she got.

'Let's walk together.'

'I'll come to the bus stop with you and we can have a chinwag while you wait for't bus.'

'I hope you don't mind that I asked Annie to

have the children,' said Nell, 'only after last time...'

'I know, love, but I'll always come round to yours if you need me to. I feel bad, seeing you having to lug a bag of their things around.'

Nell laughed. 'It's not heavy. Mostly it's a change of clothes for little madam here. She has a gift for getting plastered in water, mud or dirt even when there's no water, mud or dirt to be seen. Fortunately, Annie doesn't mind.'

They dropped off the children and headed for the bus stop. When it came in sight, Nell slowed her pace. She didn't want to have the next bit of the conversation with the queue listening.

'Could I ask your advice?'

'Course you can.'

'It's what you said before about the kids carrying their toys.'

'Oh, that.' Mrs Brent picked up speed.

'Did it look showy-offy?'

'As if my opinion matters. You do what's right for you, love. Friends don't judge one another. I'll leave you here. My arm's dropping off, carrying these books.'

She walked away – no, not just walked: hurried. Nell stared. What had she done wrong to make Mrs Brent dodge the question like that?

Leonie didn't need to go to the library. She just had to get out of the house.

Edmund had offered to take care of her money. She didn't want that, but how could she refuse? It would look like she didn't trust him; and she did trust him, of course she did. Hadn't she put his name on the rent book? What was that if not a show of trust? It meant he was the man of the house.

And now the man of the house wanted her money.

No. That made it sound like he wanted to grab it off her, when he had simply offered to look after it. She wouldn't have thought twice about handing over every farthing to Hedley, but he had never asked it of her. In fact, it had been t'other way round. He had tipped up all his wages, except for his beer and baccy money.

She was good with money. She didn't need to have it looked after ... or did she? She was a different person since losing Hedley. She used to be confident. Not pushy or bossy, but self-assured in a modest way. Now, though, she felt uncertain about everything. She kept finding herself biting the inside of her cheek, or twisting her hands together to stop them from fidgeting; and when she decided something, she was plagued by questions afterwards as self-doubt bled into every situation.

Take yesterday: Edmund had made a small observation about her cleaning.

'It's not a criticism, Mother-in-law,' he said, 'just an observation.'

But instead of explaining her rota, and how the stair carpet would be brushed tomorrow, she had felt embarrassed at having seemed to do shoddy work. Caught out: that was how she felt.

Hilda was there. She knew the stairs were due to be done tomorrow, but had she spoken up for her? No, she hadn't. There was her own mother, blushing and flustered, and she hadn't said a word.

Nell would have stood up for her.

That was another thing. She had never had the guts to call her Nell in front of her family. If she mentioned her, it was, 'Mrs Hibbert this, Mrs Hibbert that.'

She had turned her back on her young friend today, but she had needed to escape from that conversation. How could she have been so stupid as to start laying down the law about the children carrying their toys through the streets? She didn't want Nell to feel she was being criticised.

She didn't want Nell criticising her when she heard Edmund's name was on the rent book.

Leonie wasn't even sure why she had permitted that, truth to tell. No – that was a lie. She had wanted to contribute to a happy family atmosphere. She wanted them to be a proper family and that meant the head of the household being accorded due respect. And she wasn't sorry. It was right and proper; the man of the house and all that. Only...

Only it would have been so much easier if Edmund had been more of a Hedley. Oh, if he were another Hedley, she would have offered him the rent book on a plate. She would willingly have trusted her home to his care. Herself an' all.

And that sounded like she didn't trust him. Guilt thickened in her throat and self-loathing trickled down her spine, as if she had uttered the disloyal sentiment aloud. Yes, disloyal. Edmund deserved better. He was a respectable working man, who paid his bills and provided for his family. Hilda had never had to struggle without food or heat, had never had to beg for tick at the

185

corner shop; and their Posy might not have had a proper bed before now, but she had always had underwear and a pair of shoes, which was more than many could say.

Now Edmund was going to provide for Leonie an' all.

'I'll pay the coal and the gas. I'll pay the rates. Don't worry about stretching your little pension, Mother-in-law. Leave everything to me.'

Her muscles had weakened in relief. Losing Hedley had been hard – was still hard. He was her husband, her dear old softy and her best friend; but on a practical level, he had also been her provider. She knew widows, in their sixties like her, and even one in her seventies, who had had to look for work when their husbands died. Imagine going out charring at her age. But there was no danger of that, thanks to Edmund.

She almost laughed. No, there was no need to go out cleaning, because he had got her cleaning at home. The cords tightened in her neck: what had got into her today? All these disloyal thoughts. She had always kept her house sparkling clean, so why should it matter if it was her sole household responsibility?

She was thinking altogether too much since Edmund's offer to look after her money – no, before that: since his name went on the rent book; or rather, since Hilda had suggested it. Actually, it was since Edmund passed his royal decree about the cooking and cleaning. No, it was when she gave up her bedroom ... when she gave Nell a week's notice.

Stop!

Leonie went up the steps into the library. She hadn't read her library books. Her eyes had scanned every word, but nothing had sunk in. What a waste. She walked to the desk and asked if she could have books out again.

The librarian, a woman in a dark dress with long sleeves, opened them and looked at the dates in the front. 'Are you sure? You've already renewed them once. Look, here's the R.'

'Have I? Had she? She couldn't recall. What a twit she must look.

'Why not choose new ones?' suggested the librarian in a kind voice.

Leonie wandered among the shelves, trying to focus her thoughts.

'Why did you push her into having new books?' asked a soft voice on the other side of the bookcase.

Leonie froze.

'I was doing her a favour. We get these old biddies sometimes. They never learnt to read, but they borrow books so it looks like they can. Well, it can't be good for appearances if she goes home with the same two books every time, can it?'

Leonie's skin felt impossibly hot. She crept to the corner of the bookcase and peered round to check the librarians weren't looking before she scuttled to the door as fast as tiptoes permitted.

Violet came trotting to meet her. Leonie bent down to give her a fuss and Violet danced hopefully towards the front door. Leonie's heart sank. As the door opened, Violet pressed forwards and Leonie scooped her away with the side of her foot, trying not to hear the plaintive mew as she squeezed indoors.

Posy was in the hall, beside the staircase. Her hands were raised and she was reaching between the balusters onto the stairs. It looked like she was fiddling with something, but that made no sense. Only she must be doing something, because just look at that expression on her face: caught out.

'What are you doing?' Leonie asked.

'Nothing.'

'Let me see – Posy, what are you doing taking a stair rod?'

For a second, the child was rooted to the spot. Then she burst out, 'It's loose. I'm putting it back.'

'Don't be silly. Stair rods can't come loose.'

Hilda appeared from the parlour. 'She's not doing owt, Mother.'

But Hilda wouldn't meet her eye. Goodness, both of them looked guilty. Leonie's frown was swept aside by a swell of protectiveness. Her two girls were upset. She couldn't have that. Her job was to make things right.

'Is that you, Mother-in-law?' came Edmund's voice from the parlour. 'Hilda, kindly stop blocking the doorway. Let your mother in.'

She walked in. The room was the same as always; Edmund was the same as always, but the atmosphere was stretched tight.

'You haven't taken off your coat and hat, Mother-in-law. Posy, come and fetch Gran's things.'

'What's wrong?' Leonie asked. 'I know summat is.'

'It's over and done with. Posy required a small reprimand and it has been delivered.'

Leonie looked at Hilda. Hilda looked at the floor. Through the open door, Leonie watched Posy. Her back was to the room as she did whatever she was doing with the stair rod. There were red marks on the backs of her legs and a quiver in the thin shoulders. Her head wasn't held up with its customary eager curiosity. It was bowed.

Oh, no. Oh, surely not.

Leonie turned back. The room was the same: the settee where she and Hilda sat of an evening while Edmund hogged the armchair; the footstool by the fireplace, where Posy sat, learning how to make conversation.

Edmund was the same too; a big man, a strong man. A strict man.

Oh, no, please. Nausea unfurled in her stomach.

Oh, it was tempting, but he mustn't. Jim cleaned his Saturday windows on a six-week rota, so he wasn't due at Mrs Watson's again until next week. He couldn't pitch up early and expect her not to notice. It was hard, though. Uncomfortable for another reason too. What he wanted was to get into conversation with Mrs Watson, knowing that a polite enquiry after Mrs Brent would lead naturally to asking after the Hibberts; but much as he longed to learn all he could about Nell, it went against the grain to do so in a roundabout way. He wouldn't seek information via the back door. It wasn't gentlemanly.

Today, he was due to clean the windows of a couple of houses near Wilton Lane. And he wasn't going to be stupid. He knew he wouldn't see her. He knew they wouldn't bump into one another. He wasn't even going to hope.

Like hell he wasn't.

When he finished the windows, he loaded his ladder on to his barrow. He would have to walk past the top end of Wilton Lane, but he wasn't going to look along the street. He wasn't going to pay attention to the loud clumsy beating of his heart.

'Mr Franks! Mr Franks!' Young Alf Hibbert burst out of a group of boys and flew towards him. 'I've got a wooden ladder-monkey.'

Jim stopped, lowering his barrow's legs to the road. 'Well, look who it isn't. Have you done a magic spell on your sister and turned her into a wooden ladder-monkey?'

'*No,*' cried the boy. It was delightful how he took all Jim's daft words seriously. 'She's still Cassie and we have another ladder-monkey, made of wood. You should know,' he added. 'Mummy said it was your friend who made it.'

'If Mummy said it, it must be true. Are you allowed to play here instead of staying in Wilton Lane?'

'We're being minded. Mummy's gone to work. Are you at work?'

'I've finished. I'm on my way home.'

Lifting his barrow handles, he started off. Alf ran back to his game. The group broke apart with a mighty yell, boys flying in all directions, Alf among them. Jim didn't pay attention until he heard a different kind of yell. Alf! He ran across to where the child was sprawled on the pavement and lifted him to his feet. His knees were scraped and bleeding; he was crying – shock, probably, as much as pain. Jim scooped him into his arms.

'Where's he being minded?' he asked the others, who were flocking round him.

'Mrs Lipton's.'

A couple of lads ran ahead to bang on the door. A woman in her forties, with a wrap-around pinny over her dress, opened the door.

'Hey up, Alf, have you had a tumble? Bring him in here, will you?' She addressed the swirling mass of boys. 'Where's Cassie? Fetch her in an' all.' She led the way into her kitchen. 'Pop him down there.' She pulled out a chair and knelt in front of the child. 'Let's have a look. Goodness me, Alf, are you trying to paint your legs red?'

She commenced a cleaning-up operation, her manner kindly and efficient.

'You've done this before,' said Jim.

'More times than you've had hot dinners, love, though not for a good few years. Mine are all out at work now and my oldest gets the key of the door next week.'

'I'm Jim Franks.'

'Mrs Lipton.'

'I know. The boys outside told me.'

'I know who you are an' all. You do my mum's windows: Mrs Watson in Finney Lane. I'm not often called Mrs Lipton. Mostly I'm Mrs Watson's Annie. There.' She smiled at Alf. 'How's that?'

'Sore.'

'Not to worry,' said Jim. 'You'll soon have some gigantic scabs to pick.'

'I'll put the kettle on. Would you like a cup?'

'I'd better be on my way,' said Jim.

'I want to go home,' Alf announced.

'Your mum will be back soon, pet,' said Annie.

'Actually, I wouldn't mind a cup.' God, could he be any more obvious? But Annie didn't appear to notice.

Soon they were sitting at the table, with Cassie on Annie's knee. The children had beakers with a drop of milk. Annie poured Jim tea, the strength of which would do an army cook proud. How long before Nell arrived?

'The price you pay for the tea,' said Annie, 'is to tell me everything about yourself. My mum won't forgive me if I don't get every last detail. I have to say, you don't sound like a window cleaner.'

Jim smiled. 'Before the war, I was a solicitor. After the war – well, I didn't feel able to walk back into my old life.'

'You're lucky you had the choice,' said Annie dryly. 'No offence.'

'None taken.'

'I'd heard of you before my mum got her hooks in you. You help war widows and women what lost their boys. I like that. We lost our Bill. He were a good brother, but far too young to die.'

'They were all far too young to die.'

They chatted on until a knock at the door brought on an answering banging in his chest. Annie disappeared and came back, talking to Nell.

'...he carried your Alf in when he fell over.'

Nell walked in, wearing what must be her work dress. It was simple and plain, but she had an innate elegance that made the garment beautiful. She gave him a swift 'Thank you,' before she bobbed down in front of her son.

'I hear you've been in the wars.'

'Mr Franks was in the real war,' said Alf.

'Sit yourself down for five minutes,' Annie invited her and proceeded to tell Jim's story.

He was taken aback, but only for a moment. This was what he wanted: for Nell to know about him.

'...and he's going to use his legal brain to help my cousin Matt with a bit of advice,' finished Annie. 'I told Matt he were making a mistake when he didn't take one of the Dawson houses and now he's stuck with a landlord what's out for every penny he can get. Say what you like about Mr Dawson, he's a fair man.'

'The Rental Act,' said Jim when Nell looked at him. 'It was passed to stop landlords putting up rents to ridiculous levels. If it helps,' he told Annie, 'I'll accompany your cousin to see his landlord. I can't abide unfairness.'

'Hark at him,' said Annie. 'Can't abide, indeed. Not that I'm complaining. Use all the fancy words you like. I don't suppose you can help it, but you're a decent bloke and that's what counts.'

'One thing I've learnt in recent years is how little access people in the lower levels of society have to the law.'

'Does that mean you'll offer advice to others as needs it?' asked Annie.

'Yes. I make a point of keeping abreast of legal developments.'

'Gather your things, children,' said Nell. 'Say thank you to Mrs Lipton.'

'My knees are stiff,' said Alf.

'They'll loosen up,' said Nell.

'Will they bleed again if I move them?'

'Horribly,' said Jim. 'All over Mrs Lipton's clean floor, which is why I'll ferry you home on top of my barrow. Hup you come.'

He lifted the boy beneath one arm. Alf yelled with delight to find himself dangling.

'You don't need to,' Nell began, but he was already on his way out.

He dropped Alf on the barrow and scooped up Cassie, who was clamouring around his knees, and deposited her beside her brother.

'And the luggage,' he said, taking Nell's bag from her. 'Where to, madam?'

He delivered them to their door. Would she invite him in? Of course not. He had had his time sitting with her at Annie's house. What more could he want?

Quite a lot, actually.

Jim walked out of church into bright sunshine. The mild early morning had blossomed into a warm midday. He threaded his way towards his brother. Don, Patsy and the girls stood near the wall, where overhanging trees lent some shade. They were adorable, his nieces, and one day he might even be able to tell them apart. It didn't help that Patsy dressed them alike. There they were, hair shining beneath daisy-trimmed hats, forearms protruding from slits in the front of their capes, hands lost in the depths of fluffy muffs.

He shook hands with Don and kissed Patsy on the cheek she presented, then pretended to look round.

'Where are the girls today? Don't tell me they're

sick in bed.'

'We're here, Uncle James,' said one of them. They giggled and gave one another the tiniest of nudges. In years to come, these two would be picture-perfect, not a hair out of place, even after a rousing match on the lacrosse field.

'Oh, there you are,' he said. 'I thought you were a pair of princesses.'

Compared to the kids in the backstreets, they were princesses. They didn't know how lucky they were, but he knew and felt a rush of gratitude.

Patsy beamed at him. The way to her heart was definitely through admiration of her daughters. Don wasn't immune either. His transparent pride in his beautiful, fashionable wife and their twins dealt Jim an unexpected pang. If he had stuck to his prescribed path in life, he too could have had a wife and children by now.

He accompanied them home to their bay-windowed Victorian villa. The front garden was glossy and cool, with shrubs surrounding a pristine lawn that made him want to build a swing there and then and push the girls as high as they could go.

As they walked into the chessboard-tiled hall, he inhaled a delicious mixture of aromas.

'Is that ginger ... and something appley?'

'I can tell you're hungry,' said Patsy. She turned her back to Don so he could help her off with her jacket. She removed the girls' capes and sent them upstairs to play before leading the way into her elegant drawing room, all cream and blue, with pieces from Jim's parents' house mixed with modern items, and all of it glowing in the brilliant light from the south-facing windows. 'Mrs Garbutt is roasting the lamb in ginger, honey and cider. We're trying it out on you.'

He knew what that meant. A successful dish would be served at her next dinner party – to which he wouldn't be invited. Poor girl. He was a trial to her. She wouldn't have minded half so much had he become a lowly clerk or a penniless poet.

She settled herself on the striped-silk sofa. 'Ring for tea, will you, darling?'

Don reached for the bell. 'I saw Mr Winterton the other day.'

'How is he?' Jim felt a stirring of pleasure. He had started his working life in the offices of Winterton, Sowerby and Jenks. 'Retired?'

'Still in harness, though he must be the best part of seventy.' Unfastening his jacket, Don leant back comfortably in an armchair. 'He asked after you. Offered you a job, as a matter of fact.'

'Did he really?' Patsy's response came even more quickly than Jim's.

'Seriously? He offered me work?'

'More or less. He said he'd be glad to discuss it with you, anyway. His godson had a bad time in the war and hasn't been the same since, so he has a certain sympathy with why you elected to duck out of your proper life.'

'Temporarily,' added Patsy. 'Oh, Mrs Garbutt,' she said as the door opened. 'Could we have a pot of tea, please?'

Mrs Garbutt, a stout individual whose flushed cheeks suggested she had plenty to do in her steamy kitchen without fooling around with a tray of tea, withdrew before she had got fully in.

Patsy turned to Jim. 'It's worth considering, James.'

'If you're away from the law for too long,' said Don, 'you won't be able to get back in.'

'I keep up,' he said mildly.

'That's not the same. Do you want to clean windows for the rest of your life? You could end up with no choice if no law firm will have you.'

'There's your family responsibilities too,' said Patsy, ignoring Don's frown. 'We've stood by you, which is more than Roberta and her family did. Now it's time for you to consider us. Harriet and Marguerite start at Oaklawn in September. It would be a good thing all round if they didn't have a skeleton in the family cupboard.'

Both men laughed.

'Not a window-cleaning skeleton, at any rate,' said Don. He pushed himself to his feet. 'Whisky?'

'Mrs Garbutt is bringing tea,' said Patsy.

Don spoke over his shoulder from the sideboard. 'You pour the tea, I'll give him whisky and we'll see which one he drinks.'

'You're dreadful,' Patsy scolded.

'You don't want a martini, then?'

Jim lifted his eyebrows. 'Isn't it sherry for the ladies any more? What would Mother say?'

'You're behind the times,' said Don. 'It's martini or gin and it these days. Another reason for you to get back into society. I bet you can't dance the Charleston either.'

Jim accepted his brother's joshing with good grace, but later, as he made his way home, he considered matters. Was it time to leave his humble

197

life? It had only ever been intended to be temporary. Did he still need it? If he was honest, no. He had only ever needed … time. Time to think, to remember, to heal; time to come to terms, in so far as anyone could, with slaughter and destruction on such a massive scale.

Perhaps that was it. Perhaps the simple and unutterably complex fact of realising that he would never fully heal was what he had needed to face. The guilt had faded, the guilt of being alive, being spared, being whole. When he first came home, he had felt like Marley's ghost, dragging his chains and padlocks and cash boxes behind him; but link by link, the chains had dropped away until now he was aware of this phase of his life reaching its natural conclusion.

Not that he could return to his old life in the fullest sense. He couldn't walk away from his present circumstances without a backwards glance. He would carry part of it with him always, not just in his heart and his mind, but also in his professional life. He hadn't thought it through fully as yet, but he had an idea of providing legal advice at a peppercorn rate to the lower classes alongside the lucrative work that would provide comfort and security for...

For his wife and family.

He had always assumed he would marry and become a father. For a long time, Roberta had been his chosen bride, his future, but now he would have to start again and find another future.

No – not find one. He had already found it.

If Patsy wasn't keen on his window cleaning, what would she make of Nell?

# Chapter Fourteen

Monday was washday in normal households and Nell was determined that hers would be a normal household. She didn't have to leave for her first appointment until half past nine. Usually this meant taking Alf to school, dropping Cassie at Annie's on the way back; but today she had taken both children to Annie's early and Annie would take Alf to school. Was she a bad mother, dumping her kids elsewhere so she could get some housework done? It wasn't easy being a working mother with no Mrs Brent to manage the house.

Anyroad, she was going to put the washing in the copper to soak, ready to do tonight after the children were in bed; and she should have time to give the windows a going-over before she had to set off for her first lesson.

Before she could empty the linen basket, there was a knock at the door.

'Sorry, love, I know it's a bit early.' Mrs Brent sounded cheerful, but there was an odd edge to her tone. 'But you said as you were going to get your outsides done and I couldn't let you do that on your tod.'

'You're going to stand underneath, are you, and catch me if I fall? Come in.'

'I thought we'd have a cuppa and a natter an' all. I miss our chats.'

'Don't you chat with your Hilda?'

'Aye, but I miss chatting with you and I've only got the washing to tackle if I go home.'

Nell thought of her own washing, then set the thought aside. If this dear lady wanted a spot of company, the least she could do was provide it, after everything Mrs Brent had done for her. They gathered what was needed and went upstairs into the empty front bedroom. Had the water stain faded? One thing was certain. That hole in the ceiling spewed out dust faster than she could sweep it up.

The sash window squeaked and rumbled as Nell eased it up. Turning her back to the open space, she found the sill with her hands and pressed her legs against the wall beneath the window before sitting and shuffling her bottom further outside. She blew out a breath: nerves weren't allowed. Mrs Brent drew down the sash. Nell's breath caught. Some women did this every week. Could you really get used to seeing the window close in front of your eyes, with you stuck on the wrong side of it?

Leaving the window partway up, Mrs Brent bent down, then handed Nell the wet cloth. The sharp tang of vinegar-water invaded her nostrils. Mrs Brent pulled the sash down as far as it could go without chopping her legs off, then pulled the chair closer and sat bunched up, plastered to Nell's legs, her arms winding round the backs of Nell's knees.

Raising the cloth, Nell commenced wiping the glass. Vinegar-water trickled down her arm, wetting her sleeve and tickling her skin. She reached higher, her stomach swooping as her body automatically tilted back. On the other side of the window, Mrs Brent's grip tightened.

She pressed on, then dropped the cloth on the ledge and clung on with her fingertips to the window frame. The warm pressure around her legs vanished as Mrs Brent stood to raise the sash. The window didn't budge. A streak of panic speared through Nell. Then, with a soft protest, the sash moved. Mrs Brent lifted it enough to thrust out some screwed-up newspaper, which Nell grabbed. Mrs Brent drew in the cloth, pulled down the window and resumed her position clamped round Nell's legs.

Nell buffed up the glass. She might be using less elbow grease than if falling and breaking her neck wasn't a consideration, but she gave the window a good polish. When she finished, Mrs Brent threw up the sash and hauled her inside.

'To think some women do that while gabbing to the woman at the next-door window.' Nell stamped her feet on the floorboards as if she had spent a week at sea and was grateful for dry land. 'How does it look?'

'Fine; and even if it isn't, you're not going out there again. My heart couldn't take it. You should get a window cleaner.'

'Oh aye, and a char, and a nanny. Mind you,' and she made sure she was picking up the bucket, with her back to Mrs Brent as she said it, 'if Jim Franks needed the work, I'd employ him, after the good turn he did us when we moved here.'

'I don't know how he's fixed, though he can't be on his uppers, because he does his Saturday jobs for nowt.'

'He used to be a solicitor before the war.'

'Then he can't be short of a bob or two in't bank. Good for him, is what I say, if he helps the poor one day a week.'

'Oh.'

She hadn't thought of it like that. Helping her to move house hadn't been a special thing. He would have done it for anybody. She had told him it was what her brothers would have done, but of course her brothers wouldn't have picked and chosen the folk they helped. They would have helped any decent individual. Just like Jim Franks had done for her.

Mind you, it was a good thing he hadn't intended anything special. It would be playing with fire to encourage him. Stan might have done the dirty on her, but she was still his legal wife.

She carried the bucket to the back bedroom to repeat the window-cleaning process.

'At least here my fall will be broken by the coal bunker.'

'Better than the privy,' said Mrs Brent and they laughed.

When the window was sparkling and Nell slid back inside, she felt quite an old hand. Funny how you could get used to something. Like being a widow.

She wasn't a widow.

Mrs Brent looked round. 'Eh, it'll be grand when the repairs are done.'

'Aye. The children are desperate for Violet to come home.'

'I meant having two bedrooms.'

'Two bedrooms but one bed. I'll need a bed of

my own soon, or a mattress at least. I don't want the children looking back in years to come on us squashed three in a bed. It's one thing for children to share, quite another to shove the whole family in together, even if it's a small family like ours. My mum would have called that proper poor.'

'Nay, proper poor is the whole family sleeping on the floor of the one and only room they have to live in, and there were plenty of that round our way when I were a lass. Don't do yourself down. You work hard for them children. Speaking of which, where's Cassie?'

'At Annie's.' Nell laughed. 'Imagine her seeing me sitting out doing the windows. She's adventurous enough without getting new ideas.'

She carried the bucket downstairs, emptied it, then fetched the chair.

'Do you need to go?' asked Mrs Brent.

'Not quite yet.' There was time to put the wash in to soak, but she knew Mrs Brent wanted to sit and talk. 'I'll put the kettle on – if you've got time.'

'All the time in the world. I'll only be cleaning once I get back.'

'Thanks for helping with the windows.'

'Hanging onto you dangling outside made a change.'

'Then I'm glad I got your day off to a good start,' laughed Nell.

'Owt else you need, just say. I could nip down the butcher's for you while you're at work.'

Pity lanced through Nell. Poor Mrs Brent was desperate to break her monotonous routine.

'What if you bumped into your Hilda round the shops? It'd look odd, you doing my shopping. I'll tell you summat you can do. Bring me cuttings from your herbs.'

Instead of looking pleased, Mrs Brent glanced away. 'If you must know, I haven't got them any more.'

'Why not? You always cook with them.'

'But I'm not cooking any more, am I?'

Lord, she hadn't parted with them in a fit of pique, had she? No, she was too sensible, but on the other hand, that bitter note in her voice...

Nell said lightly, 'Who's got them now?' Was it presumptuous to feel miffed that she hadn't been the recipient? She poured milk and tea and pushed a cup towards her friend.

Mrs Brent looked at it. Then she looked at Nell. 'Edmund got rid.'

Nell froze, teacup halfway to her lips. 'That's disgraceful.'

Mrs Brent looked flustered. 'It makes sense when you think about it. Our Hilda doesn't use herbs because Edmund isn't fussed about them, so why keep them?'

'But–'

'There were bound to be changes when they moved in. This is a change, that's all. I'll get used to it – like the cleaning. It doesn't matter.'

Nell felt hot with indignation. 'What other changes have there been?' She only meant to express her displeasure, but Mrs Brent squirmed in her chair like a naughty child. Nell put down her cup. 'What?' she asked quietly.

'It's Violet. We put her out at night now.'

She was careful not to show her annoyance: this wasn't Mrs Brent's fault. 'She never goes out at night. She had enough of being outdoors when she was a stray.'

'Everyone puts cats out at night.'

'I'm not everyone – and neither were you when we lived with you.'

Mrs Brent looked hurt and Nell felt a stab of guilt. This was Edmund Tanner's fault. 'Brick shithouse,' murmured Doug in her head. She injected an airiness into her voice that she was far from feeling.

'I'll just have to fetch Violet here now.'

Mrs Brent blushed. 'You can't do that. What if she got out before she learnt this is her new home? And it's not cold and wet, so it's not as though she's suffering. Me and Posy have put a wooden box in the backyard, with an old piece of towel in it, so she can get cosy if she wants to.'

'Well, maybe if she stays a bit longer...'

'Good.' Mrs Brent nodded crisply. 'After all, she's only a cat.'

Tuesday meant it was meat, boiled potatoes and carrots. Or you could say it the other way round: meat, boiled potatoes and carrots meant it was Tuesday. Or Thursday. School dinners were the same, week in, week out, and you could tell today was Tuesday because Tuesday pudding was prunes and rice and Thursday's was tinned peaches and custard. Surely you were meant to have peaches with cream, but custard was obviously considered suitable for schoolchildren. They were given it on Fridays with their tinned pineapple too. Would

Violet like custard?

The school hall was filled with noise as the children chattered their way through dinner. The sound of cutlery bashing and scraping mixed with protests from the wooden floor as chair legs grated against the floorboards. Posy slid the trinket box out of her pocket under the table. She eased off the lid, glancing round casually. It was the job of those parts of her above the table to hide what was happening below by being ordinary. She was sitting at the end of a table, which was jolly good luck because you didn't get to choose where you sat. You just filed in and stood behind the next empty place and waited to say grace.

She looked across the gap to the next table. There was an invisible line across the floor and she was right beside it. Some of the girls would fake a squeal if they had to sit next to the line, because across the invisible border were the tables for the free school dinners, where the poor children sat. Posy wasn't worried about her secret activities being observed by them. This was their first, if not their only, meal of the day and they put their heads down and shovelled.

Shepherding the peaches to one side of her dish, she took a spoonful of custard. With her other hand, she drew the trinket box close to her tummy, then lowered the spoon, keeping her head up so as not to draw attention by looking down. She was so busy missing the edge of the table with her spoon that she wiped it on herself. Rats! The spoon clinked against the china trinket box. With her finger, she scooped custard off one into the other. On went the lid and she returned the spoon to her bowl, licking custard off a sticky finger.

She slipped the trinket box back into her pocket and was about to pull out her hanky when its lumpy feel reminded her about the bits of meat wrapped inside it. She scoffed some pudding left-handed so as to look normal, while her right hand fiddled about until she had separated her hanky from its contents.

Pulling out the empty hanky, she wrapped it like a bandage round her pointing finger and dipped it in her glass of water.

'Ugh! Look what Posy Tanner's doing – dipping her snot rag in her drink.'

'I'm telling on you, you dirty cow. Miss! Miss!' Up shot a hand.

One of the dinner ladies came over. She was old with a face full of lines. All the dinner ladies were old with faces full of lines.

'What's going on here? Stop screeching, Doris Eckersley.'

'Please, miss, Posy Tanner's sticking her dirty hanky in her water and then she's going to drink it, miss.'

Posy looked daggers at Doris. Looking daggers was an interesting way of glaring. Miss Clay-bourne had once given the words their very own tick in one of Posy's exciting compositions.

'Please, miss,' said Posy, 'my hanky isn't dirty. It hasn't been used.' As if she would wrap Violet's food in a snotty hanky. But she couldn't say that, even though it was her best defence.

'What are you doing?' demanded the dinner lady.

'Please, miss, I spilt custard down my front and I were going to clean it.' More daggers flew in Doris Blabbermouth's direction.

'Ugh, a dirty dress for a dirty bugger.'

Posy joined in the collective gasp that hissed round their table. Low voices expressing shock and delight started up on neighbouring tables, but no one spoke on Posy's. No one cared any more if she was a dirty cow. They were too busy watching Doris Eckersley being pulled by her ear to Mr Dickinson's office to be given the strap.

Posy skipped home with her spoils in her pocket. The front door was unlocked and she went to the kitchen to say hello to Ma. It was important to do everything as normal when you were up to secret activities. Putting food out for Violet to have at night had been easy the first few times, because she had done it under the guise of watering Gran's herbs, but then the herbs had vanished.

'Gran didn't want them any more,' Ma said when Posy had asked.

She slid into the backyard, which was half in the sun, half in shadow. Violet's wooden box stood against the back of the house. Dropping to her knees, Posy took out the trinket box and upended it beside the box, scooping out the custard with her finger.

Behind her, a flush sounded, the lav door creaked open and Gran's voice asked, 'What have you got there, Posy? That looks like … custard.'

'It's for Violet tonight.'

'Silly girl. You can't leave it there. We'll get rats.'

'I didn't know rats like custard.'

'And what's that it was in?'

Posy held out the trinket box. 'It's not one of yours.'

'Gramps and me gave you that as a christening present, and you're putting custard in it.'

Remorse – that was a good word – consumed her. 'I'll give it a good wash, I promise.'

'You certainly will.' Gran smiled. 'I'll help. We'll do it upstairs in the washstand so Ma needn't know.'

'You're a brick, Gran.' Some people called you a brick for the smallest reason, but not Posy. She used the word only when there was a particular reason. 'What about Violet's meat?' She produced her lumpy hanky.

'Oh, Posy, was there ever a child like you?'

'No, because I'd need a twin sister.'

'Put that hanky away and let's go upstairs.'

In their room, Posy poured water from the jug into the bowl and swished the trinket box about before using her fingertip to wipe its inside.

'Before you put owt else in that box,' said Gran in what was for her a stern voice, 'ask yourself: would Gran approve? If the answer's no, don't do it.'

'Cross my heart and hope to die.'

Dad had put up shelves and Posy had a whole one to herself. She put the trinket box back in its place.

'There's not much left in the ewer,' said Gran. 'You'll need to top it up – not just now,' she added as Posy leapt to do her bidding.

Gran sat on the bed, patting the place beside her; Posy hitched herself onto the bed and sat, feet dangling. She liked sitting on the bed. She liked lying on it and in it. She liked the whole room. It was a proper bedroom, not a scullery. It bothered her that Gran might not like it as much as she did. She had heard Gran mutter something about *crowded* once, but Posy didn't think the room was crowded. With Gran's big bed and dressing table, the chest of drawers and the washstand, the hanging cupboard, the chair and the bedside table, the shelves and pictures on the wall, and the rug ... it didn't feel crowded. It felt like the room was hugging them.

'We need to talk about Violet,' said Gran. 'You mustn't put food outside any more, but we'll see if we can give her a little summat extra in the evening; and we'll make her box more comfy. I've got some old pieces of sheet that I've been saving for dusters.'

'Can we make up her bed now?'

'The pieces are in the airing cupboard. We'll leave them be to keep warm and they can go in her box this evening when we give her your meat scraps. Give them to me and I'll pop them in the meat safe while Ma's busy.'

Posy hugged her. 'Me and Violet are so lucky to have you.'

'I'm lucky to have you an' all, chick.' Gran pressed a kiss into her hair. Her voice sounded thick and weepy, but that could be because some hair had got in her mouth.

'And Violet. You're lucky to have Violet too, while she's still here.'

'Aye, chick. And Violet.'

'I can't say I'm pleased about this, Mother-in-law.'

Posy went cold. Dad's displeasure did that to her, even when it was aimed at someone else.

'No need to stop what you're doing, Hilda. Posy will clear the table and you can serve the pudding. What is it tonight?'

'Stewed apple and custard.' Ma's voice wasn't much above a whisper.

'Good. Posy can have the skin. You like the skin, don't you, Posy?'

Posy's stomach rolled, but she said, 'Yes, Dad.'

She stacked the plates, gathering the cutlery on the top one, and took them to the scullery. Violet was on the wall, gazing in. Posy cracked the door open, let Violet squeeze through, then darted into the kitchen, closing the door on Violet's nose. Poor Violet, but at least she was indoors. Sculleries were uncomfortable places, as Posy knew better than most.

Ma served the pudding. Dad picked up his spoon and so did the rest of them. Posy stirred the skin, bunching it into a single lump.

'Don't pull faces, Posy,' said Dad.

She straightened her features. They didn't want to straighten. They wanted to stay screwed up with disgust. Her flesh felt clammy. She touched the spoon to her lips and forced her mouth to open. In went the spoon. Round went her stomach. She took the skin into her mouth and swallowed – almost gagged, but didn't, couldn't – Dad would be angry. Another swallow. Her gullet rippled from top to bottom. This time the skin went down. Her stomach twitched in protest. Her

211

eyes watered. The skin stayed down.

'As I was saying, Mother-in-law,' said Dad, 'I'm not pleased.'

'Why not?' Gran's voice was mild but not droopy like Ma's. Gran wasn't a droopy cowslip. 'I'm only going next door to spend the evening with Mrs Watson. What's wrong with that?'

'People might get the wrong idea. It might appear that you're not welcome in your own home.'

'As if anyone would think that,' said Gran, almost but not quite laughing.

'Since my name has recently gone on the rent book, I wouldn't want anyone thinking anything untoward about your position in my household.'

'Well, they won't, because I haven't mentioned it to anyone.'

'There's no need to keep it a secret,' said Dad. 'I'm the man of the house now in every way and it's right the neighbours should know.'

'Fine. I'll tell Mrs Watson.' Gran added in a peacemaking voice, 'I can't not go. It's arranged.'

'Very well.' Dad was like a king bestowing a gracious favour on his humble subject. 'But after this evening, perhaps you should wait a while before you do it again.'

'Well...'

'For appearances. We don't want to be talked about.' He smiled. 'Humour me, Mother-in-law. I want everyone to see us as the perfect family.'

That won Gran over. 'Very well.'

Dad and Ma disappeared into the parlour to await their tea. Posy cleared the table and helped wash up. They let Violet into the comfort of the kitchen. When Posy carried the tray to the

212

parlour, Gran opened the door for her, called, 'See you later,' and shut it quickly.

'You may sit in Gran's place,' said Dad, so Posy sat next to Ma on the settee. Ma didn't budge up closer like Gran would have, or give a welcoming smile. She carried on sewing.

Presently Posy remembered she was supposed to top up the bedroom jug. She wasn't allowed to speak unless spoken to, so she half-raised her hand. She didn't like doing that because it felt like being at school, but it was the only way.

'Yes, Posy?' said Dad.

'Gran wanted me to put more water in our jug. May I do it now?'

Dad made a *tsk* sound, like he was hissing at her. 'Very well, but don't let it happen again. Evenings are for family, not for jobs.'

She left the parlour, shutting the door behind her. Dad didn't like doors left open. She fetched the ewer, but when she touched the kitchen doorknob, she heard a mew from the other side. She couldn't open the door: Violet would be upstairs before you could say Jack Robinson and Dad would skin the pair of them.

She returned the ewer to the bedroom. Gran would understand.

Downstairs, she paused outside the parlour door. Dad was saying something about a green vase.

'It's hideous.'

'It belonged to my grandmother – Dad's mother,' said Ma. 'She gave it to Mother, but Mother hates it, always has.'

'I don't see why she should foist it on us, if she

213

doesn't care for it. Put it in her bedroom.'

Nothing important, then. Not about Violet. Posy opened the door and went in.

'Ma and I think it would be nice for Gran to have some of her special things upstairs,' said Dad. 'It can't be easy for her, having to share with a child...'

Oh no. They weren't going to put her back in the scullery, were they?

'...and it would make the room feel even more her own. That's important, because this used to be her home.'

'It still is,' said Posy.

'Of course it is, but we all live here now and we want to make her comfortable in her own room. Having her things round her will do that. Shall we take some things upstairs for her? That will be a surprise when she comes home. What about this figurine? What do you think, Posy?'

She swelled with pride. 'It's so pretty.' It was a girl with a straw hat, a wicker basket over her arm. 'I'd love to wake up every morning and see it; and if I'd love it, think how much more Gran would. If the girl goes upstairs, the boy has to as well. They're a pair.'

'Good girl for noticing.'

She almost burst with happiness. Dad's praise, Gran's forthcoming delight: what more could she ask? All she needed was for Violet to stay in at night and life would be perfect.

They chose a few more things.

'Anything else, Posy?' asked Dad.

She bit her lip. Gran might not be fond of the green vase, but choosing it would please Dad ...

or would he somehow twig she had been listening at the door?

'What about the vase?'

'Oh, that. What do you think, Hilda? I'm not keen on it myself, but if Posy thinks Gran would like it upstairs...'

Up went the selected items and down came some ornaments from the mantelpiece in Ma and Dad's bedroom.

'That's better,' said Dad. 'Some of Gran's things, some of ours, all together in the parlour. That's fair, isn't it, Posy? Not a word to Gran. Let's see how long it takes her to notice.'

When Gran returned, Posy nearly exploded with excitement. Would she notice immediately?

'Did you have a nice chat, Mother?' asked Ma.

'Aye. Mrs Watson says you should come an' all next time.'

Ma bent over her sewing as if she had suddenly gone near-sighted.

'Except there won't be a next time ... just yet,' said Dad.

'I know,' said Gran. 'I won't let you down, Edmund. Anyroad, me and Posy have a job to do.'

Violet! Posy jumped up. 'May I be excused?'

'Of course, if Gran wants you.'

Chuckling, they fetched the pieces of sheet from the airing cupboard. Some of Posy's chuckles were because of the surprise Gran was going to have, but she managed not to blab. They managed to get into the kitchen without releasing Violet. Violet yowled and tried to push past.

'We'll sort out her box,' said Gran, 'then you can give her the scraps.'

But when they opened the back door, the box was gone.

Gran went to the parlour. 'Someone has stolen Violet's box. Of all the things to take.'

Dad puffed out smoke. He leant forward to tap the ash off his cigarette, then leant back again, resting his head against the back of the chair. It was a good job antimacassars had been invented.

'Nothing to worry about, Mother-in-law. I rid us of that box earlier. We can't have our premises cluttered with rubbish like that. This is a respectable house, not a rag-and-bone yard.'

## Chapter Fifteen

If only Hilda had said something instead of letting Edmund shift her bits and pieces around. Leonie didn't doubt he was behind it, and that made it sound like she was blaming him for doing summat bad, and you couldn't call it that. It was only right that her knick-knacks should give way to Hilda's. Share and share alike, and that meant sharing space. As Edmund had pointed out, it was Posy who had chosen the pieces to go upstairs, so she had had to tell Posy what a clever girl she was and how she had made the perfect choices. She wouldn't dream of hurting Posy's feelings.

And now she was stuck with the new arrangements. The others were happy and they thought she was an' all. She felt tired, but not I've-worked-hard tired, not satisfied tired. It was a deep-down

216

inside tired ... defeated tired.

That was enough of that! Defeated tired – what twaddle. Pulling her spine straight, she looked round her bedroom. So what if it was smaller than her old room? Hilda and Edmund needed the bigger room. So what if she shared with Posy? She loved Posy. And so what if it was a squeeze? She was lucky to stay in her old home. Plenty didn't.

Anyroad, it was selfish of her to harp on about herself all the time. She had a bigger problem to think about: that stair rod. Hilda refused to discuss it; not that she could have done owt about it. And Edmund ... well, he wouldn't be swayed. Leonie fetched a deep sigh. It felt like barbed wire being pulled up her throat.

Her gaze roamed the room. Her bud-vase and the china cat playing the accordion were on a shelf, with some of Hedley's books on the shelf below. Was this why Edmund had put up the shelves? The green vase was on the shelf with the books. Well, she wasn't having that. She seized the vase and opened the hanging cupboard, intending to shove it to the back.

Wait. Why not sell it? If Posy noticed, she would say it was on top of the cupboard in the box of old letters and postcards. Hilda was out shopping for chops and cabbage. Could she get out and back before Hilda returned? And why should it matter if she didn't? She could come and go as she pleased. Besides, she had to go this morning, because it was half-day closing and the shops would be shut this afternoon. Now that she had decided, she couldn't hang on until tomorrow.

217

She took her coat from the back of the bedroom door. When it was just her and Hedley, she had hung her coat in the hall, but now there wasn't room. She didn't mind. It made sense for the others to keep their coats downstairs, because ... she couldn't call to mind why, but there had been a good reason at the time, so of course she hadn't minded. Like she didn't mind swapping bedrooms or sharing with Posy. Or agreeing not to pop out of an evening or that there was no point in keeping the herbs.

She was flaming sick of not minding.

Half-day closing was the best thing that had ever been invented. It applied to Nell even when she wasn't in the shop; so on Wednesday mornings she felt extra chipper. It was like having a tiny weekend in the middle of the week. This morning she had two new ladies to call on, one in Urmston, the other in Chorlton. Including travelling time, that was her morning's work spoken for.

She removed the apron she wore at home to protect her Ingleby's uniform of plain black dress with detachable collar and cuffs. Honestly, all she needed was a frilly cap and apron and she could serve afternoon tea at the Midland Hotel. Inglebys had provided her with work shoes, which she was paying for out of her salary and which she was required to polish every night; and she had made herself a hip-length, edge-to-edge jacket, which was the most agonised-over garment she had ever produced.

First, there was the colour.

'Black,' said Mrs Brent.

'With the black dress, I'll look like I'm going to a funeral,' said Nell. Also, it would make her look ... subservient, as if colours weren't allowed.

'Navy,' suggested Mrs O'Rourke. 'You can't go wrong with navy.'

'Not with black. I'd look like I'd put it on by mistake instead of a black one.'

'Red,' said Mrs Clancy, causing a gasp to whistle round Nell's kitchen. 'Why not? It's cheerful.'

Red and black would be dramatic, but it would take only one of her ladies to make a sniffy remark to Ingleby's and she could be out on her ear.

'Red's pushy,' said Mrs O'Rourke.

'What about fawn or beige?' said Mrs Dunnett. 'There's nowt pushy about them.'

But set against black, either would look drab. Dressing appropriately was one thing, but she couldn't bear to be drab. Why must working-class women dress soberly? Her time in the garment factory, handling fabrics in a glorious variety of hues and modern patterns, had fed her need for colour. Now she yearned for it.

'Ask Ingleby's,' said Mrs Brent. 'They'll tell you.'

That was what she was afraid of. They were bound to say black. But she would be wearing the jacket when she represented them, so they ought to be consulted.

'Forest-green,' said Miss Collier after consideration. 'Deep enough to look businesslike but striking enough to form an elegant though not inappropriate contrast to your shop dress.'

'Linen,' added Miss Moore, removing the next

question from Nell's mind.

After that, there was the style.

'Something plain, obviously,' said Miss Collier.

Why obviously? 'But not too plain,' said Nell. 'I want to tell the customers, "You'll be able to make something like this," so they have to find it pleasing.'

Miss Moore and Miss Collier exchanged looks. Had she gone too far?

'That's a good point,' Miss Moore conceded.

'Show us the pattern before you take it home,' added Miss Collier.

Nell spent a happy dinner hour sifting through pattern books before presenting her chosen pattern for inspection.

'It's a modern look without being fancy and it's straightforward to make. I'll take the pattern picture with me to show clients what can be done when they're more experienced.'

So here she was in her work rig-out, ready to set off. First, she let in Mrs O'Rourke, who was hiring the sewing machine to make a skirt for their Josie; then she left. It was a bright May morning. Actually, it was cloudy, but she felt bright inside and that was what mattered. She caught the bus to Urmston for her first lesson, then returned along the same route for her second. Mrs Marsden lived on Edge Lane and, as she descended from the bus, Nell was pleasantly aware of being halfway home.

Mrs Marsden's house had a rockery in the front garden and snowy nets at the windows. If you were lucky enough to have a garden, why would you blur your view with net curtains? Inside was smart but tired-looking. A few home-made cushions would cheer it up no end, but Nell knew better than to say so. Middle-class ladies might be discovering the pleasures of dressmaking, but make their own soft furnishings? Never! The only thing Mrs Marsden would ever do to a cushion cover with her own fair hands was embroider forget-me-nots on it.

Nell demonstrated how to thread the machine, then unthreaded it and stood aside to let Mrs Marsden take her place while she guided her through the process; then she resumed her seat behind the machine to show how it worked. She had just got the treadle moving when there was a loud ringing sound. Cold water poured through her – the machine had gone horribly wrong. But the sound was coming from elsewhere.

'Excuse me.' Mrs Marsden didn't merely smile, she smirked. 'I must answer my telephone.' The ringing cut off. 'Someone has answered on my behalf. I'll be fetched if I'm needed.'

The door opened and a dark-haired young man wearing a yellow silk tie beneath a knitted pullover sauntered in. 'You're wanted on the blower, Ma. Excuse the interruption,' he added with a nod for Nell.

'Thank you, Walter.' Mrs Marsden rose. 'Excuse me, Mrs Hibbert. It might be an acquaintance about social arrangements.'

Walter held the door for her, then smiled at Nell. 'She'll be disappointed. It's the butcher with a question about chops.' He nodded at the sewing machine. 'You work for Ingleby's, don't you?' He sat on the arm of a chair, throwing his forearm across the back and mussing up the antimacassar.

221

'I'm a writer – a journalist. Always on the lookout for a good story that will have Fleet Street begging for my services.'

'I hardly think sewing lessons would make a good story.'

He laughed. 'I'll leave you to it. A pleasure to meet you, Mrs Hibbert.'

As she got up to take another piece of cotton out of her bag, her gaze fell on a magazine, folded open on a side table. Beneath a wordy advertisement for Cyclax beauty preparations were some small ads.

Supposing she advertised her services.

Don't be daft. What, her, a girl from the backstreets, pushing herself forward like that, daring to suggest her services were worth paying for?

But they were. Ingleby's thought so; so did Mrs Liversedge and another couple of ladies who had asked for extra lessons. If she advertised – and it was a very big if – and some ladies took her up on it, it could give her more possibilities, such as going part-time at Ingleby's, if they would let her. At the moment, if she wasn't out demonstrating the use of the machines, she was in the shop. Might it be possible to give up the shop hours? Always supposing, of course, that she could find enough private teaching. If she could – if – she might have more flexibility regarding her hours, which would make life better for her children.

Could she carve out a future as a sewing teacher?

Leonie spent the afternoon on her hands and knees, wiping the skirting boards. She heaved furniture out of the way and shoved it back again. She was achy and unpleasantly warm, but she wasn't about to stop.

'You shouldn't be doing that, Mother,' said Hilda.

She sat back on her heels. Hilda rubbed her hands together like she was washing them. Her clouded eyes and downturned mouth gave her a dissatisfied expression and Leonie felt a flash of vexation. If anyone should be dissatisfied round here, it was her, not Hilda. Then she felt guilty. Hilda wasn't dissatisfied: she was anxious. Leonie sighed and something inside her crumpled. It wasn't Hilda's fault. She was just doing as she was told by Edmund. As for the skirting board marathon, Leonie was doing it on purpose to get her dander up, because then she could tell herself it was the disagreeable task she was hot and bothered about, and not ... and not the money.

Why was she het up about it, anyroad? It was her money. No one could take it off her, not even to look after it for her, not if she didn't want them to.

Another sigh. She was meant to be pleased with herself for selling the green vase. Instead, walking home with her plump purse had stirred up worries about Edmund's offer to look after her money.

'Put the kettle on, Hilda. Let's stop and have a drink.'

Let's stop – as if the pair of them were fettling. The hardest Hilda had worked today was mashing the potato topping for the shepherd's pie.

But she wasn't going to get riled about that. It wasn't Hilda's fault that Edmund had divided up the household tasks the way he had; and it wasn't Hilda's fault her mother had elected to get all hot

223

under the collar over the skirting boards.

Leonie hadn't given Edmund an answer to his offer. She didn't want to cause upset, but she couldn't bring herself to hand over her money, little as it was. Yet why not? He was the man of the house. If she gave him control of her money, wouldn't it bind them together more closely as a family?

She pushed herself to her feet and wiped her hands on her apron, feeling twinges deep inside her muscles and joints. She followed Hilda to the kitchen and took her place at the table. It didn't feel right, not being the one to make the tea. It made her feel like a visitor in her own house.

But that was the point, wasn't it? It wasn't just her house. It was their house.

'Edmund suggested looking after my money. Did he tell you?'

The tiniest pause. 'He mentioned it.'

'What do you think?'

Hilda poured boiling water into the teapot, then stirred the pot in a way guaranteed to stew the tea in two minutes flat.

'Stop faffing, Hilda. Sit down and tell me what you think.'

Hilda froze like a child playing statues. She transferred the pot to the table and sat down.

'It's up to you, Mother.'

'I'm asking what you think.'

'Edmund's good with money. He's never kept me short.'

'So you think I should give him mine?'

Hilda milked and sugared the cups. 'It's up to you.'

'You really aren't helping.'

'What did you and Dad do with money?'

'Dad handed his wages to me every week.'

'Me and Edmund aren't like that. He's always done the money side.' Hilda reached for the teapot. 'He'd give you pocket money, if that's what you're worried about.'

Pocket money? Pocket money! Like a child getting weekly spends. Not on your nellie.

Although ... would it be such a bad thing? Might it be the magic detail that would make everything fall into place? She had swallowed so many changes in the hope that each would be the one to bring about the most important change of all, the one that would create the easy-going atmosphere of her longings.

If Edmund looked after her money, would that transform this house into a truly happy and comfortable home?

Leonie held the teapot under the tap and directed a quick squirt of water into it, then took the pot outside, swilled the water round to catch all the used tea leaves and chucked them down the drain. Violet was lying on the path, stretched out in the early evening sunshine. Posy stood in the doorway, the damp tea towel hanging from her hands.

'Should we bring her in so she can lie on the kitchen rug?'

'She's fine where she is,' said Leonie.

'But she needs to be indoors as much as possible because of going out at night.'

'I know, chick, but she's happy outdoors just now.'

'She won't be happy when she gets put out at bedtime.' Posy ducked back inside.

Leonie followed her in. They joined Hilda and Edmund in the parlour.

'Well, Mother-in-law,' said Edmund.

Instant panic. Had Hilda told him of their conversation about money? Surely Hilda wouldn't drop her in it like that?

'Hilda and I have been admiring how well our things look in here. Thank you for allowing some of your possessions to be moved upstairs. That was generous of you.'

His voice was warm and rich. She relaxed. When he used that tone, she always felt better.

'Pleasure,' she said. 'I should have moved them sooner.'

'Don't apologise or I'll feel bad for mentioning it. There's nothing wrong with your possessions. You understand that, don't you, Posy? Gran's things aren't less important than ours. It was just a matter of, as Gran says, making room.'

'Yes, Dad.' Posy directed a happy beam at Leonie.

'In fact,' said Edmund, 'why don't you go and fetch one of Gran's special things, Posy? The green vase: fetch that. Carefully, mind. Gran can tell you about it and about your great-grandmother, who gave it to her.'

'This is good of you, Edmund,' said Leonie. And it was. It was more than she deserved after yesterday evening's fiasco. Why had she sold the vase? Blasted thing. She had hated it all these years and now it had caused dismay and embarrassment, not to mention Posy's distress.

'Poor Posy,' Edmund had said yesterday evening. 'She's the one who chose it to have the honour of going in your bedroom. How must she feel?'

She couldn't have felt any worse than her gran. Oh, the humiliation, the shame.

'If we'd known, Mother-in-law, that you didn't like it, we'd never have let Posy choose it.'

There was a saying about wanting the ground to open up and swallow you. That was how she had felt. There she had sat, squirming in the middle of it all – Edmund being understanding and forgiving, Hilda burying herself in her darning, Posy sitting pencil-straight, sniffing back tears – knowing she had made the worst mistake of her life.

But now, twenty-four hours later – what a difference. Edmund had invited her and Posy for a walk.

'Is Ma coming?' Posy asked.

'She has things to do. Besides, I wouldn't have enough arms.' Edmund jutted out his elbows invitingly. 'A beautiful young lady on each side.'

'Gran's not young.'

'I'm sure she was always young and beautiful in Gramps's eyes,' said Edmund and Leonie looked at him in surprise. Fancy him realising. She squeezed his arm.

They walked to Chorlton Park, where Posy went on the swings and then Edmund pushed the roundabout at top speed, to squeals of delight from half a dozen children. Was this the same man who beat his child with the stair rod every Saturday? Watching him, it was hard to believe. In spite of herself, Leonie began to feel at ease with the world. And it was all because of the green vase. Edmund had never suggested a walk before. Clearly he wanted to make her feel better. Could it be that that horrid old vase had provided the piece of magic she had longed for?

As they made their way home, she stepped lightly.

'Go and get ready for bed, Posy,' said Hilda the instant they walked through the door. Leonie felt a clip of annoyance. Not 'Did you enjoy your walk?' Not 'Where did you go?'

Posy kissed them all goodnight and pattered upstairs.

'We had a lovely walk, Hilda,' Leonie said pointedly.

'Indeed we did,' said Edmund. 'Come and sit in the parlour so Hilda and I can talk to you.'

A flutter inside her. 'That sounds serious.' She said it in a jokey way to show she didn't really expect it to be serious.

'It is and it isn't. We're concerned on your behalf. We only want what's best for you.'

Oh, lord, they hadn't bought back the green vase, had they?

Edmund held open the parlour door. 'Make yourself comfortable. Do you notice anything different?'

What was this about? She looked round. The green vase was gone. So were the boy and girl figurines; Hilda's shepherdess stood in their place. Hedley's Charles Dickenses – they were on the shelf upstairs. Her Toby jug wasn't there – wait a minute. The Toby jug wasn't upstairs. And her ornamental fan – that was missing an' all. Her gaze flew round the room. The musical box, the candlesticks, her mother's spills-jar ... all missing.

'It's for your own good, Mother-in-law. We can't have you feeling you must sell your precious things, so we've taken them into safekeeping.'

'You mean ... Hilda ... while we were at the park...'

'I hold myself to blame,' said Edmund. 'I should have realised how worried you were about money.'

'I'm not worried.'

'You obviously are, or why would you sell your treasured possessions?'

'That vase wasn't–'

No. Stop. She mustn't say it. After Posy had selected it as a special item; after Posy had been upset and confused at its being sold; how could she say that, far from being treasured, she had been glad to see the back of it? Posy would be hurt all over again.

'Wasn't what, Mother-in-law?'

She ran the tip of her tongue over her top lip. 'Nothing.'

'Selling your vase – dare I say it? – wasn't rational. You've suffered a bereavement and people do odd things in that state, especially women who aren't as young as they once were. I invited you once to put your money into my hands and I make the offer again.' He held out his hands, palms up. Did he expect her to whip out her purse from up her knicker-leg? 'If you don't trust me...'

'Of course I trust you.'

'Then you'll place your money in my keeping? I'm pleased to hear it – pleased and honoured.'

Wait a minute. All she had said was... That didn't mean...

'And your ornaments and what-have-you will remain in safekeeping. I think we all agree it's for the best. We want Hilda and Posy's heirlooms safe from being sold, don't we?'

Leonie came to her feet. It was too much. How had she got into this fix?

'Where are you going, Mother-in-law?'

'I'll let Violet in for a while.'

'Violet?'

'The cat.' Why must he pretend not to know her name? 'It'll give her a chance to have a snooze indoors before she gets put out.'

'There are no cats in this house.'

'What are you talking about?'

'That animal doesn't come in my house again. It doesn't get fed; it doesn't get somewhere to snooze. If you had spent less time fussing round that creature, and more time concentrating on your family, you wouldn't have sold the vase, you wouldn't have upset Posy, you wouldn't have embarrassed Hilda and me, and we wouldn't have had to take your things into safekeeping. You've brought it all on yourself but please don't worry. We forgive you and we'll do our best for you.'

# Chapter Sixteen

'And you've waited until now to tell me?' Nell's chair scraped as she pushed away from the kitchen table. She glared down at her friend. 'You even let me waste time making a cup of tea.'

'I'm sorry,' cried Mrs Brent. 'I couldn't come any sooner. Hilda wanted Posy to get off to school without any upset.'

'You could have come after she'd gone – and don't say I'd have been out taking Alf to school. You knew I'd be in the house till nigh-on half-nine before I had to take Cassie to Annie's.'

'And what could you have done if you had known, eh?' Mrs Brent asked with spirit. 'You'd still have needed to get to your appointment.'

'But I'd have *known;* and right this minute, I'd be out looking for her instead of–' She threw up her hands, then brought them down in a sharp slap on her thighs. 'We need to fetch her. With luck, she'll be hanging about. She must be starving hungry.'

She swept down the hallway, with Mrs Brent scuttling behind.

'I'm that sorry, and after you trusted me with her an' all.'

Nell swung round to face her. 'Don't tell me you're sorry. Tell Alf and Cassie.' She clapped a hand over her mouth. 'I'm sorry. That was a horrid thing to say. I know it's not your fault. But

231

throwing her out were downright cruel. It's got me all het up.'

'He didn't throw her out exactly; more, won't let her back in.'

'Same difference. Come on. I need to bring my cat home.'

As they turned the corner into Finney Lane, Nell felt a flurry of anticipation, but there was no sign of Violet and she pressed her lips tight to contain her disappointment.

'She could be in our backyard,' suggested Mrs Brent.

Hoping for summat to eat. Distressed because she had never gone hungry since she arrived here. Nell swallowed. She should have seen this coming. She should have fetched Violet the minute she heard about her being put out at night.

'Shall we go down the entry?' she said.

'What for? It's quicker to walk through the house.'

'Aye, and I can imagine your Hilda telling you-know-who that I came storming through.'

'Nay, she wouldn't.'

'Yes, she would. I know she's your daughter and I shouldn't speak ill of her, but her middle name is Doormat.'

Mrs Brent's face stilled and she looked away. Nell experienced a sinking feeling. She had held her tongue on her opinion of Hilda Tanner for over two years and now she had blurted it out.

Mrs Brent said, 'Well, I'm going in the front. Are you coming or what?'

As they walked in, Hilda came downstairs. Most women at this time of day would have an apron on or a wraparound pinny, but Hilda Tanner didn't do housework, did she, so there she was in a drop-waisted brown dress. She had never had her hair cut short, but that bun, worn low, wasn't flattering. She should wear it higher; that would lift her hair clear of her cheeks.

'Don't mind us, Hilda,' said Mrs Brent. 'We're going through to see if the cat's there.'

Nell followed her into the kitchen. The table was covered with a dark green oilcloth. A glass vase with decorative handles, filled with lily-of-the-valley, stood in the centre. Mrs Brent marched through the scullery and opened the door.

'Violet,' she called.

Nell joined her in the backyard, but no fuzzy black shape emerged from behind the mangle, tail erect in greeting. Nell strode to the gate and stepped into the entry, looking up and down and calling. There was no answering mew, no rush to greet her. She went back in and shut the gate. Hilda stood in the doorway, looking fretful. The flaming doormat couldn't even bring herself to set foot in the yard to help Violet.

She addressed her friend. 'Thanks for helping. I'm sorry I were sharp earlier. I have to get to my appointment now.'

Mrs Brent's face softened in sympathy. 'Far away?'

'Edge Lane. The lady I went to on Wednesday.'

'Her with the telephone that made you jump? You get along. I'll walk round a bit and see if I can find Violet.'

Nell turned to Hilda. 'Thanks for letting me look. If your mum doesn't find her, I'll try your

233

backyard again later.'

Hilda shifted awkwardly. 'Just give us a knock and I'll look for you.'

And risk Mr Brick Shithouse telling Mrs Doormat to say the cat wasn't there? Not likely.

The foliage overhanging the garden walls on Edge Lane was young and fresh. Jim pushed his barrow, enjoying the variety of greens shifting in the breeze, the deep green of the horse chestnut complete with its candles of white flowers, the glossy green of the laburnum with its fluid tassels of golden blooms, and the bright green of the good old beech. That exhausted his knowledge of trees. He ought to learn more, just as he had learnt the names of the wildflowers on the meadows. Living this simpler life had given him the time to discover an interest in nature.

Before the war, nature had been little more than a flower in his buttonhole and an account at the florist's so he could send bouquets to Roberta, but now he derived satisfaction from working the vegetable patch at the back of Mrs Jeffrey's cottage. He had learnt how to thin out young shoots, how to tend the strawberry plants, spreading short straw beneath them to keep them clean and covering them with it at night until all danger of frost was over. Turning over the soil, with the pungent aroma of earth filling the air and a brave blackbird diving for worms practically at his feet, was an unexpected joy. Whatever decisions he made concerning his future, he intended to continue gardening.

Not far now to Mrs Fielden's house, which was

next door to Mrs Marsden's, another of his customers, just a few doors along from Mrs Randall's.
Was he daft to want to duck out of sight as he
passed Mrs Randall's? A grin tugged at his mouth,
but it wasn't funny, not really. Seeing Roberta had
been unsettling – probably more for her than for
him. Poor girl.

Arriving outside Mrs Fielden's, he lowered the
barrow's handles so the wooden uprights touched
the ground. Taking his bucket from its hook, he
walked between the ornamental-topped stone-
clad gateposts and went round the rear of the
house to ask for water. He started at the back and
worked his way round to the front. When he
finished, he stowed his gear and collected his
money. As he went through the gate, someone
emerged from the gate next door. He was about
to touch his cap to Mrs Marsden, should she wish
to notice him – his heart caught – Nell Hibbert.

He covered the ground between them in a few
strides.

'Afternoon.' He raised his cap. She was lovely,
and entirely unaware of it, which made her lovelier
still.

'Were you working next door? Daft question.'

'Then we're both daft. I was about to ask you the
same thing. You've been teaching Mrs Marsden?'

Her polite smile built to something warmer.
'How kind of you to remember what I do.'

Kind? Was that what she thought? He remembered every word she had spoken, every nuance of
emotion in her face, the questioning frown, the
relaxed smile, the steady determined eye, the glow
in her cheeks as she watched her children ... the

cool politeness when he told her about his friend's wooden toys and she thought he was offering to pay for one.

A smartly painted cart drew up. The driver reined in the horse and called to them.

'Marsden residence?' He jumped down. 'I've got their new sundial. I'll go and see where they want it.'

He couldn't let the interruption end their meeting. 'How are you?'

'Fine, thank you.' She made a move.

'And the children?' That would detain her.

'Doing well, thank you. Alf loves school.'

'Long may it last.'

She had innate grace. He had known girls who had attended dancing lessons, deportment classes, the whole works, without achieving what Nell possessed. There was a woman coming along the road – a lady, rather – whose blue and cream ensemble was probably the height of elegance, but she was no match for Nell in her plain black with the striking jacket. The stranger's little girl, dressed in a confection of frills, trotted beside her, patting a hoop along with a stick striped like a barber's pole. The hoop wobbled, but kept going, just about.

Nell followed his glance. 'She needs to hit it a lot harder than that.'

'She needs your Cassie to show her how it's done.'

Little Cassie Hibbert had more gumption in one hand than this frill-bedecked child had in her entire privileged body. As if his thoughts had conjured up Cassie's energy, the girl delivered an almighty thwack, sending the hoop bouncing along. With a delighted cry, she ran in pursuit.

A motorcycle-and-sidecar was coming along the road, its throaty engine loud in the peaceful afternoon. The waiting horse shifted, its harness jingling; a hoof struck the road: the horse needed reassurance. Jim took an instinctive step towards it. There was a sharp *tap* as the child hit the hoop again.

'Look, Mummy! It's getting away!'

The hoop veered along a curving course, bouncing off the pavement onto the road in front of the horse at the same time as the motorcycle-and-sidecar chugged alongside. The horse reared – Jim dived for the harness – a cry – a crumpled heap of frills. A strangled scream from the mother. Nell darted into the road to kneel beside the child as Jim caught the harness, his arms being yanked upwards before his muscles gauged the power needed to bring the situation under control.

'Are you all right, sweetheart?' Nell's voice was urgent but quiet. 'Can you speak to me?'

'Melissa! Oh, Melissa!' The mother threw herself on her knees beside her child. 'Is she all right? Is she–?'

'She's not quite conscious,' said Nell. 'Try to stay calm. Talk to her.' She looked up at him, her eyes huge and unusually dark, belying the assured manner. 'We need a doctor – or an ambulance. Mrs Marsden has a telephone.'

The delivery man appeared. Jim left him to see to his horse, which seemed recovered from its fright. He sprinted to the front door, ringing and knocking at the same time, pushing his way past the maid.

'There's been an accident. Where's your telephone?'

She gaped at him, but a nattily dressed young man appeared in a doorway.

'This way. What's happened?'

Jim ignored the question. The telephone stood on a desk in a room that would be a lot brighter if someone would dispense with the net curtains.

The young man got there first. 'Shall I make the call for you? No offence, but...'

'None taken.' Jim lifted the mouthpiece and made the call. Window cleaners might not be au fait with the use of telephones, but former solicitors were.

When he went back outside, the child was still on the ground, Nell's jacket folded beneath her head. Nell sat on her heels beside the child, her attention fixed on her, her voice low and steady. The mother knelt on the girl's other side, holding her hand, breathing raggedly but striving for calm. There were a couple of neighbours; another joined them, offering a blanket. The delivery man stood by the horse's head – and the natty fellow was engaging him in conversation. Seeking the juicy details, presumably. Jim felt a twist of distaste.

A motor car pulled up on the other side of the road and a gentleman climbed out. He hurried across.

'I'm a doctor. Do you need assistance?'

'An ambulance is on its way,' said Jim.

'Right-o. Let me take a look. Are you the mother? What happened?'

The young fellow appeared at Jim's side. 'Yes, what happened? Are you a witness?'

'Are you a policeman?'

'Journalist. Shocking accident and all that, but I need the story. What's your name?'

'Not now. Let's make sure the child gets off to hospital.'

'And then you'll talk to me?' Without waiting for a reply, he pounced on another potential witness.

Jim edged away. The doctor had taken charge and – yes – here came the ambulance.

Time to disappear.

Nell wanted nothing more than to go home and hug her children. That poor little girl, getting knocked down like that. Chills helter-skeltered down her spine. The poor mother too. It just showed. Money protected you from a lot, but it couldn't protect you from honest-to-goodness accidents.

As the child was lifted into the ambulance, the mother turned to her. 'Thank you so much for helping my daughter.'

'I really didn't do anything.'

'Oh, you did. Just being so calm helped tremendously. You're a heroine.'

That was the emotion talking. 'I hope she recovers quickly.'

The mother followed her daughter into the ambulance. Nell stepped away, aware of someone hovering close by. She looked round, expecting to exchange glances of compassion with one of the neighbours, but it was Walter Marsden.

He held her jacket. Instead of passing it to her,

he said, 'You saw what happened.'

'No, I didn't.'

'You must have. The mother called you a heroine.'

'You'll have to ask someone else. Thank you,' she added, looking at her jacket.

He held it up for her to slip into, but she took it from him, looking round for the bag she took to lessons. It was by the Marsdens' garden wall, where someone had put it out of the way. She walked purposefully away. Would Walter Marsden take it into his head to come after her? She walked faster.

She arrived home, hoping Mrs Brent would be there with Violet, but there was only Mrs Dunnett, finishing some work on the sewing machine. Hiring out her machine was going well. Everyone was keen to learn how to use it and happy to pay the small sum she charged.

'That's the quickest sides to middle I've ever done,' said Mrs Dunnett. 'Our Ida was saying as she wants to turn her sheets an' all, so I'll tell her about your machine, if that's all right.'

'Of course.' She helped Mrs Dunnett fold her sheet. 'Will your Janey be home this evening? Would she sit with my two while I pop out? Our cat's gone missing and I need to look for her.'

'She'll be glad to. Give us a knock.'

Nell didn't want to tell the children about Violet if she could help it. Annie wasn't expecting her to collect them yet, because by rights she should have gone from Mrs Marsden's to Ingleby's to finish her working day with an hour there; but the accident had eaten so much time that if she had trailed into town, she would have had only fifteen minutes at work. She was due in the shop to-morrow morning, so she would make her excuses then.

Right now she had some unexpected free time, so she searched the neighbouring streets and entries, starting with Finney Lane, but there was no sign of Violet.

Later, when the children were in bed, she knocked for Janey Dunnett, then returned to Finney Lane. Hilda had said she would look in the backyard, but what if Edmund Tanner answered the door? Nell baulked at the thought. How could she ask the brute who had chucked the cat out to check round the back?

She went down the entry to the back gate. Taking hold of the ring-handle, she turned it and pushed. The door didn't budge. She tried again. It was locked.

It was never locked.

She looked round. Someone had dumped a wooden box along the entry. She set it down in front of the gate and stood on it, placing her hands on top of the gate and lifting herself on her toes to look over. She couldn't see Violet but called her anyway. The back door opened and Edmund Tanner emerged.

'What d'you think you're doing? What's wrong with knocking on the front door like a civilised person?'

'If I knock, will Violet answer?'

'If you're referring to that flea-bitten animal of yours, you had no business leaving it here.'

'Violet has never had fleas.'

241

'I'll remind you that you don't live here any more and you have no right to enter my premises. It's a good job I took the precaution of locking the gate. I don't like trespassers.'

'I can see the cat's not here, so I'll search elsewhere, but if I can't find her, I'll be back, because this is where she knows; and if she's in yon yard and she doesn't jump over the wall when I call her, I'll come in and fetch her and if that means shinning over the wall, so be it.'

'You set foot in my yard and I'll call the police.'

'I'll save you the bother. I'll bring a copper with me.'

He thrust out his chest. 'The law is on my side in this.'

'It wasn't the law I had in mind. You get a bobby knocking on your door and the world and his wife will want to know the reason why. I don't think you'd like that, would you?'


## Chapter Seventeen

Leonie walked home with the paper bag deep in her pocket. It was a sunny morning, but she didn't feel sunny. She felt cloudy and defiant. And rather scared, if she was honest.

Children played in the street. Three little girls sat squeezed on a doorstep, playing at school, with the 'teacher' standing in front of them on the pavement. Further down the road, a boy dashed out of hiding, yelling, 'Kickstone, one, two, three,' as he reached the pillar box. Down this end, Posy darted about in a game of ticky-it. Eh, she had said it before and she would say it again: that child was fleet of foot.

It was tempting to call Posy indoors with her, but she mustn't do anything differently. As she went inside, Hilda called to her from the kitchen, offering a cup of tea.

'I'll just take my things off.'

She shut the bedroom door before removing the paper bag and transferring it to her top drawer, as if the door might burst open behind her and she would be revealed in her secret activity. Edmund was out for his Saturday morning walk, but she still felt jumpy. Once the bag was stashed away, it was safe to go down to have tea with Hilda. It ought to feel cosy and mother-and-daughtery, but it felt stilted. There was so much they couldn't discuss, so many subjects that were out of bounds. Housework. Herbs. The possessions that had been taken upstairs, and those in safekeeping. And now Violet.

And Gerald.

Why not smack Posy if she needed it? Or send her to bed without any supper. But to beat her with a stair rod? That was plain horrible. When she found out about the stair rod, she had exclaimed against it, begged Edmund not to use it, poured out a dozen reasons why it was wrong, while Hilda alternately fluttered and drooped in the background.

'I shall discipline my daughter in any way I see fit, Mother-in-law,' Edmund had informed her. 'If Posy behaves as she ought, there's no call for it. In the end, it's Posy's choice, not mine.'

Except on Saturday afternoons.

Well, not any more.

There was a cheery rat-tat on the front door as Leonie came downstairs and she opened the door to a smiling young man dressed in a blue-grey jacket and dark-blue flannels. What was the likes of him doing here?

'Can I help you?' she asked.

'Good morning,' he said in an educated voice, raising his trilby to her. His shoes were two toning colours of leather an' all. Blimey. 'Have I come to the right house? Does Mrs Hibbert live here?'

'Who wants to know?'

'My name's Marsden. I'm a journalist. I'm writing a piece about the accident yesterday afternoon on Edge Lane.'

'Accident?' Heartbeats skittered across her chest. But Nell hadn't been injured, because she had climbed up to peer over the back gate yesterday evening; and she wouldn't have done that if anything had happened to the children.

'Yes, she was quite the heroine – and a modest one too, if she hasn't talked about it. May I enquire, are you her mother?'

'No.'

'No, you're not or no, I mightn't ask?' He made it sound like she had uttered a wonderful witticism.

'Why do you want her?'

'To talk about the accident. She did something special, and those are the injured girl's mother's words, not mine. A reassuring presence, is what I was told. I can report the accident as a series of bald facts or I can make it into a heartwarming story that will make readers appreciate what a remarkable person your ... daughter is.'

'I'm not her mother. I was her landlady.'

'Will you fetch her? I've gone to a lot of trouble to find her. I was at Ingleby's as the doors opened and persuaded a sweet young lady to give me Mrs Hibbert's address.'

'She may have been sweet, but she wasn't efficient. Mrs Hibbert doesn't live here any more.'

He whipped out a notebook and a pen – no, a silver propelling pencil. 'Can you furnish me with her new address?'

Furnish? What was wrong with plain old *give?* 'Have you got a card I can pass on?'

'If you insist; but please tell her this needs to be done while the story is fresh. You'd like her qualities to be recognised, I'm sure.'

'Well, yes.'

'Perhaps you could tell me a little about her, just to get me started.' He leant forward confidingly. He was good-looking. 'We both know she isn't one to blow her own trumpet.'

That was true. Leonie warmed to him. 'I'm not surprised she was a support to the injured girl and her mother, because she's a wonderful mother herself.'

'That comes as no surprise. Names and ages?' Scribble, scribble in the notebook. 'What job does Mr Hibbert do?'

'Mrs Hibbert's a widow, which makes her all the more remarkable in my book. Better fetched-up children you won't find anywhere, and her a working mother, an' all.'

'Indeed. My own mother is one of her pupils.'

'Really? Then she can vouch for what a good teacher Mrs Hibbert is. So can any number of women round these streets.'

He quirked his head on one side. 'How so?'

How agreeable to be listened to so attentively. 'She teaches private as well as for Ingleby's. Initiative, it's called.' Edmund had used that word, only he had said it in a sarky voice. 'She used to slog God knows how many hours a week at a garment factory in town. She works less hours for Ingleby's and she uses her extra time partly to be at home with the children, because they always come first with her, and the rest for teaching privately.'

'You mentioned the neighbours.'

'She teaches them an' all, and then they hire her sewing machine.'

'Most enterprising.' Scribble, scribble.

Enterprising: that was a good word. If Edmund was sarky again about initiative, she would counter with a calm remark about enterprise. She drew a breath, filling her lungs with satisfaction.

'She's a good girl, is my Nell. I couldn't have wished for greater help when my late husband was poorly.'

Scribble, scribble. 'So it comes as no surprise that Mrs Hibbert put herself out to assist at the scene of an accident?'

'Not one bit.'

'And your name, madam?'

That brought her up short. 'Nay, you don't need that, do you?'

'As you wish.' Burrowing under his pocket flap, he pushed the notebook inside, then slid his pencil in his top pocket, ruffling his silk handkerchief in the process. Leonie's hands itched to straighten it up. He raised his trilby. 'Many thanks. Good morning.'

'Wait a minute. What about your card?'

He gave her a brilliant smile. 'No need. You've been more than helpful.'

Her shoulders gave a small wriggle of pleasure at a job well done as he walked away with a confident stride that said everything you needed to know about privilege. What a pleasant young man, hanging on her every word like that, even though he was a toff and she was ordinary. He was right: dear Nell would never have sung her own praises. How wonderful to have done her friend a good turn.

'Before Posy goes on your errand, Edmund, could you spare her?' Leonie wished she could cast a reassuring glance at her granddaughter, but she had to keep her gaze fixed on Edmund for fear of giving herself away. 'There's a spot of tidying that needs doing in the bedroom.'

'Has she been untidy?' Edmund's displeasure homed in on Posy. 'Little girls who are allowed to sleep in bedrooms should show their gratitude by keeping them clean and tidy.'

'It's nothing, really. It's my fault, if it's anyone's. I thought Posy could–'

'Of course, Mother-in-law. It's good for children to be useful.'

She didn't wait a moment longer, but led the

way upstairs.

'I'm sorry if I made a mess,' said Posy, looking round.

'You didn't, chick, but I needed to get you up here before you go for your dad's caramels. I'm not having that stair rod–'

'Gerald.'

'–that stair rod used again in this house.'

'I know you tried, Gran, but Dad won't listen.'

Leonie opened the top drawer. 'I bought these.'

Posy gasped at the sight of the bag. Leonie up-ended it on the bed, tipping out a quarter of caramels.

'I know you get into trouble if there are only five.'

'There were always five and it never mattered,' said Posy. 'Then one week there were six and after that Dad decided that if there weren't six, I must have eaten one.'

'Rubbish. They must have been smaller sweets that week.'

Posy shrugged, dismissing the weekly beatings. Leonie felt a surge of protectiveness. Her darling little girl wouldn't suffer like that again if she had owt to do with it.

'Put one in your pocket to take with you and pop it in the bag before you get home.'

'Oh, Gran you're an *angel*. Thank you, thank you, thank you.'

She staggered backwards as Posy flung her arms round her. Leonie's arms went round the child who meant the world to her and they hugged one another. Leonie could have stayed like that for hours, but she disentangled herself, holding

Posy's chin and looking deep into her eyes.

'I wish I could get rid of that stair rod, but this is the next best thing.'

'If you did, he'd only get another.'

Posy's offhand acceptance of the situation was disconcerting. Disappointing an' all, when she had wanted to offer reassurance; but there was no time to talk about it. Posy had to go.

Leonie decided it would be best for her to be outside when Posy arrived home. She couldn't risk letting Edmund see her glee at Posy's escape from the weekly punishment, so she went to Nell's to ask about the accident, but Nell wasn't there.

'She's at work.' Mrs O'Rourke paused on the doorstep, shopping bag in hand. 'She said she had to put in extra time.'

Leonie wandered along a few roads and entries, calling Violet, until she deemed it safe to go home. In Finney Lane, several streets' worth of girls had got together and a huge circle, joined hands held up in arches, stretched the width of the road. 'In and out the fairy bluebells, in and out the fairy bluebells,' sang the girls as a chain of them wound in and out of the arches. Posy was at the end of the chain. She broke away and came running, her beaming smile telling Leonie all she needed to know.

Posy gave her a hug. 'You're the best gran in the world.'

Leonie returned the hug. 'Get back to the game or you'll lose your place.'

The leader of the chain stood behind a member of the circle. 'Pat a little girl upon her shoulders...'

went the song. Posy resumed her position, patting the shoulders of the girl in front.

Leonie felt ready to burst with happiness. Eh, but she could wind her way in and out of that circle herself, the way she was feeling. Nell would have: she was a big kid at heart. What a splendid day. She had saved Posy's neck and done Nell a good turn. Now all she had to do was find Violet. Well, why not? Things were meant to go in threes.

As she went indoors, Hilda appeared with her shopping basket.

'I won't be long. Edmund's going out shortly to play bowls.'

It was all Leonie could do not to throw her hat in the air. She was going to have the house to herself. Guilt dumped itself on her, pinning her to the spot. She was disloyal. Ungrateful. She loved Hilda and Posy, and Edmund wasn't so bad, not really. It was just that his ways were different to Hedley's.

The parlour door was open. She glanced in as she passed. Edmund was reading the paper. Her movement made him glance her way, but she didn't stop. Upstairs, she took off her coat and hat, then came downstairs to the kitchen. This was where you were supposed to live, not in the parlour. She checked the teapot. The old leaves were still inside. She poured in some water and swilled them round, then opened the back door to pour the leaves down the drain – and there was Violet.

The cat's tail went up and she trotted forward. Leonie bent to stroke her – was she thinner?

'Good girl. Wait there. I'll fetch you summat

and then we must get you to your new house.'

She hurried indoors, dumping the teapot and gathering scraps with fingers that fumbled. With the side of her hand, she swept the scraps onto a saucer and went back outside. Violet bumped her head against her before raising herself on her hind legs, sniffing and mewing. Her face was in the saucer before it touched the ground. Poor mite. When did she last eat? There was some ham in the meat safe. Would Hilda notice if a tiny bit went missing?

'Wait there,' she told the cat.

Violet followed her to the door. It was shut. Leonie turned the knob, but nothing happened. She tried again: nothing. She hadn't shut it when she came out – had she?

But it was shut now.

And locked.


It was an ordinary thing to do, wasn't it? Neighbourly. Of course he should pop round and ask after Nell, following the accident yesterday. To knock on her door on his way to clean Mrs Watson's windows: what could be more natural? Jim was certain Nell was fine. She had been level-headed and useful during the event and it was impossible to imagine her falling to pieces afterwards; but his heart wouldn't stop nagging him to make sure. Not that he needed much persuasion. It was only the concern about what the neighbours might say that gave him pause. He hadn't forgotten the nudge-nudge remarks made by the friends who cleaned her house when she moved in. It would take just one clever-clogs to give her a sideways glance and say, 'Jim came round to give you some legal advice, did he?' and she would shut the door on him for ever.

Word had spread quickly about his background. Mrs Watson's Annie was evidently as skilled at sharing other people's business as her mother. He had already been asked a couple of times for advice; he had even been asked to tell off a lad who had broken a window, rather as the local bobby might be asked to do. He didn't mind his knowledge being sought. He just wished he had offered it sooner.

In Wilton Lane, he parked his barrow and knocked on Nell's door. The door opened to reveal a stranger with apples in her cheeks.

He touched his cap. 'Is Mrs Hibbert at home?' At home? Hark at him.

'She's working. You're the window cleaner what fettles for war widows, aren't you? I've seen you about.'

'Yes. Do you know when she'll be back?'

'Nay. I just know I have to get my sewing finished by half-past because that's when Clarrie Dunnett's hour kicks off.'

He flexed his hands inside the roomy leather gloves that became more comfortable the more he wore them, grasped the handles of his barrow and set off for Mrs Watson's. He filled his bucket in her scullery and set to work. He did the front first, then hoisted his ladder onto his shoulder and walked along Finney Lane, round the corner and into the entry that ran between the backs of Finney Lane and Brundretts Lane.

Mrs Watson's gate creaked open. If she had a

spot of oil, he would see to that for her. Setting his ladder against the wall, he climbed up with his bucket, hanging it on the metal hook at the top. He dunked his chamois and reached across.

A movement in the next-door backyard caught his eye, but he affected not to see. He wasn't the nosy type and Mrs Brent wouldn't appreciate being watched on her way to the privy. But when he finished the window, she was still there and she didn't appear to be doing anything, just wandering about, forearms across her stomach, elbows clasped.

He called, 'Mrs Brent, are you all right?'

'Yes, yes, fine.' She turned away, then swung back. 'No, I'm not fine. It's so stupid. I – I'm locked out.'

'Not to worry. I'll come down.'

When he went into the entry, she hadn't opened her gate for him and when he tried it, he found out why.

'I thought you meant you were locked out of the house.'

'I am.'

So she was stuck in the backyard. Odd. 'That's a pickle.' He kept his tone cheery. 'Is the front door unlocked?'

'If it isn't, the key's on a string through the letter box.'

'Do I have your permission to enter the house?' asked the solicitor in him.

'Yes – please.' The crack in her voice pulled at his heart.

'We'll have you inside in two shakes of a lamb's tail.'

He strode round to Finney Lane and tried the front door. It was locked.

'Hey – that's our house. What are you up to, mister?'

He turned to face a group of children of assorted ages, headed by a thin girl with pale fair hair the colour of buttermilk. Her face was narrow and her chin jutted out in a challenging point.

'Are you a burglar?' demanded a ginger-headed lad.

'Don't be soft.' The girl kept her gaze trained on Jim. 'A burglar wouldn't try the door with all of us here. Are you a spy?'

'I'm the window cleaner. You can ask Mrs Watson if you like. Sorry to disappoint,' he added as there was a collective falling of faces. 'I know who you are. You're Mrs Brent's granddaughter, Posy. I've heard about you from Mrs Watson.'

'If you want my dad, he's out. So's Ma, but Gran's in.'

'Your gran is stuck in the backyard. The gate's locked and so is the back door.'

'The back door's never locked during the day unless everyone's out.'

'Well, your gran can't budge it, so I said I'd try the front, but your dad must have locked it when he went out.'

'No, he didn't, not with Gran at home and me playing in the road.'

'See for yourself.' He stepped aside.

'Maybe you didn't use enough gusto.' Posy tried the door. 'It's locked.' She didn't sound surprised so much as indignant. She lifted the letter box flap and pulled out a length of string ... with nothing on the end of it.

'It must have fell off,' said Carrot-Top.

Jim looked up. 'The bedroom window is open. I'll get my ladder.'

There was a surge of interest behind him.

'I'll shin up and climb in,' said Carrot-Top.

'No, you won't,' said Posy. 'It's my house.'

'And it's my ladder and no one goes up it but me,' said Jim. He started off down the road, only to discover how the Pied Piper felt. He turned round. 'You lot stay here and guard the house. You can come with me,' he said to Posy, 'because it's your gran we're rescuing.'

She trotted alongside him. He liked her. She was a sparky little thing. At the end of the entry, she ran ahead to her back gate.

'Are you there, Gran? I'm going to help the man rescue you.'

Jim retrieved his ladder from Mrs Watson's backyard, stopping briefly when Mrs Watson popped out to tell her what was happening.

'Ready, Posy?' He settled the ladder on his shoulder. He seemed to have a dent where it fitted.

'Don't be scared, Gran,' the child called. 'Rescue is at hand. Keep an optimistic heart.'

'You make it sound like she's fallen down a mineshaft,' said Jim.

Round the front once more, he positioned the ladder. As well as the children, various adults had come to watch. He climbed up, grasped the lower edge of the window frame and pushed it upwards. It resisted, then slid up with a shudder. There was a cheer from below.

'What the hell – heck's going on here?' came a

loud, angry voice.

Jim looked down to see a stocky man pushing his way to the front. He lifted his face, revealing a strong, square jaw and a broad brow beneath the shadow of his homburg.

'What are you doing?'

He shook the ladder; Jim made a grab for the window frame. Two or three people stepped forward. A young man in his shirtsleeves took the man's arm and tried to pull him away but was shaken off.

Voices were raised in explanation.

'It's the window cleaner. He's only trying to help–'

'Poor Mrs Brent's stuck in yon backyard with no way in or out–'

'D'you think we'd all be stood here watching someone break in? Do us a favour.'

Jim descended and faced the angry man.

'I take it you live here?'

'I certainly do and I don't take kindly to finding a stranger on the verge of breaking in.'

'He weren't breaking in,' said a couple of voices.

Jim's eyes narrowed as he assessed his opponent – yes, his opponent.

'Sir, you are entitled to be surprised under the circumstances, but you are not entitled to be unreasonable. Several people have attempted to explain the situation, but since you appear not to have heard, I'll explain again. Mrs Brent is locked in the backyard and I sought to gain access so as to let her in.'

'So you say.'

'I do say. Furthermore, Mrs Brent will say so too, since I sought her permission before I acted. My actions have been observed by Posy, Mrs Watson and, from the looks of it, by half of Finney Lane. Any attempt on your part to cast aspersions on my intentions or my integrity will be met by the strongest refutation.'

'Watch it, Tanner,' called a man's voice. 'He was a man of the law before the war did for him.'

'Dad.' Posy appeared at Tanner's side. 'We can't get in. The key's not on the string.'

'Of course it isn't. I have it here. I took it to get a copy cut.' He looked at Jim. 'Stand aside.'

Jim didn't want to give ground to this over-bearing man, but he had no option. At the same moment that he stepped aside, Tanner pushed forwards as if to shove him out of the way. Brute. Tanner unlocked the door. He went inside and turned. Everything in his manner, in the set of his shoulders, in his deliberately casual actions, said this was a fag and a nuisance: Jim's senses spiked.

'Posy!' Tanner's voice was unnecessarily loud. 'Inside.' He didn't even look at her. You wouldn't speak to your dog like that.

Posy scuttled to obey. Her father's gaze swept over the onlookers.

'Thank you all for your concern. I'll see to my mother-in-law now.'

He swung the door shut in Jim's face.

What a mess today was. Nell should have worked at Ingleby's until one and had made arrangements accordingly with Annie; but because of yesterday's events, she had ended up owing time in the sewing department. Annie couldn't keep the children into the afternoon, so Nell had had to dash down the road yesterday evening to prevail upon Mrs Clancy's good nature. Dear Mrs Clancy had cheerfully agreed to take over after Annie's stint. Farming her children out to two minders in one day made Nell feel like a bad mother, and an even worse one when Alf, the moment they came home from Mrs Clancy's, clamoured to have the bath-tub out in the backyard so they could play sea-sides.

'I'm sorry, pie-can, but we have a job to do – all three of us.'

'This isn't job time now. It's playtime.'

Nell sat at the table, lifting Cassie onto her knee. The normally wriggly child was happy to be held: had she spent the day missing her mummy? Nell swallowed another dose of bad mother medicine.

'I wish it could be playtime, but...' She had hoped they would never need to know, but after failing to find Violet yesterday evening, she had to tell them. 'Something has happened to Violet. She's not hurt, but she's got lost, so we have to find her.'

'Vi'let.' Cassie nestled her head under Nell's chin. 'Vi'let.'

Alf frowned. 'If she's lost, how do you know she's not hurt?'

Crikey. 'I don't, not for certain; but cats are clever at looking after themselves, so we have to tell ourselves she's all right.'

'Even though she might not be.'

'If we're going to do a proper search, we need

clear heads. It's no use getting upset about some-thing bad that might not have happened. Can you do that?'

He nodded. 'How did she get lost?'

Because a horrible flaming brute chucked her out of the house, that's how. 'Brick shithouse,' murmured Doug in her head. Mr Brick Shithouse versus defenceless cat: no contest.

'Maybe she went out to play and wandered too far because she was having so much fun.'

'Can we go now?'

'Good idea.'

Giving Cassie one last squeeze, Nell set her down. Cassie wobbled and clung. Nell's heart turned over, but then Cassie sprang to life, de-taching herself and making for the door. Nell couldn't help smiling. She had never been as fit in her life as she had since she started running round after Cassie.

A wild knocking on the front door brought her to her feet.

'Stay here,' she told Alf. 'Hang onto Cassie.'

She hurried down the hallway as another burst of knocking sounded. She threw open the door – and stepped forward instinctively to support Mrs Brent as she almost fell into the house.

'Oh, Nell, oh, Nell. I can't bear it any longer. Can I come and live with you?'

# Chapter Eighteen

'I'm so sorry. This is my fault.' Leonie sat at Nell's kitchen table, supping tea and trying not to splutter as she fought to stem the tears. She knew now that she had been holding them in since the Tanners moved into her house; tears of worry and exhaustion and – yes, go on, admit it – fear. Edmund, her own son-in-law, had moved into her house and pushed her around. That was the truth. She had hidden from it for as long as she could; but even she, stupid old baggage that she was, couldn't pretend any longer.

On top of everything else, she had descended on Nell's home and caused chaos. Her sobbing had scared the children; then, when Nell told them they wouldn't be going out because they had to take care of Mrs Brent, that had set Alf off crying because he wanted to find Violet; and the sight of the two of them blubbing had proved irresistible to Cassie, who had also turned on the waterworks. Nell had mopped up her children and done the only thing she could to get some peace and quiet. She put them outside in the street to play with the other kids, asking Sally Hawkins to keep an eye on them.

'What's happened to get you in such a state?' asked Nell, sinking into the chair beside Leonie. 'You said summat about living here?'

'Aye. I can't stop there no more.'

'Why? Have you had a burst pipe or summat? You can stay here as long as you like, you know that.'

'I don't mean just to stay. I mean, live here ... if you'll have me.'

She buried her nose in the hanky Nell had provided because her own was already saturated. She honked a few times and dragged her ragged breathing under control. She felt weak and shivery and her eyes were raw, but all that was nowt compared to the ache in her chest where her heart was trying to hold itself together and not crack straight down the middle.

'I'm sorry I asked you to move out. I should never have done it. We'd have managed. Look how well you've done since.'

Nell shrugged. 'You wanted your family round you.'

'But what did they want? Not me, that's for certain, just my house.'

'No, surely–'

'Posy loves me, I know that; and I suppose Hilda does.'

'Of course she does.'

'How am I supposed to tell? She does as she's told by Edmund, and when she isn't doing that, she's busy keeping her eyes down, pretending all's right with the world. Well, it isn't.' A surge of indignation made her sit up straight. 'Edmund locked me out; and before you say owt, no, it weren't an accident. He knew I was there. He knew when I went into the backyard to feed Violet.'

'Violet? She's come back?' Nell half-rose as if to

261

rush off and collect her.

'Nay, she scarpered again.' Was Nell about to abandon her in favour of the cat?

'We'll search for her later,' said Nell. 'Go on.'

'Edmund locked the back door and went out; and because he'd left the back gate locked an' all, I were stuck in't yard. You may well look shocked. I were pretty ruddy shocked myself. Anyroad, your window cleaner chap came round next door and he saw me.'

'Jim Franks.' Nell looked pleased, then rather cool. 'Yes, I can imagine him helping.'

'He went round the front, but Edmund had locked up and taken the key with him, so Jim took his ladder round the front–'

'It's Jim now, is it?'

'It most certainly is, after what he did for me today. Anyroad, Edmund came home while Jim were up the ladder. There were an almighty row, according to our Posy. Edmund came through and unlocked the back door. He says he had no idea I was home, but I know he did.'

'Why would he lock you out?'

'He wants rid of me. He's done things to make me unhappy.'

'Didn't you stop him?'

'You make it sound like it's my fault.' Doubt assailed her. Was it? 'All I wanted was a happy home, so I gave way at every turn. Only it didn't feel like giving way ... not until afterwards, when it were too late. I agreed to all kinds. Like when my things were moved upstairs. It seemed only fair to make room for their things, but now there's barely anything of mine left in't parlour.'

'That's not right,' Nell said quietly, 'not in your own house.'

But it wasn't her house any more, was it? It was Edmund's name on the rent book But she had never admitted that to Nell.

There was a knock at the front door. Hilda? Come to see if she was all right? That would make up for a lot. She followed Nell down the hall. The door opened, not on Hilda, but on Jim, with Cassie sitting upright and alert on one arm and Alf on his shoulders, legs dangling down his chest.

Jim smiled at Nell, touching his cap. 'Is this your lost property?' He handed Cassie over and lifted Alf down. 'I was oiling Mrs Watson's back gate and I found these two in the entry. Alf said they were looking for the cat.'

Nell sucked in a breath. 'Alf, you know not to wander off. I'll swing for that Sally Hawkins.'

'No harm done,' said Jim. He touched Alf's sandy hair. 'Always tell your mum where you're going in future.' He stuck out his hand. 'Shake on it?' Instead of taking the hand the small boy eagerly offered, he said, 'Shaking hands means we have a contract; and you must never break a contract.'

The sight of the little boy and the man solemnly shaking hands warmed Leonie in spite of how shaken she was, or possibly because of it. Jim Franks was a good man, and if he wasn't married with children, then he jolly well ought to be. He was born to be a dad, this one.

'We've got a pot of tea on the go,' she said. 'Why don't you come in?'

'I'm sure Mr Franks has things to do,' said Nell, turning to glare at her privately.

'Nonsense. He's been good enough to bring your children home; and I never got the chance to thank him for what he did for me.' Her throat tightened as the emotion came rushing back. 'My granddaughter tells me you got the door slammed in your face for your trouble.'

He shrugged. 'You're fine; that's what matters.'

'Come in,' said Nell. She sounded warmer now, more her usual self.

Leonie returned to her seat as Alf said, 'We tried to find Violet, but she wasn't there.'

'I'm vexed with you, young man,' said Nell, 'but just now the grown-ups need to have a conversation.'

'I happen to have about my person...' Jim delved in his pocket. 'Here we are: a couple of marbles. These are not for putting in mouths. They are especially not for putting up noses. If you promise not to do anything disgusting with them, you may play with them on the floor.'

With the children happily occupied, the adults sat round the table.

'I trust you're none the worse for your experience, Mrs Brent,' said Jim. He had a lovely way with words.

'I'm very much the worse, as it happens. I'm here to ask Nell – Mrs Hibbert – the biggest favour I've ever asked anyone.'

'Should you...?' said Nell.

'Wash my dirty linen in public?'

'If you ladies have something private to discuss...' Jim started to get up.

'Sit down, lad. If I come to live here, the world and his wife will know soon enough.'

'Of course you can come here, if you need to,' said Nell. 'But – that's your house. I know they're your family, but if things have gone badly wrong, you must ask them to look for another place.'

'I don't know what's going on,' said Jim, 'but if someone is making life hard for you in your house...'

They thought it was that simple. Tell Edmund to sling his hook. End of problem. A knot formed in Leonie's belly.

'I can't. Even if I could, I wouldn't do it to Hilda and Posy. But I can't. It in't my name on the rent book any more. It's Edmund's.' The knot tightened. She looked at Nell, afraid of seeing scorn, but the compassion and disbelief she saw was worse. 'I never told you because I knew you wouldn't like it; and you'd have been right. Please don't say *I told you so*.'

And Nell, bless her, kissed her cheek. Leaving her face close to Leonie's, she whispered, 'The only thing I'm going to say is, how soon can you move in?'

'Mother, don't do this. It was an accident.'

'Pull the other one, it's got bells on.' But Leonie only muttered it; she didn't say it out loud. She didn't want to make things worse. Worse? As if anything could make it worse. Widowed mothers were meant to live with their daughters, and here she was, about to up sticks and move in with her old lodger. She bustled about her bedroom – nay, not her bedroom. Her bedroom was the front

265

room, hers and Hedley's. This was Hilda's old room and after Hilda married, it became the lodger's room. Say what you liked about families budging up and making room for one another, but there was something shaming about ending your days in your old lodger's room.

'I've got Posy downstairs in floods of tears,' said Hilda.

Leonie stopped in the middle of folding her Sunday best blouse. Poor Posy, poor little love. If anything could make her stay, it was Posy. But Edmund had come here, determined to get rid of her – she saw that now – and he had succeeded. Not even for her precious Posy could she stop another night under this roof.

'I'll explain to Posy.' Her voice shook, betraying her.

'You won't say that Edmund–'

'What d'you take me for? I'm not out to cause trouble. You know me better than that.'

'Aye, I'm sorry.'

'So you should be.' Dropping the blouse on the bed, she grasped Hilda's hands. 'Eh, love, don't let's you and me fall out.'

'You don't have to leave,' said Hilda. 'Locking you out was an accident. Edmund's apologised.'

She returned to her packing. Oh aye, Edmund's apology. Her blood boiled. Edmund's apology, in that smooth, rich voice; the voice that used to make her feel safe and cared for. It wasn't the warm tone of kindness. It was the sound of complacency, because he had succeeded. Did Hilda really not know? Was she that stupid?

Leonie's throat was fastened so tight, she had to

move her jaw from side to side before she could speak. 'It's best I go.'

'You're being stubborn. This is your home. We want you here.'

'You might, and Posy does, but Edmund wants me gone.'

Hilda looked away, colour flooding her face. She practically dived through the door. Her footsteps sounded on the stairs; then her voice saying, 'Posy – no – leave Gran alone,' followed by a rapid patter of steps, and Posy burst in; but instead of throwing herself into Leonie's ready arms, she halted, eyes huge and brimming, face white.

'You're going. You're leaving. Please don't. I want you here.'

Leonie put her arms round her, but for the first time in her life, Posy didn't mould herself to fit snugly against her grandmother's body. She stood, stiff and miserable, not responding. Leonie felt a swell of pain. Had she lost her beloved grand-daughter? She didn't let go. With a hand cupping the back of Posy's head, she spoke into the child's ear.

'I'm only going to Wilton Lane. You can come and see me whenever you like and I can come here.'

Posy pushed free. She swallowed hard, but the light of battle was in her eye. 'Why are you going?'

She must protect Posy from the truth at all costs. 'To help Mrs Hibbert with the children. It's difficult for her, going out to work. You've got Ma here all the time.' Should she back down, ask Edmund and Hilda if she could stay?

But she couldn't stay. Not with Edmund. He

267

had won.

Pushing the suitcase across the bed, she sat down. She patted the space beside her, but Posy stayed put.

'I can't live here, Posy. I ... I miss Gramps too much.'

'It's Dad, isn't it? You want to get away from Dad.'

Surprise skittered over her skin. So much for protecting the child.

'I knew if we came here, something would happen,' said Posy. 'I knew he'd ... oh well.'

'Me and your dad–'

'I could come with you.'

'Sweetheart, you wouldn't be allowed.'

'I know that. But you could stay here with me.'

Posy was the one thing in the whole world that could make her stay. Posy needed her, wanted her. How could she leave?

How could she stay?

'I have to go,' she whispered.

Posy nodded. 'I know.'

And that was worse than if she had burst out sobbing.

Jim parked his barrow, unloaded the tea chests and knocked on the door. Curious stares came his way from a group of women chatting in the street; he gave them a polite smile and turned to the door as it opened. A woman stood there. She had a faded look about her, as if she was past her best. Could this be the mother of sparky little Posy?

He touched his cap. 'Mrs Tanner? I've brought

boxes for Mrs Brent.'

She leant out to look up and down the road. Catching sight of the neighbours, she drew back. 'She asked for boxes? Does everybody know?'

'You'd have to ask Mrs Brent that, but I don't think so.' What sort of woman was she to let things reach such a pitch that her own mother felt impelled to move out? 'Should I take them upstairs?'

'Hilda, who's at the door?'

Jim's spine stiffened. The parlour door opened and Tanner appeared.

'You again,' said Tanner.

His eyes flared, then narrowed. He covered the few steps to the door and stood in the doorway, his wife slinking into the background. Tanner threw back his shoulders as if squaring up for a fight. He was a big bloke. Not tall but thickset.

'Clear off,' he said. The words were uttered with a sneer. 'You've done enough damage for one day.'

Jim kept his voice mild. 'Firstly, I have done no damage. I did only what Mrs Brent asked me to do. Secondly, I will indeed clear off, and with pleasure, once I have delivered these boxes to her. Is she upstairs?'

'You won't set foot in my house.'

'Suits me. I'll pile the boxes here, shall I?'

Tanner looked him up and down. 'Aye, you do that, then I'll carry them up. My mother-in-law knows that I only want what she wants.'

'Is that so?' Jim loaded the words with disbelief.

Tanner smiled, his vexation wiped away. 'I made a mistake today and I have apologised several times. Even so, my mother-in-law has decided to live elsewhere, regardless of the pain this causes her daughter and grandchild. It is my belief that the best thing I can do is allow her to go, so that calm can be restored to my house ... though it will be a sad sort of calm.'

Clever bastard. Jim had to hand it to him. He had covered his back and no mistake.

'So, if you'll unload the boxes, you can...' He leant forward as if to confide. His voice dropped, the words for Jim's ears alone. '...bugger off and mind your own damn business in future.'

Jim took a step backwards, disgusted with the fellow. Tanner had had the last word. For now.

He unloaded the tea chests and Tanner carried them in and shut the door. How was Mrs Brent faring inside? Jim didn't mind taking a few verbal knocks himself, but was Tanner leaving her alone?

Carrot-Top appeared by his side. 'Mrs Watson went in to see Mrs Brent and she says she's packing to leave. Are you moving her? Where's she going?'

'Wilton Lane. A hop and a skip away. If Posy's upset, you can remind her of that to cheer her up.'

'Aye. She might be upset. She loves her gran.'

Jim waited what seemed a reasonable time, then knocked. No one came, but he wouldn't give Tanner the satisfaction of knocking a second time. He folded his arms, leant one shoulder against the wall, crossed one ankle over the other with the toe of his boot on the ground, and started whistling 'Lily of Laguna'. He had got as far as 'I know she likes me, I know she likes me, because she said so,' for the second time before the door opened.

'I didn't hear you knock,' said Mrs Tanner, not meeting his eyes.

'Is Mrs Brent ready? Shall I carry her boxes down or would Mr Tanner prefer to do it?'

'He said to go up. It's the back bedroom.'

Mrs Brent looked exhausted, poor old girl. He wanted to hug her, but all he could do was carry her possessions outside. He stood the first tea chest on the pavement and called Carrot-Top over.

'Sixpence says you'll guard Mrs Brent's boxes and not let anyone look inside.'

He flipped a tanner at the lad and returned upstairs for the next box.

'Is there any furniture to go?' he asked when the boxes were outside.

'The hanging cupboard and the chest of drawers. Nell hasn't got much in the way of bedroom furniture, so we can make use of these. But the bed is staying put. I'm not leaving Posy without a bed. I've told Edmund that when he buys her one, I'll have mine taken to Wilton Lane.'

'You look shattered,' he said gently.

'I am, and not just in my body. I can't believe this is happening.'

'Are you sure you want to leave?'

'Want to? *Want* to?' She was clinging to her self-control by a thread. 'Just get my things and go.'

'I'll need help with the furniture.'

He ran downstairs. The parlour door was closed. He knocked, opening it at the same time.

271

He felt like barging in and grabbing Tanner by the throat, but he wouldn't let Tanner accuse him of not having knocked.

'Shall you give me a hand with the furniture or should I fetch a neighbour?'

Tanner helped him and they loaded the barrow.

Mrs Brent appeared at the front door. At the sight of the barrow, she covered her mouth with her hand.

Jim went to stand beside her. 'Is there more furniture?'

She looked at him helplessly. 'Most of it's mine, but I can't take it, not until those rooms in Wilton Lane are dried out properly. Anyroad, I wouldn't leave Hilda and Posy without.'

'But you will take what's yours in the end?'

'We'll see.' She closed her eyes. 'I can't think about it now. It's too much.'

'I'll take the barrow now and come back for the boxes. Do you want to come with me?'

'What, now?' She looked startled. 'No, I... Not yet. My coat's hanging on the bedroom door.'

Jim's heart ached for her. He had seen this before. In the war, when men were overwhelmed, they sometimes latched onto a trifling detail as if it had the greatest significance. Focusing on that enabled them to blunder on through the horror.

'I'll be back before you know it.'

He trundled the barrow round to Mrs Brent's new home, then he returned to Finney Lane. A couple of men from across the road helped load the tea chests onto the barrow.

Jim knocked and Posy opened the door. He found Mrs Brent upstairs, almost in a trance, gazing round the room, evidently too drained to think what to do next. Jim fastened the suitcase.

'Come along,' he encouraged the tormented lady. 'Time to go.'

He descended the stairs ahead of her, braced to break her fall should she stumble. The Tanners were in the hall, dressed for going out. Jim followed them outside.

'Will you be much longer?' Tanner demanded.

'There are still a few things upstairs,' said Jim.

'We can't wait. We must get to the second-hand furniture shop to look for a cupboard for Posy's bedroom.'

'Before you go,' Jim said quietly.

He glanced round. Mrs Brent was where he had left her in the hall, gazing round, raw pain etched into every line of her body. Jim drew Tanner aside and spoke for his ears alone.

'Here's a piece of free legal advice. Even though Mrs Brent is quitting this house, the furniture she is leaving behind remains her property. If there is any damage to it, or if it is not returned to her when she requires it, I'll see you in the magistrates' court.'

Tanner broke away from him and addressed Mrs Brent.

'We'll say goodbye now, Mother-in-law. Are you sure there's nothing I can do to persuade you to change your mind? No? Then I wish you well in your new home. Come along, Hilda, Posy. No tearful farewells. She's only going to Wilton Lane.' He made as if to go, then turned back. 'Kindly lock up behind you, Mother-in-law, and leave the key on the string. I wouldn't want you taking it

273

with you by mistake.'

With his wife on one arm and his daughter on the other, off he went.

Jim made a couple of final trips up and down the stairs and finished loading his barrow.

Mrs Brent walked through the front door in a daze. It wouldn't have surprised him had she dropped to the pavement in a dead faint. Then her face changed, her chin hardened and she darted back inside. Great Scott, she wasn't going to take possession of the house in the Tanners' absence, was she?

She knelt on the staircase, fiddling with something. She pulled free one of the stair rods, marched out of the house and thrust it into his astonished hands.

'Get rid of this for me.'

'Mrs Brent–?'

She tramped away without a backwards glance.

'Why that man isn't married is a mystery to me,' said Mrs Brent.

Nell looked at her over the mugs of Ovaltine they were sharing before bed, or rather, she was drinking from a mug; Mrs Brent had her harebell teacup and saucer. Her special china that had lived in her own kitchen for umpteen years was now in Nell's house. Eh, just when you thought life had thrown everything at you...

'How do you know he isn't married?' Nell asked.

'He doesn't wear a ring.'

She snorted. 'That doesn't mean owt.' Even when a man did wear a ring, it needn't mean owt.

Look at Stan. One ring, two wives.

'Anyroad, I asked him.'

Nell removed the mug from her lips without taking a sip. 'You never!'

'I weren't obvious. I asked if his wife would mind him being home late because of helping me.'

'Oh aye, very subtle.'

'It's different if someone my age asks. And it is a shame, Jim not being married.'

'I hope you aren't hinting anything.'

'You must admit, he's a good 'un.'

'He's been a good friend to me and the kids; a good friend to you an' all, now.'

A good friend, and that was all he could ever be. Never mind that her skin felt tingly and glowing in his company. Never mind that funny little flip her heart did. Never mind that he was solid and dependable, that he thought of ways to help and went out of his way to do you a good turn. Never mind that the children adored him. She almost wished he would let her down ... just so he wouldn't seem so right for her.

Nell put down her mug. 'Have you finished? Let's go to bed.'

'I'll wash up.'

'I'll do it. You must be dead beat.'

'I didn't come here for you to run round after me. I'll pull my weight.'

Nell grinned. 'You wait until tomorrow. I'll give you a list of jobs as long as your arm. Seriously, it'll be a big help, having you here.'

'I hope child-minding is at the top of your list. I can't offer much by way of rent, but I can pay my way through other means.'

'I won't pretend a spot of rent won't go amiss, but you aren't a lodger. You practically brought up my children while I was at the factory. You're family.'

Mrs Brent's eyes gleamed with tears. 'After everything that's happened ... after the way I threw you out.'

'You didn't throw us out.'

'One week's notice...'

'That's forgotten. I know it's rotten, leaving your Hilda and Posy, but you've got family here an' all, if it isn't cheeky of me to say so.'

'Cheeky? There's nowt you could have said to make me more welcome. And ... here's a piece of cheek, if you please.' Mrs Brent pressed her lips into a line, looking uncertain. 'You said family just now, so can I stop being Mrs Brent? Can I be ... Aunt Leonie?'

Warmth cascaded through Nell in a series of tiny bursts. 'I'd love that. Can the children call you "Aunt" as well?'

'I always wanted to be Nana, but when our Posy came along, Edmund said I was Gran. Could they call me Nana? Only it must be Nana Leonie to show I'm not their real nana, so Posy isn't pushed out.'

'That'll be perfect.'

'Perfect? You think so?' Mrs Brent – Aunt Leonie spread her fingers across her throat. 'I've lost my home, driven out by my own son-in-law. Should I have stood my ground? I tried, honestly, I tried, but in the end... What have I done, Nell? What have I done?'

# Chapter Nineteen

She must go through the motions of ordinary everyday life – ordinary? That was a joke. It would never be ordinary again. Yes, it would, Leonie tried to reassure herself, though her ears rang with panic. Given time, this new life would become normal and acceptable. It must. Until then, she must be cheery, helpful and sensible. She could manage that – couldn't she?

She and Nell spent most of Sunday unpacking.

'It's lovely to have your things here,' said Nell. 'It makes this house feel like home, Aunt Leonie.'

Nell called her Aunt Leonie at every opportunity, and Leonie knew this was to make her feel welcome, but would she ever feel anything again, other than stunned and sick and disbelieving? Even her muscles were overwhelmed. They were sore and sluggish. Everything was an effort.

On Monday Nell went to work, setting off early because she was in Ingleby's today, and Leonie looked after the children. She delivered Alf to school, then took Cassie round the shops.

'Eh, is it true you've moved in with Nell Hibbert?' she was asked a dozen times.

'That's right,' she answered, 'and I'm glad my Hilda and our Posy have my old house to live in. It's a lucky house, that is.'

Aye, ruddy lucky for Edmund Tanner. Give up two rooms and a scullery, move into a nice two-up two-down, install yourself in the parlour, get your name on the rent book and Bob's your uncle.

She spent the morning baking. The house filled with the scent of ginger and apples and sugar. Her house had always smelt of baking, of pastry and onions and warm, juicy fruit. And herbs. She must start again with a few herbs. Edmund had taken her to pieces bit by bit. She had to rebuild herself. She needed chives to sprinkle on smoked haddock flan, rosemary to add a tang to her roast potatoes. The thought of cooking and baking gave her a little boost. No, it didn't, because she was in the wrong kitchen.

That afternoon, she summoned all her self-control and returned to Finney Lane. She didn't walk in. It stung not to walk through her front door of forty years, but she didn't. She knocked and waited for Hilda to do the honours. Hilda was embarrassed. Well, so she rotten well should be.

No, she mustn't get bitter, not against Hilda. This was Edmund's doing.

'Did you have to bring the little one?' Hilda asked.

Leonie promptly dumped Cassie on the floor to run amok. 'I'm minding her. I must keep an eye on the time so I'm not late fetching Alf from school. I can fetch Posy an' all.'

'She doesn't need fetching.'

'It'll give me the chance to see her. I want to see you and Posy as much as I can. You still want to see me, don't you?'

'Do you need to ask?'

Well, yes, she did, but she couldn't say so.

They had a pleasant chat after that, a bit stilted in places, but that was only to be expected; and later, when Posy saw her at the school railings, she hurled herself at her, not minding at all that she had come to collect Alf. Posy was such an easy child.

And to prove it, when they were back in Wilton Lane, Posy offered, 'I'll bring Alf home for you in future. That way, I can come and see you every day.'

Was there ever a dearer child than this? Leonie looked round to make sure neither of the Hibberts was in earshot. 'On Fridays, I'll have a quarter of caramels waiting. One each for you three children and one for you to take home for Saturday. It'll be our secret.'

'You're a marvel,' said Posy. 'I wish – never mind.'

'I wish an' all, but things are the way they are.'

'What about the fifth caramel? Will you have it? You should, as thanks for being a marvel.'

'I think Mrs Hibbert should have it. She's a marvel an' all.'

'She's your marvel,' said Posy, 'and you're my marvel.'

And right then, with Posy's eyes shining at her, full of love, Leonie was a marvel. She tried to cling to the feeling, but soon she felt like a wrung-out dishcloth again. But Nell had made her welcome, and she was on reasonable terms with Hilda, and Posy loved her. Count your blessings.

Tomorrow she would pop in on Mrs Watson. They had lived next door to one another all these years and been good neighbours. But she wouldn't go during the day; she didn't want to be accused of haunting Finney Lane. She would go in the evening. She and Mrs Watson often used to snatch a quiet hour together in the old days when the kids were in bed and their husbands were enjoying a pint, and they had carried on with their evening visits once or twice a week until Hedley was so ill, so dropping round was something she would have done anyroad.

Except that, if she had stayed in her old house, she wouldn't have done it any more, because Edmund had wanted her in the parlour of an evening.

All the more reason to do it now.

Nell was out and about all Tuesday; and that evening, a neighbour came for a lesson, which made it a good time for Leonie to visit her old neighbour. Walking down Finney Lane, she kept enough of a smile on her lips to make her look pleasant and untroubled. Folk must be dying to tattle about how miserable she was and how awful the Tanners were, but if they did, it would be none of her doing.

Her smile froze as her old front door opened and the Tanners spilt out.

'Gran!' called Posy.

'Good evening, Mother-in-law,' said Edmund. He sounded pleased to see her. He could afford to be pleased, couldn't he, now he had got shot of her.

'Were you coming to see us?' asked Hilda.

'No, but I'm glad to catch you. There are some things of mine still in the house.'

280

'Only the furniture,' said Edmund, 'and I understand it's staying until such time as Mrs Hibbert's house is no longer riddled with damp.'

'It isn't riddled with damp.' Leonie stopped. She mustn't rise to the bait. 'Some small things were left behind, the ones you took into safekeeping.'

'Oh, those, yes. Don't worry. They're secure where they are.'

'I'd like to have them back.'

'What do you say, Hilda? It was worrying when your mother sold that vase, that heirloom, for no good reason.' Edmund's brow crinkled into a friendly frown. 'Trust me, Mother-in-law. We had to put those items into safekeeping because you were upset and it made you unreliable. Who knows what else you'd have sold?'

Her ribs squeezed her heart so hard they nearly smothered it. 'I'm not upset now.'

He laughed indulgently. 'Upset enough to move out. Let us do this for you. All we care about is what's right for Gran – hey, Posy?'

Posy nodded. 'Yes, Dad.' Did she think her father was acting for the best?

Leonie summoned up a brave smile specially for Posy. 'Are you going for a walk?'

'Would you care to join us, Mother-in-law?' Edmund offered.

'Another time.' When hell froze over. 'I'm on my way to Mrs Watson's.'

'Perhaps you'll call on us next time,' said Edmund. 'There's always room for you at my table.'

At his table? His table? Hedley bought that kitchen table in 1887. The drop-leaf table in the parlour was hers an' all, inherited from Auntie

Mary. The only table Edmund owned was the one they had brought with them from Withington; but she couldn't say so, because she needed to keep on good terms with Hilda and she wanted to keep everything smooth and easy for Posy.

Nay, that wasn't the reason. Well, it was, up to a point. The real reason was because Edmund would get the better of her. He would get the better of anyone.

It was wonderful having Leonie living with them. Sad, obviously, when you thought of how it had happened; but even so ... wonderful. Nell felt guilty for appreciating it so much when Leonie was in such a distressing situation, but she couldn't help herself. In the weeks since she and the children left Finney Lane, child-minding arrangements had taken up residence at the forefront of her mind and she had farmed Alf and Cassie out non-stop, or so it seemed. If she wasn't hurrying them round to Annie's, she was rushing them down the road to Mrs Clancy's; so unlike the past two years with the Brents, when they had been cared for without leaving the house.

Now, with Leonie in their little household, the children already had a settled routine, and this was only the second Monday. Nell felt settled too. She might even stop feeling like a bad mother.

But what a price Leonie had paid. Nell hoped that the children's devotion would help her come to terms with her new life.

Alf had stumbled over the name Nana Leonie

the first few times, but now rattled it off so quickly Leonie said, 'You make me sound like an Italian ice-cream seller,' and 'Oh, Oh, Antonio' became their new bedtime song, with Alf jubilantly bellowing the final line, 'Then up will go Antonio and his ICE-CREAM CART.'

'Hm,' said Nell wryly, 'it's not exactly a lullaby, is it?'

'You won't go away, will you, Nanaleonie?' begged Alf. 'Not like Antonio and his ice-cream cart.'

Nell and Leonie exchanged glances.

'No, pie-can.' Leonie tucked him in. 'I'm here to stay.'

Nell spent Wednesday's half-day closing with Mrs Liversedge's friend Miss Vine, who was eager for private tuition. It was a shame to miss her afternoon off, but earning extra was important too; and with all due respect to Annie, she felt better about leaving the children with Leonie, her adopted aunt.

Miss Vine's lesson went well and Nell returned home feeling heartened. She greeted the children with hugs and dropped a kiss on Leonie's cheek. Leonie put her fingers to her skin and Nell couldn't tell if she was pleased or not.

'I hope you don't mind, only if my mum lived here, I'd kiss her; and you're my aunt now.'

Leonie smiled, a proper smile that plumped her cheeks and crinkled her eyes, not the brave, empty smile that Nell had seen too many times since she moved in ten days ago.

'This came by the one o'clock post.' Leonie

reached for a postcard. It was a couple of lines from Miss Collier, dated *Wednesday 9 a.m.*

*Please attend this afternoon to explain the item in yesterday's Evening News. I will expect you at 4 o'clock.*

'Four o'clock?' Nell glanced at Leonie's carriage clock that stood on the kitchen mantelpiece, though she didn't need to look. She knew it was gone five.

'I didn't know what to do. I knew you were going straight from Mrs Edge Lane to your new lady.'

Nell tried to shrug it off. 'It's my afternoon off. They can't expect me to be at home to collect the post. I'm due in the sewing department tomorrow, so I'll see her then.'

But she felt uncomfortable. She hadn't been here because she had been teaching her first truly private client. Her conscience gave a twinge. Why was she required at such short notice, anyroad?

'What does she mean about yesterday's *Evening News?*' Oh no. 'Unless…'

'What?' asked Leonie.

'Mrs Edge Lane's son is a journalist. He wanted to write about that accident; and he knows my name because I teach his mother; but what could he have written that…?' She waved the postcard. 'This sounds disapproving.'

'Oh,' said Leonie.

Nell looked at her.

'I'm sure he won't have written owt unflattering about you. I mean, how could he?' Leonie looked flushed. Bless her for being indignant.

There was a knock at the door. Nell opened it to find Jim. Now it was her turn to flush as her heart took the next few beats at a sprint.

'Evening.' He touched his cap. 'I saw you in the paper yesterday.'

She had to know. 'Did it say anything un-flattering?'

'On the contrary, it sang your praises. Haven't you seen it? I'd have brought my copy round if I'd known. I've come to see how Mrs Brent has settled in.'

'Come in.' She led the way. 'Aunt Leonie, look who's here.'

'Aunt Leonie?' he questioned.

'We've decided to be family.'

'Good for you, though I shouldn't be surprised, after that newspaper piece.'

'What do you mean?' asked Nell.

'I'll tell you later,' said Leonie. 'Tea, Jim?'

'If it's convenient.' He glanced at Nell, seeking agreement.

'Have a seat,' she offered.

'Thanks. How are you, Mrs Brent?'

'Oh, you know, getting used to things.'

'Moving house is a big undertaking.'

'And it's not over yet,' said Leonie. 'Once this place has been repaired, I'll bring my furniture – not all of it, that wouldn't be fair on Hilda, but we'll get this place fixed up nice.' She poured his tea. 'But I've left some things behind. Do you remember my musical box, Nell? And my pretty cake stand? Some other bits and bobs an' all.'

'I'll fetch them,' Jim offered.

Leonie bit her lip. 'It's not that simple. Edmund

took them into safekeeping, because I sold a vase. He said it would stop me selling owt else.'

'He took your possessions?' Nell couldn't believe it. Or maybe she could. This was Edmund Tanner they were talking about.

'The vase you sold was your own property, I assume? And Mr Tanner knew it was your property?'

Suddenly they had a solicitor at their table. No longer Jim Franks, the well-spoken window cleaner, but Mr Franks the solicitor, crisply spoken, with an intentness in his eyes that showed he was taking in every word. Nell's heart swelled ... and then shrank. She had no business being attracted to the likes of him. He might be living out of his class now, but he wouldn't stay here. She was a fool to like him in that way.

Not to mention the small matter of not being quite as widowed as she might be.

His face, which she had only ever seen genial and smiling, set in grim lines as he asked, 'Have you requested the return of these items?'

'Yesterday. Edmund said he would keep them for now.'

'Did he provide a reason?'

'He said moving out proved I were still upset.' Leonie's voice hitched.

'Did he indeed?' He came to his feet, tall and serious. 'With your permission, Mrs Brent, I'll pay a call on Mr Tanner and discuss the legal situation with him.'

Leonie gazed at him admiringly and Nell felt an unexpected flicker of annoyance. Yes, Jim Franks had proved himself a good friend, but that didn't mean they should lean on him. It was different for Leonie; she had had a good husband and maybe she found it natural to depend on a man; but that hadn't been Nell's experience. Her marriage had taught her to stand on her own two feet.

'I don't think that's the right thing to do,' she said. 'Sending you round is bound to cause bad feeling. Aunt Leonie doesn't want to fall out with her Hilda.'

Leonie sighed. 'It's only a few things. I can live without them.'

'Let's you and me go and have a word,' said Nell. 'He won't find it so easy to fob off both of us.'

'Thanks, Jim,' said Leonie. 'I still might need your help if ... well, you know.'

'Just say the word.' He hesitated. 'Do you know Riley's Farm, along Beech Road? There's a row of cottages behind and I live in the one furthest from the road. My landlady is Mrs Jeffrey. If you need assistance for any reason, that's where you'll find me.'

What a generous man he was. A true gentleman, decent and considerate and ready to do the right thing. If she had found a husband like him, how different her life would have been.

'Thank you,' she said, careful to be cool. 'I'll see you out, then I'll pop next door and ask Mrs O'Rourke to sit with the children.'

In a few minutes, she and Leonie were on their way to Finney Lane, taking a roundabout route in the hope of spotting Violet. The lingering warmth made it a pleasant evening, or would have done.

Honestly, Edmund Tanner was the limit.

With a nod of encouragement for Leonie, she knocked on the door. Hilda answered it. Good. She would be on her mother's side, wouldn't she?

'Evening. Me and your mum–'

'*You!*' exclaimed Hilda. 'I don't know how you have the brass neck to come here.'

Nell caught her breath. Was this because she had peered over their back gate?

'Hilda, what's the matter?' asked Leonie.

'As if you didn't know.'

'Hilda, who is it?' Edmund Tanner appeared. He stepped into the doorway, but instead of squeezing Hilda aside, he put an arm around her shoulders. 'I don't know how you have the nerve.'

'What's this about?' Nell asked.

'I'm not addressing you,' he replied contemptuously. 'You're the one who has come between my wife and her mother. I'm speaking to my mother-in-law. I hadn't read the *Evening News* when we saw you yesterday, but I've read it since and I'm disgusted. Flaunting your admiration for this creature for all of Manchester to read about, and never mind what you owe your family.'

'Edmund–' Leonie began.

'What was it you said? *She's another daughter to me,* wasn't it?'

'I never ... did I?'

'You were quoted and poor Hilda can't hold her head up again in public. Go away, the pair of you. Come inside, Hilda. They're not worth it.'

Usually Nell enjoyed walking along Market Street first thing in the morning when she started her working day at Ingleby's. The road was quiet apart from shopworkers like herself; and the early sunshine glinted on the vast windows behind which wares were tastefully displayed. There was no end of red, white and blue at present, because of the British Empire Exhibition down in London; but she didn't waste time admiring anything. She wanted to reach Ingleby's early, as evidence of her keenness to explain to Miss Collier why she hadn't come yesterday at four. She didn't know what Miss Collier would say about the piece in the paper. Jim had called it flattering, but perhaps Ingleby's took exception to an employee appearing in print. She would have to make it clear she hadn't sought the publicity.

She was vexed with Walter Marsden for cornering Leonie and asking questions, and she wasn't best pleased with Leonie for answering them, though she hadn't had the heart to say so to her friend. Poor Leonie had been beside herself last night.

'I never called you a second daughter. It would be disrespectful to Hilda. I'm sure I didn't say it.' But her fidgety hands and wrinkled forehead showed she wasn't certain. 'Edmund sounded so sure.'

'We need to read that article for ourselves.'

Nell had knocked on one or two doors where she knew they took the evening paper, but each time she got a similar response before she could ask.

'Are you still looking for your cat? We've looked in our coal hole and she's not there. Sorry we can't help.'

She hadn't liked to ask for the paper after that in case it looked like she didn't care about Violet.

'Aunt Leonie.' She had felt rotten for asking when Leonie was preoccupied and distressed, but she needed to know. 'What else did you tell Walter Marsden?'

'Nothing you should worry about. It was all good.'

'I'm sure it was, but it would help me to know before I see Miss Collier.'

Leonie sighed. 'About being my lodger, and working at Ingleby's, that sort of thing; and how much I admire you. But I'm sure I never called you a second daughter. I'll never forgive myself.'

That was as much as Nell had been able to glean. It didn't seem to warrant that disapproving postcard; or had it been disapproving? Had she mistaken professional formality for censure?

She turned down the side street that provided access to the backs of the row of shops. The door-man let her in. There were various cloakrooms. Which you used depended on whether you were male or female and how important you were. Nell hung up her jacket and hat and stowed her hand-bag inside her small cupboard, taking out her shop shoes. As well as the shoes Ingleby's had provided for her to wear while out and about, they had also given her – sold her – a pair to wear inside the shop.

There were common rooms on the other side of the corridor. Most people would be having a final sit-down and a chat before presenting themselves at eight forty-five sharp in their various depart-ments for their appearance to be inspected and the day's duties to be allocated, but Nell went in search of Miss Collier, knowing she and Miss Moore would already be in the department.

She found them deep in conversation over some paperwork, but not so deep that they didn't glance her way. They didn't acknowledge her, just carried on talking, making her wait. Keeping her in her place.

When Miss Moore moved off, Nell approached Miss Collier.

'Good morning, Mrs Hibbert. You're late.' Miss Collier lifted the gold timepiece pinned to her blouse. 'Sixteen hours and thirty-five minutes, to be precise. I expected you yesterday at four.'

'I'm sorry, but I wasn't in when your postcard arrived. I didn't see it until after five.'

'You were out all afternoon?

Her heart bumped. Was this the moment to confess?

'Were you by any chance teaching a private pupil?'

Nell's cheeks burnt. If only she had spoken up instead of hesitating. Now she looked deceitful. Well, she had been deceitful, hadn't she?

'I don't expect to read about my sewing machine demonstrators in the newspaper. I particularly don't expect to read about the private work they are doing. I take it from your silence that what I read was correct.'

'I haven't read the article myself, but if it referred to private teaching, then ... yes.'

Miss Collier withdrew to the office, signalling her to follow. Miss Collier took a seat. There was another chair but Nell wasn't offered it. It was

291

like being hauled into the headmaster's office.

'Tell me,' snapped Miss Collier.

Nell gave details of the additional teaching she had provided for which ladies, but she didn't mention Miss Vine. She was in enough trouble already without admitting to this fresh way of branching out.

Miss Collier made a note of the ladies' names, as if they too would be sent for to have their knuckles rapped. 'Unfortunately, nowhere in your contract does it say that you may not take on private pupils; though, believe me, any future contracts for demonstrators will say so. You will work here in the department, demonstrating the use of the sewing machine and teaching this week's workshops. If you're not needed, work will be found for you in the back, tidying or stocktaking. The lessons you are due to teach in customers' homes will be taken by another demonstrator. Your pupils will be informed that you are indisposed.'

Nell clasped her hands together. At least she hadn't lost her job. Just the part of it she loved best.

'May I ask if this is a permanent arrangement?'

'It is for the remainder of this week,' said Miss Collier, 'while we decide what to do with you.'

Leonie sighed – again. She had spent the whole day sighing. She sounded like a train blowing off steam. How could she have hurt Hilda like that? She had gone round to Finney Lane this morning, but Hilda had already gone out.

Or maybe she was in. Just not answering the door.

Leonie had been consumed by an absurd compulsion to call through the letter box, but she restrained herself. She needed to find someone with a copy of Tuesday's *Evening News,* but she was too ashamed. She wanted to hide in the coal bunker and never come out.

She couldn't face going round the shops in case word had got round. She had intended to buy chops today, but they would have to make do with whatever she had to hand. Potato rissoles; she could do those, but it would have to be with onions instead of spring onions. 'The green part of the spring onions, not the white,' she had taught Hilda years ago, and now here she was, making potato rissoles with ordinary onions because she was too ashamed to show her face.

It was an exhausting day. Her head was crammed full of what she had done and so was her heart.

As home time approached, she watched the clock, anxious to see Posy, but Alf walked in on his own.

She looked past him. 'Didn't Posy see you home?'

'She saw me to the corner. She's not allowed to come here.'

The pain that caused was so huge, she didn't know how her skin held it in, but she mustn't show the children how distressed she was.

When it got to the time for Nell to come home, there was a knock at the door. Leonie walked down the hall. Nell must have her hands full. Maybe she had brought some shopping home. It would be just like her to realise Leonie had cowered indoors all day. She was so considerate.

There was a man outside, a stranger. He lifted his cap to her. Blue eyes, sandy hair. Something vaguely familiar, though she had never seen him before.

'Evening, missis. I was sent here by a woman in Finney Lane. Is this where Mrs Nell Hibbert lives?'

'Who are you?' After getting into hot water for talking to that journalist, she was never going to spill information again.

Before he could answer, she noticed Nell coming along Wilton Lane. The man turned, following her gaze. She expected Nell to smile or quicken her pace if she knew him.

But she stopped dead.


## Chapter Twenty

You were supposed to sit down after a shock, weren't you? Mum used to say that and she was right. Your legs gave way under you. Nell was lucky she didn't plonk down right there on the pavement. Somehow she managed to walk towards her house. There was a buzzing in her ears and her skin was slick from scalp to soles with a cool beading of sweat. She didn't want to move; she didn't want to come face-to-face...

He had found her house. Her children were inside. Leonie was on the doorstep. She couldn't let Leonie find out who he was. Sickness rose inside her. Had he already told Leonie?

She halted a few feet away. He seemed so big. Had she forgotten his height, his size? In her thoughts, in her memories, she hadn't allowed him to intrude much, not as a person, two arms, two legs. It was his actions that had mattered, that had created the thoughts: who cared what he looked like? But here he was now and his looks startled her. Sandy hair, blue eyes, an oval face. His physical presence, after two years of nothing, two years of unwelcome memories that she had learnt to dismiss, shocked her to her core. She wanted to grab Leonie's arm, drag her indoors and shoot the bolt.

'Nell, are you all right? Look at you, you've got no colour.' Leonie reached out to her, then instead clapped her hand over her own mouth. 'Is this – this is never one of your brothers that's meant to be dead?'

Her throat closed, hot and tight. Not that she wanted to speak. Once she spoke, goodness knew what would be unleashed.

'Well,' he said, 'aren't you going to introduce me?'

She couldn't make it unhappen. Her knees felt like beaten eggs.

'This is...'

Saying it would make it real. It was already real. 14 Vicarage Lane and a little lad who was the spit of her son.

'I know who you are.' Leonie clapped her hands together and Nell's insides turned to ice. 'I knew you put me in mind of someone. It's young Alf, isn't it? You have a look of him about you – or he has a look of you, I should say.'

Stop it, stop it, don't say it, don't realise. Too late. Leonie had already realised.

'You must be ... his uncle? His late dad's brother? No wonder Nell looked so shocked, you turning up out of the blue. He's your brother-in-law, isn't he, love?'

His gaze was on her face. Would he let her get away with it? She swallowed. And nodded.

Leonie smiled, delighted. 'I knew it. Pleased to meet you. I'm Mrs Brent. I live here an' all.'

He shook her hand, then looked at Nell. 'Aren't you going to ask me in?'

The skin on her face felt stretched tight. She didn't want him in her house, but if she didn't agree, would he announce his real identity? 'Would you keep the children busy in the kitchen?' she asked Leonie. 'We – we haven't seen one another for a long time and...'

Leonie disappeared indoors. Nell went in too, slipping sideways through the door. Not that walking in forwards would have put her in danger of touching him, but she went sideways, anyroad.

'Bloody hell,' said Harold in her head.

'I'll wash your mouth out if you're not careful,' said Mum.

Bloody hell. Bloody, bloody hell. Sorry, Mum. But, honestly – bloody hell.

Nell sat on the chair they used for the sewing machine. She had worked jolly hard to get that sewing machine, had been so proud of her achievement, but Stan had tracked her down. Her muscles had turned to putty and any minute now

296

she might slither to the floor.

Stan stood there. He had paced the room. There wasn't much to see. The sewing machine and chair. A second-hand bookcase with deep shelves, which they used for putting sewing things on, bobbins, pieces of fabric, big dressmaking shears, pincushions. Some of the neighbours kept their works in progress on the bottom shelf. That was it, really, apart from a second chair for the next woman in the sewing queue to sit on while she waited, and a pair of figurines and an ornamental dish of Leonie's that they had put on the mantelpiece to brighten the room. Oh yes, and the shadowy remains of the patch where the water had caused damage.

Stan didn't look impressed. What did he expect? He should be ruddy impressed. She had fed, clothed and housed his children for two years on a woman's wage.

'How did you find me?' Her voice was dull. So was her heartbeat, and her brain. She had to pull herself together. Stan had the upper hand, taking her by surprise and getting into her house. She mustn't let him win.

Win? Win what?

'There was a newspaper article,' he said. 'It even said which road you lived in – well, the one you used to live in.'

'What do you want?' No: the question gave him control. She had to fight back. Something stirred in her blood. 'Does your other wife know you're here? Did you tell Mrs Vicarage Lane you were coming?' Or was she Mrs Lark Street now? Had he moved her into their old house?

A dull flush crept into his face. His hands fisted, then loosened. 'If I can explain–'

She surged to her feet. 'If? That's a bloody big if. I don't want to know. I don't want to hear about her and them, your other children, your other family. Weren't we enough, me and Alf? Even if you couldn't keep it in your trousers, even if I weren't enough... Your own boy, your own son: wasn't he enough?'

She grabbed the shears off the shelf, her fist closing round the handles, knuckles hard and white. The blades glinted. Stan's mouth fell open. He retreated a step, holding up his hands.

'Nay, lass, nay, Nell. This in't like you.'

'Isn't it? What am I like? Cleaning the pub: is that me? Swilling out stinking urinals: is that me? While *she* sits indoors like Lady Muck.'

'Don't call her that. She has a name–'

'Don't you dare say it – unless you want your ear sliced off with these scissors, and don't kid yourself I wouldn't. You have no idea what I'm capable of. What I've gone through these past two years, what I've done, what I've achieved – you know nowt about me. Nowt!'

'I know what a success you've made of yourself. I read that piece in't paper, remember.'

A thud of resentment stiffened her body. 'How did you get hold of it?'

He shrugged. 'One of Mother's friends. Her son is a porter at the station. Someone came on the train from Manchester and left it on't seat. He gave it to his mum and she saw the bit about you and...'

Oh, perfect. So Olive Hibbert had read it an' all.

298

Stan took a piece of newspaper from his pocket. He unfolded it and ran his gaze over it. 'Aye, it makes interesting reading.'

Her hands itched to snatch it from him, but she couldn't bear him to know she hadn't read it.

'For what it's worth,' said Stan, 'Mother's reet impressed. She's never took to–'

'Don't say her name, not in front of me. I mean it.'

'Anyroad, Mother's never got along with... She's always took your side.'

Well, that was a turn-up. Not that she wanted Olive Hibbert's support. Mrs Hibbert had had plenty of chances to make her feel loved and wanted when she lived in Annerby; but once she had married Stan, Mrs Hibbert's goodwill had soured.

'In fact,' said Stan, 'she even used this newspaper piece to taunt–'

Nell crashed the shears onto the shelf. 'Taunt who? Your fancy woman? Your tart? Your bit on't side? Except she wasn't on the side, was she? She was all fixed up in a nice little cottage in Vicarage Lane. She could spend all flaming day polishing her horse-brasses while some of us went out cleaning urinals.'

'Will you stop going on about urinals? It in't ladylike.'

'It were ladylike enough for me to clean them when we needed the money. And what did we need the money for? Remind me. Oh, I know: to support that female in Vicarage Lane, her and her ruddy front door.'

'Her what?'

'You heard. I know how you used our paint on her front door, leaving my back gate peeling.'

'Well, if that's all you care about–'

'Don't be stupid. It's just easier to think of that than – than those children. Oh, Stan, how could you? You had two of us expecting at the same time, and not just the once neither. Can you imagine how I felt? I'll never forgive you. Never.'

He pulled himself up straight, lifting his brows and tilting his head, for all the world like a man who had been on the receiving end of an unreasonable onslaught but had taken it on the chin, like the good fellow he was. Nell clenched her fists.

'Then you'll be glad to see the back of me, I reckon,' he said.

'Too bloody right I will. Too bloody sodding right.'

Her language made him jerk his head back, but his shock was quickly replaced by a set jaw and a steady eye. 'You want rid of me and I'll go gladly, but not until you've heard why I've come.'

'I don't care why you've come. All I care about is that you go – and don't come back.'

'Oh, I'm going – but I want money off you first.'

'You what?'

'You're doing well for yourself. A sewing machine, a job, extra work on't side. You're bringing in enough to rent a house: how many women on their own can say that? I want your savings.'

Nell gasped. His brass-necked cheek poured down her throat into her lungs, threatening to choke her.

'You'll soon build up more,' said Stan. 'You

always were a grafter.'

'You'll get nowt from me.' In her head she was shouting from the rooftops, but all that crept out of her mouth was a whisper.

'What's your reputation worth? I'd say it's worth your savings. You can keep your savings or you can keep your good name, but not both. That shop you work for, and them ladies you teach: how pleased will they be to employ a runaway wife? Your neighbours won't be best pleased neither. Want to be the talk of the wash house, do you?'

Nell flinched. 'If you dare...' Her eyes were brimming and she had to wipe her nose. God, how pathetic. She pulled herself up as tall and straight as she could. She had walked out on this man. She had made a life for herself and her children. She wouldn't back down now. 'Having two wives is against the law. You've got comfortable with your bigamy. Your neighbours in Annerby have chosen to look the other way, so you think you've got away with it. Your mother disapproves, but she hasn't done owt about it. But I will. I'm known as a respectable widow here. You do anything to damage my reputation and I'll get you sent to prison.' She marched past him and threw the door open. 'Get out and don't come back.'

He walked out – no, he stopped right beside her in the doorway. She felt hemmed in, but she wouldn't duck away. If he touched her, if he laid one finger on her, she would scream the place down.

He was going to speak. Well, let him have the

last word, for all the good it would do him. She didn't care. She just wanted him gone.

'You think it's so simple.'

She looked into his face. How had she ever loved this man? 'Things are simple when you're respectable. You just do the right thing.'

He bent his head closer. 'Well, in that case, you've done the wrong thing. The right thing would have been to give me the money. I hope for both our sakes you don't live to regret it.'

Jim did a deal with old Mr Pomeroy in the cottage next door. He couldn't use his vegetables as trade because Pom's vegetable patch was less of a patch and more of a flourishing garden; but old Pom was fond of his pipe, so Jim had purchased a few ounces of Golden Virginia.

'You're a gentleman,' said Pom, accepting it.

'And you're a fine gardener. I hope you'll give me some of those tall daisy plants in exchange.'

'Marguerites,' said Pom. 'You didn't need to give me the baccy to have 'em. Not that you're getting it back.' He clutched the tin to his chest with a mischievous gummy grin.

Jim used his pen-knife to cut some marguerites, fastening them into a bunch with a piece of twine, wondering that such a simple offering should please him so much. Then he dug out Tuesday's *Evening News* and set off.

A bunch of daisies and an out-of-date newspaper. Roberta would have chewed his head off.

With a light heart, he strode through the evening streets in the direction of Wilton Lane. Would Nell realise that bringing the newspaper was the

302

act of a man desperate to see her? Or would she think it just a neighbourly gesture?

He wanted to speak out. He wanted her to see his interest. And yet he couldn't be interested in her. He mustn't. They were poles apart socially, and it wasn't as though he was going to stay in this lower-class life indefinitely. He knew he had recovered, as much as any man could, from his experiences and the time was approaching for him to resume his old life and social position.

But how could he leave Nell Hibbert behind?

He knocked on her door. He sucked in his cheeks, pulling his smile under control. God, he'd got it bad. As the door opened and he saw her, he couldn't help letting his smile widen – until he caught the barely controlled anger in her face.

'Have I called at an inconvenient time?'

'No. I thought you were someone else.'

Edmund Tanner? Had there been more trouble?

'I come bearing gifts. Flowers for Mrs Brent in case she's in need of cheering up, and the paper with the piece that mentions you. I can hand them over and go away or...' Please, please.

'Come in. Aunt Leonie will love the flowers and you ought to give them to her yourself. I'll be interested to read that article and see what caused all the trouble.'

'Trouble?'

She shrugged it off, calling, 'Aunt Leonie, you've got a gentleman caller bringing you flowers.'

Mrs Brent looked round, puzzled and then transparently pleased as he entered the kitchen.

'How lovely. Are those for me?'

He presented them to her, wishing a fabulous

bouquet of roses and baby's breath had been appropriate, though her delight couldn't have been any greater had he offered her the florist's finest.

'To bring a smile to your face,' he said.

'They've certainly done that. Look, children.'

Alf's eyes widened. 'Giant daisies. Are they magic?'

'No, they're just giant daisies,' said Jim, 'but think of the size of the daisy chain.'

'Look at this, Aunt Leonie.' Nell held up the newspaper.

Mrs Brent's breath caught. 'Let me see what–'

'We'll read it later,' said Nell. 'For now, let's enjoy your flowers.'

'They're marguerites,' said Mrs Brent. 'Can you say marguerite, Cassie? Mar-guer-ite.'

'Mar-geet.' Cassie reached for a flower head.

Jim settled into the family atmosphere. 'I have a niece called Mar-geet.'

'Really?' asked Alf. 'Even though Mar-geet is a made-up word because Cassie can't say marguer-ite.'

'My mistake. She's Marguerite. Marguerite is a girl's name as well as a flower, the same as Daisy.'

'Plenty of flowers are girls' names,' said Nell.

Alf's face screwed up thoughtfully. 'Is there a Cassie flower?'

'If there isn't,' said Jim, 'there jolly well ought to be.' He scooped up the little girl, lifting her high in the air, confident she would laugh out loud. He settled her on his hip; it felt right and comfortable to do so. He had loved holding his nieces when they were tiny – when he was allowed to. Patsy had teased him that it wasn't the done thing to elbow Nanny out of the way: a joke, but a warning as well.

Had he overstepped the mark here? He blew a raspberry on the child's forehead and popped her on her feet. She grabbed his trouser leg for support, then waddled off.

'No, you don't, miss.' Nell swung her up into her arms. 'It's way past your bedtime.'

'We're running late because of having a visitor – not you, Jim,' said Mrs Brent. 'Earlier on.'

'Not in front of the children.' Nell looked off into space, as if this would prevent the children from hearing.

'I don't see why not, but you know best.'

'Yes, I do.' Nell shut her eyes for a moment. 'Sorry to snap, but I've already told you, I don't want certain people to know.'

'Don't want certain people to know what?' asked Alf.

Nell threw Mrs Brent an exasperated look.

Jim stepped in. 'That I'm looking for Violet this evening.'

'You, young man, are going to have a wash and go to bed,' said Nell. 'Cassie too. Fancy her being up at this hour. Disgraceful!' But she said it in a way that made the children laugh. 'Aunt Leonie, could you see them to bed and we'll look for Violet.'

Jim's heart leapt. Courting Roberta had involved elegant dinners and trips to the theatre and here he was, grateful to look for a lost cat.

Leaving her to say goodnight to the children, Jim waited outside. Who had come visiting to cause such a stir? Someone Nell didn't want the

305

children knowing about; and yet Mrs Brent clearly didn't understand the fuss. He wanted to ask, to offer help, if needed. He wanted to trounce the fellow who had ruffled Nell's calm. But if she was in the mood to snap at the woman she loved enough to adopt as her aunt, she would undoubtedly bite the head off a mere window cleaner if he dared pry.

She joined him outside.

'Shall we start in Finney Lane?' he suggested.

She fell in step beside him. 'Violet's been gone a fortnight now.'

'Perhaps this will be our lucky evening. Did Mr Tanner return Mrs Brent's belongings?'

'Oh, that. I'm sorry; I'm a bit distracted today.'

Should he? Shouldn't he? 'The visitor you mentioned?'

'Yes; and no, we haven't got Aunt Leonie's things back. I'm not sure we will, the way things stand at the moment.' She spoke with a note of finality.

Down Finney Lane, there was a tabby on a window ledge and a black cat with white socks lazing on a doorstep, but no little black cat. They turned the corner to try the entry.

'I hope it was all right that I picked up Cassie and flew her around,' said Jim.

'She loved it.'

'I didn't mean whether she minded; I meant whether you did. I don't want to overstep the mark.'

'I didn't mind,' said Nell, or I'd have said. The children like you. You're a friend of the family. Like now, looking for Violet.'

He couldn't contain it any longer. He had to tell her. He had to pour out his hopes and promises. It ought to be done somewhere appropriate, somewhere romantic, somewhere as beautiful as she deserved, but so what? Here and now, social differences be damned. Here and now, he could wait no longer. With brick walls and wooden gates on either side, he stopped and turned to her. The cinder path crackled beneath his boots. It was a warm evening. The entry was half in sun, half in shade. She stood in the shade, tall and slender. With the evening sun in his eyes, he couldn't see her face, couldn't read her expression, her eyes.

But he didn't need to read her eyes. If he could look into them, there would be no spark of hope or interest, no answering glow. The words died in his throat. He was a fool to think they could ever be spoken.

## Chapter Twenty-One

'Serves her right, getting caught out,' Nell heard a voice say as she pushed open the door to the women's lavatories. She caught the door before it could open further and give her away. 'If someone gave me a jammy job like that, I wouldn't take advantage.'

She closed the door and scurried away, giving the gossipers time to disappear before she returned to the Ladies' to get changed. Yesterday Miss Collier had had her dusting various cupboards, so this morning she had brought an old skirt and blouse with her, and a headscarf to cover her hair. The look on Miss Collier's face when she said she was going to get changed!

Soon she was busy giving the sewing department's stockroom a severe bottoming. If Miss Collier imagined this was a form of punishment, she was sorely mistaken. Bashing about with mops and brooms was precisely what she needed to let off steam. Now that she had emerged from the fog of shock, she was furious with Stan. How dare he demand money? How dare he appear on her doorstep? She was angry with Walter Marsden too, for pouring personal details into that article. It had been more about her than about the injured girl. *Mrs Nell Hibbert of Finney Lane, Chorlton-cum-Hardy,* indeed!

Jim had been right: the article was nothing if not flattering, and it was doubly flattering to know that dear Leonie, the aunt of her heart, was the one to have made these remarks about her, only she hadn't had a chance to say so last night. Leonie was preoccupied with the words that had upset the Tanners.

'I didn't call you a daughter. See?' But triumph was quickly replaced by a weighty sigh of doubt. 'But I did call you *my Nell.* I wish that young man hadn't written that.'

'I wish he hadn't written any of it.'

'I should never have spoken so freely. Look at the trouble it's caused. I wonder what the next thing will be. Things always happen in threes. There's your trouble at Ingleby's and mine with Hilda. I wonder what the third will be.'

Nell had stayed up half the night, thinking about the third thing: Stan.

Anger built up inside her now and she had to leave the stockroom and march away, because if she stayed, she would scoop everything off the shelves onto the floor and jump on it. There were so many thoughts crashing around in her head, she didn't know where to start. Oh, heck. She couldn't afford to be away from her work. She was in enough hot water already.

Turning on her heel, she bumped into a woman emerging from a back room. Thirties, reddish hair, a smattering of freckles. Nell knew her – no, she didn't – yes, she did.

'You came to the interviews for the demonstrator positions.'

The woman smiled warily. 'You got the post for South Manchester, didn't you? There were two of us for the north post. I didn't get it.'

Yet here she was, wearing an Ingleby's dress. Oh. Nell's hand reached towards the wall to steady herself.

'You've been brought in to do my calls.'

'Yes. I'm sorry.'

'No need. Not your fault.' She forced herself to say something gracious. 'It's a good opportunity for you.'

The woman relaxed. 'You can say that again. It's a lot of travelling, because I live up Crumpsall way, but I don't mind.' Her eyes glazed over, as if she realised she had been tactless. 'I'm Matilda Pugh.'

'Nell Hibbert.'

'Yes, I know.'

Of course she knew. Nell smiled: with luck, it wouldn't look as ghastly as it felt. 'I mustn't keep you. Good luck.'

Tears blinded her as she retreated, but she pushed her shoulders back and persuaded her chin to stay up, though what she really wanted was to curl up in the furthest corner of the stockroom. She was already curling up on the inside, her thoughts shattering into a hundred jagged fragments.

But she had to face this. Miss Collier had said her visits would be covered, but she hadn't said by whom and Nell hadn't given it any thought. But she thought about it now. Was Matilda Pugh's appointment permanent? She should have asked – no, she would have died of humiliation.

What lay ahead for her at Ingleby's? If she was dismissed, would the factory take her back? Her stomach clenched, rebelling against the idea of returning to the old punishing round.

Her children deserved better and it was up to her to do something about it.

Leonie hadn't gone shopping yesterday because of being a coward, but today she could hold up her head, which was fortunate because she had no option other than to go to the fishmonger's and the grocer's. Herrings in lemon sauce, then sponge pudding with tinned peaches, would do nicely. She had a bright feeling about today. Now that she knew the exact wording in the newspaper, she could set Hilda straight and make peace with her.

*She's a good girl, is my Nell.*

Her bright feeling wobbled. All right, so she

hadn't claimed Nell as a daughter, but her words did have a motherly ring. *My Nell.*

Shops first and Hilda later, or Hilda first? No, shops first, so as to leave the rest of the morning for Hilda.

Arriving in Finney Lane, she settled the handle of the wicker basket comfortably over her arm, knocked on her old front door and waited. The moment it opened, she said cheerfully, 'Morning, Hilda. I've come for a chat.'

Hilda's mouth was a prim line. 'You'd best come in.'

She put down her basket and took off her coat, hanging it on top of Hilda's. Hilda put the kettle on. That was a good sign, surely? Leonie sat down. She ran the palms of her hands over the nearest part of the dark green oilcloth, as if it were linen in need of smoothing.

'I've been anxious to see you.'

'Oh aye? So anxious you did the shopping first, not to mention you never came yesterday.'

Blast. She should have come here first. There was nowt quite so vexing as being told off by your own child.

'There was no answer yesterday; and today I went to the shops first to give us the rest of the morning. If you're stopping in,' she added.

There was an obstinate tilt to Hilda's chin. She had Hedley's chin. It felt disrespectful to Hedley that Hilda would make his chin look obstinate.

'I've got my shopping to do an' all,' said Hilda.

'Then it's a good thing I didn't miss you again.' She kept the smile plastered on her face for all she was worth. 'I've come to say I'm sorry your feelings were hurt by what was written in the paper.'

Hilda fiddled with the tea caddy and put the crockery on the table. Her chin had gone crinkly. Hedley's chin had never done that. Hedley never struggled with difficult thoughts and feelings. He was honest and considerate, qualities that had given him a quiet confidence that the best-educated, most beautifully fetched-up gentleman would have admired. Pity he had never met Jim Franks. They would have taken to one another.

Leonie spoke quietly, as if Hedley was whispering the words in her ear. 'You're my one and only daughter and I wouldn't change you for anything. Me and your dad thought the world of you, and I still do.'

Hilda reddened. 'You don't have to say that.'

'I want to. And I never said owt about having a second daughter. I know you was upset t'other evening when you'd just seen it, but now you must know I never said it.'

'I know nowt of the kind.'

She hadn't expected that. 'You must have read–'

'I didn't need to. Edmund told me.'

Ah. 'He may have ... exaggerated.'

'I can't bear to read it, if you must know. Fancy my own mother saying–'

'I never said it.'

'Edmund says you did.'

Oh, the temptation to blurt out what she thought of that troublemaker. Hedley would have told her to concentrate on Hilda. 'I expect Edmund were upset on your behalf, as any good husband would be, and maybe that made him exaggerate.'

312

Hilda looked at her as if she had gone mad. 'How can you exaggerate what you read out of the paper?'

Annoyance bubbled beneath Hedley's influence, but she kept her voice calm. 'Clearly he did, since that isn't what was written. 'What I said was...' Oh lord, now she was for it. 'I called Mrs Hibbert a good girl.'

'A good girl?' Hilda looked baffled.

'I said how hard she works and what a loving mother she is and I finished up calling her a good girl.'

'Oh.' Apparently unable to think what else to say, Hilda warmed the pot. Would this teach her not to take Edmund's word as gospel?

'Have you still got the paper?' Leonie asked quietly, careful not to rub it in. Hedley would be proud.

'No. Some of it got used for wrapping a piece of broken glass and Posy had the rest for paper chains for Lyddie Foskett's birthday. Did you bring your paper with you?'

'No.' It would have felt like gloating, but now she wished she had. It was proof of Edmund's lie – sorry, his exaggeration.

'So you just called her a good girl?'

Hilda sat down and Leonie felt a weight lift. She was back where she should be, on good terms with her daughter.

Hilda frowned. 'Why would Edmund get it wrong?'

'I told you. Exaggeration.'

'But to jump from summat about a good girl to another daughter.'

There was nothing for it. Why hadn't she said it at the start? Because Hilda might not have listened to another word, that's why.

'My actual words... What I said was...'

Hilda, who had grown into such a drip, suddenly had a gleam in her eye that Leonie hadn't seen for years. 'What?'

'I said, *She's a good girl ... is my Nell.*'

Hilda lurched to her feet. 'And you dare to say Edmund exaggerated? How about you? Pretending all you said was, *She's a good girl,* and conveniently forgetting to mention *your Nell.*' Her breath caught in a gasp. 'Your Nell! If that doesn't make her sound like family, I don't know what would.'

'Hilda–'

'And that's another thing. You've always called her Mrs Hibbert to me. You've never once referred to her as Nell.'

'Well, no. You and her aren't on first-name terms.'

'But you obviously call her Nell to her face.'

'She lived with me and your dad a long time, two whole years, and she were so young...'

'Younger than your own daughter. Dad said you'd always wished for more children. If I'd been the oldest of a family, like I were meant to be, there could have been one her age, the baby of the family.'

'Nay, Hilda, stop it, please. The last thing I want is for us to fall out.'

Too late.

'You needn't bring cleaning clothes to change

314

into on Monday, Mrs Hibbert,' Miss Moore told Nell when she finished for the week. What did that mean? That she was returning to normal duties, or that she would be out on her ear? Whatever happened on Monday, she must have a plan ready. That gave her tomorrow and Sunday to prepare herself.

It had been an uncomfortable couple of days at Ingleby's, and she was glad to get home, though the atmosphere was strained here too. Things had gone from bad to worse between Hilda and Leonie. Nell had every sympathy until Leonie shocked her by saying, 'I don't know why you sent your brother-in-law away, but you should think again. I'd do owt to make up with my Hilda.'

'I'd rather not discuss it, if you don't mind.'

'Happen I do mind. He's made the effort to come here. You should give him a chance. What's he done to upset you, anyroad?'

Nell's heart beat faster. 'Leave it be – please. He's the black sheep.'

'If you say so, but what about yon children? The only family they've got is you and each other.'

'And you.'

Leonie's eyes softened. 'Aye, they'll always have me. But don't you think an uncle would be a good idea?'

'No, I don't. Please don't say owt to them. You haven't, have you?'

Leonie looked offended. 'Certainly not. I wouldn't go behind your back.'

'Of course you wouldn't. I'm sorry.'

'I'll put the kettle on,' said Leonie. 'You're teaching tomorrow morning, aren't you?'

'Yes – Miss Vine.'

Should she feel guilty for not telling Miss Collier about the private client who hadn't come to her via Ingleby's? No, she would have been mad to let on. If she lost her job, Miss Vine's custom would be her one source of income until she could find more pupils.

Or maybe not her one source.

'I have an acquaintance who is interested in lessons,' Miss Vine said as Nell tidied up at the end of the lesson. 'Here's her name and address and a list of days and times that would be suitable. Send her a postcard to let her know, there's a dear.'

Nell took the sheet of paper. An address in Victoria Park, no less. 'Did you tell her my rates?'

'Good heavens, no. Ladies don't discuss such matters.'

More fool them. Nell put the details in her handbag. Next week, she would send either an appointment or her apologies. Which would it be? One thing was certain. With an address in Victoria Park, this new lady could afford a higher fee.

'Thank you for suggesting me.'

'I'm happy to recommend you to anybody who invests in a sewing machine.'

Recommend. She made a mental note to say, 'Thank you for recommending me,' next time.

Next time. That made it sound like she could build a business by word of mouth. If only it were that simple! If she lost her position at Ingleby's on Monday, she must advertise. What she must do beforehand was prepare her advertisement just in case. She started composing it in her head on her way home.

That was all she could do for now. It didn't feel like much.

Nell vowed to devote the rest of the weekend to the children. The band was going to play in the rec that afternoon, so what could be better than a picnic?

'Run round to Finney Lane and ask if Posy can come,' she told Alf, but he wound his arms around his Nana Leonie's neck as she sat at the table. Standing on one foot, he kicked his other toes on the floor.

Nell and Leonie exchanged glances.

'Josie O'Rourke is in the same class as Posy, isn't she? If we invite Josie, we can ask her to call for Posy – but you'll have to go too, Alf, because it's our invitation, though you won't have to say owt.' She bent down and put her hands on his shoulders, looking into his troubled face. 'It'll be Mrs Tanner that answers the door and it would mean a lot to Nana Leonie to have Posy with us.'

When Josie and Alf had gone, she said to Leonie with a sigh, 'I hate to send him, but it wouldn't do much good if you or I went.'

Leonie clapped a hand to her mouth. 'It's Saturday!' Her face crumpled. 'Posy never came yesterday for her caramels.'

Was that all? 'You can give them to her this afternoon if Hilda lets her come.'

'You don't understand.'

'So tell me.'

'I can't. It's a family matter.'

What a fuss over some sweets. But if Leonie

mentioned her so-called brother-in-law again, she might remind her that the Tanners weren't the only ones to have a family matter. Or would that be mean?

'Posy can't come, Nanaleonie,' Alf announced, running in, spirits high now that he had knocked on Edmund Tanner's door and lived to tell the tale – or stood behind the girl who had knocked, anyroad.

Damn Hilda! 'Never mind,' said Nell. 'Josie can still come.'

She spread fish paste on barm cakes and cut them into quarters to make them stretch further. Leonie sliced her cherry cake and poured home-made lemonade into a bottle.

Soon they were on their way, Alf clutching the ladder-monkey and Josie carrying a length of old washing line in case there were other girls to skip with. There were plenty of other families in the rec. Well-to-do folk sat in deckchairs near the bandstand, or laid their picnics on tablecloths. They must be well-heeled if they could afford to lay a tablecloth on the ground.

They found a place beside a bench so Leonie could sit on the end of the bench while the rest of them sat on the grass. The band played 'I'm Twenty-One Today' and Nell and Leonie hummed along.

'See the hedge over there,' Leonie said to Alf. 'Over the other side of it is Beech Road, and on the other side of Beech Road is Riley's Farm, and behind that is where Mr Franks lives.'

'Can he come to our picnic?' Alf asked.

Nell squashed that immediately. 'He's probably

busy working.'

'I don't think he works the whole day on Saturday,' said Leonie. 'We should ask him. He's been good to us.'

'It wouldn't be respectable,' Nell objected in a voice she hoped the children couldn't hear. 'People might jump to conclusions.' Or was it her thumping heart that was jumping to conclusions?

'Nonsense,' said Leonie. 'We'll ask his landlady an' all. Is that respectable enough for you? Besides,' she added with a twinkle, 'I wouldn't mind seeing that Mrs Jeffrey. Is she an old biddy? She might be a beautiful young war widow.' Before Nell could object, she was on her feet. 'Come along, Alf. Let's find Mr Franks. You come an' all, Josie.'

Nell stayed behind, playing with Cassie. Would Jim be there? Would he come? She didn't want him to. Oh yes, she did. But she shouldn't.

Presently, a small party trooped across the grass: Leonie and the children, with Jim carrying a pair of folding chairs, an old boy with a cheery smile and no teeth, and – an old biddy. Nell had no business being relieved, but she was.

Mrs Jeffrey carried something wrapped in a tea towel, which turned out to be a chunk of pork pie. The old fellow, who was introduced as Mr Pomeroy – 'Call me Pom; everyone does' – produced apples from his pocket and buffed them up to a shine on his jacket. And Jim, as well as the folding seats, had carried a box of Huntley and Palmers.

It turned into quite a feast and the mixture of ages added to the family feeling.

'Any sign of the cat?' Jim asked Nell.

'Not yet.'

'When we were searching on Thursday, you said Mr Tanner still had Mrs Brent's things. Has he returned them since?'

'We never asked. Summat else happened. That piece in the paper has caused all kinds of ructions.'

'Between Mrs Brent and the Tanners?'

'For one; and with my job, for another.' She explained about the trouble at Ingleby's. 'So I don't know what to expect on Monday, but I'm not sitting around feeling sorry for myself. I've made a plan.' She told him about it.

'Tell me the wording of your advertisement.'

She looked at him. He had pushed his cap right back on his head and the sun played on his face. 'Are you serious?'

'Entirely. I gave you and Mrs Brent my address so you could come to me for help. The people around here have allowed me to live among them, so any assistance I can provide – advice, legal information, looking for lost cats – is given freely and gladly.'

She shared her wording, not looking at him in case he found her attempt laughable.

'May I make a suggestion? It would be better if you could say *References available.* Can you provide references?'

'I have the one from Miss Lockwood at the factory.'

'You need some from pupils.'

'Miss Vine might write one. She recommended me to a friend.'

'Anyone else?'

320

'Mrs Liversedge, definitely – but she's an Ingleby's lady. If they sack me, I might not be allowed to approach their pupils.'

'Of course you can; and if Ingleby's try to tell you any different, inform them that you'll refer the matter to your solicitor.'

Nell laughed, then realised he meant it.

'Another thing,' he said. 'I suggest you prepare some postcards with relevant details, so you can give them out; and you'll need a post office box for enquirers to contact you.'

Panic flared. 'There's so much to do.'

'It's nothing you can't manage, I'm sure. If you prepare some details, I'll get them typewritten for you. A lady who worked in the office where I had my first position is now retired, but she makes extra from typewriting jobs. Bashing out a stack of cards would be easy for her.'

'Would she charge much?'

'I'll ask, shall I? You ought to look businesslike.'

Her – a businesswoman! Nell Pringle from the backstreets, giving out cards with her business details and *References available* at the bottom.

'Of course, it might not happen,' he reminded her. 'Ingleby's might reinstate you.'

'Fingers crossed.'

She held up her crossed fingers, but she didn't cross them very hard. She might feel differently later, but just now she didn't want to be reinstated. She wanted to meet the challenge of working for herself. Was she having a mad moment or could she really give it a go?

Had it been respectable, she would have squeezed Jim's hand. 'You've been so kind.'

'I'm not doing it out of kindness,' he said. 'I'm doing it because–'

'Oh, listen.'

Her face swung towards the bandstand, where the musicians had struck up 'Take Me Back to Dear Old Blighty'. Nostalgia swelled inside her and her throat clogged. She could almost hear Vi's clear voice singing the words.

'It's not easy, is it?' Jim said softly.

His compassion, his understanding, curled around her heart. She wanted to speak of her lost family, but the pain in her throat made it impossible.

'Mummy.' Alf appeared at her side. 'Can we–?'

'Come on, kids.' Jim jumped to his feet. 'Bet you can't catch me.'

He jogged away, with Alf in pursuit and Josie helping Cassie to toddle after him. And this man said he didn't act out of kindness. He was the kindest person she knew.

The music finished to warm applause and was followed by– Alf's face turned to hers in astonishment and joy and Nell's heart responded with a beat of pure happiness. Her son's pleasure meant more to her than her own. 'Oh, Oh, Antonio'. She jumped up and caught his hands, dancing him in a circle as they sang along. She had lost so much, but that made what she had now all the more precious.

'Then UP will go Antonio and his ICE-CREAM CART.'

Miss Moore and Miss Collier squeezed side by side behind the desk. Nell stood in front. The least they could have done was provide her with a chair; or maybe she didn't deserve one because she was about to be sacked. She composed her features into what was intended to be a pleasant but non-committal expression and folded her hands in front of her.

'You let us down, Mrs Hibbert,' said Miss Collier. 'You took advantage of your position and we can no longer trust you to visit customers' houses.'

Nell's fingers twisted tighter. Dismissal, then.

'You will tutor for Ingleby's here in the sewing department,' said Miss Moore. 'You're a good teacher and we're prepared to give you a chance. Besides, your friend might run to the newspaper if we dismiss you. *Ingleby's Sacks Accident Heroine.* We can't have that.'

Nell stared. 'Mrs Brent wouldn't do that.'

'On the contrary, it seems entirely likely she would do something similar again.'

'You'll run our classes,' said Miss Collier, 'which will provide you with regular work, though not to the extent of employing you full-time.'

'We provide up to four classes per week,' said Miss Moore. 'These are held between two o'clock and four. You will start at one. It will be your duty to prepare everything and greet the pupils. Afterwards you will answer questions and advise on purchases, for which you will receive no commission. You will then tidy up and finish at five.'

'Four hours,' said Nell, 'four afternoons a week.'

'Up to four afternoons,' Miss Moore corrected her, 'and some weeks there may be none. You will receive ample notice of the lessons and you will not be excused from attending.'

'And the rest of my time?' asked Nell.

'What you do with that is up to you. We assume you'll teach privately, in which case you may say or do nothing to suggest those lessons are connected to Ingleby's.'

'And,' added Miss Collier, 'you may not offer lessons to ladies whom you taught previously for Ingleby's; neither may you offer lessons to ladies you teach here in the department. Moreover, should your private work in any way bring discredit upon yourself, this will result in your instant dismissal.'

So many conditions. So much control. And no time for her to take it in.

'We have two lessons for you to teach this week, on Thursday and Friday afternoons. We will expect you here at twelve forty-five on Thursday, ready to start at one. Good morning, Mrs Hibbert.'

Nell untangled her fingers to open the door. Her head was spinning. She hadn't been sacked, but she had hardly any hours left. Sixteen in a good week. And all she had in her diary was lessons for Miss Vine; and, after she had sent the postcard making arrangements, Miss Vine's friend, Mrs Fairbrother, but that wasn't until Thursday of next week.

She needed heaps more private work, and quickly.

# Chapter Twenty-Two

The Fairbrothers' front door stood beneath a protruding porch at the top of a flight of stone steps. To either side was a vast bay window, above each of which was another bay; and above those was a floor with ordinary flat windows. You could get the population of Wilton Lane in this house and still have room to wriggle.

Nell knocked. The door was opened by a maid wearing a black dress not unlike an Ingleby's dress, only she had a bibbed apron over it, and a white cap.

'Good morning. Mrs Hibbert to see Mrs Fairbrother.'

'I shouldn't think so,' was the blunt reply.

Be professional. Nell kept her smile in place. 'She's expecting me. I have an appointment.'

'I'll see if madam is home. Wait here ... please,' she added at the last moment, and flounced away.

Ridiculous. As if she didn't know whether her mistress was in. Nell turned to admire the garden. Imagine having a garden that size. It must be a lot of work, but the Fairbrothers wouldn't care about that. They would employ a gardener. The lawn was a square with four paths leading into the middle, creating four smaller squares. In the centre was a fountain, with spray spurting from a fish's mouth. Sunshine caught the water, transforming it into a shower of diamonds.

The door swished and she turned back to the maid.

'You're here to see madam's lady's maid, Miss Preston. Round the back.'

The door shut, leaving her stranded. No point being vexed. No time either. Her appointment was for ten o'clock and if she didn't find this Miss Preston in two minutes flat, she would be late. She ran down the steps and found her way to the back door. It was standing open on this fine June morning. She knocked and walked in.

'...the front door, bold as you please, and asked for madam herself – oh, look who it isn't. Visitor for you, Miss Preston.'

'Thank you, Daphne.'

A middle-aged woman with an oval face above a double chin rose from the pine kitchen table. She wore black with white collar and cuffs – did everyone in the lower orders wear black with white? It was the uniform of the respectable work-ing woman; Nell had run up a black-with-white dress for herself. Miss Preston wore a narrow black belt and Nell caught a flash of silver hanging from it that brought to mind housekeepers in novels, who carried the keys of the house about their person, before she realised the objects in-cluded a pair of scissors and a small box, like a cigarette case, only it must contain pins and needles.

'Mrs Hibbert? How do you do? I am Miss Preston, lady's maid to Mrs Fairbrother. I'm sorry about Daphne's manners. She picked up some unfortunate ways in the munitions.'

She gave Daphne a look; Daphne gave her one right back.

Miss Preston led the way upstairs by a back route into a room with a child's bed – but what a bed! A four-poster, only not a four-poster; a two-poster, if there was such a thing, with an arch of delicate voile over the head of the bed; and a coverlet that cascaded in lacy frills to the floor. Nell would have given five years of her life for Cassie to have a bed like that. Mind you, the little minx would probably use the posts for climbing practice and build a nest in the fabric at the top. Even then, it would be worth it. Any mother would think so.

'This used to be the nursery,' said Miss Preston.

'Used to be?' Nell wrenched her gaze away from the fairy-tale bed.

Miss Preston sounded amused. 'Miss Roberta hasn't slept here for a long time.'

What did she have now? A real four-poster? With a wooden chest at the foot, crammed with toys and puzzles and dolls with real hair and eyes that shut when you laid them down?

'Here comes Miss Graham, who is Miss Roberta's maid.'

Nell exchanged nods with the newcomer. The young miss was grown-up enough for her own maid. Sixteen? Seventeen?

'You'll be teaching both of us,' said Miss Preston.

'I see,' said Nell. Start the way you mean to go on: by making money. 'If you're both to have supervised practice, our sessions will have to be longer.'

'That will be satisfactory,' said Miss Preston.

'Shouldn't you ask Mrs Fairbrother?'

Miss Preston's eyes showed understanding. 'Please don't worry about your bill not being paid.' She said it kindly, not as a put-down.

'I'll show you the basics of the machine and we can talk about what you want to make.'

'We shan't be making clothes,' said Miss Graham in a snooty voice.

'Mrs Fairbrother and Miss Roberta are dressed by Mademoiselle Antoinette,' Miss Preston explained.

'Mademoiselle Antoinette's is one of the most exclusive salons, if not *the* most exclusive, in all Manchester,' added Miss Graham.

'I see,' said Nell. 'So you'll be...?'

Did Miss Preston smother a sigh? 'In the attics, there are trunks upon trunks of old garments of the highest quality but hopelessly out of date. Mrs Fairbrother wants to adapt some of them into new garments.'

'It was Miss Roberta's idea,' said Miss Graham. 'She thinks that because styles today require less fabric, it shouldn't be difficult to make use of the old stuff.'

Really? This young girl was dressed by Mademoiselle Antoinette, and she still wanted more clothes? Miss Roberta was beginning to sound like a spoilt brat. Just wait until she got home and told Leonie.

'We know how to mend and do alterations,' said Miss Graham. 'All we need from you is a lesson on how to use this machine.' She eyed the Singer with dislike – and wariness. Another of

Miss Roberta's ideas?

'I'm afraid it's not as simple as that,' said Nell. 'You have to know how to use it for different fabrics. I used to work in a garment factory and believe me, you wouldn't set a beginner to work on velvet. But don't worry: there's nothing to be scared of.'

'I'm not scared.'

But she was. Nell had seen the uncertainty in her eyes.

One thing soon became clear. Teaching the two ladies' maids side by side was a clumsy arrangement.

'Instead of longer shared lessons,' she said, 'I suggest separate sessions.'

Miss Preston agreed. 'Could you do two two-hour lessons next time? We'd provide luncheon, naturally.'

'I have my diary with me.' Nell spoke calmly, though fireworks were going off inside her. 'What a start to her venture.

Nell left the Fairbrother residence as soon after midday as she could without looking like she was rushing, but she was actually in a tearing hurry. She had to get to Inglebys for a one o'clock start, which meant presenting herself promptly at twelve forty-five, having changed into her shop dress. If she was lucky, there would be time for a bite to eat as well.

Just before quarter to one, she headed upstairs. As she opened the door, footsteps came running upstairs behind her. She waited, holding the door open. Matilda Pugh rounded the bend and flew

329

up the last few steps.

'Here.' She thrust something into Nell's hand. 'For you.'

And in she went.

Nell's fingers clutched an envelope. 'Wait,' she called and would have said more, but Matilda raced back.

'Hush, you fool, or we'll both be for the chop. Put it in your pocket and forget about it till later.'

Nell did as she was bid, weaving her way between the counters of haberdashery, feeling bewildered and curious; but she had to push it to the back of her mind and concentrate on her work.

The moment she sat down on the bus to go home, she pulled it out. Who could be writing to her?

It was from Mrs Liversedge, who wanted to see her and could she possibly call tomorrow morning? Indeed she could. It would be an Ingleby's afternoon, but her morning was free.

Horribly free. She needed more clients.

And, as she discovered, Mrs Liversedge intended to be one of them.

'I'd be delighted to come back to you,' said Nell, 'but Ingleby's say I can't teach anyone I met through them.'

'Fiddlesticks! I had my six lessons off them and it's none of their business what I do now. I went to such trouble to track you down. My friend has just got a sewing machine and is having her six lessons from that new girl with the frightful hair. I've told her that as soon as her six lessons are over, she has to call you in.'

'That's good of you,' Nell began.

'So don't tell me you're not allowed to teach me.'

Nell remembered Jim's advice. 'I can't give you an answer today. I'll have to refer the matter to my solicitor.'

'You have a solicitor?' Mrs Liversedge's surprise might have been insulting if it hadn't been comical.

'Of course. Everyone in business should.' How Leonie would laugh when she heard that. 'I wonder, since you're pleased with my work, if I could ask you for a reference.'

'A testimonial? Happy to. I'll write it now – and you can look at that piece of sewing and work out what I've done wrong.'

'Happy to.' She would take her time, allowing Mrs Liversedge ample scope to dream up suitable phrases.

Mrs Liversedge slipped the paper in an envelope and handed it to her.

'Thank you,' said Nell, 'and thank you for recommending me to your friend. Might I give you this postcard of my details to pass on to her?'

'So you're going to teach her?'

'If she requests it. She has come to me by word of mouth, not via Ingleby's.' Or would Ingleby's not see it like that, given that Mrs Liversedge was an Ingleby's connection? How complicated.

'But you're not necessarily going to teach me?'

'I hope I will.'

When could she see Jim? More to the point, how could she? If she went to his cottage, it might look like something a respectable widow had no business doing. She would have to take Leonie with her; and the children. But if she turned up with a posse, it wouldn't look businesslike. In fact, she might look like a widow dangling her family hopefully in front of a marriage prospect.

Suppose she got Alf to write thank-you notes to Mrs Jeffrey and Pom for coming to their picnic and bringing food. She always had a few sheets of good paper in the house. As Mum used to say, 'Being working class doesn't stop you being writing class.'

Taking the thank-yous round would be a legitimate reason to go. Wasn't her work a legitimate reason? But she still had to obey the proprieties. Her respectability was even more important now she was working for herself.

On her way home that evening, she made a detour down Finney Lane and its entry, hoping to see Violet. The little corner of her heart where she kept her worry for the cat nudged an inch closer to despair, but she put on a cheerful face when she reached home.

As she opened the door, a buttery, herby smell wafted out. The children ran to her. She hugged and kissed them, then chased them down the hall to the kitchen, where she kissed Leonie too.

'That smells gorgeous.'

'Get changed and it'll be on the table when you come down. Oh, there's a letter for you, with a typewritten address, no less.'

'It's probably from Miss Quinn. She said she'd send a list of her rates in case I wanted more typing.'

She took it upstairs and threw it on the bed

while she got changed and freshened up at the washstand, then she sank onto the bed and picked up her letter. It was hardly worth opening. She was a long way off needing anything else typed, but she opened it anyway.

Cold hit her right at the core of her being.

It was a letter from the magistrates' court. She had to attend – *summoned* was the word they used – to answer her husband's complaint against her.

Early in the morning, Posy reached across the bed to the empty space where Gran used to be. She wished Gran hadn't gone. No, that wasn't it. She wished Gran hadn't needed to go, wished they could all have lived together as one happy family, but that wouldn't ever be possible with Dad, would it? Now she wasn't allowed to go and see Gran, because Ma was upset with her. Posy wasn't meant to know why, but she did. She wasn't just an eavesdropper; she was now a reader of secret things. Maybe she could be a spy when she grew up. Not that a newspaper could be considered to have secret information, but it had apparently never occurred to Ma that Posy would see that bit about Mrs Hibbert and the accident when she made paper chains.

She had heard things too. She had heard Dad saying, 'We always knew your mother was altogether too fond of the Hibbert woman, but this is a great blow, to us as a family.'

Another time, he said, 'I know how distressing this is, Hilda, but you must put a brave face on it. Otherwise we'll look like fools.' He didn't say it in a snappy, bossy way either. He said it in his kind voice that wrapped itself round you and made you want to please him.

Posy watched Ma after that to see what her brave face looked like, but it didn't seem any different to her normal face. Maybe she was being brave on the inside, though that seemed unlikely. More likely she was pretending it hadn't happened, the way she pretended not to see when Dad sent for Gerald.

That was another thing. Gerald had vanished. It happened the day Gran moved out and it was obvious she had taken him – it. Did she think that would end the beatings? No, she wasn't stupid. Besides, she had promised caramels every Friday, which proved she knew the beatings would continue.

And that was yet another thing: the caramels. Now Posy wasn't allowed to go to Gran's, there were no more caramels. It had been a wonderful plan while it had worked ... which made it sound as if it had worked for months when really it had hardly happened at all.

Poor Gran. She had done her best, but nothing helped. There were no caramels and there was still Gerald – or Gerald the Second. Posy had been the first to notice Gerald's disappearance. She hadn't said a word, because of getting Gran into trouble. Then Dad saw. He froze and his face darkened. He looked at her and she had nearly wet her knickers in pure terror, but he must have known she would never dare hide Gerald.

Would he storm round to Wilton Lane and give Gran what for? But he never said a word and in due course, a new stair rod appeared. With hatred and curiosity vying for position inside her, Posy waited to see what its name would be, but Dad called it Gerald, as if the real Gerald had never vanished.

And today was Saturday; and this afternoon she would get a clobbering.

The Finney Lane kids were preparing for the Paris Olympics by running races up and down the road.

'What about doing the long jump down the entry?' suggested Lyddie.

Posy and Lyddie each slung an arm around the other's shoulders and they walked round, singing, 'Hands in the band for long jump, hands in the band for long jump...' Others joined on before they broke the line and ran round to the entry.

Some boys from Brundretts Lane were further along, clustered together, laughing but not in a nice way.

'Ignore them,' said Lyddie. 'We'll do our long jump up here.'

Horace used a twig to draw a line across the path. 'That's where you jump from.' He walked back and drew another line. 'Here's where you start running. I'll be umpire and mark where everyone lands.'

Posy joined the line waiting to jump, but she couldn't take her eyes off the Brundretts Lane lads. They were up to summat. You could always tell, even though they were facing the other way. A couple of them broke away and picked up stones. What was going on? Amidst more laughter, they started chucking the stones, but Posy couldn't see who their victim was. All at once the boys broke ranks and, with yells and whoops, started running. Posy bounced on her toes, anxious to see what was happening. Would their victim escape? Bullies!

A small black blur leapt onto Mrs Watson's back wall and the hairs on the back of Posy's neck stiffened. Violet!

She darted forwards, cinders sliding beneath her feet. 'They're attacking our cat! Come on!'

Leading the charge, Posy belted down the entry. The Brundretts boys were bigger, but they were outnumbered. With laughter and taunts, they ran away, but in an easy, loping way to show they weren't scared.

Posy skidded to a halt where Violet had gone over the wall. She opened the gate and went in. Violet was on the wall between here and Posy's house, her gooseberry-green eyes enormous as the children burst into Mrs Watson's backyard, then she jumped down the other side. The children surged back into the entry. Posy called, 'Be quiet! You'll scare her,' but they were making too much noise to hear. It was the locked gate that stopped them. Dad had never unlocked it. He said Mrs Hibbert might come back and he wasn't having her trespassing on his property.

'I can get over the gate dead easy,' bragged Jimmy. 'Give us a bunk up, Horace.'

'No,' said Posy. Dad would go mad if hordes of children appeared. 'You boys, stop here and watch for Violet. Maggie and Joan, go round the front and ask my Ma to look in't back. Me and

Lyddie will run to Wilton Lane.'

It was a good job they had done their Olympics training. She and Lyddie hared off, arriving breathless on Gran's doorstep. They hammered on the door, surging forwards as Mrs Hibbert opened it, looking vexed at the racket.

'It's Violet,' cried Posy. 'She's in our backyard. Some boys were throwing stones.'

Mrs Hibbert didn't need telling twice. She shouted over her shoulder, 'Aunt Leonie!'

Aunt Leonie! Posy banked that to think about later.

'Violet's in Finney Lane.' And Mrs Hibbert ran off.

Gran appeared, wiping her hands on her apron. 'Violet? What's happened, Posy?'

'She's in our backyard. Are you coming, Gran? Lyddie will mind the children.' Posy shoved her friend over the threshold. 'Come on, Gran.'

'Wait – I've got caramels–'

'We need to go now,' Posy insisted. Who cared about caramels? She tugged Gran outside, almost dancing round her in frustration at her slower pace as they returned to Finney Lane.

There was no sign of Mrs Hibbert, but Maggie and Joan ran to meet them.

'Your ma said the cat weren't in't back; and when Mrs Hibbert knocked, your dad told her to sling her hook.'

'Where is she now?' asked Gran.

'Up the entry.'

Gran knocked and Dad opened the door.

'Not you as well, Mother-in-law. As I've already told *your* Nell, the cat is long gone.'

337

'I'd like to see for myself, if you don't mind.'

'I do mind, as it happens. I mind very much that you're publicly doubting my honesty. Not content with snuggling up to the Hibbert woman and casting aside your own daughter–'

Gran crumpled. 'Edmund! Please, not in front of Posy.'

His head swivelled and his gaze bore into Posy. 'Inside.'

A chill speared through her stomach. She wanted to say goodbye to Gran. It would be rude not to, but with the look on Dad's face–

Posy went in. The door clicked shut behind her, a tiny click but a sound of doom all the same. She wanted to keep walking, down the hall, through the kitchen and the scullery, out the door. Walk walk walk. Keep going. Leave trouble behind. Don't get blamed.

'Posy.'

She turned round. You had to do as Dad said.

'You went to Gran's house.'

He strode past her into the parlour, his bulk brushing against her, making her stumble.

'Bring Gerald.'

One thing Jim would be glad to return to when he resumed his old life was indoor plumbing. A daily strip-wash did the job, but not with any sense of luxury, especially in winter. On Wednesdays, Mrs Jeffrey went next door for an evening with Pom while he had a bath in front of the kitchen fireplace; and on Saturdays after work he took his wash things to the public baths.

He strode along Beech Road with his towel

rolled under his arm, heading for home. Sparrows chirped in the privet that surrounded the rec and the fresh aroma of newly mown grass filled the air. He felt cautiously hopeful. If Nell could establish herself as sewing tutor to the middle-class, this would bring her a step closer to him socially ... wouldn't it?

He had some of Miss Quinn's postcards, which he planned to give to Patsy tomorrow in case any of her friends had sewing machines.

'How come you're handing these out?' Patsy would ask. 'What's this Mrs Hibbert to you?'

'She's someone I met on my window-cleaning travels,' he planned to say, followed by a brief outline of Nell's circumstances; and that would tactfully introduce the idea of Nell into the family.

He turned into the path at the side of the farm and there she was, coming towards him. His heart gave a bump of delight. Surprise too.

'I was thinking of you,' he called.

Her face was pale, her expression unreadable.

He walked up to her, anxiety sharpening his voice. 'What's wrong?'

'You said – you offered help.'

Gratification warmed him. 'Come to the cottage.'

'Can we talk privately?'

'There's a patch of garden in the front.'

They walked up the path. Mrs Jeffrey's kitchen door stood open; she was across the path in the vegetable patch, picking runner beans from a wigwam smothered in red flowers and dainty but vigorous tendrils.

She smiled at Nell. 'You found him, then?'

'Mrs Hibbert needs a spot of business advice,' said Jim. 'We'll sit in the front garden.' To Nell, he said, 'I'll pop my things upstairs.'

He deposited his towel and washbag in his room and ran down again. Picking up a folding chair from behind the back door, he ushered her round the side of the cottage into the small, cheerful garden, if 'garden' was the right word for something not much bigger than a handkerchief. It could do with tidying up and cutting back, but not too much. He liked the casual abundance. He set the chair down for Nell in the ankle-deep grass in front of a plant with plentiful tall stems adorned with small trumpets the colour of apple blossom. If he had hoped to please her, she didn't notice, any more than she seemed to notice Pom's marguerites nodding next door.

He leant against the hip-high garden wall, crossed his ankles and folded his arms.

'Is there a problem at Ingleby's?'

'No – well, yes, but that's not why I'm here.' Her shoulders sagged and she let out a sigh that sounded almost painful. 'I've been summoned to appear at the magistrates' court.'

Ankles and arms uncrossed of their own accord and he stood upright. 'Why?'

'A complaint has been made against me.'

'By Ingleby's?' Preposterous.

'By...' She covered her mouth with her hand, then let it drop uselessly to her lap. Rising, she turned her back to him, then swung round again, her glance briefly brushing across his. 'By my husband.'

'Your husband!'

A dozen conversations replayed in his head. Alf's voice: 'My daddy was buried with ham.'

Her lips pressed together so tightly they had gone white. Jim leant against the wall again. He rubbed the back of his neck. He couldn't breathe.

'I thought you were a widow.'

'Everyone thinks I'm a widow.'

Half a dozen bees concentrated their efforts on the fuzzy purple flowers of the lavender bush.

'If you want my help, you'll have to be more forthcoming.' He spoke more crisply than he had intended. Intended? He didn't know what he intended, not now she was married. *My daddy was buried with ham, but I'm not old enough to remember.* No wonder. There had never been a funeral.

'He's a bigamist. I found out about the other wife and I left him.' She lifted her chin and there was defiance in her eyes. 'Do you blame me?'

Shock rolled through him. 'A bigamist? Are you certain?'

'Oh aye. I saw his other son. Sandy hair and blue eyes: does that remind you of anyone? So I ran away. I brought Alf here and made a new life; Cassie was born a few months later.'

'How did Mr Hibbert find you?'

'Through that newspaper article.'

'What does your husband want?'

'Don't call him that! He isn't my husband.'

'If he married you first and the other woman second, then he is your husband. I repeat: what does he want?'

'He turned up a fortnight ago, demanding money. The article made me sound successful. He wanted my savings.'

341

'Is the magistrates' hearing to do with money?'

'I don't know. It just said I have to answer his complaint. Here, read it for yourself.' She pulled out a letter.

He read it, then continued staring at it. She was married. She had captured his heart and she was married. She had let him believe she was a widow. She had let everyone believe it, including her children.

'Can you help me?' she asked.

And, God help him, he didn't want to. He wanted her to go away and leave him to get to grips with what she had done and to nurse his injured heart. But he cared about her and nothing could change that. Of course he would help. But ... but he wouldn't hope any more. He would help her because she was in a bad situation and the original fault wasn't hers.

But the ensuing fault was hers. The lies about being widowed.

Put that aside. Be professional. Treat her as a client. That was all she could ever be from now on: a client.

'I'll accompany you to court and represent you. I also need your permission to confide–'

'You can't tell anyone,' she cried.

'I was going to say I'll confide in an old colleague, but if you imagine this is going to remain a private matter, I think you'll be disappointed.'

She sank onto the chair. The colour had abandoned her face, leaving a grey tinge. That was the despair, but he couldn't afford to soften.

'Do you have a copy of your marriage certificate?'

'I left it behind when I ran away.'

'Where did you live? I'll write to the registrar to request a copy, and also a copy of your husband's second marriage certificate. Before you leave, you must furnish me with all the relevant information, names, dates, addresses.'

'I don't know when he married ... her.'

'I'll ask for a search to be done for the second certificate.'

'Why do you need it?' she asked.

'To prove the bigamy. Whatever your husband's complaint against you, this is going to put the court on your side, but we have to prove it.'

'I see.'

While he thought it through, he placed his hand over the lower part of his face, drawing his fingers and thumb together, pushing in his cheeks and squeezing his mouth. Then, with a sigh, he let his hand drop. 'Unfortunately, there isn't time for us to receive the certificates before you have to appear in court, especially as there has to be a search for the second set of marriage lines.'

'Will that matter?'

'It won't stop me accusing your husband of bigamy, if that's what you mean. That's what I don't understand. He must know that you'll counter any complaint by revealing his bigamy.'

'I told him that when he demanded my savings.'

'Yet here he is, taking you to court. He must believe he has good reason. Is there anything you have neglected to tell me?'

'Of course not.'

His eyebrows climbed up his forehead. 'Of

course not? After two years of pretending to be a widow, I don't think you're in a position to be indignant.'

Her glare collapsed into bewildered blinking. Jim scrubbed his face with his hands.

'I apologise. That was uncalled for.'

'No, it wasn't. I'm sure you won't be the only one to throw it in my face.'

Quietly he asked, 'Is there anything you can think of to explain this summons?'

'No ... honestly.'

He nodded. He felt stunned, but he had to ignore that. 'If you'll excuse me a minute, I'll fetch a pen and paper and you can give me the details I require.'

When she had written them down, he took the sheet from her without looking at her, then he stepped back and waved her ahead of him out of the garden. She walked away down the path to Beech Road. He didn't watch her go. He went upstairs into his small sitting room. He had a schoolmaster's desk, a battered old piece with a lift-up lid. He couldn't manage without a desk and this one had seemed in keeping with Mrs Jeffrey's humble home.

He lifted the lid, took Miss Quinn's postcards from the shelf above and placed them inside the desk, right at the back under a couple of books.

Then he closed the lid and went downstairs.

# Chapter Twenty-Three

Nell stood outside the magistrates' court. Jim had offered to call for her, but she had refused. No one in Wilton Lane knew where she was and she wanted it to stay that way. Being exposed as a bigamist would put paid to Stan's scheme, whatever it was, and no one else need ever know.

A black motor car drew up and Jim climbed out. He was dressed in a well-made suit and the discreet gleam at his collar was undoubtedly repeated at his cuffs. How handsome he looked. Nell felt warm inside, but the warmth was quickly swamped by a chill as his smart appearance brought home to her the seriousness of her situation.

He leant across to pay the driver, then joined her, awarding her an approving glance. She was wearing her smart black work dress with her forest-green jacket. She had taken the precaution of substituting her white collar and cuffs with cream, so her dress looked less of a workwear garment.

'I thought I'd try it out,' she had told Leonie – another lie to add to the list.

'How are you?' Jim asked. 'Nervous?'

She waited for him to add, *There's no need,* but he didn't.

'When we tell the court about Stan's bigamy–' she began.

'Let's hope so.' He opened the door for her. 'We won't be in court as such. I've managed to get the matter heard in one of the rooms.'

'That's good.'

'The price we pay is that certain formalities have been set aside.'

She let out a breath. 'Better and better.'

'One of which is that I haven't been informed of the nature of your husband's complaint.'

'All I care about is the privacy.'

'The room will still be open to the public.'

'Who will want to see? Nosy parkers who come here to gloat over the burglars and vagrants won't care. They'll want to see the good stuff in the courtroom.'

'Or the attempt at privacy could make your matter more intriguing. I'm sorry, but it's my duty to warn you.'

She said lightly, 'You aren't being very reassuring.'

'I should have thought you would find it reassuring to be told what to expect. Would you prefer me to pretend you have nothing to worry about?'

She felt a sting of vexation, underneath which swished something scary. She wasn't in the company of Jim Franks any longer. It was more than the absence of the cloth cap and the working man's boots. Gone was the good-hearted friend who would do anything for anyone, replaced by a keen-eyed, superbly tailored professional gentleman. She had glimpsed James Franks the solicitor that time in her kitchen when he had advised Leonie. Now she was seeing the real thing.

He took her across the lofty foyer, their footsteps ringing on the tiled floor. There was a wide stair-case with shallow treads. At the top, Jim escorted her along a couple of door-lined corridors.

An older, soberly dressed gentleman came to-wards them, his red sagging cheeks lifting as he smiled. 'Mr Franks, what a pleasure to see you again, sir. Permit me to show you the way.'

'Thank you, Robbins. It's good to see you too. This is Mrs Hibbert, whom I'm representing.'

Mr Robbins led them back the way he had come, rounding a corner and opening a door. 'You're early, sir. Do you wish to go in now?'

Nell suppressed a shudder. 'I don't want to sit in there waiting.'

'If you wait elsewhere,' said Jim, 'you may find yourself walking in under the public gaze. If you go in now, you can sit with your back to the public seating, and when people are admitted, no one need see your face.'

She walked in. Well, this room was nothing to worry about: there was hardly any space for on-lookers. Then she realised it was an anteroom and Mr Robbins was showing them to the door on the other side, which opened onto a disappointingly spacious room. A splendid desk at one end faced the room and everything else faced the desk. To the side at the top end of the room were smaller desks in front of a bookcase containing leather-bound volumes. In front of the desk were two tables, each with two chairs, and behind these were three rows of wooden seats. Nell hoped no one would be ghoulish enough to occupy any of those.

Jim indicated the table further away and pulled out a chair for her. He said, 'I shan't be long,' and left.

She half-rose, then sank back, heart thumping. She was perfectly capable of sitting at a table on her own. The sound of the door opening made her look round. A lady and gentleman walked in. Nell pulled her handbag onto her knee and took a great interest in its contents. By the time Jim took the seat beside her, there were several murmured conversations going on behind her and she was frozen with shame.

He spoke quietly. 'Your husband's solicitor is Bernard Norton and the magistrate is Mr Aitcheson.'

'What is he like?'

'He's a bit of a stuffed shirt, but that's only to be expected in a magistrate of his age.'

'A stuffed shirt will be horrified by Stan's bigamy.' Stan was going to be sorry for dragging her here. Before the morning was out, she would have ground him beneath her heel.

'I don't mean to knock your confidence,' Jim murmured, 'but don't forget that we still don't know the nature of Mr Hibbert's complaint.'

'It can't be anything bad because I've never done anything bad. A trumped-up matter: that's all it can be. He was stupid to demand my savings and now he's added to his stupidity by doing this.'

'Whatever it is, Bernard Norton doesn't think it's stupid. Here they are.'

Nell looked across to where Stan and a balding gentleman were taking their places at the other table. Stan wore his campaign medals on his jacket. Whose idea was that? A fat lot of good it would do him once Mr Aitcheson got wind of his bigamy.

He winked at her and her mouth dropped open in astonishment.

'Mrs Hibbert,' said Jim and she turned to find him on his feet, 'may I present Mr Fairbrother?'

'How do you do?' Mr Fairbrother was a distinguished gentleman with important-looking whiskers. He had a rumbly voice, which made him sound kindly – until you noticed his eyes. They weren't cold or unkind, but they were sharp and would miss nothing.

Nell murmured a greeting. He gave her a courtly bow.

'Mr Fairbrother is a former senior colleague of mine,' said Jim. 'I have informed him of your situation and he is here as an observer in case I need to consult him.'

Fairbrother! But she could hardly ask.

'All rise.'

A door behind the handsome desk opened and two men took up their positions at the desks at the side of the room. A dumpy man with a hooked nose marched in and permitted a minion to pull out his chair. The minion also placed some papers on the desk.

'You may sit.'

A discreet rustle whispered around the room as everyone obeyed. How many watchers were there in the public seats?

Mr Aitcheson spread out the papers. 'The Hibbert matter: unfortunate business.' He looked up without raising his head, as if he were peering over the tops of non-existent spectacles. 'Are there ladies present? Kindly remove them.'

Jim was on his feet in an instant. 'Mr Aitcheson, I must protest–'

'Duly noted.' He glanced towards the rear of the room. 'Show the ladies out, will you? Not fit for their ears.'

Not fit? There was a kettledrum inside Nell's chest, delivering deep, echoing thumps that reverberated through her body and packed her ears. She turned to Jim, but he silenced her with a glance. From behind her came the muted sounds of departure, and something else too, an alertness in the air, as if the men were sitting up straighter.

Mr Aitcheson eyed Nell. Her skin prickled.

'Mr Franks,' the magistrate began.

Jim stood up again. 'Sir, if you're about to suggest that Mrs Hibbert should be required to leave, I'd like to state for the record that this would be highly inappropriate. As one of the people concerned in this matter, and as the person against whom this case has been brought, she is entitled to be present. Indeed, her presence is essential.'

'Is it?' replied Mr Aitcheson. 'She has you to represent her interests.' His gaze slid between Nell and Jim to someone behind them – Mr Fairbrother? – and then he glanced over to the clerks at the desks in front of the bookcase. 'Very well. She may remain, but you'll be accountable for her good conduct. I don't want any hysteria or suchlike.'

'Mrs Hibbert's conduct will be impeccable, sir,' said Jim. He resumed his seat.

Nell's muscles quivered with rage. She moved a

fraction, slanting her body away from Jim. It wasn't his fault, but she couldn't help it.

Mr Aitcheson poised his pen over a sheet of paper, as though about to take down every word in Pitman's shorthand. 'This seems to me a straightforward matter. I hope it can quickly be brought to a conclusion, so I can have my luncheon.' He looked over his non-existent spectacles at Nell as if it would be her fault if his lamb chops got cold, then waved his hand in Mr Norton's direction. 'Proceed.'

Mr Norton rose. 'Thank you, sir. My client, Mr Stanley Hibbert of Annerby, Lancashire, is here to make amends with his estranged wife, Eleanor Margaret Hibbert, late of Annerby, now residing in Chorlton-cum-Hardy. I'm sure Mr Hibbert joins you in wishing for a speedy resolution, not least because his presence here means he is absent from his long-time employment and hence he is not receiving his salary. I hope the court will take this into account as a sign of how serious this matter is to him.'

'Duly noted.' Mr Aitcheson wafted his pen over the paper, but didn't write anything. 'Proceed.'

Mr Norton favoured Nell with a smile – signifying what? – before addressing the magistrate. 'My client and his wife have been estranged for over two years. I say *estranged* and yet I hesitate to use the word, as it might be taken to suggest mutual agreement, which is not the case. The fact is, Mr Aitcheson – and may I at this point offer my gratitude for your delicacy in having the ladies removed from the proceedings – that Mrs Hibbert left her husband.'

A frisson ran round the room and darted up Nell's spine, shaking droplets of disapproval inside her.

Jim was on his feet. 'Sir, the circumstances–'

'–are about to be explained by Mr Norton.' The pen wafted two or three inches above the paper. 'Proceed.'

'The circumstances are indeed distressing,' said Mr Norton. 'Mrs Hibbert not only left her husband, but flat out ran away. There was no discussion, no argument, no gradual disintegration of the marriage. This gentleman,' and he stepped aside as though to allow Stan ample space to soak up everyone's sympathy, 'arrived home one evening at the end of an honest day's labour to find his home cold and empty. This man, this former soldier, who served his country in the Great War, found himself abandoned.'

Mr Aitcheson's gaze flicked in Nell's direction. 'Is this true?'

'Well ... yes, but–'

'Proceed.'

'Furthermore, Mrs Hibbert took with her Mr Hibbert's son and heir.'

Murmurs and movements from behind her made Nell squirm. Why didn't Jim stand up for her?

'Mr Hibbert has not laid eyes on his son from that day to this,' Mr Norton added.

'He didn't need to,' Nell muttered. 'He's got at least one other son to keep him occupied.'

Mr Aitcheson addressed Jim. 'Do you dispute this, Mr Franks, or may we accept all this as fact?'

Jim rose. 'What Mr Norton says is true, but

these are not all the facts. Mrs Hibbert–'

'–will have her turn in due course,' said Mr Aitcheson, wafting his pen.

'Rather than continue with his heavily biased view of events, sir,' said Jim, 'perhaps Mr Norton would be good enough to explain why my client has been summoned here today.'

About time too! Those disapproving men behind her would change their minds about Stan when they heard the truth.

Mr Norton inclined his head. 'Mr Hibbert has lodged a complaint against Mrs Hibbert that she abandoned him and deprived him and their son of a normal family life.' He spoke directly to Mr Aitcheson. 'It is Mr Hibbert's wish, sir, that his family should be returned to him.'

How was she to make amends with Hilda? The lively, laughing girl who had brought such pride and happiness to her and Hedley's lives might have grown into a disappointing droopy-drawers, but she was still Leonie's beloved only child and she couldn't bear to have bad blood between them. Knowing it was her own fault made it harder. How could she have been so carried away by her admiration for Nell as to say something that was bound to hurt Hilda?

Mind you, trust Hilda to take it the wrong way. Leonie pressed a hand to her breast. Where had that treacherous thought sprung from?

Well, she was going to put things right. Talking to Hilda hadn't helped. In fact, it had made it worse. So that left one possibility: Edmund.

Reluctance, tinged with resentment, uncoiled inside her. Edmund was the last person she wanted to turn to, but no one else could make a difference. Besides, wasn't she the one who had urged Nell to make amends with her brother-in-law? She had no business pressing Nell to do the decent thing if she wasn't prepared to do the equivalent, and that meant approaching Edmund.

No time like the present. She would take Cassie round to Annie's, and that would free her to tackle Edmund.

Nell sucked in her breath so sharply, it felt like sandpaper scraping her throat. Did Stan really imagine she would go back to him? And why did he want her? What about Mrs Vicarage Lane?

'Silence!' called a voice.

Jim was on his feet. 'Mr Aitcheson.'

'If I might trouble you to restrain yourself,' said Mr Norton, 'I haven't quite finished.' He looked at the magistrate.

Mr Aitcheson nodded. 'Proceed.'

'In making this request, Mr Hibbert extends it to include his wife's young daughter, even though there is a question as to the child's paternity–'

Nell's chair crashed over backwards as she sprang up. Her palms slapped the tabletop as she glared at Stan. She felt like upending the table.

'How dare you! I left you in the February and Cassie were born in September and I've got the birth certificate to prove it.'

'So you left your husband, knowing you were carrying his child,' said Mr Norton, 'a child of whom he knew nothing until he read about her in the newspaper.'

'Mr Franks,' said Mr Aitcheson, 'kindly control your client. You assured me there would be no hysterics.'

Jim had hold of her arm, but she wouldn't sit down. He said quietly, 'You aren't helping yourself.'

'At least I'm trying, which is more than you are.'

His expression didn't change. 'If you don't calm yourself, he'll make you leave.'

She yanked her arm free and resumed her seat.

'I apologise for my client,' said Jim, 'but I'm sure every respectable, right-minded gentleman present can appreciate her indignation and distress at hearing herself maligned in that way.'

'Perhaps,' suggested Mr Norton, 'the gentlemen present would be more inclined to be sympathetic had Mrs Hibbert not deserted her husband in the first place.'

'Yes, let's discuss that, shall we?' said Jim. 'It's time Mrs Hibbert's side of the story is heard.'

Mr Aitcheson coughed. 'If you don't mind, Mr Franks, we'll proceed at my pace, not yours. Mr Norton, have you anything to add on behalf of Mr Hibbert?'

'Not at this time, sir.'

Mr Aitcheson looked at Jim over the rims of his invisible glasses. 'Proceed.'

'It is true that Mrs Hibbert left her husband; it is true that she did so as a matter of suddenness.'

'On a whim, you mean?'

'No, sir. She did it in response to the discovery that Mr Hibbert is a bigamist.'

More murmurs and rustling from behind. Nell

355

started to feel vindicated, but it didn't last. The atmosphere wasn't one of sympathy so much as fascination. The audience was lapping up the show.

Mr Aitcheson lifted his head properly. 'A bigamist? Are you certain?'

'Allow Mrs Hibbert to tell you herself.'

'Not if she's going to fall into another fit of the vapours.'

'I assure you, sir, my client has full control of her senses.' Jim sat down.

Nell stood. 'Stan's other wife had a baby and the district nurse came to my house by mistake. I went to the nurses' station and found the other wife's address and when I went round there, she said she was Mrs Stanley Hibbert.'

'Are you the wife of Mr Hibbert's first or second marriage ceremony?' asked Mr Aitcheson.

'The first.'

'How do you know?'

'I saw it with my own eyes. My Alf – my son is older than her son.'

'So you are the legal wife.'

Nell lifted her chin. 'Yes, sir.'

'Which makes it all the more unreasonable that you left your husband and broke up his family.'

'He had another family to console him,' she snapped. Jim softly cleared his throat: a warning. 'Real wife or not, sir, I were shocked and furious at the bigamy. I wanted to rescue my son from any danger of seeing his father's other family.'

'Does your son know of the bigamy?'

'No, sir. He believes his father was a good, hard-working man, who loved us and served his country.' Please let that be sufficient.

'Where does your son think his father is now?'

Oh, lord, now she was for it. 'He thinks– I told him his father is dead, sir.'

There were exclamations from behind, low-voiced but full of consternation. One of the clerks called 'Silence!' and the room subsided.

'That's disgraceful,' declared Mr Aitcheson.

'She had to tell him something, I suppose.' Mr Norton was on his feet. His voice was reasonable, but his eyes were sly. 'Who else has been told this lie, Mrs Hibbert?'

She froze. What could she say that wouldn't damn her?

'Perhaps I might spare the lady's blushes,' said Mr Norton. 'Should we assume everyone you know in Manchester believes you to be a widow?'

'And what if they do?' Jim came to his feet. 'How else was Mrs Hibbert to cope? You may frown upon her decision to leave her bigamous husband, but you cannot deny the steadiness of character and the honest maternal love that prompted her to extricate her child from a situation that would in time result in scandal and lasting shame. Mrs Hibbert values her respectability and everything about her life in Manchester attests to that.'

'I'm sure it does,' said Mr Norton, 'if you over-look the fact that her husband is alive and well.'

'One moment,' said Mr Aitcheson.

One of the clerks had come forward to offer him a piece of paper. He read it, then had a whispered conversation with the clerk before lapsing into thought. Nell was ready to leap up and strangle him by the time he looked over his non-existent glasses and addressed his listeners.

'It has been brought to my attention that higher courts than this have shown leniency to bigamists in recent years in cases where the bigamy was committed by a man who served his country in the Great War and made the so-called marriage after returning from active service. This isn't to say bigamy is ever acceptable, but no one benefits if two families are left without a breadwinner.'

It beggared belief. Was Stan going to get off scot-free?

Mr Norton stood up. He looked pleased with himself. Too pleased.

'Mr Aitcheson, I understand, indeed I share, the court's distaste for the leniency you have described. It is, however, by the by in this instance.' He paused, extending the moment. 'Mrs Hibbert may have felt at the time that she had ample reason to believe in her husband's bigamy, but she was mistaken. Mr Stanley Hibbert never went through a second marriage ceremony with the other woman.'


## Chapter Twenty-Four

Leonie felt tense and trapped, but more than anything she felt determined. The hooter sounded and she walked through the gates and across the yard. Inside, the building smelt of ink and wooden floors laced with the tang of oiled machinery.

A young fellow in a brown overall stopped to

speak to her. 'You look lost. Can I help you?'

'No need,' came a familiar voice. 'I'll take care of our visitor.' And there was Edmund in his shirt-sleeves, with elbow-garters up his forearms to prevent his sleeves from sliding down. 'What brings you here?' His voice was rich and deep, pleasing to listen to. No one overhearing him would imagine that he had as good as slung her out of her home of forty years.

'I'm sorry to interrupt your dinner hour, but I have to speak to you.'

'About Hilda?'

'I'll take five minutes of your time.'

'I can do better than that, Mother-in-law. There's a little place down the road. It doesn't look like much, but it's clean and the food is good. I'll fetch my jacket and take you there.'

He was gone before she could object, returning in his jacket and hat. He opened the door and bowed her out. She felt vexed and uncomfortable. All she wanted was to talk and now look at her, being escorted along the road to be treated to a meal. How did he always turn things his way?

'In we go, Mother-in-law.'

A bell jingled above her head. Edmund was right. The place didn't look anything special, but her eyes, which always became razor-sharp in the presence of someone else's housework, found nothing to object to in the simple furnishings and the cakes and scones under glass domes on the counter. She scuttled to a table and sat down before he could annoy her further by pulling out her chair. The menu was written on a piece of card.

'What would you like?' Edmund offered.

Anything. She didn't care. 'Poached eggs.'

He glanced at her.

'Please,' she added.

'Kedgeree for me, I think.' He gave the order to the waitress. 'And tea for two, if you would be so kind.'

Leonie seethed. It wasn't fair that he could be charming and attentive. Smarmy bugger. He ought to be rude and critical like the scheming bully he really was. He ought to hurt everybody, so they would all know what he was like behind his front door.

Her old front door. Her heart dipped. She mustn't let that upset her. She needed him on her side.

'You said you wish to discuss Hilda. I assume you're here to seek my assistance?'

Why couldn't he let her make the request herself? Goaded, she said, 'It's the least you can do after the way you misquoted the newspaper.'

His black eyebrows climbed up his broad forehead. 'When I read your words in the paper, I was vexed and hurt on my wife's behalf; so perhaps it's understandable if I misquoted you. Besides, what I mistakenly told Hilda and what you actually said weren't so very different, were they?'

She wasn't here to discuss that. 'I want to make amends, but Hilda won't listen.'

'Tell me what you want me to do. Now that we no longer live together, it's even more important that we're on good terms.'

'If you ask Hilda to give me another chance, she will.'

'I'm flattered you think so highly of my powers of persuasion.'

'Will you do it? Please. You say you want us all to get on.'

'It will be my pleasure to intervene, Mother-in-law, for the benefit of the family.'

Relief gushed through her. 'Thank you, Edmund.'

'Here's an opportunity for you also to do something for the good of the family.' He moved and she expected him to lean forward confidingly, but instead he leant backwards. 'Will you consider doing something too?'

What did he mean? She thought of Posy. She would do anything for Posy. 'Of course.'

'It's a matter of trust. Families are built on trust. You trust me to talk to Hilda on your behalf, and I trust you not to take advantage of my good nature.'

'I don't follow.'

'Will you do me the honour of allowing me to keep your precious things in my safekeeping? Do you trust me that much?' He held up a finger. 'Say nothing now, but think about it. I hope that soon you'll come to me and make your request and I'll be proud to consent, and I'll also sort things out with Hilda.' He sighed and nodded. 'What a splendid day that will be – for the whole family.'

The waitress appeared with their plates.

'Thank you,' said Edmund. 'This looks delicious. And here's our tea. Will you pour, Mother-in-law? Oh dear, is your hand trembling. Would you mind pouring?' he asked the waitress. 'I've just given my mother-in-law the good news that a misunderstanding can be resolved and she's feeling overcome.'

Nell wasn't able to eat. She sat hunched in her seat at a corner table in the restaurant, feeling as if the stuffing was pouring out of her. Jim had spent the duration of the meal quizzing her about Stan, obliging her to resurrect all kinds of small details.

'Is it true?' she asked. 'Is Stan really not a bigamist?'

'Presumably. When I hear back from the registrar in Annerby, that should confirm it.'

'I shan't go back to him.'

'You might have to, if Mr Aitcheson awards him custody of the children.'

She sat upright, knocking the table. A cut-glass water goblet toppled, spilling its contents on the linen. Mortified, she made a grab for the goblet and started dabbing with her napkin, only for a waiter to appear at her elbow. Before she knew it, her napkin was gone from her hand.

'I'll arrange for fresh linen, sir,' the waiter murmured, 'or would you prefer to finish your meal at another table?'

'No to both, thank you,' said Jim. He waved the waiter away.

'I'm sorry,' said Nell.

'No, I should apologise for giving you a shock.' The sympathy in his face scared her.

'Can Mr Aitcheson take my children off me? That's cruel.' She cast about for something to cling to. 'He's only a magistrate. Surely he's not important enough.'

'Believe me, we don't want this referred to a higher court. Being in the magistrates' court gives us a little leeway.'

'Leeway? My children are at risk and the most you can offer is leeway?'

'I suggest we get back to court. I need to speak to Mr Fairbrother. I expect Robbins can find you somewhere private to wait.'

'I should be there when you talk to Mr Fairbrother.'

'I don't doubt your ability to hold your own, but he and I can cover more ground by ourselves.'

An objection hovered on her lips, but she thought better of it. If this Mr Fairbrother was the gentleman paying her bill in Victoria Park, it was better all round if he didn't have the chance to realise who she was. She couldn't risk being sacked because of this.

Soon she was closeted in a small office deep inside the court building. Every time she sat down, she jumped up again like a jack-in-the-box. She was a married woman. Well, she had been that all along, but it hadn't felt like it. Stan's bigamy had freed her from the marriage, in her own eyes if not in law. But now she wasn't free after all.

Mr Robbins came to escort her to the magistrates' room. Jim joined her.

'Where are the public?' she asked.

'Mr Norton and I prevailed upon Mr Aitcheson to hear the afternoon session in private.'

'Mr Norton?' She glanced beyond Jim to where Stan and his solicitor sat.

'It is in no one's interests for this to be heard in public.'

That was something, but she found no comfort in it. She had come here so sure that Stan would get the trouncing of his life, but everything had been turned upside down.

'All rise.'

Mr Aitcheson walked in and settled himself. 'Mr Hibbert, you wish your wife to return to you?'

Stan stood up. 'Yes, sir. I've seen the error of my ways and I want to do right by my lawful wife and family.'

Mr Norton rose. 'Mr Aitcheson might find that commendable, except that you hardly did right by Mrs Hibbert before.'

'If the gentleman orders her to return to me, I promise to be a good and faithful husband.' He added in an almost jokey voice, 'I know my Nell, sir. She won't let me get away with owt after this.'

'What can you offer her?' enquired Mr Norton.

'A decent home in the town where she grew up, the place where her parents and grandparents are buried. She has a strong sense of family, does Nell, especially for her poor dead brothers who gave their lives for this country, and her sister. It's grieved me these past two years that she felt obliged to leave her family home behind. It's where I'm from an' all, and it's right that my child-ren grow up there.'

'Indeed, Mr Hibbert,' said Mr Norton. 'What else can you offer?'

'A warm welcome from my mother, who is willing to forgive and forget that Nell left without a word.'

'Are you in a position of financial security?' asked Mr Norton.

'Yes, sir. I'm an upholsterer by trade and I've been in the same works all my life, from being an apprentice.'

'One more question,' said Mr Norton. 'What of the other woman?'

Stan cleared his throat. 'She no longer resides in Annerby, sir.' Resides? That wasn't Stan talking. He was repeating what he had been told to say.

'You're separated?'

'Yes, sir.'

'Permanently?' asked Mr Aitcheson.

'Yes, sir.'

'And the children of the liaison?' asked Mr Norton.

'Gone as well, sir. Permanently. We're no longer a couple.'

'You never were a couple,' snapped Mr Aitcheson, 'not in any way deemed acceptable by respectable society.'

'The *soi-disant* Mrs Hibbert has left with another man,' said Mr Norton, 'and they're no longer in the district.'

Mr Aitcheson's pen made rapid passes above the paper. 'Mr Franks, do you wish to ask Mr Hibbert anything?'

Jim stood. 'So now we know why you wish for Mrs Hibbert's return. Your – let us be polite and refer to her as your common-law wife – has departed and you're in need of a housekeeper.'

'That's not it, sir,' said Stan. 'My Nell is a good woman and I want her back – and the children. I want to put things right. She deserves that.'

'Yet when you went to see her in her house, it

365

was to demand money. Correct me if I'm wrong.'

'No, no, no,' exclaimed the magistrate. 'I won't have that. As her husband, he is entitled to her money.'

'At the time she left her husband,' said Jim, 'Mrs Hibbert had good reason to do so. Since then, she has worked hard to provide a home for her children, who are fed, clothed, clean and happy.'

'As happy as children can be whose father is dead,' said Mr Norton.

'The children are settled, thanks to Mrs Hibbert's devotion.'

'Settled?' demanded Mr Aitcheson. 'Without their father? Nonsense. It's a hand-to-mouth existence at best without a man's wage. If the son doesn't grow up tied to his mother's apron strings, he'll be a tearaway. A boy needs a man's hand to guide him and a man is entitled to expect his wife to look after his home. Mr Hibbert's conduct in setting up the second household was disgraceful, but if higher courts can show leniency to actual bigamy, it behoves me to overlook the common-law arrangements, unsavoury as they were. Therefore...'

Nell caught her breath. Was he about to order–?

'One final question for Mr Hibbert,' said Jim.

Mr Aitcheson sighed. 'If you must.'

'Mr Hibbert, if your family were to return to you, where would they live? In Vicarage Lane?'

'What is the significance?' demanded the magistrate.

'I'm sure Mr Hibbert will be pleased to explain.' Jim sat down.

Stan shifted awkwardly. 'It's where I lived with

my other family, sir.'

Jim rose in a fluid movement. 'You mean your bit on the side and her bastard offspring? I beg your pardon. I forgot we were being polite about your extramarital arrangements. I mean, your common-law wife and her illegitimate brood. Mr Aitcheson, your remarks suggest you're in favour of Mrs Hibbert's returning to her husband, but please consider the impropriety, the injury and the injustice in asking her to move into 14 Vicarage Lane.'

The room went quiet. Nell held her breath.

Mr Aitcheson looked at the paper in front of him, as if he had spent the day making important notes. At last he looked up properly, not over his invisible spectacles.

'Of Mr Hibbert's private life, the less said the better. 'Whatever justification Mrs Hibbert believed she had in abandoning him, she had no business separating her children from their father. As for telling them their father is dead, that is the act of an unnatural mother. She is fortunate her husband is willing to have her back. If she returns to him, she can live her life in the home, as a decent wife and mother ought, and possibly she will eventually live down her wrong and inappropriate actions.'

'*My* wrong and inappropriate actions?' cried Nell. 'What about Stan's?'

'Really, Mr Franks, not another fit of the vapours.'

'I apologise.' Jim looked at her.

She subsided, but she was seething. Or rather, she tried to seethe. She tried to keep the anger

367

burning, but how could she when she was quaking with fear? This man could order her to return to Stan. Whether she obeyed was another matter, but how could she not obey if Stan was given the children?

Mr Aitcheson threw down his pen. 'This woman is a runaway wife and an unnatural mother. As such, she doesn't merit any special consideration, and yet even she cannot be expected to move into that other female's house. Mr Hibbert, you must make alternative arrangements to house your family.' He snapped his fingers in the air. 'Diary, please.'

One of the clerks took a book to him. They flicked pages to and fro, whispering as they did so.

'Today is the 1st July,' said Mr Aitcheson. 'We shall reconvene on Friday 25th. By that time, Mr Hibbert, I expect you to have made adequate arrangements, so that I can make my decision without any further objections from Mr Franks.'

## Chapter Twenty-Five

'How could you? How *could* you?' Through Leonie's tears, the kitchen blurred as if it was starting to melt. It might as well melt. It wasn't anything like as smart as her old kitchen. 'You lied to everyone. You lied to me and Hedley.'

'Aunt Leonie, I'm sorry–'

'Aye, now you've been found out. Me and

Hedley trusted you; we loved you.'

Nell squeezed her eyes shut for a moment. She looked so vulnerable that Leonie's heart ached, but she wouldn't be swayed. She absorbed the ache into her own misery.

'I could never have hoped to live with anyone kinder than you and Mr Brent,' said Nell.

'You lied all along.' It all came bubbling up. She couldn't stop it. 'I were piggy-in-the-middle for two whole years, I were, between you and Hilda and Edmund. They could see how fond me and Hedley were of you and the children and they weren't best pleased, I can tell you. The number of times I had to soothe ruffled feathers, and all along you was playing me for a fool.'

'You know that isn't true. If you and Mr Brent loved me and the kids, we loved you back, and I wasn't stringing you along.'

'Yes, you were: me, Hedley, the neighbours, the grocer, the milkman, the–'A laugh burst out of her. 'I were going to say the window cleaner, but you did tell him, didn't you? How long has he known?'

'Only since–'

'And there was me thinking he was coming here out of concern for me, but really he was–'

'No,' Nell exclaimed. 'Say what you like about me, but I won't hear a word against him. He never knew a thing until I had the letter from the court. Without him there today, I'd be packing to go to Annerby now; either that or I'd have lost the children if I wouldn't go back to Stan. How do you think that feels? I know you're hurt and angry and you've every right to be; but I'm hurt

369

and angry too after what Stan put me through today. Maybe you think I deserve it, and maybe you're right, but it still hurts.'

They stared at one another across the table. Across it. That said a lot. Normally they cosied up, side by side, enjoying a good natter or sharing their woes, supporting one another like ... like family.

'Don't turn this round,' Leonie hissed. What was she saying? She loved Nell. But she couldn't help it. It wasn't just Nell and the lies and the disgrace. It was everything, flaming everything. 'Don't make out we should all be sorry for you. Do you have any idea what I did today? And I did it partly because of you, because how could I encourage you to make amends with your black sheep brother-in-law if I wasn't prepared to go cap in hand to Edmund? Practically prostrated myself on the floor, I did, and he walked all over me an' all. None of that would have happened without you and your so-called family feud.'

'I'm sorry you've had a bad day, but–'

'But what? It wasn't as bad as yours?' The gristle in her bones popped with indignation. 'That's probably true, and you know why? Because I'm a decent, honest body and I don't keep secrets, not like some folk what tell great hairy lies and then have a three-act drama when the truth spills out.'

A brisk tattoo on the front door brought them both to their feet.

'That'll be your solicitor, I suppose, come to see how his client is.'

Emotion propelled Leonie down the hall to fling open the door. She blinked. Not Jim.

'Oh!'

The soft cry came from behind her. She looked over her shoulder, a pang spearing through her at the sight of the naked anguish in Nell's face. She and Hedley had given heart and home to this lass and she had deceived them from start to finish. Leonie rounded on the Hibbert man.

'If I had the carving knife in my hand, I'd stab you in the heart.' She snatched her popping-next-door shawl from the peg. 'I expect you two need to discuss your mucky secrets, so I'll leave you to it. I've got my own muck to sort out.'

'Stan...' Nell faltered. 'Aunt Leonie, don't go,' but it was too late; Leonie was marching, rigid-backed, up Wilton Lane. Nell glared at Stan. 'Haven't you done enough damage for one day?'

'What sort of a greeting is that after the magistrate as good as said you had to come back to your husband?'

'Shut up!'

Mrs O'Rourke and Mrs Dunnett were chatting in the street, or rather not chatting but frankly staring.

Mrs O'Rourke came forward. 'Are you all right, love? Only I couldn't help overhearing.' She flicked a look at Stan, curious, ready to wade in.

Nell's face felt red-raw. 'It's fine, thanks.' She grabbed Stan's sleeve and yanked him indoors. 'You've just made me the talk of the wash house.'

He shrugged. 'You won't be here much longer.' He walked down the hall to the kitchen as if he owned the place, taking in the room at a glance and resting a hand on the back of Leonie's chair.

'D'you mind?'

It was her turn to shrug. 'Suit yourself.'

So he sat. She could have crowned him.

'Aren't you going to sit down?' he asked.

She stayed on her feet, arms folded. 'I'm not coming back to you.'

'You will when I'm given the children.'

The enormity of the magistrate's decision reared up and pain twisted through her. 'Don't take it lying down,' Harold had advised when a spiteful girl at school was teasing her. Gentle as a spring morning, was her lovely brother, but that didn't make him a pushover. 'Fight back.'

'She's upped and left you, then?'

Stan looked away. Good: she had scored a point. But when he looked at her again, his face was rueful, only not sorry-rueful. Smug-rueful.

'I did warn you. I said you'd be sorry if you didn't give me your money.'

Her curiosity was hopping up and down, but she wouldn't give him the satisfaction of asking.

'She were never happy not being properly wed, weren't Alice–'

Alice! Nell's arms unfolded. Her fists landed on the table, knuckles down, sending a stab of heat through the bones in her hands. It sizzled round her wrists like a too-tight bracelet before singing up her arms and jarring her elbows. She wanted to lean over him, to be bigger than he was, to make him squirm, but all she managed was to bring them eye to eye. She had loved his blue eyes once.

'I told you never to say her name.'

'I'm sorry, but let's face it–'

'Face it?' She swung away, almost spinning in a circle in frustration. 'I did face it, Stan. I faced *her* and I saw her son.'

'I never meant to hurt you,' said Stan. 'I met her after I came home from the army. She weren't a local lass. She'd come to Annerby to nurse her old auntie through the Spanish flu, but the aunt died and she was alone in the world. She ... she needed comfort.'

'Comfort, and a couple of kids, and a green front door.'

'What's the door got to do with anything?'

'I don't want to hear about you and her.'

'You brought her up. You said she left me. You threw it in my face.'

Nell drew a breath. 'What did that have to do with you asking me for money?'

Stan scrubbed his face with his hands. 'Like I say, she were never happy not being married. After you left and I moved in proper-like, I thought she'd feel more settled, only...'

'Only she was scared you'd do the dirty on her the way you did it on me. I don't know why she thought being married would have stopped you doing that.'

His mouth turned down mulishly. 'I'm not say-ing owt else.'

'Yes, you are.' She made a show of leaning against the cupboard, looking relaxed. 'If you think I'm coming back to Annerby, the least you can do is tell me what the talk is in the wash house there.'

Rising to his feet, he faced her. 'The other bloke offered marriage and he said he'd have the children. I thought if I could get money off you, I could make things better for us and she'd want to stay.' He jabbed a finger at her. 'So you've got to come home, and that's not me talking, that's the court.'

Still with her hips leaning against the cupboard, Nell leant forward to speak in a soft, confidential voice. 'I would sooner stick pins in my eyes.'

'You'll beg me to take you back when I come to fetch the children.'

She jerked upright. It was hard to breathe. Her lungs felt tight.

'Speaking of the children,' said Stan, 'I want to see them.'

'You can't. They're asleep.'

'I can. I'm their father. This way, is it?'

Darting after him, she made a grab for his arm, but he shook her off without breaking his stride.

'Stan – no!'

But he was halfway upstairs.

Leonie banged on her old front door. Then she banged again. She wasn't in the mood to wait. The door opened and there was Hilda.

'It's you, Mother. Why are you making such a racket?'

'Is Edmund here? I want to speak to him.'

'Just a minute.'

Hilda turned away. What? Wait on the step while Hilda went crawling to Edmund? No fear. Leonie marched in, swept past Hilda and entered the parlour. Edmund sat in the armchair, cigarette in hand. Posy bounced up from the footstool by the hearth.

'Gran!' Her face shone with delight.

'Sit, Posy,' said Edmund, adding fuel to Leonie's anger. Did he think he was speaking to a dog? He stood up. 'Mother-in-law, to what do we owe the pleasure?'

'I've come to see you about – you know.'

He came forward to draw her into the room. She tried to step out of his way, but trod on Hilda's foot behind her.

'Come in, Mother-in-law. Hilda, this is private. Go and do something in the kitchen. Posy, help your mother.'

The door shut behind them.

'Take a seat.' Edmund was at his charming best. Or his smarmy worst. 'Make yourself comfortable.'

That set her nerve-ends jangling, being invited to make herself comfortable in her own home – in what should be her own home. 'I don't need a seat to say what I've got to say. I've been thinking about what you said earlier.'

'Ah yes.' He made it sound like he was drawing the memory from the depths of his mind. 'My offer to restore good relations with Hilda.'

'Your offer to keep my personal possessions against my will.'

'But it wouldn't be against your will, would it? It would be a sign of trust.'

'Trust? Is that what you call it? Me, I call it blackmail.'

'That's rather extreme, Mother-in-law.' He sounded amused.

'Is it? I wouldn't know. I speak as I find. What I find is that your idea of trust is blackmail, pure and simple. Well, you can take your blackmail, Edmund Tanner, and stick it where the sun doesn't shine.'

Nell belted up the stairs, then tried to switch to creeping as she crossed the bedroom threshold, nearly falling over her feet in the process. Stan looked round the room. Nell did too, seeing it through new eyes: the big bed with the upturned tea chest beside it that served as a table; the battered old washstand from the second-hand place; Leonie's hanging cupboard and chest of drawers, squashed in together; Leonie's stack of boxes. Suddenly it looked like a dumping ground. Stan's lip curled and she felt a flare of angry shame.

Stan looked at the sleeping children. Cassie was curled in a ball, only the top of her head showing, Alf flat on his back, one arm flung out. Was Stan seeing his other son? He reached out.

'Leave them,' said Nell.

He glanced at her, a glance that said he had made up his mind. The hair lifted on her arms. The lies she had told the children—

Stan gently shook Alf. The boy stirred. Nell held in a wail of distress. The lies she had told—

Alf mumbled and settled again. How young and small he looked. How vulnerable. She wanted to plead with Stan. The lies—

Stan sat on the bed. He stroked Alf's cheek. 'Wake up, son.'

When Alf moved and blinked, Stan scooped him into a sitting position. He was clearly used to handling children. Well, of course he was. Alf stared, then shrank away, scrambling backwards until he was sitting on the pillow.

Nell's heart ballooned. 'Don't be scared. I'm here.' She clamped her hands to her sides so as not to shove Stan to the floor.

'Hello, Alf,' said Stan. 'Do you remember me?'

Alf pressed himself against the brass bedstead, his eyes big and frightened but not focused.

'He's not properly awake,' said Nell. 'Leave him be.'

Stan ignored her. 'We've not seen one another for a long time, Alf. You've grown up.'

'Mummy...' Alf scrambled into her arms. She cuddled him close, kissing his hair.

'This man isn't anything to be scared of, pie-can. He's...' She looked at Stan. 'He's your uncle.'

'Nell.' It was a quiet warning.

'He needs time to get used to you.'

Stan stood up. Hope quivered through her.

'He needs telling,' said Stan.

'This is good of you, Mrs Fairbrother,' said Jim. He hadn't expected ever to be in this drawing room again. It was essentially the same old room, with its handsome furniture and grand piano, but the lighting was different. The ornate brass and glass hanging oil-lamps had been replaced by hanging electric lights.

'Marjorie doesn't mind,' said Mr Fairbrother. 'I used to spring guests on her with no warning. Now she receives advance notice by telephone.'

'I'm pleased to see you again, James,' said Mrs Fairbrother. Was she genuinely pleased or was old Fairbrother going to get a wigging for bringing home the son-in-law that got away? 'Roberta is out this evening, so it will be just the three of us. I expect you'll want to be left alone later to discuss the case. It must be intriguing if it has brought you back into the law.'

'It's a shabby affair, I'm afraid,' said Mr Fairbrother. 'A woman left her bigamous husband, but apparently he isn't a bigamist after all and he wants her back.'

Mrs Fairbrother shuddered delicately. The silvery threads in her ankle-length evening gown caught the light in a cascade of minute twinkles. 'How unpleasant. Well, my dear,' she said to Jim, 'if you will mix with the lower orders.'

Jim wasn't having that. 'The woman concerned showed courage and initiative and she's built a decent life for herself. If anything, she's to be admired.'

The door opened and Roberta walked in. Roberta! She looked gorgeous in a magenta and gold dress with a floaty layer over the top. Jim's breath caught. At the top end, the dress was cut to display the line of her elegant collar-bones, while at the other end it was daringly short and might even reveal her knees when she sat down. She wore a sparkly headband that showed off her short fringe and the blonde waves that covered her ears and brushed her cheekbones, leaving exposed the long line of her jaw and her slender neck. She carried a vast ostrich-feather fan that ought to look idiotic, but instead added a cheeky touch that he found – crikey – endearing.

He stood up, excuses at the ready.

'Bobbie darling.' Mrs Fairbrother's poise slipped for a fraction of a second. 'We weren't expecting you. James is here.'

'So I see.' A rosy blush filled her cheeks beneath the fine layer of powder. 'How are you, James?'

'I'm well, thank you.' He looked at his hostess. 'Perhaps–'

'You have to discuss the case, so of course you must stay.' She extended a hand to her daughter, inviting her onto the sofa. 'Bobbie darling, what brings you home?'

Roberta sank gracefully beside her mother and yes, there was a glimpse of knee. Jim kept his gaze fixed on her face. The girlish fullness of her cheeks was now refined to a sleek, high-bred line. She snapped her fan closed.

'Oh, it's too tedious for words. Never mind it now.' She looked at James. 'I didn't know you were expected.'

'It was a last-minute invitation.'

Roberta pretended to administer a long-distance slap to her father's wrist with the fan. 'You're very naughty, Daddy.'

'I know your mother will always cope.'

What about the cook? Did she keep extra portions on stand-by?

'Bobbie, darling, why don't you show James the garden?' Mrs Fairbrother suggested. 'Get the awkward bit out of the way and if it's still awkward, Daddy and James can dine in the library.'

The evening air was warm, the light softening into a gentle fade. In the centre of the lawn, the water pattered in the fountain. Roberta stopped at the foot of the front steps, using her slender bare arms to indicate what lay before them.

'Behold, the garden.'

'I'm sorry, Roberta. I'd never have come if I'd known you'd be here.'

'I don't mind if you don't.' She shrugged one shoulder with continental elegance.

'Then I'd be delighted to stay.'

'Don't go all formal on me, James. We know one another better than that – or we used to.'

She strolled down the path and he fell in beside her. There was something sweet in the air. The garden's scent or a discreet dash of perfume?

'I'm sorry I caught you by surprise that time at Mrs Randall's,' he said.

'Yes, it was rather a blunder, wasn't it? I must say, I prefer the look of you this evening. Very spiffy.'

He started to relax. 'You don't look so bad yourself.'

'Why, thank you, kind sir.' She pointed gracefully with her fan. 'White flowers. Tall blue flowers. Mummy said to show you the garden, but honestly, the only thing I know the name of is the fountain.'

'I can go one better. The big green thing is a lawn and,' he added impressively, 'I believe it's made of grass.'

'Oh, you!' Roberta laughed. 'Better not keep the olds waiting. Let's go and tell Mummy we'll all be dining together, shall we?'

Nell sat at the kitchen table with Alf on her lap. Stan was in Leonie's chair, looking thoughtfully into his son's face while Alf sneaked curious glances. There was a dead weight in Nell's chest.

'Alf,' said Stan, 'I'm your dad.'

'No, you're not,' said Alf. 'My daddy's dead.'

'You mum thought I was dead, but she made a mistake.'

Alf looked up at her, puzzled, trusting. She nodded, her neck stiff and creaky.

'In bed, you said he was my uncle.'

'I know.' What could she say? 'Sometimes, when something is difficult to say, you say it a bit at a time, to get used to it.'

'Is he really my daddy?'

'Yes, pie-can.'

He pushed himself closer to her. 'I like being here with you and Cassie and Nanaleonie.'

'So do I,' said Nell.

'There isn't enough room in the bed for Daddy.'

'Not to worry, son,' said Stan. 'We'll soon–'

Nell shook her head at him. There was a furious ache in her throat.

'Soon what?' asked Alf.

'Soon nothing,' said Nell.

'Are you saying it a bit at a time because it's difficult?'

'Aye,' said Stan. 'I reckon she is. Maybe you and me should have a talk man to man.'

Alf sat up straight. Nell felt a thrill of fear as their cuddle loosened. Was Alf warming to Stan?

'Other boys have daddies,' said Alf.

'You do an' all now,' said Nell, though it tore at her heart to say it.

'You had one all along,' said Stan, 'but your mum made a mistake.'

'How?' asked Alf.

Nell stared at Stan. Her mind was blank.

'Never mind that now,' said Stan. 'You need to plan what to tell your mates at school and in the street. I'll tell you something else an' all. You've got a nanny who can't wait to see you again.'

'Nanaleonie? Why isn't she here?'

'Nanalee...?' Stan looked at Nell.

'Mrs Brent. Nana Leonie.'

'The children call her Nana?' He sounded displeased.

'Don't, Stan.'

He smiled at Alf. 'Your real nanny.'

Alf wriggled round to look at her. 'Did you think she was dead too, Mummy?'

She needed to get her answers worked out. 'I can't remember at the moment. I'm so surprised at Daddy turning up.'

'Are you going to have more children? Then I can wear the *I have a baby brother* badge or the *I have a baby sister* badge at school.'

'We'll see.' Stan's smile verged on a grin.

'Mummy, you said I was too young to remember Daddy dying.'

'That's right, pie-can. You were too young when I thought it happened.'

'You said Daddy was buried with ham. How could he be buried with ham if it was a mistake and he wasn't dead?'

# Chapter Twenty-Six

Alf hated her.

Her darling son, with whom she had had such a close and loving bond since the day he was born, had turned against her. He was a thinker; and once he had thought through the ramifications of his daddy's supposedly being buried with ham, she had lost him.

She had never seen him erupt like that, red in the face, incoherent, shaking. Stan was as taken aback as she was. As they tried to calm him, he became more distraught.

In the middle of the rumpus, Leonie came home.

'You woke him up to tell him?' she demanded incredulously. 'Couldn't it have waited?'

She got rid of Stan and took charge of an exhausted Alf. She got some warm milk down him and took him upstairs, soothing his tear-encrusted face with a damp flannel while Nell hovered in the background, reduced to the role of bystander.

When Leonie pulled back the covers for him, Nell couldn't bear it any longer. Inserting herself between Leonie and the bed, she sat on the edge, drawing Alf to her, but instead of curling into her embrace, he went stiff, his limbs shooting out to shove her away, thin arms and surprisingly strong legs pencil-straight and unyielding as they fought against her. When his feet started pummelling her stomach and ribs, Leonie pulled her away.

Downstairs, Nell paced the kitchen, hugging herself. When Leonie came in, she ran to her.

'He's asleep, fair worn out with it all, poor lamb. Whatever possessed you to wake him up and tell him?'

'Don't rub it in. I feel bad enough already.'

'Things will look different in the morning.'

'Will they?'

'Who knows?' Leonie's skin was faded and tired, her lines deeper. 'You hurt me, lass.' She held up a hand. 'I don't want another apology. You did what you did and I have to get used to it, but what you've done to me is nowt compared to what you've done to them children.'

'Alf hates me,' she whispered.

'He loves you. He'll come round. Children are like that.' Leonie sat down. 'Well, the little 'uns are. The grown-up ones...'

'You mean Hilda? Is that where you went?'

'I told Edmund I won't give in to his blackmail.'

'Good for you. You stood up for what's right.'

A gleam of defiance appeared in Leonie's eyes. 'I were magnificent. I told my son-in-law he could stick his blackmail where the sun doesn't shine.'

'You never,' said Nell.

'I were magnificent.' Leonie's shoulders drooped. 'But I'm still not back together with Hilda.'

Walking Alf to school was one of the joys of Nell's life, but this morning he wouldn't let her.

'Normally I'd say to give him a smack and

make him do as he's told,' said Leonie, 'but today I'll take him. A day at school is what he needs. It'll get him back to normal.'

Nell stood on the step to see them off. Alf wouldn't kiss her; he didn't even wave from the corner when Leonie did. The palms of Nell's hands felt clammy. What had she done? She gave Cassie a saucepan and wooden spoon to play with while she washed up, then tried to give Cassie her attention until Leonie arrived home, but her mind was churning. Alf. Annerby. Stan. The trial. It wasn't a trial, but that was how it had felt. Stan's mother wanting to welcome her back – really? She couldn't go back, yet how could she not if Stan took the children? Why hadn't he told her why he wanted her savings? If he had, would she have handed them over or would she have told him to get lost? Would she have stood up for what was right, like Leonie? Aye, and ended up suffering the consequences.

When Leonie returned, Nell rushed to meet her.

'He didn't repent at the school gates, if that's what you're hoping,' said Leonie. 'The best thing you can do is keep busy.'

Leaving Cassie in Leonie's care, 'helping' her donkey-stone the step, Nell got ready in the front room. She had two new pupils coming at half-ten, friends of Annie, and this afternoon she was due at Ingleby's. Would Alf be upset when he came home from school and she wasn't here?

'Nell,' Leonie called.

Outside the open front door, Leonie was sitting on her heels, donkey-stone in hand, while Cassie made squiggles with her own sliver of donkey-stone in a corner of the step. Beside Leonie stood a middle-aged woman, plainly dressed, but Nell recognised good dressmaking when she saw it.

'Here's a new pupil for you,' said Leonie.

'Mrs Hibbert?' said the stranger. 'I'm Miss Neville. I saw your postcard in the newsagent's window. I'm a dressmaker. I've got an ancient sewing machine and I'd like to try out yours to see if it's worth getting an up-to-date one. Could I book a couple of sessions?'

'Come in and I'll look in the diary.'

Miss Neville hopped across the wet step and Nell showed her into the front room.

'If you don't get your own machine, you could hire mine. We could work out a suitable fee.'

'I'll bear that in mind,' said Miss Neville. 'I have a friend in Fallowfield, who is also a dress-maker. If I like your machine, she'll want to try it too.'

Nell booked two sessions for Miss Neville, and later, when Annie's friends had finished their lesson, she booked them in for more. One of them had three sisters who were all interested in home-sewing.

'Your front room enterprise is expanding,' said Leonie.

Nell smiled, determined to look pleased, but would she still be here to build up her business?

As soon as they sent for her, Nell knew. She had presented herself in the sewing department promptly at quarter to one, ready for inspection. Instead, Miss Ashton approached.

'Miss Moore and Miss Collier would like to see you in the office.'

And she knew.

She ought to feel weighed down by impending doom, but what she actually felt was a strangely offhand sensation of getting it over with. They didn't want her any more? Fine. She needed to get home and start drumming up more business.

More postcards in shop windows. And she could seek out more dressmakers to the genteel poor, women like Miss Neville, who still used ancient sewing machines bequeathed to them by their mothers. The chance to use a modern machine would enable them to offer a speedier service. Her mind dashed through the possibilities, unleashing a flutter of eagerness.

Eagerness? She was about to be kicked out of a semi-regular job and the rent man wouldn't wait while she built up her private work.

But even so – eagerness. She could do this. She could make a success of it.

If she was still here. If Stan hadn't dragged her back to Annerby.

For a child who loved to make mud pies, Cassie was a fastidious eater. As long as you cut everything up for her, you could safely leave her to get on with it. Nell gave her daughter a few words of encouragement and ruffled her fine brown hair, then tucked into the poached egg on toast Leonie had put in front of her.

'How did they know?' Leonie's face darkened. 'That young journalist wasn't at court yesterday, was he?'

'It hasn't been in the paper, thank goodness. It was Miss Ashton who told tales. Her brother is out of work and he passes his time by following cases in court.'

'I see. Mind you, his sister could have kept her trap shut.'

Nell shrugged. 'It's to do with Ingleby's reputation.'

'Talking of reputation, Mrs O'Rourke wanted a word with me. She overheard you and Stan on the doorstep yesterday.'

Nell's heart dipped. 'What did you say?'

'The truth.'

'You didn't.'

'I did.' Leonie's voice sharpened. 'Don't look so scared. You aren't the first round here to have scandal attached. When Ivy Arthur at the sweet shop found out her husband was getting cosy with another woman, she grabbed a bottle off the shelf and pelted the pair of them with gobstoppers; and we've had our fair share of so-called premature babies; not to mention that family what used to live next door to Mrs Clancy.'

'You told Mrs O'Rourke everything?'

'I laid it on with a trowel, all about your courage in the face of heartbreak. Now get next door and open your heart to her. Before you know it, the whole neighbourhood will be on your side. I told Mrs Watson an' all; I wanted her to hear it from me, and d'you know what? Her first question was, if you go piking off up north, what's going to happen to me? And she offered me a home with her. Eh, you find out who your friends are, don't you?'

'That's good news.'

388

'You get round to Mrs O'Rourke's and I'll fetch Alf.'

'I thought I'd collect him.'

'And what if he's still in a strop? You don't want that in public.'

'Surely he'll have calmed down by now?' She had pictured him running to her across the playground.

'Let's not put it to the test, eh?'

So when Leonie and Cassie set off to fetch Alf, Nell knocked next door.

'I've come to apologise for letting you think I was a widow.'

'I take it kindly that you've come to say so. Come on in, love.'

Leonie had prepared the ground well. All Nell had to do was expand on a few details and soon Mrs O'Rourke was her staunch supporter.

She excused herself so as to be in when Alf came home. She stood on the doorstep, her eyes glued to the corner. Alf appeared at a run, spinning round to look back the way he had come.

'I won,' he cried.

Nell's hands trembled. Bless Alf's good nature, and bless Leonie for giving him a spot of fun. But the person who came round the corner next wasn't Leonie. It was Stan.

Jim mopped up the last of Mrs Jeffrey's Irish stew. To most people, the stew might not be a patch on the breast of lamb with mint stuffing followed by orange fool, not to mention the fine wine and twelve-year-old port that he had savoured last night at Mrs Fairbrother's table,

389

but to him, after a long day's work in the fresh air, it was every bit as delicious.

'Rice pudding for afters,' said Mrs Jeffrey.

He wished he could tell her about yesterday's meal, but it would make her feel awkward. When he returned to his old life, would it be possible to remain on genial terms with her? He was fond of her, even felt a certain responsibility for her. It would be a shame not to see her again.

He knew what Patsy would say. 'James, you can't be serious. Not the old duck in the cottage.'

He loved Patsy dearly, but their social ideas didn't coincide any more. Or maybe he should follow her lead. If he were to return successfully to his old life, he had to have the right attitude. It wasn't as though Nell would be part of his life.

He had to see her this evening. He would make it brief. No point in lingering with an unattainable woman.

When he knocked on her door, he took a step backwards, keeping his distance. Nell answered the door, a bright smile on her face. It vanished at the sight of him.

'I thought you were Alf. Stan's got him.'

'I assumed Mr Hibbert had gone back to Annerby.'

'I don't want him here. I'll ask him when he's leaving.'

'Don't say anything that could be construed as encouragement to find a new house.'

'He wants the children to get to know him. He's taken Alf to look for Violet. Come through.'

'Aye, come in, Jim,' called Mrs Brent. 'Have a seat.'

'I won't, if you don't mind. I can't stay. I've come to tell you I spent yesterday evening with Mr Fairbrother and the best advice we can give is to continue living a respectable life.'

'Unfortunately,' said Mrs Brent, 'Nell's been sacked.'

'Ingleby's got wind of the case,' said Nell.

'Concentrate on building up your private work. That's all you can do. Now I must go.'

He had never been in and out so quickly. He strode away, needing to get clear of Wilton Lane and its complications. It was time to forget Nell Hibbert. Maybe she would end up making the best of things with her husband. Why else would she permit him to take Alf out looking for the cat? Was she starting to accept what looked like being the inevitable outcome?

He felt a pang of guilt at not having found Violet himself. But he had no reason to find her now, other than as an act of kindness to a lost animal. There was no benefit to be had in terms of gaining acceptance by the Hibbert family. Well, he had already gained it from Mrs Brent and the children. It was Nell's acceptance he had craved. Had. But no more.

Acceptance was a funny thing. How easily he had slid back into favour with the Fairbrothers. That had surprised him, warmed him too. It was thanks to Roberta, of course. Had she objected to his presence, the evening would have been very different. As it was, they had all enjoyed a pleasant time and he had stayed longer than he had expected to.

Back at home, he sat at his schoolmaster's desk,

opening it to extract a sheet of paper to write his bread-and-butter letter to Mrs Fairbrother. He thanked her and made a couple of flattering but not sycophantic remarks about her hospitality; then he sat back, tapping the end of his pen against his teeth.

*...seeing you again?* Or ... *seeing all of you again?* Why not?

*I hope to have the pleasure of seeing all of you again—*

He pulled his hand away before he could add the full stop. Should he, shouldn't he?

*soon.*

Other children were out playing after tea, but Posy was out for a walk with Dad and Ma. Dad liked to do that sometimes. 'It's good to be seen out together,' he said. Sometimes, as he ushered them out, he said something about going out with his two best girls, which made Posy stand up straighter. How she would love to be Dad's best girl. Then he would never again make her hold her hand over the candle to test her truthfulness and he would never again send for Gerald.

They walked along with Dad in the middle. Up ahead, a child emerged from an entry. Alf! Was he with Gran? When Gran had come round yesterday evening, Posy had come over all optimistic, but after Gran spoke to Dad, she had marched off without so much as a goodbye.

Later, Posy had crept downstairs to do some honest-to-goodness eavesdropping. She had heard Dad say, 'Your mother seems to attach more importance to her precious possessions than she does to you and Posy.'

Posy's fists had clenched and if she had had any nails to speak of, the palms of her hands would have been torn to shreds. She had run back upstairs, determined not to hear anymore, because it wasn't true. It couldn't be true. Gran loved her and she loved Gran. Always and for ever.

Alf turned to watch the person he was waiting for. Please be Gran.

A man. As they grew closer to Alf and the stranger, Alf slipped his hand inside the man's. Ma and the man exchanged glances. The man touched his hat to her.

'Evening.'

'Who's this?' Dad asked.

'He came to our house a while back, looking for Mother because he wanted Mrs Hibbert's address.'

Alf beamed his head off. 'This is my dad.'

'Your dad?' said Posy. 'But–'

'He's not dead,' said Alf. 'Mum thought he didn't love us any more, so she ran away, but she was wrong.' He curled his lip. 'Mum's stupid.'

## Chapter Twenty-Seven

Nell gave Miss Preston and Miss Graham their separate lessons, coaching them in the sewing of the plumpest velvet and the slipperiest silk; then a tray of sandwiches was brought in.

'Afterwards we'll show you some of the gar-

393

ments we've brought down from the attics,' said Miss Preston. 'We'd value your opinion as to how we might use them. They're hanging in the old schoolroom.'

'I'd be happy to make suggestions,' said Nell.

'I'm the best judge of what suits Miss Roberta,' said Miss Graham.

Stroppy so-and-so. But if Miss Graham thought she was giving Nell a hard time, she should come to Wilton Lane and take lessons from Alf.

Having only ever been inside a classroom for sixty, Nell was intrigued to see what a school-room for one looked like, but it was impossible to tell. It had been transformed into an Aladdin's cave of silks and satins, velvets and furs, poplin and lace.

'You can't cut these garments down,' she exclaimed. 'They're beautiful.'

'They're also old-fashioned. If we don't use them, they go back into the attic.'

Nell drifted round the room, touching with reverent fingers as she went from a golden-brown floor-length coat with enormous leg-o'-mutton sleeves; to an off-the-shoulder evening creation of shimmering forget-me-not silk with the bunched-up layers and flounces of the bustle at its biggest; to a colossal crinoline that made her think she could curtain her entire house.

Daphne came in. 'Good, you're here. Miss Roberta asked me to check. She'll be up in a min-ute.' She disappeared.

'Should I leave the room?' asked Nell.

'No, stay,' said Miss Preston. 'Miss Roberta may wish to speak to you.'

'She's Miss Fairbrother to you,' said Miss Graham.

Nell wasn't sure she could bring herself to address a young girl in such a formal way, but there was no choice. The door opened and she just had time to wonder if Miss Roberta had a glamorous young stepmother before the two ladies' maids murmured, 'Good afternoon, Miss Roberta,' and dipped little curtsies.

Roberta Fairbrother had started off in her imagination as a sweet little girl with a fairy-tale bed; then she had grown into a pushy sixteen-year-old; and here stood a woman a few years older than herself. She was beautiful in a sharp-edged way, high cheekbones, crisp chin, lean arms, her slender figure highlighted rather than disguised by the smooth lines of her loose-fitting dress. And what a dress! Minute pin-tucks edging the boat-neck; narrow clinging sleeves with a sudden flare at the wrist; low-waisted straight skirt of devastating simplicity: if that was a Mademoiselle Antoinette day dress, what must their evening gowns look like?

'Good afternoon.' Even her voice was sharp. Not nasty-sharp, but brisk. Her gaze landed on Nell. 'This must be the person teaching you the mysteries of the sewing machine.' A brief dazzling smile. 'I'm anxious to see what can be done with all this old stuff.'

'We're about to discuss that,' said Miss Graham, 'if you would like to hear some ideas.'

'Not today. I've come to heap more work on you, I'm afraid.' Dazzle, dazzle. 'There are masses of day dresses upstairs, aren't there? I'd like to help the poor clothe their children better. If there are garments in appropriate fabrics that can be cut up, and if there are simple patterns... Goodness knows how many little dresses could be made out of a crinoline. Please find some suitable garments and I'll make arrangements.'

Dazzle, dazzle; and she left.

'Well!' said Miss Graham. 'I hardly think that's fit work for a lady's maid. Perhaps it's more suited to Mrs Hibbert, given her background.'

A dig at her working-class roots? 'If you mean–'

'I was referring to your experience as a seamstress. What did you think I meant?' She gave her version of her mistress's smile. Not so much dazzle, dazzle as brittle, brittle.

Nell addressed Miss Preston. 'I'd be happy to assist. Shall we put some dates in the diary?'

More hours, and doing what promised to be an agreeable task. This time last week, she would have been thrilled. This time last week, she had her hours at Ingleby's. This time last week, Stan was a bigamist.

This time last week, her son loved her.

Oh, the temptation to tell Alf about Stan and Mrs Vicarage Lane, but of course she would never crush him like that. Let him think she had made a foolish mistake. Let him punish her. Better that than tell him about the other family. Alf was hurt now and taking it out on her; but he would come round and give her his trust again.

Wouldn't he?

Nell pinched the bridge of her nose. She kept her back to the kitchen table, where Stan and

Leonie were sitting.

'Bad head?' asked Stan.

She placed the kettle over the heat, faked a smile and turned.

'I'm fine.'

Fine? When she had to look at her son standing pressed close to his father? At least Cassie wasn't impressed by this stranger. When he picked her up, she had let out an almighty roar and wriggled until he put her down.

'Dad's taking me to look for Violet again,' said Alf. 'When did you last look for her, Mum?'

'You mum's been working hard,' said Leonie. 'She hasn't had time.'

'Dad's got time.'

'Now then, son,' said Stan. 'No answering back. Be polite to your mum and Nana Leonie, you hear?'

'Yes, Dad.'

Nell didn't know whether to be furious or humiliated. Her smile dropped. She hoisted it back into place.

'Is Violet really lost?' asked Alf.

'You know she is,' said Nell.

Alf shrugged. 'You said Dad was dead.'

'Violet's lost,' said Leonie. 'It's not your mum's fault. If it's anyone's fault, it's mine, because I should have fetched her here the moment I knew Mr Tanner didn't want her.'

'Isaac Tupman in my class has a cat and she had kittens and Isaac's mum drowned them. That's what you do with kittens, his mum said.' Alf looked straight at Nell. 'Did you drown Violet?'

397

'Lovely day for it, isn't it?' Jim had heard the words a dozen times. He even used them himself as a conversational opening to a smiling couple whom he stood beside during the PT display.

'Have you got daughters here?' they asked him.

'I have nieces starting in September.'

'So you have plenty of these garden parties ahead of you. This is our last.'

The gardens of Oaklawn School were busy with parents and girls enjoying the convivial atmosphere as they waited for the country dancing display to begin. A plump man with a fiddle under his chin struck up a jolly tune and led a crocodile of young girls onto the lawn where they formed a circle, ready to start.

Jim and Don picked up the twins so they could see better.

'That'll be you this time next year,' said Jim.

At the end of the display, the audience clapped and Miss Martindale walked into the centre of the circle. 'Thank you, girls. We'll allow some time for everyone to enjoy refreshments, then our older pupils will perform extracts from Shakespeare.'

Jim and Don put the girls down and they skipped off to play at country dancing.

'Don't look now,' said Patsy, 'but I spy Roberta and Mrs Fairbrother. Lord, I hope this isn't going to be embarrassing.'

Jim felt a rush of pleasure. 'On the contrary.'

She gave a little gasp. 'Don't say you two have made it up, and after the way you threw her over.'

'I didn't throw her over. She called it off.'

'If you say so. Look, they're coming over.'

Among all the prettily dressed women, Roberta

cut a dash in a turquoise dress with matching shoes and a lacy parasol with a turquoise ruffle. Greetings of the 'You remember So-and-So', variety were exchanged. Mrs Fairbrother engaged Don and Patsy in conversation; she had always liked them.

'What brings you here?' Jim asked Roberta.

'I'm an old girl. They like us to come back, preferably with fee-paying daughters, but you can't have everything. That wasn't a dig at you, however it sounded.'

'Believe me, I have a dig at myself every time I see my nieces.'

'Really?' She tilted a glance at him, but all she said was, 'Speaking of children, I'm organising a project to provide clothes of good quality to the poor. Just in a small way, you understand. I can't claim to be solving the nation's problems.'

'If enough people worked in a small way...'

'I knew you'd be pleased. Mummy's given me some advice; she used to serve on the old Deserving Poor Committee before the war.' Roberta twirled her parasol. 'But it was you who provided the inspiration. Daddy said you've helped various lower-class people with legal advice, and now you're involved in this case, and it made me think. I'd like to make a difference in my own small way.'

When she explained how the ladies' maids had been allocated the job of cutting down old dresses to provide fabric, he had to chew the inside of his cheeks to stop himself smiling. Roberta evidently meant it when she said she was doing the organising. Clearly the donkey-work had been delegated. Then he lost the desire to smile. Who was he to criticise? He might have helped a few folk with advice, but it hadn't involved any effort on his part. He looked at Roberta with kinder eyes.

The others' conversation ended. It was time to part.

He didn't want to.

He took out the postcards he had intended to give to Patsy. They had been in his desk since the day Nell had told him the devastating truth about her past; but now, if she were to have any hope of making a good impression on Mr Aitcheson, she needed all the help she could get.

He offered half the cards. 'Roberta, would you give these to your lady's maid? It's a woman from Chorlton who teaches the use of the sewing machine. I believe she's rather good.'

Roberta took them. 'Graham and Preston have a woman who teaches them, but they'll know of any other ladies' maids who need lessons.'

With parting smiles, the Fairbrothers moved off. Jim affected not to see Patsy's eyes, packed full of meaning.

'May I give some cards to you?' he asked.

She took them, glancing at the wording. 'What's she to you, this Mrs Hibbert?'

Not so long ago, he would have blessed her for asking. 'She's someone I know from my window cleaning.'

'Respectable or backstreet?'

'Both.'

'That sounded rather sharp. Have I touched a nerve?' Her eyes widened. 'You've not got yourself entangled with her, have you?'

'Certainly not.'

'I'm pleased to hear it.' Her gaze followed Roberta. 'There's a far more appropriate entanglement to be had.'

Jim went down on one knee and held out his arms to Marguerite and Harriet as they ran to him.

'Uncle James,' said the one with the pink ribbons.

'If you marry that lady with the parasol,' said the one with yellow, 'can we be bridesmaids?'

Posy bounced on her toes, awaiting her turn. As she neared the front, she did her serious preparation, jogging on the spot. Miss Claybourne had called it limbering up. This coming Saturday, she would be limbering up for real at the sports jamboree in Chorlton Park. All the schools were attending. But today she was the champion of the England Rounders Team and the world championship depended on her performance. The judges were watching. She glanced at where Ma was chatting with some other mothers. Ma wasn't looking at her, but she would when it was Posy's turn, wouldn't she?

Posy took her place in front of Lyddie, who was back-stump, and prepared her bat, shaking her arm and extending it, fist clenched, tucking in her thumb. As Jimmy bowled, she kept her eyes on the ball, drew back her arm and thwacked with her curled fingers. She didn't look to see how far the ball went: she ran. First base was easy. She skidded round and pelted for second. The air streamed past her ears. Mike was second base. He jiggled on the spot, ready to catch the ball. He leapt up, but the ball went over his head and a dozen fielders piled on top of one another. Posy darted past and made it to third base. Now for the fourth – she was going to do it. She hurled herself forwards. Success!

Her team jumped up and down, cheering. Posy looked at the mums. Ma had her back to the game, but maybe she had watched Posy's glorious rounder and then returned to her conversation.

Dad came round the corner and Ma broke away and went inside. Soon the game ended as children were called in for their tea. Posy usually stayed out until the last minute, but today she wanted to find out if Ma had seen her rounder.

She went in. Dad and Ma were in the kitchen, talking, so she waited. You didn't interrupt grown-ups. Rupert had taught her that.

'The others are getting at me,' said Ma. 'They know about Mrs Hibbert's court case. If she gets sent back to her husband, what happens to Mother? I know Mrs Watson has offered, but everyone thinks she should come back to us.'

'Really? You can tell "everyone" to mind their own business.'

'I wish me and Mother hadn't fallen out.'

'It wasn't your fault, Hilda. If the Hibbert woman leaves, and your mother moves in next door, she'll be close enough to keep an eye on, but at a distance so we don't tread on one another's toes. I'm sorry to say it, Hilda, but she wasn't good at coping in a family household.'

Posy squeezed her mouth tight shut to hold in the indignation. It wasn't fair to talk about Gran like that. Creeping back along the hall, she opened the front door and shut it with a bang.

'Did you see me score my rounder, Ma?'

Not that she needed to ask.

It would be wonderful if Gran lived next door. It would be sad too, because it would mean the Hibberts had moved away, but would that be altogether bad, given how Dad disliked them? If Mrs Hibbert left, maybe he would like Gran more.

Mrs Hibbert wanted to stay, but Alf wanted to leave. He was going round school, saying he couldn't wait. He had even said he didn't care if his mum went. That shocked Posy. Ma might be a droopy cowslip, but you didn't turn your back on your mum.

But Ma had turned her back on Gran – or had she? Did she want Gran back? It had sounded like it yesterday after the rounders, or had that just been because some of the neighbours had had a go at her?

This evening, Dad sent Ma out to Mrs Watson's Annie's house, where a gang of knitters got together every Friday. Ma hadn't been before because Dad had never let her. Not that Ma had ever said she wanted to go, but somehow they all knew she wasn't allowed.

Until this evening, when Dad suggested it, but instead of jumping up and racing gleefully out of the house before he could change his mind, Ma – wouldn't you know it? – had hedged.

'What if they have another go at me about Mother?'

'Say she was difficult to live with.'

'I can't say that.'

'Then you'll have to let them have a go at you.' Ma picked up her knitting bag and left.

'Go to bed, Posy,' said Dad. 'I fancy an evening on my own.'

'May I read in bed?'

'You may.'

Posy raced upstairs, gave herself a lick and a promise, and threw on her nightie. It was a warm evening and still light. She left the curtains open and pushed the sash up further before climbing into bed with *Just William*. She hadn't read more than a few pages when a creaky sound caught her ear and she slid out of bed to peep outside. Dad was opening the back gate. Good! It was a nuisance, having it locked all the time.

He did more than unlock it. He left it standing open and returned to the house. Posy ducked back in case he looked up. When she heard the back door shut, she looked again.

After a while, a man came along the entry. Mr Hibbert: he must be looking for Violet. But when he reached their gate, he came inside. Was he a burglar, taking advantage of an open gate? Pulling on her cardy, she crept onto the stairs. Voices came from the kitchen, not loud, angry voices, not Dad demanding to know what the heck Mr Hibbert was doing, but ordinary talking voices.

Posy sat on the stairs, pressing herself against the balusters.

'We want the same thing,' said Dad. 'You want your wife back and I want her gone from here.'

'It looks like the magistrate will order her to come home, but she's determined to stop here if

404

she can.'

'That's why she needs to be persuaded,' said Dad. 'It has to be impossible for her to stay.'

'I've been thinking.' Had they talked about this before? 'A few words from me to the newspaper would ruin her professionally, then she'd have to come back.'

'That's your idea of persuasion, is it? She'd hate you for ever. It needs to be something she can't trace back to you.'

'What about damaging her sewing machine?'

'She'd still have her other teaching, which in any case earns more. Besides, the sewing machine isn't hers. She hires it. If it gets damaged, the repairs will have to be paid for and, as the husband, you'll be liable for the debt.'

'I suppose that means damaging the house is out of the question an' all,' said Mr Hibbert.

'Theft of money: that'll do it,' said Dad. 'Take away her money and Bob's your uncle. She'll have to accept that she can't stay. Where does she keep it?'

'Dotted around the house, knowing her. She used to have a Mazawattee tea tin that I wasn't meant to know about.'

'And my mother-in-law keeps her money in my father-in-law's fireproof tin box, with birth certificates and whatnot. If her money vanishes too, she won't be able to help out. But the tin box will have to be found later. I won't be forced to have her back here because she's destitute. When her money is returned, she'll move in next door with her head held high; and you, my friend, will have a wife with a crushed spirit, plus a wallet

405

stuffed with money, which is rightfully yours any-way, as her husband.'

Posy pulled up her knees into a protective huddle. Mr Hibbert was indeed a burglar.

No – wait.

'There's a sports event on Saturday for the local schoolchildren,' said Dad. 'You must take your family. Before you go, make sure the back gate is unlocked; also, leave the scullery window open. Spend all afternoon with your family. That's your proof you were nothing to do with the theft. And while you're at the park...'

Silence.

Posy nearly wet herself. What was Dad going to do?

## Chapter Twenty-Eight

'I don't want to go with you,' sulked Alf. Nell's erstwhile sunny little boy looked like he might dash out of the back door and run away at any moment.

'Don't be silly, pie-can.' She kept her tone light. 'Of course we're going together, you, me, Cassie and Nana Leonie. We want to see you in the egg-and-spoon race.'

It was Josie O'Rourke who had told her about Alf's race. He hadn't uttered a word. It was all Nell could do to hang onto the pieces of her heart.

'Don't want to go with you,' Alf muttered. He

stood on one foot, swinging the other, the swings getting bigger and bigger. Any moment now he would kick the table leg. Would he really push things that far?

Patience hadn't worked. It was time to be firm. 'Alf, I've had enough. I know how upset you are, but it's time to be sensible. You know how to behave properly and that's what I expect you to do.'

His eyes welled up; her heart did too. Were they about to be reunited? But with a roar of anger and distress, he broke away and pounded upstairs.

Nell pressed her hands to her cheeks, trying to compose herself. 'I don't know what to do,' she told Leonie. 'I wish I'd never lied.'

'But if you hadn't, what would you have said instead? A small child, knowing you'd left his dad, would have blurted it out all over the place, and you couldn't have had that.'

'You've changed your tune. It's not long since you were shouting the odds at me for lying to you.'

'If I'd kept my mouth shut instead of yakking to that journalist, none of this would have happened, but you haven't once said you blame me.'

'It never occurred to me.' Nell kissed her. Leonie smelt of rosemary and lemon.

'Tell you what,' said Leonie. 'You don't blame me for tattling and I won't blame you for keeping secrets.'

Part of Nell's burden lifted, but she still felt guilty about Leonie's precarious future. Mrs Watson was a true friend to offer her a home, but it would make Leonie beholden in a way she wasn't here in Wilton Lane, where she enjoyed the position of honorary aunt and grandmother, an altogether different situation to being the homeless friend.

Footsteps thundered downstairs at the same time as there was a knock at the door. Nell found Alf trying to open it.

'It's Dad,' he yelled and there was only one way he could have known that. He had looked out of the front bedroom window, which meant he had been close to the water damage, an area he knew was off-limits.

She reached over his head to open the door. He flung himself at his father. Nell's muscles tightened in jealousy.

Stan laughed. 'Steady on, young fella. I hear there's some sports going on in the park this afternoon. Are you taking part?'

'I'm in the egg-and-spoon race,' said Alf. 'Are you coming to watch? You can take me and bring me back.'

'I've already told you,' said Nell. 'I'm taking you.'

'Listen to your mum, son. She knows best.' Stan crouched down. 'I want to have a talk with her, but I'll see you later, eh?'

'Are you going to tell her to let me go with you?'

Nell glared at Stan, daring him to undermine her. How could he be so cheery when she was struggling to control her son?

'Like I say, Mum knows best.'

It wasn't exactly a ringing endorsement.

'Go to Nana Leonie,' said Nell, but it wasn't until Stan nodded that Alf went. 'What do you want? I'm busy.'

'Too busy to talk to your husband?'

'You stopped being my husband the moment the door to 14 Vicarage Lane opened.'

Even that didn't rile him. 'You aren't doing yourself any favours. You know you'll have to come back to me.'

She wanted to say, 'Not in a million years,' but if Mr Aitcheson handed over the children, what choice would she have?

'We need to get on better,' said Stan, 'for Alf's sake.'

She sighed. 'All right, we'll talk, but not here. Let's go to the rec. Wait here while I tell Aunt Leonie.'

She set off for Beech Road at a brisk pace that failed to walk off her displeasure. In the rec, there were children playing and couples strolling and men heading for the bowling green. Over to one side was a bench with no one nearby. Nell sat on the very end.

Stan's smile was almost a smirk. 'Don't worry. I don't think we'll be mistaken for a courting couple.'

'What do you want?'

His sigh said she wasn't helping but he would struggle on manfully. 'I want to be a family again. The kids need stability.'

'They had plenty of that before you turned up.'

'I let Alf down and I want to try again. Rather like you letting him down and wanting to try again.'

Neil caught her breath. 'How dare you compare the two?' Was he right?

'He's a grand lad and our Cassie is a sweetheart.'

'It's our Cassie now, is it? Have you forgotten about accusing me of having her out of wedlock?'

'Mr Norton said it was important to make an impression.'

'It did that, all right.'

'It were a shock to see in't paper I had a child I knew nowt about, and I admit that when I saw her name, I thought she must be someone else's. I thought if she was mine, you'd have called her Olive.'

'Why in heaven's name would I do that? Even if I'd still been married to you when Cassie was born–'

'You never stopped being married to me, lass.'

'If I'd still been living with you, I wouldn't have called her Olive.'

'Why not? You were happy enough to call Alf after my father. Alfred Stanley Hibbert, for his grandfather and his father.'

'Only because I couldn't use Dad's name. He couldn't be Alfred Frederick.'

He laughed as if it was a great joke. Didn't he know the sorrow she had felt at not using Dad's name? And she hadn't felt able to use one of her brothers' names, because how could she choose?

'If you're so keen for us to move to Annerby,' said Nell, 'shouldn't you be there, making arrangements?'

'I've written to the landlord, giving notice, and Mother is going to sell the furniture and what-have-you from Vicarage Lane, so don't try telling Mr Aitcheson you can't live surrounded by Alice's things. We'll move in with Mother for a

410

spell while we find somewhere of us own.'

'You're kidding.'

'You should be flattered, having me down here getting to know the children while Mother sorts things out up there. It shows how keen we are. We had a good marriage, you and me.'

'So good you went off and got another one.'

He took her hand, keeping it when she tried to pull away. 'Let's make a fresh start by taking the children to this sports thingummy. The sooner we're on the same side, the sooner Alf will start behaving himself. Have you thought of that?'

He let go of her hand. She meant to yank it away, but his final words made her stop – literally – and think. Would it be better for Alf if she gave in? And yet, while there was even the smallest chance of remaining free, how could she walk back into the cage?

Her hand lay on top of Stan's. She pulled it away and stood up.

'That's blackmail; and you know what blackmailers get told, don't you? Take your blackmail and shove it where the sun doesn't shine.'

His mouth dropped open. She headed across the grass to the gate closest to Riley's Farm. Using Leonie's words had made her want to ask Jim to tackle Edmund Tanner about Leonie's precious things. Would Jim be there at this time on a Saturday? It was worth a try. He didn't think much of her any more and she didn't blame him. Aside from the odd flash of kindness, he had been purely professional in his dealings with her since she told him about Stan. But he would help Leonie gladly. She knew he would.

Had he ever been fond of her? Irrelevant. He was lost to her now. Whatever happened, whether she was forced to follow the children to Annerby or grudgingly permitted to remain here, she was still a liar and a married woman. Jim would be glad to forget her.

Would she ever be able to forget him?

Mrs Jeffrey was out when Jim arrived home from work. Chucking his cap on the table, he helped himself to a glass of cordial from the jug on the marble slab in the pantry, glugging down a few mouthfuls. A knock at the door made him look round, expecting it to open as a neighbour walked in, but it stayed shut. He opened it but no one was there. It took him a moment to realise the knock must have been at the front door, which was never used.

Curious, he walked round the side of the cottage.

'Roberta! What are you doing here?'

'Paying a call.' The offhand confidence in her voice was belied by the anxiety in her eyes. 'If it's convenient.'

He glanced down, indicating his casual attire. 'You'll have to take me as I am.'

Her gaze skimmed up and down him. This was the moment when she came to her senses and wondered why she had bothered being civil to him recently.

She smiled. 'You'll do.'

Cripes. She meant it.

'Have you been out window cleaning this morning?' she asked.

'Normally I'm out all Saturday, but most of my Saturday people are going to a sports jamboree this afternoon.'

'Lucky for me.' She trailed her hand across the top of the lavender, releasing its fragrance into the air. 'I've come to apologise for being unsympathetic when you came home from the war. I was so dreadfully hurt and disappointed. I know that seems like a feeble excuse.'

'Not at all. I let you down.'

'I was too upset to appreciate how deeply your experiences had affected you. I hope you'll give me credit for trying to understand now.'

Her dress, which was of a colour Patsy had once scolded him for calling off-white when really it was ivory, made her look cool and lovely. She wore a straw hat with a gauzy scarf tied round it. He had always liked her in a straw hat.

'It's generous of you to say so,' he told her. 'It makes me feel worse for having let you down.'

Her hand reached out as if to touch him, but fell away, brushing her skirt and causing a silky ripple. 'I didn't intend to make you feel bad.'

'As a matter of fact, I feel rather good.'

'Then I'm glad I came. I mustn't outstay my welcome. I'm sure you have things to do.'

Dash it! 'As a matter of fact, I have,' though he rather wished now that he didn't. 'It's the court case. I'm going to call on my client's landlord and ask him to have the repairs seen to. It's a small detail but it could make Mrs Hibbert look better in court.'

'Mrs Hibbert? Isn't that the name on those postcards?'

'Yes.' Damn. 'I shouldn't have mentioned her name.'

'James, I understand all about discretion and confidentiality. I'm not a solicitor's daughter for nothing.'

'I know you wouldn't say anything inappropriate.'

'The only inappropriate thing is you handing out her postcards.' But she laughed as she said it.

Was it inappropriate? He had wanted to help. But whereas he would gladly tell Mr Fairbrother he had asked about the repairs, he wouldn't mention giving out Nell's cards. Roberta was right.

'Maybe,' he said.

'Just the teensiest bit.'

'She deserves a chance. That's all I can say.'

'You're a good judge of character, James. I wondered about her when you gave me the cards.'

*It's a woman from Chorlton who teaches the use of the sewing machine. I believe she's rather good.*

A woman from Chorlton who taught me to love again. I believe she's rather...

Rather married.

'My interest is purely professional. Now, if you'll excuse me, I must get changed.' He softened the words with a smile.

'You mean you're not seeing Mr Landlord dressed like that?'

'Absolutely not, you wretched girl. I'll walk you to your motor. Is it parked on Beech Road?' He offered his arm and she took it. He pressed her hand against his ribs. There were times when his skin yearned for another's touch. 'If we walk round the back of the cottage, there's a proper

414

path, which will be much kinder to your shoes than this track.'

They walked round to the path between the cottages and their gardens. She moved to stand in front of him, facing him.

'I was nervous about coming today, but I'm glad I did.'

'So am I.'

She lifted a coquettish eyebrow. 'I could stay and straighten your tie after you get changed.'

Did she move nearer or had she always been that close? Her eyes were wide and trusting. Her lips parted. She touched the tip of her tongue to the centre of her top lip. His heart thumped. Did she have any idea how desirable she was?

He leant his face down to hers, moving slowly, giving her every chance to break the spell. His eyes fluttered, wanting to close, but he forced them to stay open in case the kiss didn't happen. The side of his nose brushed the side of hers. Their lips touched, slipped away, touched again. Memories flooded him of old embraces as their mouths joined in tender little movements that deepened. The kiss was familiar but also exciting and new. His hands twitched by his sides, but he made no attempt to take her in his arms.

When the kiss ended, she gave a breathy little laugh and glanced away, as if shy. Maybe she was feeling shy. He was in too much of a whirl to analyse his own feelings.

Over her shoulder, down the path, something caught his attention. Nell Hibbert. She stood stock-still. Then she turned and hurried away.

Nell rushed home. She was breathless, but it had nothing to do with her speed. She had no business being upset. She was married. Even if she didn't return to Annerby, she was still married. What mattered now was going to the jamboree with Leonie and the children ... and Stan. She hated including him, but if he wanted to go, and Alf wanted him there, what choice was there?

'I'm home,' she called. Smile. Be cheerful. Do it for the children.

Stan was at the kitchen table. Why wouldn't he push off and leave her alone? Even after what she had said in the rec, he was still here, still being marvellous with Alf, who was playing with Cassie and glancing at Stan to make sure he was watching.

'You're back,' said Stan, as if he was part of the family and she had kept everyone waiting. 'Time to go. You'll come, won't you?' he asked Leonie.

'Aunt Leonie was always coming with us,' Nell said stiffly.

'The children are ready,' said Stan. 'I just need to nip out the back.'

He vanished through the scullery. It was tempting to march off and leave him, but Alf would dig his heels in. Leonie ushered the children to the front door. Nell hovered in the kitchen, all kinds of dark feelings bubbling away inside her.

When Stan returned, she pounced. 'You can walk with us to please Alf, but once we're there, get lost.'

'What will Alf say to that?'

'He'll be with his team and he'll neither know nor care.'

'I think he'll care. I think the best bit for him will be being watched by his dad.'

Anguish speared through her. 'I'm not having you telling Mr Aitcheson how we went together as a family.'

'You never used to be this stubborn,' said Stan. 'After you.'

'No, thanks. This is my house and it's my responsibility to shut the doors.'

With a shrug and a maddening smile, he preceded her along the hall. Nell shut the kitchen door behind her. She felt like slamming it but had to make do with a brisk click.

'Dad, can I hold your hand?' said Alf.

How was she to bear it? Her son hated her. Her resentment against Stan crumpled into a petty heap. He said resuming their marriage was what Alf needed. Was he right?

What about what she needed?

## Chapter Twenty-Nine

Posy had been looking forward to the jamboree, but now she was bunking off to creep after Dad while he did whatever he was going to do. She sort of knew what it would be, but she didn't want to think about it. Her stomach couldn't stop thinking about it, though. Forget butterflies. She had a flock of pigeons in her tummy.

'I'll see you at the park, Ma,' she said. 'My team wants to be there early for a practice.'

She ran out, looking round to make sure no one was watching as she slipped into Mrs Watson's backyard. Mrs Watson had gone over to her Annie's earlier to shepherd some kids whose parents couldn't go because they were working. Or blind drunk. Everybody knew the Bradburys were out cold every Saturday after drinking Mr Bradbury's wages on Friday night.

She hid in the outside lav, which turned out to be a good place, because twice she needed a wee. Excited voices came and went in the entry. Then all was quiet. She opened the door and listened. Sure enough, there were footsteps in the yard next door. Dad! The gate opened without a creak, so he must have oiled it. The latch clicked as it shut. Posy opened Mrs Watson's gate. Dad's footsteps on the cinder path already sounded fainter, the crackle dying away. She peeped out to see him disappear. She started to scurry after him when—

'Violet!' It came out as a joyful whisper. 'Oh, Violet, you're so thin.'

Violet skittered away, but not far. She came back. She needed kindness. She needed food.

But Posy needed to follow Dad. It was a wrench but she made herself leave the cat. Violet trotted after her, mewing, and Posy accelerated. At the end of the entry, she peeped out. No sign of Dad. She ran to the next corner, catching up with him – well, catching sight of him, down the entry behind Wilton Lane. Gone was his usual stride. He moved purposefully but softly.

He went through a gate. Posy ran that far, switching to tiptoe-running as she drew near. He had shut the gate. With her heartbeats swelling inside the back of her mouth, Posy pressed down the latch and opened the gate to look at the back of the Hibberts' house. Their backyard was a lot smaller than the ones in Finney Lane, which made the house much closer, as if it might fall on top of her.

Next to the kitchen window was a sticky-out bit of building where the scullery was; and the scullery window was open. Had Dad climbed in? Should she follow? She hadn't planned what to do when she got this far. She only knew that something bad was happening and she needed to see it for herself in case ... in case what?

There was nowhere to hide in the yard unless she went in the lav, but that wasn't a good idea. If Dad was as nervous as she was, he might need to use it on his way out. She returned to the entry. A few houses along, in the opposite direction to the way Dad would go, someone had left their gate open. Posy hopped onto the step and stood just inside, ears straining.

At last, the Hibberts' gate opened. She gave Dad time to go on his way, then peeped out. He had something under his arm. Buggeration. Dad was a thief.

She followed him home. The thing under his arm was covered in a piece of cloth. Gran's fire-proof box? Posy hovered outside their back gate after he went in. She had to follow. She had to know what he did with the box. The back door was ajar; that meant he didn't mean to be inside for long. She crept through the scullery and the kitchen. She couldn't hear him. Her skin cooled and it took her a moment to realise it wasn't from fear: the cellar door was open. She could hear sounds. Dad was down there. What now? She couldn't go down without being seen. Was it enough to know the cellar was the hiding place? It would have to be. Oh, the relief of leaving the house. She made a dash for the gate and fell into the entry. She had to get to the park and behave as if nothing had happened.

A mew made her look up. Violet was on the wall.

'Wait there, Violet,' she called.

But Violet had other ideas. Facing Posy, she leant over the edge, touching her paws experimentally against the brickwork before half-jumping, half-running to the ground.

'No, Violet. Go and hide. Shoo.' But she couldn't say it in a cruel voice. 'I have to go.'

She ran away. She must be gone before Dad emerged. She had to reach the jamboree and pretend she had been there all along. She ran all the way to Chorlton Park, then slithered through the crowd of grown-ups and headed for the children.

Her team dived towards her.

'Where the heck have you been? It's nearly our first race.'

'Don't make a fuss,' hissed Posy, trying to be invisible.

There was loud applause from the parents for the egg-and-spoon race for the babies' classes. A couple of kids had made it over the line. Most of the others were scattered about, picking up their eggs.

Posy spied Alf. 'Come on, Alf!' she yelled.

Lyddie nudged her. 'You're not meant to cheer

for him. He's not on our team.'

'Back in a mo.' Posy dashed round the side of the track to the far end, where Alf was hurrying to cross the line, trying to look as if his thumb wasn't clamped on top of his egg.

As he finished, Posy grabbed his arm. 'Alf, I've seen Violet down our entry. She might still be there when we go home.'

She ran back to her team, scanning the crowd for Ma. But instead, it was Dad she saw; and the look on his face said he was displeased with her for breaking ranks.

Gerald would have something to say about that.

When the jamboree ended, the older children were allowed to wander off, but the little ones were kept on the other side of the white-painted running lanes to be collected by their families. Spotting Alf, Nell was about to fetch him when Stan appeared and took his hand. Alf babbled at him in excitement and Stan bent down to listen, then he gave her a cheerful wave and walked away.

'I'm fed up to the back teeth with Stan,' she fumed. 'How dare he waltz off with Alf like that?'

She picked up Cassie. She had already lost one child; she wasn't losing this one. They made their way slowly with the crowd towards the gate. It wasn't until they got out of the park that they could walk at a normal pace. Nell kept a sharp eye out for Stan and Alf, but there was no sign of them.

'They'll be waiting outside the house for us to

let them in,' said Leonie.

'That might teach Alf not to go off with his dad,' said Nell, but she knew it wouldn't; and didn't she sound petty?

No one was waiting outside the house, which made her feel even more annoyed with Stan. As she walked into the house, she looked straight along the hall into the kitchen, and her insides turned icy cold. The kitchen door was open.

She pushed Cassie into Leonie's arms. 'Wait here.'

'What is it?'

'We've had an intruder.'

'How do you know? Don't do owt rash. I'll see if Mr O'Rourke is back.'

Nell had no intention of waiting for reinforcements. She strode into the kitchen. Everything looked as it should, but she knew someone had left that door open. She threw open the doors to the pantry and the broom cupboard, then the scullery; she went into the backyard. Opening the gate, she stepped out into the entry, looking up and down. The blood felt warm in her veins. Someone had been in her house. That was a threat to her children and Leonie, and she was ready to fight like a lioness. Back inside, she looked – yes, it was daft, but it was her duty to search thoroughly – under the kitchen table, then she marched into the front room. Nothing had been disturbed.

'What's going on?' Mr O'Rourke marched in, followed by his grown-up son, with Leonie bringing up the rear. 'Mrs Brent says someone broke in. Are you sure?'

'Positive. I was about to check upstairs.'

'We'll do that.'

They were closer to the stairs or she would never have let them go first. One of them burst into the bedroom, the other into the front.

'No one here.'

'No one here,' said Mr O'Rourke. 'Is anything missing?'

Nell walked into the bedroom. She made herself stand still and look carefully. Her breath caught. Leonie's box was missing from the top of the cupboard. Pushing past the two men, she ran downstairs to the pantry. Her hand shot to the back of the bottom shelf. Her Mazawattee tea tin was missing.

'Mr O'Rourke, will you please fetch a policeman? We've been burgled.'

'Burgled?' Leonie cried.

'I'm sorry. Your fireproof box has gone.'

Leonie pressed a hand to her mouth. 'No. That's got ... oh, no.'

By the time the copper arrived, Nell had discovered the rent money was missing from the pot on the mantelpiece, as was the jar into which she put the fees from the neighbours who used the sewing machine.

'I'll ask up and down the street if anyone else has been burgled,' said the policeman, but when he returned, he said no one had. 'Why would someone choose your house?'

'My bad luck, I suppose.'

'An old lady from further along, who didn't go to the jamboree, said she saw a man walking along the entry, but she didn't have her glasses

423

on, so she couldn't see him clearly, just that he was stocky.

'Edmund!' Leonie exclaimed.

'Edmund who, madam?' The copper produced his notebook.

'Edmund Tanner, my son-in-law.'

'I'll need his address.' He wrote down the details, then asked Nell, 'Do you have any idea who might burgle your house?'

Yes, she jolly well would say it. 'Stanley Hibbert, Constable. My estranged husband. It's in his interests to see me strapped for cash. He walked to the jamboree with us, but I didn't see him again until the end. Aren't you going to write it down?' she demanded. 'I think you should question him. I want to see justice done.'

'Justice? You're asking for justice? I know who you are. My mate is a copper in town and he does duty in the magistrates' court. He told me about a Mrs Hibbert, who ran away from her husband, thinking he'd done the dirty on her with another wife.'

'Then you understand how difficult the situation is between me and my husband.'

'But he wasn't the only one to do the dirty, was he? You told your kids he was dead, and you dare to stand there demanding justice. What justice did you show your children, eh? Tell me that.'

Nell was stunned. There was a knock at the door, but she didn't move. It was followed by a series of rapid knocks. Leonie hurried down the hall.

Alf burst in, followed by Stan, who was carrying his jacket rolled up in his arms, holding it firmly.

424

'It's Violet,' yelled Alf. 'Dad's found Violet and brought her home. He's a hero. I want me and Cassie and Violet to go to Annerby and live with Dad for ever.'

Posy kissed Gerald and thanked him, then put him away. 'Nasty bugger,' she breathed as she fixed him in position.

'Go upstairs, Posy,' said Dad. 'You're all red and dishevelled from running about in the sun.' Oh aye, and being thrashed had nowt to do with it. 'Your hair's a mess as well. Don't come down until you're presentable.'

Posy looked at Ma. An offer of help, perhaps? An 'I'll brush your hair for you' would be nice. Huh! Being looked in the eye would be nice. The droopy cowslip lifting her head and facing what was happening would be nice.

She trudged upstairs. She had to go slowly because her body was roaring with pain and she felt dizzy and sick. And angry and scared. Dad was a thief and she was a coward. But Dad had said he would make sure Gran's box was found, so he wasn't really a thief. Thieves kept things for ever.

She stood at the foot of the bed, leaning over, arms resting on the foot of the bedstead, head on her arms. The sickness subsided, but the pain was still fresh. It stung her flesh and beneath that, it was a deep, dark ache inside her bones. As weak as she felt, she mustn't lie down or her body would go stiff and getting moving again would be reet buggeration.

She splashed her face and hands and patted

them dry, then combed her hair. She didn't want to go downstairs, but in the end she had to. She wound her arms round the newel post at the top of the stairs. The staircase looked ever so steep. What if she came over all woozy partway down and missed her footing and fell to her doom?

Someone knocked on the door. Ma appeared and opened it.

'Good afternoon. Mrs Tanner?' A man's voice. A voice with authority. 'Is Mr Tanner in? I'd like a word.'

Ma fluttered; Posy felt a rush of shame. It wasn't easy being descended from a ditherer. Ma turned to the parlour and the man – the *police*man – followed. Posy sank down the side of the newel post and landed with a bump on the top stair.

A policeman. In their house. Wanting Dad. Oh cripes.

The parlour door had been pushed to, but not fastened. Posy forced herself to her feet and crept halfway downstairs. For once in her life, she didn't want to listen, but she had to.

'Mr Tanner? Constable Shore, sir. There's been a burglary in the area and I'd like to ask you some questions.'

'Of course, Constable. Anything I can do to help.' Dad didn't sound worried. He didn't need to. Posy was worried enough for both of them.

'Where were you this afternoon, sir?'

'At the sports jamboree, along with half of Chorlton. I was there all afternoon – wasn't I, Hilda?'

'Did you and your husband go to the park to-gether, Mrs Tanner?' asked the copper.

426

'Well—'

'No,' Dad cut in smoothly. 'We walked there separately, but I was only five minutes behind you wasn't I, Hilda?'

Posy held her breath. He took longer than that. Go on, Ma. Say it. Tell the truth.

'...Yes.'

Posy crumpled.

'And before you ask, Constable, no, I didn't spend the whole afternoon at my wife's side. I watched my daughter's races, naturally, but I wasn't interested in the others, so I walked about, passing the time of day with various neighbours. I can provide a list of names, if it helps, though I don't see what this has to do with me.'

'Do you know a Mrs Hibbert of Wilton Lane?'

'She used to be my mother-in-law's lodger.'

'It was her house where the burglary took place.'

A faint cry from Ma.

'I'm sorry to hear that,' said Dad. 'Was much taken?'

'I'm not at liberty to say, sir.'

'Mrs Brent, who lives with Mrs Hibbert, is my mother-in-law. Is she all right? Has she had anything stolen? Don't be alarmed, Hilda. I saw her from a distance in the park, so I know she's safe.'

'No one has been hurt, Mrs Tanner,' said the policeman.

'So this is what brings you here, Constable,' said Dad. 'You're here to inform us of my mother-in-law's misfortune?'

'Not exactly, sir. A man answering your description was seen near where the crime took place.'

'Indeed?' said Dad.

'And your name was suggested to me, sir.'

'By that Hibbert woman, no doubt,' Dad said sharply. 'She has a grudge against me.'

'Actually, it wasn't Mrs Hibbert, sir.'

'You mean it was my mother-in-law?'

'I'm not at liberty to say, sir.'

Posy clutched her elbows. Had Gran split on Dad? But how could she? She wasn't there. The only person who knew it was Dad was Posy – oh, and Mr Hibbert, but he didn't count.

A few more questions and answers were batted to and fro. Posy could tell things were winding up and she retreated to the landing. Dad saw Constable Shore out and went back into the parlour, shutting the door.

Posy waited a couple of minutes, then went down. She meant to walk right in, but, catching a few interesting words, she stopped to listen.

'Edmund, when you said you were five minutes after me...'

'What of it, Hilda?'

'Well...'

'Well, what?'

'Nothing.'

'I'm surprised at you if that's your main concern. I should have expected you to be more bothered by your mother's betrayal. Imagine her giving the police my name. How's that for family feeling? She as good as accused me of theft.'

'I'm sorry, Edmund.'

'You can't possibly want to make friends with her again after this – can you?'

Sundays were meant to be quiet, but someone was hammering on Nell's door. She had barely started to open it when it was shoved from the outside, sending her stumbling backwards, and Stan barged in.

'How dare you!' they exploded in unison.

'How dare you force your way in?' Nell demanded. 'This is my home. It's my name on the rent book.'

'And mine on the marriage lines, which gives me every right to be here – even if you've accused me of theft.'

'Oh.' Guilt flooded her – and uncertainty, then she rallied. 'You must admit it would suit your purposes if I lost my savings.'

'You stupid article.' His face was flushed with temper. 'That magistrate is going to order you to come back to me, so why would I need to steal your money?'

'The policeman asked if anyone had a reason—'

'And you thought: let's get Stan into trouble. Thanks very much, Nell.' He jabbed a finger at her. 'D'you know where I spent this morning? At the cop shop, that's where.'

'Don't point your finger in my face.' She slapped his hand aside, turning to march up the hall.

He grabbed her wrist and swung her back. 'Don't turn your back on me when I'm talking.'

She wrenched herself free. 'Don't touch me – at all – ever.'

'Don't be so dramatic. You tried to get me locked up and you failed, because I'm innocent – which you knew perfectly well, but you thought you'd try your luck.'

429

'I knew nowt of the kind. It *would* suit you if I lost my savings.' She stuck her hands on her hips. 'You went missing yesterday afternoon. I never saw you from when we arrived at the park to when you went off with Alf. You could easily have come here.'

He laughed derisively. 'If you didn't see me, you need spectacles. I offered my services to the teachers and spent the afternoon counting heads and picking up the poor little beggars in the sack race who couldn't even make it to the starting line without falling flat on their faces. Not only was I there all afternoon, but I have umpteen witnesses.'

'Oh.'

'I've tried to make amends and this is how you repay me. What will Alf say when he hears you accused his dad of theft?'

Her hand flew to her throat. 'You wouldn't tell him.' Thank goodness the children were at the park with Leonie.

Stan's mouth set in a grim line. 'Why would I tell him? Haven't I told him over and over to be polite to you? I'm trying to mend the damage you did by telling him I was dead and meanwhile you're doing your best to blacken my name. And that's what I'll tell Mr Aitcheson next time I see him.'

# Chapter Thirty

Nell had to run for the bus because Mr Miles had dropped in unexpectedly to look at the damaged areas.

'Downstairs is ready to be made good. Upstairs, I'm not so sure. Mr Dawson employs Perkins and Watson, a highly reputable firm. I'll ask the foreman to inspect the upstairs room and decide.'

Leonie was delighted. 'Well, that's good news and we're overdue for some of that – aren't we, Nell?'

'Yes,' said Nell. 'Thank you, Mr Miles.'

But after he had gone, their smiles faded.

Leonie sighed. 'Let's hope that when the work is done, we'll still be living here to benefit from it.'

'Assuming we can still afford it when the rent goes up.'

It was a relief to get out of the house. She hadn't recovered from her confrontation with Stan. Discussing it yesterday evening with Leonie had only served to make her friend jumpy about her own suspicions about Edmund.

'You didn't exactly give his name,' Nell had tried to comfort her. 'It was surprised out of you.'

As she travelled to Victoria Park, she tried to clear her mind of her troubles and concentrate on the work ahead, work that was even more important now her money had been stolen.

431

She entered the Fairbrothers' house by the kitchen door, exchanging good mornings with the cook and the gardener. They were used to her coming and going and she was left to make her own way up the back stairs without the formality of being shown by stroppy Daphne.

'We don't require any more lessons,' said Miss Graham while Nell fought to maintain a cheerful expression.

'You've taught us so well that we're confident we can manage,' said Miss Preston. 'But we still need you to sort through the clothes Miss Roberta mentioned. They've been put in what used to be Nanny's room.'

What had happened to Nanny? Had she hung on for years, hoping for another generation to care for? Was Miss Roberta one of those surplus girls you heard about, who had no hope of finding a husband after the terrible loss of life in the war?

Miss Preston took her along the landing.

'This used to be Nanny's bedroom.'

It still was, by the looks of it. Bed, hanging cupboard, a modest dressing table. Did rich people have so many rooms that when one outlived its use, they simply closed the door and forgot about it?

Clothes hung on hangers from the picture rail, others were piled on the bed. A royal-blue coat with tiered shoulder capes and huge cuffs; a pale-lilac dress with tiny white dots that made it look paler still; a ruby-red costume with a flared and pleated jacket ... and these were the ordinary clothes, the daywear! Fringing and piping, accordion pleating, lace and bows and ruching filled the room. The only truly simple clothes were the unfussy, but still beautifully tailored, silk blouses and linen skirts that said someone had enjoyed tennis or golfing.

'I'll leave you,' said Miss Preston. 'Remember, we're looking for things that can be cut down to make basic garments for children. The more children's things we can get out of a single item the better.'

'The children who get anything of this quality will be lucky.'

Miss Preston sighed. 'I do question the wisdom. The schools will have to be given a selection for the poorest children to change into in the morning and give back at home time. Otherwise there'll be jealousy in the streets and no doubt many of the garments would end up being pawned. But,' she said briskly, 'Miss Roberta has set her heart on it.'

She withdrew. Nell looked round. She would start with the sporty-looking skirts, as having the most appropriate fabric, and then move onto the crinolines, as being able to produce the greatest number of garments. When she finished, would that be the end of her work here? It looked like it.

A prickly feeling sprouted across the back of her neck. She turned to find Roberta Fairbrother, boyishly slim yet utterly feminine in a pale-green dress, the slender tiers of the skirt echoed in the daintily tiered short sleeves. She couldn't have looked more captivating if she had set out to make Nell feel dowdy in her respectable work dress.

'Good morning, Miss Fairbrother. I'm–'

'–Mrs Hibbert, the woman in the court case, whom Mr Franks is representing.'

Goodness. She hadn't realised before. Roberta Fairbrother was the woman she had seen kissing Jim. She had been too shocked and embarrassed at the time to recognise that slender, graceful figure, but the moment Miss Fairbrother spoke Jim's name, it fell into place.

'I know all about you,' said Miss Fairbrother. 'I asked my father. He didn't say much, because he's so discreet, but he did say it's a contemptible business involving bigamy that turned out not to be bigamy after all. Do tell: was it you or your husband who ... didn't commit the offence?'

Nell gritted her teeth. 'As you rightly point out, neither of us did; but for two years, I believed my husband had. Not that it's any of your concern, Miss Fairbrother.'

Roberta Fairbrother smiled. Dazzle, dazzle. 'I wouldn't say that. Daddy doesn't know he's employing you. I wonder what he'd say? No, that's not true. I know exactly what he'd say.'

'Are you going to tell him?' Thank goodness this looked like being her last time here ... but there was still the matter of the outstanding bill.

'And have you dismissed? I've considered it, I must admit, but I decided not to. There's no reason for Daddy to know and once you've served your purpose, you'll be gone.'

Her purpose? Roberta Fairbrother was toying with her. But she was Nell's employer's daughter, so the utmost politeness was required.

'Thank you,' said Nell.

'Don't thank me.' Miss Fairbrother waved her words away with a graceful sweep of her hand. 'Thank Mr Franks. He thinks highly of you; too highly, if you ask me. Men can be so susceptible. Darling James, he's going to be grateful to me when he hears that, in my own way, and even though it meant keeping a secret from my father, I was able to give you some support.'

Dazzle, dazzle. She turned to leave and a flowery scent wafted in Nell's direction.

Had Roberta Fairbrother just warned her off Jim Franks? She caught her breath and the floral scent went down her throat.

Maybe Nanny would be called out of retirement after all.

Jim knocked on Nell's door, worried about the news he had to impart. When she opened the door, the evening sun struck her hair, adding a bronze tinge to its autumn-leaf brown. Her smile of greeting couldn't hide her anxiety or her tiredness. She couldn't have had a good night's sleep in a considerable time. A feeling of protectiveness stirred; he hid it beneath a brisk manner.

'I've brought news. May I come in, if Mr Hibbert isn't here?'

A flush stained her cheeks. 'He's never here by my invitation. Come in. It's just me, Aunt Leonie and the children.'

'Mr Franks!'

Alf came belting down the hall, followed by Cassie. Jim let Alf crash into him, then pretended to box with him, before sweeping Cassie into his arms.

'Thank you for the warm welcome, young Master Hibbert,' he said. 'Go and hold the kitchen door open for us, there's a good chap.' As Alf scampered off, he murmured to Nell, 'I don't recall him being so boisterous before.'

The expression in Nell's eyes flattened. 'He hasn't forgiven me for lying to him about his father.'

They joined Mrs Brent in the kitchen. Aware that Stan Hibbert could turn up at any time, and also not wanting to spend more time with Nell than he had to, Jim elected to forego the chit-chat.

'Mrs Brent, I need to speak privately with Mrs Hibbert.'

She rose at once and clapped her hands. 'Time for bed, miss. Alf, come and help me with Cassie.'

'I don't want to.'

'And I don't want to give you a clip round the ear, but I will if I have to. Up the wooden hill – quietly, Alf, or you'll scare Violet.'

She picked up the little girl. Alf ran upstairs, but at least he didn't sound like he was wearing hobnailed boots.

Jim looked enquiringly at Nell.

'I don't get goodnight kisses any more from my son.' She sat, waving him into a seat. 'What did you want to tell me?'

'I've had two letters. One was from the magistrates' court. The date of your hearing has been brought forward. Instead of being held on the Friday of next week, it will be heard this Saturday. Mr Aitcheson has to go away unexpectedly next week, so he's fitting in all his work this week.'

Her face had gone white, turning her hazel eyes brown. He wanted to take her hand, just to reassure her, nothing more. He removed his hands from the table.

'If Stan hasn't had time to move out of Vicarage Lane, will it make a difference? No, it won't. He said we're moving in with his mother.'

'Mr Aitcheson is certain to wind up proceedings this week.'

She sagged. She was usually so upright, a slender figure with innate grace; but now, with her shoulders curving forwards in despair, her posture was clumsy. She looked...

It was the one thing she had never looked before.

Defeated.

'Do you need time to think about this? I could leave the other news for now.'

She came to life. 'No! I need to hear everything.' She pulled her shoulders back.

'The other letter is from the registrar in Annerby. There is no record that your husband entered into another marriage after the date of your marriage.'

'I should have expected that after what Stan said in court, but...' She sighed.

'You may remember I also asked for a copy of your own marriage certificate. One has not been provided.'

Her hand moved impatiently. 'So what? It was only needed to prove my marriage came first.'

Jim took the letter from the inside pocket of his jacket, unfolded it and laid it on the table. 'Here.' He pointed. 'That's the important bit.'

She bent her head. '...*the information provided*

*does not match that on the certificate.*' She looked up. 'Does not match? What does that mean? Are you telling me you made a mistake in the letter you sent the registrar?'

'You don't understand.'

She half-laughed. There was a glint in her eyes. 'I'd have written the letter myself if I'd known. I placed my trust in you. I never thought you'd let me down.' Her voice hardened. 'Or maybe, after all my lies about being widowed, I don't deserve your best attention.' It was a challenge.

He bridled. He had fallen in love with this so-called widow and had stood by her when she turned out to be married. Was she calling his professional integrity into question? He had intended to share his suspicion as to the letter's meaning; but if he did, and then he turned out to be mistaken, that would be worse. He rose to his feet. Perhaps if he made to leave, it would bring her to her senses and she would back down; but she let him go, without a word.

He returned home and started packing, ready for his journey tomorrow.

He slept badly. He felt vexed with Nell for flying off the handle. She had as good as accused him of being unprofessional. But then, she had every reason to be upset, after everything she had gone through and with her future being decided this weekend. Actually, it had in all probability already been decided, as she must realise. Moreover, it wasn't as though she had any idea of what the registrar's letter could mean. But that was the point, wasn't it? She hadn't asked. She hadn't trusted him. She had immediately fought back.

Women weren't supposed to do that. They were supposed to let you look after them. But who had Nell Hibbert had to look after her since she left her husband? Only herself. She had been responsible for everything.

It was too late now. There wasn't time to see her in the morning. The little time he had would be spent with Mr Fairbrother, who was entitled to hear about the latest developments.

He knew Mr Fairbrother didn't set off for his office until nine-thirty, so he took the liberty of calling at the Fairbrother residence shortly after nine, with profuse apologies for dragging Mr Fairbrother away from his devilled kidneys.

They talked over coffee in the study.

'You'll have to excuse me now, James,' said Mr Fairbrother when the clock struck the half-hour. 'I'll leave you to finish your coffee. I hope things go well in Annerby.'

Jim rose to shake hands and his old colleague left. Jim stood at the window with his cup and saucer. Behind him, the door opened and he turned, expecting Mr Fairbrother had forgotten something.

Roberta stood there.

'Daddy says you're going away.'

'A business matter.'

'To do with Mrs Hibbert? Don't worry. You haven't been indiscreet. I've put two and two together. She's working here, your Mrs Hibbert.'

'She isn't my Mrs Hibbert.'

Roberta smiled. 'I'm pleased to hear it. Even so, you'll be glad to know I've given her a helping hand. Daddy wouldn't be pleased to have her

439

here, what with the bigamy and all, so I'm keeping quiet. I know you have a good opinion of her.'

'You're a brick, Roberta.'

'Aren't I just? How long will you be away?'

'I need to get back here as soon as possible. The court case has been moved to this Saturday.'

She came closer to him and he inhaled her floral scent. 'Hurry back, won't you?' Kissing her fingertip, she brushed it against his lips. 'And not just for the court case.'

'Don't I get a proper kiss?'

'Not while you taste of coffee.' She walked to the door, twinkled her fingers at him and left.

Jim put down his coffee unfinished. No doubt about it. Roberta was behaving a lot better than Nell was.

The palm of Posy's hand was red and stinging where she had been given the strap for not paying attention in class. She sat up straight, ignoring the sniggers that said some children were pleased to see her being punished. She had a reputation for being a hard worker and there was a contingent in the class that didn't like that, but that was their hard luck.

If giving her the strap was meant to make her pay attention, it wasn't working. It just reminded her of the clobbering she would get tomorrow from Dad when yet again there were five caramels in a quarter of a pound.

That wasn't the only thing that would happen tomorrow. Alf's mum and dad were seeing the magistrate. Alf had paraded round the playground, telling everyone he was going to live with his dad. How could he want to leave such a loving, capable, playful mum as Mrs Hibbert? Daft little beggar. Mind you, he wouldn't actually be leaving her behind, because she would be moving too, but Alf didn't care about that.

Anyroad, tomorrow wasn't just about what happened to the Hibberts. It was about Gran. She was going to live with Mrs Watson, which would be wonderful but wrong. You were meant to live with family, not the neighbours. It was all right for Gran to live with the Hibberts, because she was treated as family; but for her to live with Mrs Watson wasn't right. It would be the biggest snub in the world. It would make Gran look unwanted. Posy couldn't bear that to be inflicted on her lovely gran. She didn't have Gramps to protect her any more. That was Dad and Ma's job now, but they weren't doing it, which left Posy.

It was her job to make things right for Gran.

'What d'you mean, Mr Franks is unavoidably detained?' Anger coursed through Nell – no, not anger: fear. She forced steadiness into her voice. 'I'm sorry, Mr Robbins. I knew he'd gone away. I assumed he would be back for this.'

'He intended to be,' said Mr Robbins. 'Mr Franks would never let down a client.'

Never let down a client? Pull the other one! 'What else did his message say?'

'Just "unavoidably detained". It was a telegram, you see. Essential words only.'

Her heart doubled in weight as she walked into Mr Aitcheson's room and took her place. Jim's absence was the worst possible disappointment.

441

Mr Aitcheson placed a husband's rights above all else and she had little hope of a favourable resolution; but she had trusted Jim with her future, with her children's futures. Even when Stan played his trump card of monogamy and her situation had instantly been redrawn into something far more dire, she had still trusted Jim to do his best, no matter how hopeless her case. Having him at her side had made her feel that, whatever the outcome, she had had the best possible chance.

But he had made a pig's whisker of his letter to the registrar and now he couldn't even organise himself to turn up.

Well, what of it? She was used to facing her troubles alone.

Rather than dwelling on Jim Franks's shortcomings, she must prepare what to say to Mr Aitcheson. She took out her appointment diary. On a plain page at the back, she listed everything that provided security for the children.

*Child-minding – A. L.*
*2 bedroom house*
*Decent neighbourhood*
*Work hours = with A & C for b'fast & in evenings*

Was that all? It didn't seem much, and yet in real life it was a huge amount that added up to a stable background for Alf and Cassie to grow up as happy, healthy, confident individuals. Would Mr Aitcheson be swayed?

The clerks appeared and took their places. Stan and Mr Norton took their seats. She glanced across, but Stan didn't look her way.

The door opened at the top of the room.

'All rise.'

In came Mr Aitcheson, carrying a file under his arm. There was an impatient air about him, as if he was fed up with the extra work he had had to plough through and couldn't wait for it to be over. Nell sensed movement behind her. Onlookers? Didn't they have anything better to do?

Mr Aitcheson opened the file and spread out the papers. Then, tilting his chin upwards a fraction, he scanned the room before looking at the clerks.

'I had all the women removed last time. What makes you think I want any here today?'

A clerk hurried to his side. 'There's just one, sir.' He bent his head and whispered.

'I suppose so,' said Mr Aitcheson. 'But at the first sign of hysterics, out she goes.'

Who was this woman? Nell reminded herself not to look round.

'Mr Norton, has your client found alternative accommodation for his family?'

Mr Norton rose. 'If I may be so bold, I suggest he did better than that. In order to make the best provision for Mrs Hibbert, who, as we are all aware, is woefully reluctant to return to him, he made arrangements for his family to take up temporary residence with his mother, specifically so Mrs Hibbert could choose her new house at her leisure.'

'And Mrs Hibbert senior is happy with this?'

'Delighted, sir. She wanted nothing more than to forgive her errant daughter-in-law and welcome her home to the place of her birth, along

443

with the grandchildren whom she longs to see.'

'That seems satisfactory,' said Mr Aitcheson. 'In that case, I have no hesitation–'

'Wait!' Nell sprang up. 'What about me? What about the stability I offer my children?'

'Sit down, woman,' said the magistrate. 'If you have a case to put, your solicitor should put it. Where is Mr Franks?'

'He's not here.'

'I can see that. I asked where he is.'

'I don't know.'

'Given up on you, I expect.' He held up a finger to forestall her. 'One more word from you and I'll have you removed.' He cast a glance at the ceiling. 'Women! I am satisfied with the arrangements Mr Hibbert has made and therefore–'

'If I may, sir,' said Mr Norton.

Mr Aitcheson glared. 'What now, man?'

'If it is your intention, sir, to order Mrs Hibbert to return to her husband, Mr Hibbert wishes you to know he has had a change of heart.'

'A what?'

Nell gasped and then seemed to freeze. Stan had changed his mind. She had won after all. She should be shaking with relief, crying out for the good news to be repeated; but she couldn't move. Just when she ought to be rejuvenated, she was so overwhelmed that she turned to stone.

'A change of heart,' said Mr Norton, 'and one that I think you will find understandable, Mr Aitcheson. Mr Stanley Hibbert's greatest wish is to have his children, Alfred and Cassandra, restored to him; but he no longer wants his wife.'

# Chapter Thirty-One

Outside the sweet shop, Posy unfolded the top of the white cone-shaped paper bag with infinite care and lifted it to her face to inhale. Even in their wrappings, the caramels smelt rich and sweet. She upended the bag into her cupped hand. Out tumbled the sweets. Five – naturally. There were only ever five, except for that one time.

Her heartbeat was calm. She popped one caramel back in the bag and looked at the other four. She had thought when she planned this, that she would eat the lot; but now it came to it, she didn't want them. Perhaps she should give them to other children before she got home. That would be a generous thing to do, but somehow wrong. She had to concentrate and she couldn't do that with children crowding round her, everyone suddenly her best friend.

Better to drop the sweets down the drain. One … two … three … four. Goodbye, caramels.

She couldn't change her mind now.

Carrying the bag carefully so as not to crease it, she went home. Dad was sitting in the parlour, reading the paper. Ma was knitting.

Ma stood up. 'I must–'

Oh no, you don't. 'Hang on, Ma. Dad, here you are.'

She had never handed over the sweetie bag so

boldly before. As soon as he felt it, Dad's expression darkened and a furious heat took up residence in Posy's chest. What had she let herself in for?

She knew what she had let herself in for. It was the only way.

Dad stood up. He opened the bag and shook the contents into his hand. One caramel. Dad's mouth twisted. Posy felt sick, but there was only way to do this and that was with gusto.

'You're going to beat the living daylights out of me anyroad, so I thought I'd make it worth my while. Count yourself lucky you didn't get an empty bag.'

There was a great roar and after that Posy couldn't quite tell what was happening. It was like falling down a rocky mountainside, all bumps and bruises and the breath whooshing out of her. The first heavy slap had thrown her to the floor. Now he stood over her. He had the scruff of her neck in one hand and in amongst the power of the blows he dealt with his other fist was the sharp pain of having her hair pulled tight. The blows pounded into her. Her ribs creaked as they bowed inwards, but they didn't snap.

Watch, Ma, watch what he's doing...

Her arms curled round her bent head, but they couldn't protect her from a hefty blow that sent pain jangling from her neck up into the back of her skull at the same time as out across her shoulders.

Watch, Ma, watch...

Her body throbbed inside and out. That wasn't a fist on the end of his arm. It was a brick.

Nell waited in Mr Robbins' office. He had produced a ham sandwich, a slice of Dundee cake and a cup of tea, but Nell couldn't face any of it. Damn Mr Aitcheson. As soon as Mr Norton had made his shocking announcement, he had declared, 'I have two other matters to deal with today, which I know can actually be dealt with, unlike this one, which, every time it appears to draw to a conclusion, skids off in a new direction. I want everyone back here at two o'clock.'

Bewildered, Nell had made a dive for Stan's table, but Mr Norton had ushered him out, leaving her standing there. She might still be standing there now, had Mr Robbins not taken pity on her.

Stan didn't want her. Night after night, she had lain awake, picking over the possibilities that lay ahead, but this one had never occurred to her. Stan wanted to take the children and leave her behind. Would Mr Aitcheson permit that?

'It's time,' said Mr Robbins.

Dread pressed her into the chair. From somewhere she found the strength to heave herself up and return to her lonely place in the magistrates' room. Stan and Mr Norton were already in their seats but didn't look at her.

'All rise.'

Mr Aitcheson resumed his place.

'My other business is concluded. There is just this repugnant matter left. Let's begin. Not you, Mr Norton. Mr Hibbert, on your feet, if you please. You no longer wish to have your wife returned to you.' He made her sound like a parcel. 'Why not?'

'I've tried, sir. I've done my best to set things right between us. I've corrected my son when he's been rude to her. I've told her how a proper marriage would be best for the children, and I meant it. I even tried to put things right after she accused me of stealing her savings, only we had a bit of a slanging match and I caught her by the arm and she said I was never to touch her again, not ever. It was the way she said it, sir. Until then, I thought she'd come round eventually, but when she said that, I knew she meant it ... if you get my meaning.'

'I see,' said Mr Aitcheson. 'You realise you are entitled to your conjugal rights?'

Stan coughed. 'I don't want what isn't freely given.'

'This is most irregular. From start to finish, Mrs Hibbert, you have caused nothing but trouble. Your husband started the shameful process by consorting with another woman, but since then you've blundered through life in a haphazard and disgraceful fashion that beggars belief. Here you had the opportunity to reinstate yourself and your children in a respectable married home, but you have refused to enter into a proper married life with your husband. Therefore, it is my decision–'

'You can't,' cried Nell. 'I haven't had a chance to speak.'

'Are you going to tell me about the stable life you provide for your children?'

'Yes.'

'Have your savings been stolen?'

'Yes.'

'Then you cannot provide security. Not that it would be of any relevance if your savings had not been stolen, since, after the way you lied to your children and pretended their father was dead, you are without question an unnatural mother. My ruling, therefore, is final. Mr Hibbert is awarded–'

The door – a disturbance – 'Mr Aitcheson!' Jim! Nell didn't know whether to be thrilled or furious. He hurried forward, followed by Mr Robbins, who peeled off and went to the clerks at the side.

'Forgive the intrusion,' said Jim, 'but I must be heard.'

'You're too late, Mr Franks. You should have been here this morning.'

'I was travelling here by train, sir. You must hear me out.'

'On the contrary. I have made my decision and shall not be swayed. Your late arrival does you no credit. Neither does your client: I suggest you choose more wisely in future.'

One of the clerks, watched anxiously by Mr Robbins, came to the magistrate's side and murmured to him.

'Great Scott!' grumbled Mr Aitcheson. 'I've a good mind to withdraw from this and leave it to someone else to mop up. In all my days on the bench, this is the unholiest mess...'

'Mr Aitcheson.' Jim spoke firmly. 'This matter can be settled in a matter of minutes.'

'It better had be. Proceed.'

'Thank you,' said Jim. 'The facts are simple.

When Mrs Hibbert believed herself to be married to a bigamist, she was correct.'

Posy came to her senses to find herself on her feet. Well, not precisely on her feet, more slumped against someone else, against Ma. Ma's arms were around her and she was saying something, but it was like listening underwater. Her body was sore and smarting. She wanted to crumple to the floor. She started to crumple, but Ma's arms wouldn't let her. They tightened round her and pain shot through her ribs. Vomit surged up her gullet. The world swooped around her or was it the inside of her head that was swooping?

One of Ma's arms let go. There was the sensation of falling, not falling, leaning, being held, feeling crushed, Ma's arm squashing into her tender body. Then she went blind. Fresh air enveloped her. Ma had opened the door. Not blind – dazzled. Afternoon brightness. Her skin went slick with relief. Not blind. Whatever he had done to her, he hadn't done that.

Voices, people, commotion. She flinched away from the hands, the concern. The ground vanished as she was scooped up. A man's arms lifting her. Dad? Reet buggeration. No – someone else's dad. He carried her up, up. The footsteps on the stairs were loud, ringing. No stair carpet. Not their house, then. They had a strip of carpet up their stairs. Very posh. Not everyone had stair carpet.

Another swoop and she was in a bed. Covers were drawn over her. Voices surrounded her. She wanted to sink away, but she had to finish what she had planned. What had she planned? Her brain was like scrambled eggs.

Voices faded, leaving two voices, urgent and thick with distress. Ma. Mrs Watson. She was next door in Mrs Watson's house. Was that good? Was it part of the plan?

She heaved her eyes open. 'Ma...' Pulling an arm out from under the covers made her muscles roar, but she had to reach out. 'Ma.'

'Posy! You're safe now. Mr Foskett has gone for the doctor.'

'Dad...'

'He's not here. He stormed out.'

'Ma...' She couldn't hang on much longer. 'Did you see? Did you watch?'

'Hush, Posy.'

'Did you see?'

'Of course I saw. You're all right now. The doctor's on his way.'

'You didn't...'

Didn't what? What hadn't Ma done? Ma hadn't done something and Posy had put herself through all this to make her do it. What was it?

'I couldn't, could I?' said Ma. 'He's so big and strong. I couldn't have stopped him. Why did you provoke him like that? You know what he's like.'

'Nay.' Mrs Watson now, agitated and determined. 'Are you saying yon lass asked for it? Shame on you, Hilda Tanner.'

'No, of course not.'

'No one deserves a beating like this,' said Mrs Watson. 'I'm going next door to fetch Posy's nightie. She's stopping here until she's better and I'll tell that husband of yours if you haven't got the guts.'

A bustling sound, a click: she was gone. The room smelt of beeswax and warm wood. Ma held Posy's hand. Her head was bent. It was always bent. The droopy cowslip, not seeing what was in front of her, because if you didn't look, it wasn't your responsibility. Stir the custard, do the darning, anything, anything, rather than look at what was happening.

'Ma ... you lied to the police.'

'What are you talking about? You're confused. Does your head hurt?

'The policeman asked where Dad was during the burg – burg–' *How did you say it?* '...burgle-ry. You said he was with you.'

'He was.'

'Five minutes behind, you said.'

'How do you know that?'

'Dad said he were five minutes behind and you said yes.' A feeling darker and more bitter than any physical pain twisted inside Posy. 'You lied.'

'I never–'

Ma looked away. She always looked away. Well, not any more.

'I followed him, Ma. He weren't with you. He were up Wilton Lane, stealing Gran's box.'

'No, Posy.'

'I was there. I saw him walk back with it, and Mrs Hibbert's money. I know what he's done with them an' all.'

Ma let go of Posy's hand and covered her face. She rocked to and fro. The mattress moved with her, a slight motion but enough to stir up Posy's nausea. It would serve Ma right if she vomited all over her.

Ma dragged her hands away from her smeared face. 'I had to say what he wanted.'

'Did you? Do you still?'

Nell's thoughts scrambled to take in Jim's words. Stan was a bigamist after all. Her lungs felt tight; it was hard to breathe. Was it safe to feel relieved? But there had been no trace of a marriage certificate for Stan and Mrs Vicarage Lane. Had one turned up? Did she dare hope?

'Silence!' called the clerk.

'Proceed, Mr Franks,' said Mr Aitcheson.

'I applied to the registrar in Annerby for copies of the marriage certificates for Mr and Mrs Hibbert and for Mr Hibbert and the woman from Vicarage Lane. It was my intention to prove Mr Hibbert's bigamy, but, as we subsequently learnt, he never went through a marriage ceremony with the woman from Vicarage Lane. I was more surprised, however, not to receive a copy of Mr and Mrs Hibbert's certificate.' Jim produced a piece of paper. 'The registrar wrote to me saying that *the information provided does not match that on the certificate*. Odd wording, I think you'll agree; but what it means is that the copy couldn't be issued because the letter requesting it assumed a marriage had taken place.'

Nell couldn't contain herself. 'A marriage did take place.'

He turned to her. 'A ceremony took place and everyone believed it was a legal marriage; except Mr Hibbert, who knew he was already married to someone else.'

Nell's head jerked back in shock and her pulse

ran riot. Married to someone else!

'Permit me to explain.' Jim glanced at Mr Aitcheson, but Nell knew his words were for her. 'At the start of the war, Stanley Hibbert joined up. After his training, he was sent to work in stores in an army base in the south of England for six months, during which time, he met and married – his wife. Never mind her name: she wouldn't wish it to be made public. He was shipped over to France in 1915. In 1917, on leave in Annerby, he met and married our Mrs Hibbert.' He indicated Nell. 'Later, he took up with a third woman, though without benefit of clergy.'

Three wives? Three! Nell was stunned. He was reasonably good-looking and he had a pleasant manner, but – three wives!

'The real Mrs Hibbert, the lady from down south, tracked down her husband in 1919. Judging by the expression on Mr Hibbert's face, he was unaware of this. Upon discovering he was "married" to another woman, namely our Mrs Hibbert, and that they had a son, the real Mrs Hibbert decided not to pursue the matter publicly, since it would bring disgrace on her as well as on our Mrs Hibbert and her child. She did, however, inform the registrar, who decided to let the matter lie; but his position required him to place a notification on the certificate that recorded the illegal marriage, which meant that when I requested a copy, it could not be supplied because there is no legal marriage.'

'Are you saying the registrar knew about this?' demanded Mr Aitcheson. 'Disgraceful! This Hibbert fellow has committed a crime.'

'He has, sir, but the real Mrs Hibbert declined to be involved in a court case and the registrar decided to leave our Mrs Hibbert and her son with their good name intact.'

Mr Aitcheson looked at the clerks. 'Send for a policeman.'

Stan lurched to his feet. 'You said yourself, sir, that higher courts have shown leniency.'

'Yes, to former soldiers who married legally before the war and bigamously after it ended; and the leniency was never intended to condone the practice of bigamy, but to keep the breadwinner out of prison to fulfil his family obligations.'

'Mr Aitcheson,' said Jim, 'will you state for the record that the Hibbert children are to remain with Mrs Hibbert?'

'Yes, yes, the clerks will make a note. Not that any of them has the right to call themselves Hibbert any more.'

'What?' Nell began.

'Which won't go well for them when they end up on the parish, as they undoubtedly will, and all the faster now she has had her savings stolen.'

Mr Aitcheson pushed himself to his feet. There was a call of 'All rise', but something was happening at the other table.

Jim moved to block Nell's view. 'Best if you don't see.'

'Don't be ridiculous.' She moved. 'Oh.' She was in time to see Stan being led away.

'I'll take you home,' said Jim.

'Home. Yes.' She shook her head. 'It's a lot to take in.'

As they walked into the anteroom, Roberta

Fairbrother stepped forward and Nell's heart stopped. Miss Fairbrother was as beautiful as ever in a glorious dress of chiffon with a print of dramatically large flowers. Instead of a fashionable cloche hat, she wore a pretty straw with a scarf tied round the crown.

'There you are, James. I waited for you.' Dazzle, dazzle.

'I didn't expect you to.' Jim turned to Nell. 'On my journey back from Annerby, I had to wait for a connection so I took the opportunity to have a call put through to Mr Fairbrother to keep him abreast of developments.'

Miss Fairbrother took his arm, which just showed what a bold piece she was. 'Lo and behold, when he arrived, who should be waiting at the station to spirit him straight to court?'

Jim looked uncomfortable. Served him right. 'Roberta, may I present Mrs Hibbert? Mrs Hibbert – Miss Fairbrother.'

'No need for introductions, James. Mrs Hibbert and I are old friends.' Dazzle, dazzle. 'May we drive you anywhere, Mrs Hibbert? I've got the motor waiting. It would be our pleasure, wouldn't it, James?'

'No, thank you,' said Nell. Miss Fairbrother was beautiful and cultivated and she had never felt more ordinary in her life. 'I'll catch the tram.'

'If you're sure.' Dazzle, dazzle. 'James, Mummy made me promise faithfully to bring you home with me. We'll have tea first, then you can rehash the case with Daddy before dinner.'

'I'd like to, of course, but I did say I'd see Mrs Hibbert home.'

'No need,' Nell said quickly.

'I think Mrs Hibbert has her own engagement,' said Miss Fairbrother. She looked past Nell. 'That woman seems to be waiting for you. You mustn't let us keep you.'

Nell turned and found herself face-to-face with Olive Hibbert.

## Chapter Thirty-Two

Jim disliked leaving Nell stranded. She had taken an emotional battering and he wanted to see her home safely. It was the gentlemanly thing to do and the least she deserved. But she was focused on the stranger. It didn't look like a comfortable meeting. He should go to her side, but Roberta drew him away.

He felt a rush of gratitude. 'Thanks for meeting me at the station. It made all the difference.' He couldn't help glancing at Nell. Should he–?

'Are you ready, James? Mummy and Daddy are expecting us.'

Roberta attracted admiring looks as they made their way out of the building, making him proud to be her escort. Her kid-gloved fingers rested in the crook of his arm. In his other hand he carried the Gladstone bag with the clobber he had taken on his travels.

'I haven't got evening togs to change into,' he warned her.

'Mummy won't mind this once.'

Outside, Mr Fairbrother's beloved old Austin was waiting. The chauffeur jumped to attention and opened the door. Did he recognise Jim as the window cleaner who had passed the time of day outside Mrs Randall's a few weeks ago? If he did, he couldn't afford to show it.

The motor drew away and Jim settled back.

'I'm proud of you, James. After your telephone call, Daddy said what a remarkable job you've done. He's hoping to lure you back into the firm.'

He laughed. 'I'm sure you're not supposed to tell me that.'

'He'll ask you this evening. And I want to discuss my scheme for providing clothes for poor children. I hope you'll provide valuable insights.'

'After living among the working class, you mean?'

She looked at him. 'I won't pretend that part of your life never existed.'

Good. It was an important part of him.

The motor pulled up and the chauffeur got out to open Roberta's door, but she preferred to skim across the seat and follow Jim. He gave her his hand and she slid out gracefully, coming to her feet in a fluid rippling of floaty fabric.

Jim opened the garden gate. The fountain tinkled in the centre of the lawn. Large-leaved shrubs cast purple shadows round the edges. Instead of heading up the path, Roberta lingered.

'Do you remember Mummy sending us out here to make up our differences or declare eternal hatred?'

'I'm glad you didn't opt for the latter.'

'Shall I tell you a secret?' She danced a few

458

steps along the path, then turned to face him with a provocative little smile. 'It's a bit naughty.'

He laughed. 'Then I definitely want to hear it.'

She walked backwards. Her skirt floated around her. 'That evening, I said I came home early because my plans were cancelled.'

'I remember.'

'That was a teeny little lie. When I was out, I heard about you and Daddy working on a case and I thought Daddy might invite you for dinner.' A light shrug; a sensuous ripple of material. 'So I came home.' She tilted her head to one side. 'Do you mind?'

Leonie rushed for the front door at the first scrape of its opening. Nell! She reached out her arms, expecting her dear adopted niece to collapse into them, but Nell walked straight into the house.

'Where are the children?' she asked.

'With Mrs Clancy. I thought you'd need to have a good cry.'

Nell grasped Leonie's hands. 'It's good news. I'm keeping them.'

'You won? You won!'

'I can hardly believe it. I'm shaking.'

'You and me both.' Leonie clutched Nell's hands. 'I need to sit down. I want to hear every detail.'

Seated at the table, she listened in amazement.

'So you're not married and never were? And you'd never have known if Jim hadn't gone digging through the records.'

'I gave him such a telling off for bungling his enquiry, as I thought.'

'He'll understand. You can apologise next time you see him.'

'I'm not sure I will – see him, I mean. He has other commitments.' Something in her tone closed the subject.

'If you and Stan were never wed,' Leonie said, treading delicately, 'the children are...'

'Don't say it.' Nell rubbed a hand across her mouth. 'I don't mind losing my respectability – well, I do, obviously, but I'd throw it to the winds if the children could keep theirs.'

'One thing at a time,' said Leonie. 'The children are yours.'

The darkness receded from Nell's eyes and they filled with an inner glow. Leonie's emotions welled up, crowding her chest with gratitude. Nell was keeping her children, which was what she deserved.

'I'll fetch them,' she offered.

'No, leave them. There's summat else. Mrs Hibbert was in court today – Olive, Stan's mother. He didn't know she was coming. She wanted to tell me she would make me welcome.'

'She'll have a lonely journey home.'

Nell sighed. 'I fetched her back here with me. I didn't know what else to do. She was that shocked about Stan.'

'Where is she now?'

'I pointed out the house and told her to get lost while I talked to you.' Nell groaned. 'I must be mad. I should have stuffed her on the first train heading north.'

A knock on the door made them both freeze, gazes locked.

'Speak of the devil.' Leonie stood up. 'You stop here. Hold your horses,' she called as there was another knock. She opened the door, intending to give Mrs Olive Hibbert the sharp edge of her tongue.

'You took your time,' said Mrs Watson. 'Come quick. I've got your Posy tucked up in bed. The doctor's been.'

Someone walked over her grave. 'Is she all right?'

'That son-in-law of yours gave her a leathering.'

Emotion flared, a mixture of fury and despair. She should never have left that house. She should have been there to stand between Edmund and Posy and suffer the blows herself.

'Is our Hilda all right?'

'He never laid a finger on her, but when Mr Foskett came back from fetching the doctor, she sent him off again to find a bobby and right now she's howling her eyes out at my kitchen table. Now come on. Your Posy needs you.'

'Sounds as if Hilda does an' all,' said Nell, appearing behind her.

Mrs Watson snorted. 'Stuff Hilda.'


As Roberta preceded him into the drawing room, Jim heard words of welcome from more voices than those of her parents. He walked in and there were Don and Patsy.

'James, my boy, welcome, welcome.' Mr Fairbrother was all bonhomie. 'Let me be the first to congratulate you.' He pumped Jim's hand. 'James saw off a tricky case today. Splendid work.'

Don shook his hand and clapped him on the shoulder. 'Congrats. We've heard all about it.'

Patsy rose to her feet in a shimmer of silk and brushed his cheek with a kiss. 'You saved the day, James.' Releasing him, she turned to Roberta and they kissed one another. That had never happened before. 'Roberta, how wonderful to see you. We were delighted to receive your mother's invitation to share James's victory dinner.'

'Patsy, you look marvellous,' said Roberta. 'Look at me, all crumpled. I've been James's chauffeur all afternoon.'

Jim bowed over Mrs Fairbrother's hand. 'Thank you for the invitation.'

Afternoon tea was brought in on pretty cake stands. There was a well-bred flurry of activity as tea was poured and plates were passed round. Jim found a seat and let it all happen around him. He wasn't comfortable, but why not? His family and Roberta's family were getting along famously. It should be perfect.

Should be.

Some things didn't change. Olive Hibbert walked into the kitchen and said, 'This is ... nice,' and that hesitation catapulted Nell back to all the times her mother-in-law had done her down. She had put up with it back then, but not now.

'It didn't take you long to get started,' she commented. 'You're barely through the door and you're criticising my kitchen.'

'If you must know, it were my intention to walk in and say summat complimentary to get us off on the right foot. But what could I say? It's so bare.'

'Shall I tell you summat? I'm sick to death of

this kitchen table. A proper kitchen should have a pair of armchairs beside the hearth, but I couldn't afford that when we moved in, not without digging into my savings, and I couldn't do that, so we've had nowt but this table to sit at.'

'Savings mean security.'

'That's why I was so upset when I thought Stan was drinking.'

Silence. Why had she brought this woman here? Nell wanted to be in Finney Lane. Poor Posy. Well, Olive was here and she couldn't ask her to leave, not yet.

'Park yourself,' said Nell. 'I'll put the kettle on. Do you want to take your coat off?'

Olive smiled grimly – not a smile at all. 'Will I be here long enough?'

'I'll hang it up.' She warmed the pot and set out the crockery.

'I never knew about Stan's other wife down south,' said Olive when Nell sat down and poured the tea. 'I'm that ashamed. My son, a bigamist.'

'You sound surprised.'

'Aren't you?' asked Olive.

'About the wife down south, yes; but I've spent the past two years or more thinking he was a bigamist. So must you – unless you knew him and Mrs Vicarage Lane never had a ceremony.'

'I'll have you know I thought the same as everyone, that Stan had had two weddings. Alice called herself Mrs Hibbert right till the end.' Olive leant forward. 'I never approved of her.'

'But you never did owt about it, did you?'

'Like what? Report Stan to the law? What for? You'd vanished, and I might not have approved of Alice and her kids, but they had to be provided for.'

'So what was the big shock about discovering he really is a bigamist?'

'Because I thought he was married to you,' cried Olive, her emotion taking Nell by surprise. 'I thought you were his real wife. I thought that was how it were meant to be. When Stan said he were fetching you back, it felt like everything was going back to normal. That Alice never set foot in my house, no matter how much Stan went on at me, and I never set foot in hers until Stan wanted me to sell the furniture. I came to court today so you'd know it wasn't just Stan that wanted you.' Olive looked at her. 'I can see that doesn't mean owt to you.'

'It's not as though you liked me much when I was there before.'

'Actually, I thought you were a mardy little cow, begrudging your husband a pint of an evening.'

'You what?' Nell sat up. 'I thought he was drinking a lot more than a pint.'

'And I could see he wasn't. Drinkers get puffy faces and big bellies and that wasn't Stan. It riled me; you, the destitute little orphan we'd took to our hearts, moaning about your husband when he never deserved it.'

'I had no idea you thought that.'

'I know, and that were ruddy annoying an' all.' Olive lifted her eyebrows at her. 'Go on: say how much you hated me, and then we'll call it quits.'

'Actually, I was thinking that Stan has even more to answer for than I thought, and that's saying something.'

464

They looked at one another. Nell couldn't recall the last time she had been in agreement with Olive Hibbert.

'Come back to Annerby,' said Olive. 'You'll be the talk of the wash house if you stop here.'

'I'll be the talk of the wash house if I go there. I belong here now.'

'Then at least let me help you. I've got the money from selling the contents of the Vicarage Lane house. I'll keep a bit, but the rest is yours.'

'I don't want it.'

'Well, the offer's there. It could give you back your sense of security.'

'Look, I don't know what time the last train north is...'

'I don't blame you for wanting to get rid of me, but there's summat you should know. I did a lot of thinking while I were walking round and round the block, waiting for you to let me in.'

Olive lifted her chin. Nell swallowed. What now?

'I'm like you: I'll be the talk of the wash house wherever I am, so I've decided to be the talk of the wash house closest to my grandchildren.'

## Chapter Thirty-Three

'That was a delightful tea, my dear,' said Mr Fairbrother, as if his wife had personally sliced the sandwiches. 'If you'll excuse me, I'll take James into the study to discuss the case. Would you care to join us?' he asked Don.

'With pleasure, sir.'

The men got up. Jim cast a general smile round the room, not wanting to acknowledge Roberta in particular. Graceless? Possibly. Probably. But that satisfied, knowing look on Patsy's face made him edgy. Please don't let Roberta say something arch like, 'Hurry back.' That would be too much. She didn't, but as he left the room, he caught the way she and Patsy leant towards one another.

Mr Fairbrother led the way across the hall and opened the door. 'Make yourselves at home. I'm going down to the wine cellar to find a bottle of my best brandy.'

Jim shut the door and rounded on his brother. 'What's going on?'

'Right now I imagine the cook is having a seizure at being asked to produce a celebration dinner for six at no notice whatsoever.'

'Don't kid around. Why are you and Patsy here? And don't say because you were invited.'

'What's got into you?'

He turned away. It was a good question. What difference did Don and Patsy's presence make? It was thoughtful of Mrs Fairbrother to include them. Or was it? Two families dining together: you could be forgiven for thinking of ... an engagement.

He turned back to Don. 'It wasn't luck or coincidence that brought Roberta and me back together. She engineered it.'

'Is that a bad thing?'

Was it? Oh hell. 'It's not how I thought it happened.'

'Most men would be flattered. She's a beautiful

heiress. And don't say you're not most men. You asked why Patsy and I are here. We were surprised to get the invitation, last minute and all that; but I'm here to celebrate your success.'

'And Patsy?'

'You said yourself you and Roberta are back together.'

Yes, he had said that, hadn't he? His breath bottled up in his chest and his heart woke up. The feelings he had suppressed since Nell told him she was married poured through him, igniting every nerve end, taking possession of him.

He wasn't most men, after all.

Nell rushed to Finney Lane. As if she didn't have enough on her plate, now she faced having Olive Hibbert permanently on her doorstep: Olive, the critical, nowty mother-in-law with her judgemental sniff and scarcely concealed scorn. But that had been when Olive believed her to be a nowty, critical wife. It was a shock that anyone would have thought that of her.

Nell sensed the disturbance before she saw it. A door thrown open, an indignant voice. A copper stepped out of the Tanners' house, followed by Edmund Tanner. After him came that snotty copper who had been sent to investigate the burglary. He had something bulky under his arm, but Nell's attention was distracted by a sharp glint in the sunshine, a sudden brightness in front of Edmund Tanner. Handcuffs! Really? She looked again, but he turned away as the policemen guided him down the road.

He must have half-killed Posy if they had handcuffed him. She ran to the door and pushed her way in.

'Hello? Hello?'

The house was still and silent. It stilled her too. The house felt as if it had stood empty for a dozen years. Instinct drew her to the kitchen. Hilda sat at the table, her face a mask of misery. Nell started towards her with a comforting arm, but stopped. Hilda had never liked her and probably resented her more than ever now for taking Leonie in.

She sat down. 'Mrs Tanner? I saw–'

'Pleased, are you? Come to gloat?'

'You don't know me very well if you think that, but that's the point, isn't it? You don't know me, because you never wanted to. If you were jealous of me and your mum, you'd no need to be.'

'Hark at you, being all gracious. You've no idea what it's like, being snubbed and cast aside by your own mother.'

All the indignation and concern Nell felt for Leonie's unhappiness surged to the fore. 'Your mum thinks the world of you, Hilda Tanner. She's beside herself that you've fallen out.'

'That's not how it looks from where I'm standing,' retorted Hilda. 'She's as good as abandoned me.'

'Abandoned? You don't know the meaning of the word. Shall I tell you what it is to be abandoned?' What was she saying? She had to stop. She had never – never– 'I had four brothers and a sister. When war was declared, the boys joined up. They were so proud of themselves and we had to pretend to be proud too; and we were proud, but

468

we were scared an' all; and we were right to be scared, because they all died; and then my sister copped it ... and Mum faded away and died.'

'I'm sorry to hear that.'

*I'm sorry.* That was what everyone said. 'Will you listen to what I'm saying? My mum wasn't ill; she didn't have an accident; she just died. A broken heart, everyone said, and they said it like it was right, like any loving mother would have died. No one said, "She's left Nell." No one said, "She should have hung on for Nell." I wasn't a good enough reason for her to stay in this life. I wasn't asking to be the favourite. I just wanted... I just wanted my mum. She was all I had left and she wasn't meant to leave me, but she did.'

'I'm sure she loved you. She was your mother.'

'But she didn't love me enough to stay alive, did she? So don't you dare tell me you've been abandoned, not when your mum is desperate to make up with you.'

'All right. You've said your piece. Now clear off.'

'I will if you want. I never came to see you, any-road. It's Posy I came for. But you think on before you throw me out, Hilda Tanner. I'm the best bet you've got of finding someone who understands. Your husband's just been took away in handcuffs; and my husband turns out never to have been my husband after all.'

That got a reaction, a startled look.

'Aye, I'm an unwed mother. So the way I see it, you and me can either go into competition over whose man has caused the greatest shame or we can join forces and bolster one another up.'

'I don't know as I want to join forces with an

469

unmarried mother.'

'And I don't know as I want to with a mother who lets her husband knock seven bells out of her little girl; but I'll stretch a point if you will.'

They stared at one another. Hilda looked away first.

'I take it,' said Nell, 'that Mr Tanner was arrested for what he did to Posy?'

Hilda fidgeted with the edge of the oilcloth. 'Edmund was taken away because ... because he stole those things from your house.'

'He what?'

'Posy told me. She taunted him into giving her the hiding of her life to make me sit up and take notice. I sent for the police and I suppose the neighbours thought I wanted to report him for child-beating. I brought the copper in here and told him everything. Posy said her dad hid the things in the cellar, so the copper went and looked, but then he came back and said they weren't there.'

Nell's heart ached. 'So Posy suffered a beating for nothing.'

'The policeman lied to me, so I couldn't mess things up.' Hilda made a bitter sound. 'He ordered me to tell Edmund to go to the police station about hurting Posy. I went next door to sit with Posy and I came back here when Edmund came home. I were such a coward. I said Mr Foskett had reported him to the police and he must go down the station, but he said there was something he had to do first, and he went into the cellar.' Hilda's eyes filled. 'That was when I knew for certain what he'd done. Being sent for by the police must have put the wind up him and he wanted to take the things and get rid of them.'

Oh, that feeling of certainty. For Nell, it had come when she saw Mrs Vicarage Lane's little boy.

'While I was next door, a bobby had come in and hidden in the cellar and there was another in the backyard; so when Edmund went down there to get the stolen things...'

'It showed he knew where they were, so he must have put them there.'

'The police lied to me.'

'They had to. It was part of their plan.'

'They didn't trust me not to blab to Edmund.' Hilda banged a fist on the table. 'It's not even as though they got him for what he did to Posy. All they care about is the theft. I want him to be done for hurting Posy.'

'I know, love; but the law will be harsher on him for the stealing than for beating his own child. That's the way of the world.'

The fire went out of Hilda. 'What's going to happen to us? Edmund were a good provider. If he gets sent to prison, what's to become of me and Posy?'

It might make him the most frightful cad, but he was going to sort this out now. A gentleman would wait. A gentleman would let today's special occasion run its course. A gentleman would probably find himself engaged before he knew it.

There was only one woman he wanted to be engaged to, and it wasn't Roberta Fairbrother.

When he, Don and Mr Fairbrother returned to the drawing room, Mrs Fairbrother said, 'Let's take a turn around the garden before drinks.'

Jim hung back, smiling a message to Roberta.

'This is naughty of you,' she said when they were alone. 'What will the others think?'

'If they aren't sure, I'm sure Patsy will tell them.'

'That's a little harsh, isn't it?' But she was obviously pleased. 'Darling Patsy. She longs to see you back in your proper social setting.'

She sat on the sofa and patted the space beside her, but Jim went to the window, standing with his back to it.

'Oh dear, have I done something wrong?' she cooed.

'No, you haven't, but I'm afraid I have. I should never have let things–'

She was on her feet in a flash. There was steel in her eyes, but the next moment she came towards him, smiling and fragrant. 'Don't say that, James. You're just having a little panic. Is it a bit much, having Don and Patsy here? Two families, all cosy, almost like ... one family.' She glanced away, as if too modest to contemplate the implication.

'Was it your idea to invite them?'

'Of *course* not.' A smile and a glance to the heavens, or was that just a way of not meeting his eyes? 'Poor Mummy would be devastated if she knew she'd rattled you.'

'I need to talk to you. I'm sorry, Roberta–'

'No!' She swung away from him, then back again. 'You're doing it again, aren't you? Well, I won't have it.'

'I've changed from the man I was before the war.'

'I understand about your window cleaning phase

472

and I've forgiven you. Please be sensible.' She moved closer. 'I've changed too. Why do you think I started my scheme to clothe the poor children? I've developed a social conscience, just like you. We're meant to be together. Why else would we have been thrown together as we were?'

'We weren't thrown. You made it happen.'

'Can you blame me? Oh, the chance to see you again–'

'You could have sought me out at any time during my window-cleaning phase, as you call it, but you chose not to. Roberta, I apologise. Meeting you again has been delightful and I'm sorry for letting things go too far–'

'Don't tell me: I was so delightful that you couldn't help yourself. It won't do, James. What did you imagine would happen to me when you dumped me? Did you think I'd waltz straight into another man's arms? Believe me, I wanted to, but there's a shortage of men now and I've no intention of spending the rest of my life as my father's daughter.'

'Is that why you wanted me back? Any man will do?'

Her hand flew up and cracked him hard across the face. For a moment, he felt nothing, then a stinging sensation bloomed inside his cheek. Roberta's eyes were hard and narrow.

'You're right, James. You have changed. You've turned into a fool. You could have had the perfect wife. Why else do you imagine I've got my maid hacking old clothes to pieces to make things for the poor? I even took to wearing that stupid straw hat because you always liked straws. You look shocked. You don't imagine I wanted to do those things, do you? God, you're impossible!'

'I think I should leave.'

She grasped his arm, her nails sinking into his sleeve. 'Oh no, you don't. You're going to spend the evening here. You'll laugh at Daddy's ghastly jokes and smile modestly when everyone toasts your success; and tomorrow I'll tell Mummy I turned down your proposal.'

'As you wish.'

'And when Daddy offers you a job tonight, you'll say no.'

'I'll go along with the social requirements, Roberta, but I won't be told what to do professionally.'

'You cannot work for my father,' she hissed.

'I have my own ideas about my future in the legal system. We'll see what your father says about them.'

'You're going to do something lower class, aren't you?'

'If I did, would you still want to marry me?'

Her hand shot out again, but he was too quick for her. She glared at him and wrenched herself free, rubbing her wrist as if he had hurt her, though he knew he hadn't.

She turned on her toes and went to the door. She looked back at him and her gaze was pure ice.

'Don't stand there like an oaf. You have your social duty to perform and you shall not, I repeat not, make a fool of me.'

Posy dozed off during the doctor's visit. 'She'll be black and blue in the morning,' he said, 'but there are no broken bones, luckily.'

474

While Mrs Watson showed him out, Leonie watched over her beloved grandchild. Never mind being black and blue tomorrow, she was well on the way now. Lovely Posy, funny and spirited and full of big words, looked tiny and broken in the bed that had once been occupied by the Watson boys.

Leonie was awash with sorrow and concern and rage. Aye, and guilt. She had known about the stair rod; and even though it hadn't been used today, the fact that it existed showed what kind of brute Edmund was underneath the smarm. She had removed the stair rod the day she moved out, and hadn't she thought herself the clever one? She had known it would be replaced, but she had felt it was one in the eye for Edmund. More fool her.

Where was Hilda? She should be at her daughter's bedside. Instead she had gone piking off next door and what was that about? Leonie knew Hilda had sent for the police, but what would they do, other than give Edmund a dressing-down for being too heavy-handed? You were allowed to hit your children. You were expected to.

Or had Hilda made herself scarce so as to avoid her own mother? Surely, in a situation like this, all differences should be set aside. Would Hilda be that petty? Did Hilda hate her that much?

The bedroom door opened behind her.

'Look who's come,' said Mrs Watson.

Hilda! Leonie looked over her shoulder. In came Nell and a stranger, a beady-eyed woman the same sort of age as Leonie, but meatier, though at the same time her face had a gaunt, tired look. Mind you, Leonie's face probably had that same look right now.

'You're Mrs Hibbert,' she said.

'This is Mrs Brent,' said Nell. 'I used to lodge with her and now we live together in Wilton Lane.'

'And this'll be your Posy I've been hearing about,' said Mrs Hibbert. 'Eh, poor little mite.'

She leant over Posy like the bad fairy in *Sleeping Beauty*. Leonie wanted to shove her aside. She didn't want the mother of the villainous Stan anywhere near her precious girl. But then Mrs Hibbert looked up and the sight of her troubled eyes rattled Leonie's defences. This was a mother, a grandmother, who understood the pain of watching a child suffer.

'I'll fetch chairs,' said Mrs Watson.

'Not for me,' said Nell.

'She's getting rid of me,' said Mrs Hibbert, 'so she can fetch her children home. She doesn't want me around.'

'Who can blame her, after what your son did?' Leonie retorted. The cheek of this one!

The Hibbert woman shrugged. 'I've never held with measuring folk by what their relatives do.'

Leonie was about to say – well, never mind, because she suddenly pictured Posy being judged according to Edmund's behaviour.

'Mrs Watson says Mrs Hibbert can stop here for a while,' said Nell.

'Shouldn't you be on the train by now?' Leonie challenged the visitor.

'I'm hoping to see my grandchildren, but that's up to Nell.'

Behind her, Nell rolled her eyes. She eased herself forwards in the cramped space and leant down to murmur to Leonie.

'Your Hilda needs you next door.'

'She should be here with Posy.'

'Believe me, she'd rather be here. I were round there a bit earlier and I had to leave because the police came to talk to her.'

'About Edmund hurting Posy?'

'It's not my place to say, but she needs her mum.'

Nell slipped away, leaving Leonie feeling torn in two. What if Posy woke up and found neither her mum nor her gran at her bedside?

'You go, love,' said Mrs Watson. 'She's safe with us.'

Leonie went downstairs and knocked next door. The door opened to reveal a bobby. She stepped forward but he blocked her way.

'I'm Mrs Tanner's mother.'

'When we've finished questioning her, I'll tell her you came round.'

Leonie might have been in two minds as to whether she should come, but being prevented filled her with determination. She stepped purposefully over the threshold. The copper made a move and she gave him the evil eye.

'Lay one finger on me and I'll scream blue murder.'

Hilda was sitting at the kitchen table with a man in a suit while a uniformed officer stood in front of the range with his arms folded. In that moment, Leonie knew that Edmund was gone. If he had been here, or if his influence had been here, Hilda and the policemen would have been in the parlour.

'I've come to be with my daughter,' she announced.

'Mrs Brent?' The man in the suit consulted his notebook. 'Your box was stolen.'

'Edmund took it,' Hilda said dully. 'He's the thief. They've got proof.'

'Edmund?'

'You sound surprised, Mrs Brent,' said the suit, 'and yet I believe it was you who suggested him as the possible culprit.'

'Only because someone saw a stocky man. I didn't really think it was him.' Edmund! It was hard to take in.

The suit stood up. 'Thank you for your help, Mrs Tanner. We'll speak to your daughter when she's up to it. Mrs Brent, your belongings will be returned in due course.'

The officers saw themselves out.

Hilda and Leonie stared at one another.

'So now you know,' said Hilda. 'We must get back to Posy. She's what matters now. I'll lock the back door and follow you in a minute. And Mother – thank you for coming.'

'Of course I came. You're my daughter. I love you, Hilda.'

'I know,' said Hilda. 'I love you an' all.'

Leonie would have liked a hug, but Hilda went to lock the door. Leonie returned next door with a full heart. She and Hilda had a lot to talk about – or did they? Had they simply gone back to normal?

She crept upstairs so as not to disturb Posy, only to find her awake, looking fragile.

'How are you feeling?'

'Stiff and sort of not really here.' Her mouth barely moved as she spoke and every time she swallowed she had to blink. 'But it's been interesting. I've been listening to this lady telling Mrs Watson about all Mr Hibbert's wives.'

'Didn't you see she was awake?' Leonie hissed at them.

'Ma,' croaked Posy as Hilda walked in.

'Look who I found outside,' said Hilda. She looked behind her through the open door. 'In you come.'

Alf appeared, looking pouty.

'I've run away,' he said.

'Oh!' The exclamation came from Mrs Hibbert. She looked dazed, her gaze fixed on Alf.

'Come here, chick,' said Leonie.

She held out her hand and he came to her. She put an arm round him, angling him away from his grandmother. That poor woman needed time to recover. Lord, Nell would throw a fit when she found out Alf had stumbled across Mrs Hibbert.

'What's happened to Posy?' Alf stared.

'I was trampled by a runaway horse,' said Posy.

'I'd better take him home,' said Leonie.

'No! I don't want to. Mum says Dad won't come to see us any more, so I've run away. I don't want to live with her.'

'Alf, Mummy will be very unhappy if you don't go back,' Leonie began.

But Alf all too obviously didn't care about that. 'I want to live with Dad.'

Posy swallowed and blinked hard. 'Your dad's an arsehole.'

'Posy!' It was the combined cry of all the adults. Leonie glared at Mrs Watson.

'Don't look at me,' her friend retorted. 'I don't use language like that.'

Swallow, blink. 'It's what the big boys in the top class say. And he is an arsehole. He's done bad things. It's all right, Alf.' Swallow, blink; a clicking noise in her throat. 'My dad's an arsehole too. He did this to me.'

'You said it was a runaway horse.'

'Posy,' said Hilda, 'that's enough. You need to rest.'

'I don't care,' said Alf. 'I've still run away.'

'Alf, listen to me,' said Mrs Hibbert.

'Who are you?' asked Alf.

'I'm–'

'Mrs Hedley,' said Leonie. 'She's Mrs Watson's friend.'

Mrs Hibbert leant forward as if she might reach for Alf; Leonie braced herself to intervene.

'Sometimes grown-ups do stupid things,' said Mrs Hibbert. 'Your dad loves you, but he did some things he shouldn't have done, and he made a lot of people unhappy. He isn't as good at being a dad as your mum is at being a mum.'

'She said he was dead.'

'Everyone does wrong things and everyone makes mistakes. She said that because she thought it was the best thing to do.'

'No, she didn't–'

'Oh, but she did.' Mrs Hibbert spoke with authority. 'Hate her if you must, but don't tell lies about her. I knew her before you were born, young man, and I know what a good person she is; and you know it too, I can tell. You know that it doesn't matter how horrid you are to her, she'll still love you and never turn away from you. I knew you when you were a tiny baby and your mum was the happiest, proudest mother I ever met.'

'Was she?' A stirring of interest.

'She was, because she had you. She was unhappy before that, because all her family had died, but then you came along and made her happy again. I know she hurt you by letting you think your dad was dead, but you're behaving as if everything she has ever done was wrong, and that isn't fair. You're more grown-up than that, Alf Hibbert.'

'I'm six not next Wednesday, the Wednesday after.'

'There you are, then. You're a big boy. Your dad has done something bad and has had to go and explain to the police. So that leaves you and your mum.'

'And Cassie,' said Alf.

'And Cassie,' she agreed.

'And Nana Leonie.'

'And me,' said Leonie, with a look that dared Mrs Hibbert to make something of it.

'Are you going to go back to normal, Alf, and love your mum again?' asked Mrs Hibbert. 'Or are you going to carry on behaving like an arsehole?'

'Mrs Hibbert!' Leonie exclaimed.

'I thought you said she was Mrs Hedley,' said Posy. 'And that's interesting because Gramps's name–'

'Thank you, Posy,' said Hilda.

Footsteps on the stairs, someone panting. Nell appeared.

481

'Have you seen–? Oh, *Alf!* I've got half the neighbourhood out looking.'

She stepped forward instinctively, then stopped. Leonie's heart ached for her. He had rebuffed her so many times. But Alf launched himself at her, arms outstretched, and she bent to scoop him up with a cry of joy. He clung to her. She nuzzled his neck and when she finally looked up, her face was bright with happiness.

'What brought this about?' Nell's voice was thick with tears.

Leonie indicated Mrs Hibbert. 'She knew what to say.'

Nell turned to her mother-in-law. 'Thank you, thank you.' Giving Alf a final squeeze, she set him down. 'We must go home. Goodness, you gave me a shock. I went to put Cassie to bed and when I came down, you were gone.' She took his hand, then turned to Mrs Hibbert. 'Perhaps you deserve a chance.' She smiled, looking oddly shy. 'Perhaps I do too.'

## Chapter Thirty-Four

In Jim's bedroom under the eaves, the warm night air was as dense as port wine, and as heady, thanks to the honey-rich scent of the sweet peas in the half-barrel outside the back door. He lay on top of his bed, his heart lighter than at any time since that fateful afternoon when Nell had told him about her marriage and shock had crushed

482

all his hopes, swamping his feelings and shutting them down. Except they weren't shut down, not really. He had thrown up a wall around his heart, which had allowed him to fool himself he could manage without her and making him vulnerable to Roberta's beguiling advances. But the truth had brought him back to his senses.

Rolling off the bed, he stood at the dormer window. The ink-black sky was dotted with stars. How soon could he present himself at Nell's door? He would cheerfully arrive for breakfast, but she would be mortified. He would do better to go to church and see Don and Patsy afterwards, as usual.

Pulling on his slippers and his old dressing-gown, he crept downstairs, trying to cause no creaks, and unbolted the back door. It was warm outside, but compared to under the eaves, it was refreshing.

Behind him, Mrs Jeffrey said, 'Can't sleep?'

He looked round. Beneath a shawl, her night-gown was buttoned all the way up her throat and she wore a lacy nightcap that covered not just her hair but the sides of her face and tied under her chin.

'I'm not sleepy.'

'You won't be stopping here much longer, will you?' she said.

'What makes you ask?'

'I've got eyes in my head. You've been Jim the window cleaner for a good spell now. Every now and then, you'd put on your fancy suit and go off somewhere; then you'd come back and be Jim again. But this is different, in't it?'

He wanted to take her hand and tell her how right it had been, living here in her simple cottage, fortified as much by her acceptance as by her hearty meals. He wanted to say that, whatever happened, he would make it his business to watch over her just as she had watched over him.

'Mrs Jeffrey, he said, 'if you'd asked me that question this time yesterday, I'd have said yes, this is entirely different; but now I think – I hope – that things aren't going to be quite as different as you imagine.'

Posy woke early, having slept surprisingly well, probably because of the tot of whisky Mrs Watson had given her last night. The whisky had smelt of burnt toffee and had frizzled the insides of her cheeks and taken the surface off the roof of her mouth before setting fire to her gullet. Before she dozed off, Posy had silently sworn a great big swear never to let a drop of the hard stuff pass her lips again.

She wriggled. Below the neck, she was one giant ache, but her head was clear and that made her feel better, though the best thing of all was having Ma beside the bed. She was slumped over, deeply asleep. Her mouth was open and she was snoring, which tempted Posy to laugh, only a dark twinge around her ribs warned her not to. If this was what it felt like when your bones were still in one piece, then heaven help you if they ever got broken.

Ma delivered a gigantic snort and jolted herself awake. Her gaze met Posy's and she leant forward anxiously.

'How are you today?'

'Fine, thank you, Ma.' That was what she had been taught to say, but it was true too, in spite of the soreness that made her feel hot and the bruises, each of which had a pulse in the centre, sending out a red-hot vibration with each beat of her heart. 'Having you here makes me fine; having you looking at me.'

Ma frowned. 'You mean, looking after you.'

'No, looking at me.' Posy suppressed a sigh. It was rather a blow not to be understood. 'When Dad was punishing me, you never looked. You did the mending or the cooking so you didn't have to look.'

'Oh, Posy...'

'I'm not stupid. I knew you couldn't stop him, but I always wanted you to look. Why didn't you?'

'I don't know.'

'If you'd looked, I'd have felt you were on my side,' Posy persevered.

'It weren't a question of sides.'

'Yes, it was. Dad wasn't fair. He punished me for all kinds that weren't my fault; and if I did deserve a smack, he still wasn't fair, because he used Rupert or Gerald or I had to hold my hand over the candle.'

'There was nowt I could do.'

Oh, here we go. Three cheers for the droopy cowslip. Resignation settled over Posy like another layer of bedding. What was the point? For as long as she could remember, she had wanted Ma to understand, but all Ma could do was bleat a few lame words. Didn't she realise how much this

485

mattered? Typical ruddy, droopy, flaming cowslip.

She would have one last go and if it didn't work, she would give up for ever.

'All those times you didn't look, it was like – it was like you were letting it happen.'

Ma's mouth fell open; there was a hiss of air as she breathed in.

'That was how it felt.' Posy's muscles quivered and it was nowt to do with the hammering Dad had given her. It was a wave of anger. 'You stuck your nose in the darning and pretended nothing was happening; but it did happen and it was right in front of you, only you never looked. And every time you didn't look, every time you pretended not to see, not to know – it felt like you were letting it happen. If you'd looked at me, if you'd behaved as if you were in the same room – that was all I wanted. I knew you couldn't stop him, but I wanted you to look like you cared.'

Ma pressed her hand to her mouth. 'I always cared...'

Posy shrugged one shoulder and all the muscles down that side groaned in protest. 'Not enough to look. Why didn't you?'

Ma's eyes shifted. 'I don't know.'

'Why did you pretend?'

Ma was silent for a long time.

'I hated what Dad did to you. You're right: it was never fair. I ... I didn't know what to do. I could never go against him. He was always so clever and I felt ... useless. I never managed to do anything right unless your dad told me exactly what to do.'

'Well, you'll have to start managing now,' said

Posy, 'if Dad goes to prison.'

Patsy led the way across the lawn to a shady corner, where a pretty ironwork table and chairs had appeared since Jim's last visit. Mrs Garbutt stood ready to follow with a tray of iced cordial. Jim took it from her.

'Allow me. I'm sure you've got plenty to do in the kitchen.'

'Thank you, sir.'

He carried the tray to the table, with the twins skipping beside him. He balanced the tray on one hand and gave Harriet and Marguerite a glass each. 'Give that one to Daddy, and that one to Mummy, and say, "Five shillings, please." If they say no, we'll run away with the jug and keep it all to ourselves.'

'You're good with children,' said Patsy approvingly.

'Patsy.' Don's voice was a gentle warning.

'Girls, go and play. I'll call you over for a drink in a few minutes,' said Patsy. 'What am I supposed to say? If I can't say that, I'll have to scold him for carrying the tray.'

'You're a good girl, Patsy,' said Jim, 'but you sometimes forget you've got a cook-general on her own these days and the maid and the bootboy are long gone.'

'She has a daily char to help her,' said Patsy and looked miffed when Don and Jim laughed. 'Never mind me. What about you?'

'What about me?' asked Jim.

'You know. Yesterday. We were expecting the evening to end with an announcement of your

487

engagement. Why do you think I wore my sapphires?'

Here goes. 'Roberta and I won't be seeing one another any more.'

'What! You've dumped her again, haven't you? Oh, James, how could you?'

'She called it off, actually.'

'Fiddlesticks. No one believed it last time and they won't believe it this time.'

'What happened?' asked Don.

'I never meant to lead her up the garden path. I really thought...' He waved his hand vaguely. That wasn't what he wanted to say. 'There's someone else.'

Patsy leant across the table. 'How? There hasn't been time. Did you meet her in Lancashire while you were doing your legal digging?'

'I met her in April.'

'You dark horse,' said Don.

Patsy furrowed her forehead. 'That makes no sense. If you've known her that long, you were definitely stringing Roberta along.'

'To start with, I didn't know if she liked me, and then it turned out she was unavailable.'

'At which point you succumbed to Roberta's wiles,' said Don. 'Don't tell me. Then your new lady turned out to be available after all.'

'Has she a name?' Patsy's tone was clipped. She wasn't ready to forgive him.

'Nell Hibbert.'

'Nell?'

'Eleanor.'

'I'll call her Eleanor,' said Patsy.

Don took the glass of cordial from her hand

and set it on the table. Then he took her hand and raised it to his lips. 'You'll call her Nell, my darling Patricia.'

She pulled a face, but it was easy to see the gallant little kiss had beguiled her. Jim felt a pang of envy. Would he ever have the chance of that kind of closeness with Nell?

Patsy gasped. 'Hibbert! That's the woman on those postcards. Don, James has taken up with someone *out of our class.*' The final words emerged on a scandalised breath.

In for a penny. 'It's worse than that.' He fought to keep his tone light when his whole body was tense with resentment. 'That bigamy case...'

'*No!*'

'Yes. She believed her husband was bigamously married to another woman, but it transpired he was bigamously married to her. And before you say anything else: she's a decent person through and through. She's beautiful and clever and kind and she's worked damned hard to maintain a respectable life for herself and her children.'

'She has *children?*'

Don laughed. 'Well, you keep saying how good he is with them.'

'I meant with ours, and the hope of his own.'

'I hope Alf and Cassie will be mine.' Jim looked squarely at his brother and sister-in-law. It was time to set some ground rules. 'I hope you'll accept them as your nephew and niece.'

A look passed between Don and Patsy.

'When you talk about ... Nell and her children,' said Patsy, 'you sound...'

'He sounds,' said Don, 'like a man talking about

489

the love of his life. Just like I sound when I talk about you.' He turned to Jim. 'It isn't easy, crossing the class barrier to get married. I've watched you these past few years and I'm relieved and proud to see you've emerged from whatever darkness you were in. I know you're more than capable of facing whatever challenges life brings. As far as Nell is concerned, you have my blessing. Eh, Patsy?'

She looked thoughtful. Don normally sat back and let her go her own sweet way, but when he spoke up, she listened. Jim could see the cogs turning. She was already working out how to unite the two families.

'Girls,' Don called. 'Come and have a drink.'

The twins scampered over, clean and uncreased. They were in for a shock when they met the ladder-monkey.

'Uncle James, Mummy says if we're lucky, we might be bridesmaids.'

'If we're all very lucky indeed,' said Don, 'you might be bridesmaids and I might be best man and your mother might be the most beautiful guest at the wedding. But we must all cross our fingers, and our toes, and our eyes, even when we're asleep.'

'Steady on.' Jim faked a laugh to hide a sudden onslaught of nerves. 'I haven't asked her yet.'

'She'll say yes, won't she?' clamoured the children.

'I hope so, but you'll have to cross your arms and legs as well.'

Patsy caught his eye. 'I hope so too.'

490

## Chapter Thirty-Five

It was stuffy in the bedroom. Leonie opened the
window to its fullest extent. This was the room
she would have occupied if she had come to live
with her old friend. But, it wouldn't have been
easy lodging next door to the house she had
shared so happily with Hedley.

'When can I get up?' asked Posy.

'You can get up when you can do it without
saying "Ooh" and "Ouch" every time you move,'
said Hilda.

Mrs Watson came in, followed by Lyddie and
Josie.

'Look who's come to see you, Posy.' To Hilda
and Leonie she said, 'Get off next door, you two.
I'll stop here with this lot and make sure there's
no clog-dancing.'

The girls giggled. Leonie drew Hilda away and
they went next door.

'You're weary, Hilda. Sit down and I'll make
some tea.'

'We're both weary. I'll do it.'

They made the tea together and sat down.
Leonie could see Hilda was building up to saying
summat.

'I had no idea Edmund would hurt our Posy
that badly. She said something to me earlier.' She
put her cup down.

'Oh aye?' Leonie prompted.

'I've been a bad mother.'

Leonie caught her breath. 'Posy said that?'

'No, that's me talking.'

'Nay, love, you've done your best. No one's perfect.'

'Perfect, imperfect.' Hilda shrugged. 'I've been ... nothing. I've been married to Edmund for all but twenty years and I've been nothing. I thought my marriage was going to be like yours, but Edmund was so in charge of everything. I tried to do the right thing all the time, but I didn't always know what it was. I didn't used to be this way when I was young. I remember being cheerful and knowing what to do, and it's like thinking of another person. Now, I shrink away from everything.'

'You were such a lively girl, but you changed after you got wed and I'll be honest, I blamed you for not having more gumption. But these past weeks, I've started to see what you lived with. It's enough to wear anyone down. It would have wore me down an' all, if I'd had to live with it for a long time.'

A knock at the door: damn. Just when Hilda had started confiding.

'I'll go.' Leonie got up.

But Hilda was on her feet too. 'It's my house. Sorry, Mother. I meant, it's my responsibility.'

She answered the door and Leonie heard Jim's voice. She had to squash the wish to call to him to come in.

He followed Hilda into the kitchen.

'I went to see Mrs Hibbert about ... something else and she told me about Posy. How is she?'

'Black and blue,' said Hilda, 'but she'll get better.'

'She also told me about Mr Tanner's arrest. She asked me to help you. I'd be happy to ask questions at the police station on your behalf.'

'I'd be grateful,' said Hilda, 'but I'm coming with you.'

'You don't have to.'

'Yes, I do.'

And off she went. Well! That was more spirit than their Hilda had shown since Leonie couldn't remember when.

She went round to Nell's to see how she was getting on after the kerfuffle of the court case. Mind you, that was probably forgotten in the joy of Alf loving his mum again. But then there was Olive Hibbert to throw into the mix. Olive and Nell had looked yesterday like they might be reconciled, but you never could tell. Mrs Olive Hibbert was on the pushy side and a little of her would go a long way.

Most of all, Leonie wanted to know what the 'something else' was that had taken Jim round there.

She had her hopes. She felt a flutter in her belly. Oh yes, she had her hopes.

In Wilton Lane, the children were out playing in a restrained kind of way, this being Sunday. A game of marbles was permitted, or French skipping as long as the chanting was done at low volume, but nothing that involved running about. Some of the mothers and grandmothers were outside, having a chinwag, but Nell's family was nowhere to be seen. Leonie found them in the backyard, sailing paper boats in the bathtub. Nell was on her knees, her arm around her son, the two of them so obviously restored to their rightful closeness that Leonie welled up. Olive Hibbert sat on a kitchen chair, watching and encouraging. Cassie was intent upon finding things to put in the water.

'You look happy,' said Leonie as Nell came to her.

Nell looked at Alf. 'Thanks to Nanny.'

Leonie raised her eyebrows.

'No more lies,' said Nell.

'Afternoon, Mrs Hibbert,' said Leonie. 'Lovely day.'

'It is that, and all the better for spending it with the children.'

'Nanny likes playing at boats,' said Alf.

'If you two want to chat, I'll stop here,' said Mrs Hibbert.

'Come and see Violet,' said Nell.

Alf looked up. 'You can't disturb her if she's asleep and you mustn't touch her if she's washing, because that's when she does her thinking.'

'I promise,' said Leonie.

Upstairs, the bedroom door was shut. Nell opened it and they slipped inside, though there was no danger of Violet springing out. She was curled up fast asleep on the bed.

'So how are things with Mrs Hibbert?' asked Leonie.

'She and I have learnt a few things about one another in the past twenty-four hours, and then there was the way she spoke to Alf.' Nell pulled in a breath and let it go. 'We'll rub along. She's going back to Annerby tomorrow. I don't know what to do with her tonight. She sat up with you watching Posy last night, but she needs a bed tonight.'

'Leave her to me. Hilda wants to get Posy carried home to her own bed today, so Mrs Hibbert can have Mrs Watson's spare room.'

Nell laughed. 'You can't foist her on Mrs Watson.'

'Do you think Hetty Watson would miss the chance to stay up half the night getting all the gossip? We'll be doing her a favour. I'll take Mrs Hibbert back with me now.'

'It's rather early.'

'Aye, but a little bird tells me you'll want her out of the way soon.'

'Why? She should get to know the children.'

'But you wouldn't want her earwigging on you and Jim. What did he want earlier?'

'I told him about Posy and asked if he could help.'

'Thanks for that, but what actually brought him here? He said there was "something else" he came for.'

'I've no idea.'

'Well, I have.'

'Please don't. You couldn't be more wrong.'

'We'll never know if you don't let him speak.'

'There's nothing to say. He – he has a lady friend. I've seen them together. It's Roberta Fairbrother.'

'Fairbrother? As in...?'

'So if I were interested,' said Nell, 'which I'm not, he's spoken for.'

She turned away, but not before Leonie had glimpsed the desolation in her eyes.

'Here's our Hilda now.' Leonie left Olive Hibbert at Hilda's kitchen table and went into the hall to meet Hilda. 'Come in, love. The tea's brewed. Are you coming in, Jim?'

'No, thanks,' he answered from the front door.

'Go on through, Hilda. Mrs Hibbert will pour your tea. I need a quick word with Jim.' A gentle push saw Hilda on her way. Leonie stood in the doorway, eyeing Jim. 'What's this I hear about you and Miss Fairbrother?'

'How do you know about that?'

'It's true, then? You've got yourself hitched to someone from the top drawer?'

'No, I–'

'I'm pleased to hear it. This is the lie of the land, see. My Nell's so-called husband treated her summat shocking and she deserved better. The question is: are you better? Because if you're not, you can sling your hook toot sweet.'

'I–'

'It were Nell what told me about Miss Posh Lady.'

'Oh–'

'Not much good with words today, are you, Mr Lawyer? Tell you what. I'll walk to the corner with you and then watch which way you go. If you walk past the top of Wilton Lane, that's fair enough and I'll wish you well with Miss Top Drawer, even though I'll think you need your bumps feeling; but if you turn down Wilton Lane, and later my Nell ends up hurt, well, I won't be responsible for my actions.' She smiled. 'Shall we go?'

They walked up Finney Lane in silence. The poor chap probably didn't dare say a word. At the corner, she gave him a prod.

'Off you go. And mind – I'm watching.'

He surprised her with a warm smile. 'You're a hard woman, Mrs Brent. Nell's lucky to have you.'

'Get gone. I can't stand here all day like a flaming lamp post.'

He bent to kiss her cheek. As he walked away, she pressed her fingertips where the kiss had been. The cheeky lad!

Would he? Wouldn't he? Yes, he turned into Wilton Lane: good.

Now she must get back to Hilda.

'Where have you been, Mother?' Hilda asked as she walked in.

'Just summat that wanted doing.' She sat down. 'Is there another one in the pot? Now, Hilda, tell us what the police said.'

'They expect Edmund to go to prison.' Hilda got the words out, sounding calm, but then she pressed her hand to her chest, breathing rapidly. 'He'll be up before the magistrate in't morning and the matter will be referred to a higher court, which will mean...' She swallowed. '...a stiffer sentence.'

Leonie's heart ached for her child. 'Are you all right, love?'

'I'm that ashamed. My husband, a jailbird. But it's a relief too. Knowing he won't come back for however long – it's a relief.'

'You're very brave,' said Mrs Hibbert.

'What will we do now, me and Posy, with no

one to support us?'

'I could come back here with my pension and my savings,' said Leonie.

'We both know it wouldn't be enough.'

'I've an idea,' said Mrs Hibbert. 'I've enough to see me out and I want to live near my grand-children. What if I took on this house and you and Posy live with me? What do you say?'

Hilda placed an elbow on the table and propped her chin on the heel of her hand, fingers covering her mouth. Her eyes had a faraway look. At last she took her hand away.

'I've got a bit of time to think about it. Edmund paid the rent monthly, not weekly. It made him feel superior to everyone else. So it's paid in full until the end of July. Me and Posy have got till then.' She looked at Mrs Hibbert. 'Thanks for your offer, but the answer's no. I'm sure you're a good person, but you seem a managing sort to me, and I've had my fill of being managed. I don't know what I'm going to do or how I'm going to do it without being scared to death, but I do know I'm not going to let someone else be in charge of it.'

## Chapter Thirty-Six

Had she ever been this happy? Stan was gone; her children were safe with her; and Alf was restored to the genial, affectionate child he was meant to be. He had asked her to tuck him in last night and that had felt like all her birthdays rolled into one. Of course, there were still problems, but the pressure to find more work and earn more money was just part of life and she would tackle it with pride and determination, doing her best for her children.

The game in the backyard had moved on from paper boats. Nell scooped water into her cupped hands and chased the children round. They were wet, she was wet, but who cared? It was fun.

Mrs O'Rourke's face popped over the wall. She must be standing on something. 'Goodness me, is it just the three of you? With that amount of noise, I thought you were holding a party for the whole street.'

'Were we being rowdy? I'm sorry.' It was hard to sound apologetic.

'Nay, love. It's good to see all is well. Me and my George are glad you're stopping next door.'

'Thank you,' said Nell. 'I like living next to you too.'

'Yon window cleaner fella is knocking at your front door, only you can't hear him. I can't imagine why not,' she added, eyeing Alf with pretend-sternness, making him giggle.

What did Jim want? He had already been round once and she had got rid of him pretty sharpish.

'We'd best answer the door,' she said to the children, 'but first,' and she looked at the water in her cupped hands, 'I need to find somewhere to put this.' The children quivered expectantly. 'I'll put it back in the bath.'

The children crept behind her as if they were playing what time is it, Mr Wolf? She held her hands over the bath, then swung round and gave chase to two squealing children, dumping the few drops she had left on Cassie's head.

'Now let's get that door.'

Maybe he had got fed up of waiting.

No such luck.

He stood outside her house, smiling and handsome and engaged to another woman; or if they weren't engaged, they jolly well ought to be, after the way Miss Roberta Fairbrother had helped herself to his arm in public yesterday. If they weren't engaged – well, there was a word in the backstreets for women like that.

His smile made her heart turn over. No, wait: there was something different, a flicker of uncertainty at the corners of his mouth and in his eyes, though what he had to feel uncertain about, she couldn't imagine. He was obviously on the brink of returning to his old life, and with a beautiful, upper-crust wife in tow. She wished he would clear off and leave her alone.

Or – oh heavens – had he realised she had feelings for him? Decent, considerate man that he was, had he come to let her down kindly? 'Ruddy heck,' said Eric in her head.

'Mr Franks!' yelled Alf and the two children flung themselves at him, clinging to his legs. 'We're having a water battle.'

'That's a relief. I thought you had a burst pipe. Who's winning?'

'Mum, I think.'

'If the winner is the driest, it's Mum; if it's the wettest, that's this young lady.' He picked up Cassie. 'Is this Cassandra Hibbert or is it a sponge?'

'It's a sponge-monkey,' hooted Alf.

Nell rolled her eyes. 'They're excited, I'm afraid. I think they caught it off me.'

The sight of her little girl in this man's arms was irresistible and also exquisitely painful. Nell reached for Cassie and took her onto her hip. The familiar feel of her daughter's sturdy little body gave her confidence. Whatever had brought Jim here, she would cope with dignity and good humour. When he left, she would never see him again. She would live for her children, just as she had before he came along.

'Did you see Mrs Tanner?'

'We went to the police station and were given some information.'

'Good.' What else was there to say? 'I didn't thank you properly yesterday. I'll always be grateful.'

'You're welcome.'

He looked at her. Nell dropped her gaze. She took a step backwards. She needed to get the door shut.

'Wait,' he said. 'I heard something at the police station–'

'I don't want to hear Mrs Tanner's business.'

'This is very much your business,' he said.

Couldn't he take a hint? She put Cassie down. 'Children, go into the yard. I'll be there in a minute – don't climb in the bath!' She turned to Jim. 'If it's who the thief was, I know that.'

'It's something else.'

'You'd best come through.' She led him to the backyard so she could keep an eye on the children. Standing outside the back door, she folded her

501

arms. 'What is it?'

'There's no doubt, apparently, that Edmund Tanner was the thief; I gather young Posy was a witness, though the police haven't spoken to her yet. What you should know is that Tanner is busy blaming Stan Hibbert, saying it was all his idea.'

'Never! Stan?'

'That doesn't make it true, of course, but I thought you should know. Presumably, when Hibbert hears what Tanner's been saying, he'll return the compliment.'

'Stan was furious with me for naming him. And you're saying he might have been involved?'

'I'm just sharing what the sergeant told me.'

'Thank you. It's better to hear it privately.' She turned to the door, ready to show him out. 'I mustn't keep you.'

He looked startled. 'You haven't asked what I came for.'

'To tell me about Stan, obviously.'

'That was just to get me over the threshold. I didn't think you were going to let me in otherwise.'

She forced a laugh. He wasn't going to leave until he had said his piece, so she had better get it over with. 'So what brings you here?'

He looked at her. 'Do you really not know?'

'Does Mr Franks want to come and play?' called Alf.

'In a minute,' called Jim. 'When you told me about your marriage, I turned away from you.'

'No, you didn't,' she exclaimed. 'You turned towards me. Look at all you did.' She had to keep talking. She couldn't bear to be told about his engagement. 'Yes, you were rather cool, but I deserved that, and it didn't stop you working hard on my behalf. If you hadn't dug into Stan's past, my children would be in Annerby by now. It gives me goosebumps just to think of it. Anyroad,' she said, forestalling him, 'I shan't keep you. I have two children who aren't nearly wet enough and I expect you have to get to Victoria Park.'

'You know about Roberta.'

'Indeed I do.' She made herself laugh. 'I saw you kissing her, remember, and then she spirited you away yesterday. I wish you every happiness. You deserve it– What are you doing?'

He was heading for the bath. He climbed in and sat down, with Alf and Cassie hooting and laughing around him.

'What does it look like?' he asked. 'I'm playing with your children.' Looping an arm round Alf, he lifted him into the bath in a tangle of arms and legs. 'Come on, miss, there's room for you too.' He picked up Cassie and squeezed her in as well.

Nell ran across, then didn't know what to do, just stood there helplessly, trying not to laugh.

'One thing I know about you, Nell Hibbert.' Jim stood up, leaving the children jumping and splashing in the confined space around his feet. 'The way to your heart is through your children. Will you let me speak now, instead of interrupting me? What I've been trying to say, only you won't let me get a word in, is that I was shocked about your marriage, not just because anyone would be, but for personal reasons; the most personal reason of all. I love you. I started to love you that very first day, when Cassie climbed the ladder and you told me off for picking her up.' He lifted Cassie out of

503

the water and she nestled confidently against him. 'Come on, mate, you as well.' He held out a hand to Alf and heaved him up onto his other hip. 'The thing is this, Alf Hibbert. Your mum has an admirer. That means there's a man who wants to marry her. Now this is what we have to consider: I've got a ladder and you, Mr Alf, have got a pet ladder-monkey, so don't you think that makes me the perfect man to marry your mum?'

'Instead of her admirer?' asked Alf.

'What do you say, Nell?' asked Jim.

The uncertainty was gone from his expression. Standing there, holding her children, he looked confident and natural and trustworthy and *right*. From the start – well, almost from the start – she had associated him with the same basic decency she associated with her lost Pringle family. Never mind the class distinction. Never mind that she had learnt the three Rs in classes of sixty while he had probably had a private education, maybe even a degree. Never mind that he had money behind him. Having grown up as a daughter of the proud poor, she could tell someone's financial state by looking at their eyes; and Jim Franks's financial situation wasn't one that kept him awake at night. For her, on the other hand, money worries were a part of everyday existence.

All these differences between them; and yet, at heart, where it mattered, they were the same.

It was why she loved him.

'Well, I don't know,' she said. 'It depends who this other admirer is.'

# Chapter Thirty-Seven

## August, 1924

The house on Beech Road, near where the old beech tree hung far over the street, was perfect – big enough for their purposes without being too grand. The women from Wilton Lane and thereabouts would be comfortable coming here for lessons and to use a sewing machine. Her forthcoming marriage might be about to take her up in the world, but Nell was determined it wouldn't take her up too far. That was the way Jim wanted it too. He valued his experiences of recent years too highly to walk away from them.

They stood at the front gate looking at the house.

'Fancy me moving into a place with a room on each side of the front door.' She laughed. 'That's proper posh, that is.'

'It won't put off your backstreet pupils?'

'They understand we have to have a certain number of rooms if I'm to have my sewing school.'

They went inside. There were four rooms downstairs, plus the kitchen at the back. Each front room was spacious, the ones behind smaller.

Jim waved his hand towards those on the left. 'Your sewing school room at the front, my study behind.'

'Will you let people needing advice call on you

505

here?' asked Nell.

'Yes. The kind of people I want to help aren't the sort to traipse into town and knock on the door of Winterton, Sowerby and Jenks.'

'Isn't it wonderful that they asked you back?' said Nell. 'I'm so proud of you.'

He smiled. 'Isn't it wonderful that they agreed to my doing PPD work? But you can still be proud of me, if you like.'

PPD. Poor Person's Defence. But Jim intended to expand his work way beyond representing poor people who couldn't afford representation when they had to appear in court. He wanted to offer advice on simple matters free of charge or for a nominal sum. Just being with this man made Nell feel taller and stronger, such was her pride.

'Folk in the backstreets haven't had access to legal information and advice before,' she said, 'and now they're to receive it from my husband.'

'I'm not your husband yet.'

'Just a couple of weeks. I can't wait to drop the Hibbert name. Mr Aitcheson said I wasn't entitled to use it any more, anyroad.'

'Legally, you can use whatever name you please, as long as your use of it is above board,' said Jim, 'though maybe I shouldn't tell you that, or you might not be so eager to get married.'

Nell pretended to consider. 'It's time for a change. I'll have a go with Franks and see how I like it. I want the children to be called Franks too. Is that allowed?'

'With their father in prison, I don't think anyone will argue, but we'd better ask Alf if he minds.'

'Minds? He'll love it. He worships you.'

'What I'm really hoping for,' said Jim, 'is to adopt them – if you and they would be happy with that.'

What had she done to deserve all these good things? A wonderful husband; a comfortable home for her children; her own sewing school for her backstreet friends and her middle-class clients; an unexpectedly good friendship with Stan's mother, who wanted nothing more than to make up for lost time not only with her grandchildren but also with the daughter-in-law she had spurned back in Annerby. And now Jim wanted to make their family complete by adopting Alf and Cassie.

'There are going to be new adoption laws,' he said, 'making adoption a formal legal process, complete with certificates, so it would be in our interests if I were to adopt them before that. Afterwards, the fact that they have a father living might cause complications.'

'Alf Franks,' she said. 'Cassie Franks.'

'The name I'm keenest on is Nell Franks.'

Delight shivered through Nell's body. The Franks family. That was what she wanted. She had suffered dreadful butterflies before meeting Don and Patsy, but Don was a sweetheart who had done all he could to make her feel welcome and accepted. Nell wasn't stupid. She could see the reservations in Patsy's eyes and didn't blame her, but Patsy had been civil and kind, gradually unbending and becoming friendlier. Nell hoped she and Patsy would become genuine friends in the not too distant future. Stranger things had happened: look at her and Olive.

'Aunt Leonie will like this house too,' she said.

'We're just along the road from Riley's Farm, so she can pop across and see Hilda and Posy as much as she wants; and they can come here.'

Hilda – doormat Hilda, droopy-drawers Hilda – had surprised them all by finding herself a job serving in the grocer's further along Beech Road, which was ideal for her and Posy's new home in Mrs Jeffrey's cottage.

They went upstairs in their new house. Jim was already living here. Nell, the children and Leonie would move in after the wedding.

'Are you sure it's all right, me coming?' Leonie had asked anxiously.

'Of course it is.' Nell hugged her. 'I'm going to work during the day, so I need my dear aunt there to keep house and mind the children.'

Later, she had said to Jim, 'Make sure Aunt Leonie knows you want her to live with us.'

And Jim, bless him, had gone one better. 'I wish your Hilda and Posy would move in as well. We could make room.'

Leonie's eyes had glowed. 'Oh, you've got a good man here, Nell.'

'I know,' she said.

'I'll tell Hilda,' said Leonie, 'but I know already what she'll say. She's determined to pull herself together and do her best for Posy. They'll be poor as church mice, but working in a grocer's means she'll get the bruised stuff for next to nowt. Eh, I'm that worried about our Hilda, but I'm proud of her as well. She turned into another person after she married Edmund. I hope the old Hilda comes back.'

Now, Nell and Jim walked into the room that

was to be the children's.

Nell gasped. 'You never told me you'd organised this.'

'Do you like it?' asked Jim. 'Aunt Leonie told me how much you loved the bed in the Fairbrothers' nursery. From what she said, it sounded like a half-tester.'

Nell caught his hands, but she couldn't take her eyes off the bed. A fairy-tale bed for Cassie. Fabric spread across the top of the tall frame over the head of the bed and hung down the sides in gauzy folds that were scooped back by tasselled silver cords.

'It's perfect,' she breathed. 'I love it.'

'You do realise she's going to use it as a climbing frame?'

'I don't care. I just want her to have it.'

'Down there,' said Jim, pointing from the window, 'is where I'll have my vegetable patch. Alf can help me. And I thought we could plant violets for your sister.'

'Oh, yes,' breathed Nell. She forced a laugh before her throat could clog with sorrow. 'I'd like that. She'd like that.'

'More than she'd like having the cat named after her?' Jim suggested and this time Nell's laugh was real.

'Let's go round the garden,' she said. She was going to live in a house with a garden. Her children were going to grow up with a garden.

'In a minute,' said Jim. 'There's something I want to tell you first. I need to know if I've done the right thing. I can cancel it if I haven't.'

'Should I be alarmed?' Daft question. She

509

trusted him far too deeply to be alarmed.

'It's to do with our honeymoon. You've been happy to leave arrangements to me so it would be a surprise, but you ought to have the chance to prepare yourself.'

'For what?'

'I've been in touch with the Imperial War Graves Commission.'

Her skin tingled all over; her heart forgot to beat.

'I want to take you to visit the war graves in France. I can show you the final resting places of three of your brothers, but I haven't been able to track down Tom. It may be that his remains will never be formally identified. If that is the case, then I want you to know that official memorials to the missing are also going to be constructed; and visiting one of those in due course will be our way of paying our respects to him.'

'Oh, Jim...'

'I've also found the village cemetery in Picardy where your sister was laid to rest. We'll take her flowers.'

Vi, dear stage-struck Vi. What fun the children would have had with her. What love and support Nell had had to live without.

'Is that what you'd like?' he asked.

She couldn't speak. She walked into his arms and he held her for a long time. Then he kissed away her tears.

'Come along,' he said. 'Let's go and see our garden.'

'And choose where to plant the violets,' said Nell.

# Acknowledgements

I should like to express my gratitude to: Laura Longrigg, my agent, and Lesley Crooks, my editor; Fliss and Simon Bage, whose superb copy-editing of *The Deserter's Daughter* taught me a thing or two about planning *A Respectable Woman;* Christina Griffiths, who has an eye for the perfect cover; Susie Dunlop and all at Allison & Busby, especially Kelly Smith and Ailsa Floyd; Becky Curtis, Aimée Hogston and all at Isis Soundings; Julia Franklin, who knows how to tell a compelling story; Carol Rivers, for her support and encouragement; Kirsten Hesketh, Karen Coles, Christina Banach, Catherine Boardman, Maddie Please, Jane Ayres, Chris Manby and Vanessa Rigg, for support, advice, being excited at all the right moments and generally making the world of writing a better place; Jen Gilroy for naming the cat; but please note, Jen: I have been asked to suggest that next time, you choose Elsie; and Wendy Martyn, who is, of course, a highly respectable woman.

Susanna Bavin has variously been a librarian, an infant school teacher, a carer and a cook. She lives in Llandudno in North Wales with her husband and two rescue cats, but her writing is inspired by her Mancunian roots.

susannabavin.co.uk
@SusannaBavin

This Large Print Book for the partially sighted, who cannot read normal print, is published under the auspices of

## THE ULVERSCROFT FOUNDATION

The publishers hope that this book has given you enjoyable reading. Large Print Books are especially designed to be as easy to see and hold as possible. If you wish a complete list of our books please ask at your local library or write directly to:

**Magna Large Print Books**
Magna House, Long Preston,
Skipton, North Yorkshire.
BD23 4ND